In Bad Company and Other Stories, Vol. 1

Rolf Boldrewood

IN BAD COMPANY
AND OTHER STORIES
THE WORKS OF
ROLF BOLDREWOOD
UNIFORM EDITION
Crown 8vo. 3s. 6d. each.

ROBBERY UNDER ARMS.

A COLONIAL REFORMER.

THE MINER'S RIGHT.

A MODERN BUCCANEER.

NEVERMORE.

THE SQUATTER'S DREAM.

A SYDNEY-SIDE SAXON.

OLD MELBOURNE MEMORIES.

MY RUN HOME.

THE SEALSKIN CLOAK.

THE CROOKED STICK; OR, POLLIE'S PROBATION.

PLAIN LIVING.

A ROMANCE OF CANVAS TOWN.

WAR TO THE KNIFE.

BABES IN THE BUSH.

IN BAD COMPANY, AND OTHER STORIES.

THE SPHINX OF EAGLEHAWK: A TALE OF OLD BENDIGO. Fcap. 8vo. 2s.

THE GHOST CAMP; OR, THE AVENGERS. Cr. 8vo. 6s.

MACMILLAN AND CO., LTD., LONDON.

IN BAD COMPANY

AND OTHER STORIES

Volume 1

BY

ROLF BOLDREWOOD

AUTHOR OF

'ROBBERY UNDER ARMS,' 'THE MINER'S RIGHT,' 'THE SQUATTER'S DREAM,'

'A COLONIAL REFORMER,' ETC.

London

MACMILLAN AND CO., Limited

NEW YORK: THE MACMILLAN COMPANY

1903

All rights reserved

First Edition 1901

Re-issue 1903

CONTENTS

IN BAD COMPANY

MORGAN THE BUSHRANGER

HOW I BECAME A BUTCHER

MOONLIGHTING ON THE MACQUARIE

AN AUSTRALIAN ROUGHRIDING CONTEST

THE MAILMAN'S YARN

DEAR DERMOT

THE STORY OF AN OLD LOG-BOOK

A KANGAROO SHOOT

FIVE MEN'S LIVES FOR ONE HORSE

REEDY LAKE STATION

A FORGOTTEN TRAGEDY

THE HORSE YOU DON'T SEE NOW

HOW I BEGAN TO WRITE

A MOUNTAIN FOREST

IN BAD COMPANY

CHAPTER I

Bill Hardwick was as fine a specimen of an Australian as you could find in a day's march. Active as a cat and strong withal, he was mostly described as 'a real good all-round chap, that you couldn't put wrong at any kind of work that a man could be asked to do.'

He could plough and reap, dig and mow, put up fences and huts, break in horses and drive bullocks; he could milk cows and help in the dairy as handily as a woman. These and other accomplishments he was known to possess, and being a steady, sensible fellow, was always welcome when work was needed and a good man valued. Besides all this he was the fastest and the best shearer in the district of Tumut, New South Wales, where he was born, as had been his father and mother before him. So that he was a true Australian in every sense of the word.

It could not be said that the British race had degenerated as far as he was concerned. Six feet high, broad-chested, light-flanked, and standing on his legs like a gamecock, he was always ready to fight or work, run, ride or swim, in fact to tackle any muscular exercise in the world at the shortest notice.

Bill had always been temperate, declining to spend his earnings to enrich the easy-going township publican, whose mode of gaining a living struck him as being too far removed from that of honest toil. Such being his principles and mode of life, he had put by a couple of hundred pounds, and 'taken up a selection.' This means (in Australia) that he had conditionally purchased three hundred and twenty acres of Crown Land, had paid up two shillings per acre of the upset price, leaving the balance of eighteen shillings, to be paid off when convenient. He had constructed thereon, chiefly with his own hands, a comfortable, four-roomed cottage, of the 'slab' architecture of the period, and after fencing in his property and devoting the proceeds of a couple of shearings to a modest outlay in furniture, had married Jenny Dawson, a good-looking, well-conducted young woman, whom he had known ever since he was big enough to crack a stockwhip.

In her way she was as clever and capable; exceptionally well adapted for the position of a farmer's wife, towards which occupation her birth and surroundings had tended. She was strong and enduring in her way, as were her husband and brothers in theirs. She could milk cows and make excellent butter, wasn't afraid of a turbulent heifer in the dairy herd, or indisposed to rise before daylight in the winter mornings and drive in the milkers through the wet or frozen grass. She could catch and saddle her own riding-horse or drive the spring cart along an indifferent road to the country town. She knew all about the rearing of calves, pigs, and poultry; could salt beef and cure bacon—in a general way attend to all the details of a farm. Her father had acquired a small grant in the early colonial days, and from its produce and profits reared a family of healthy boys and girls.

They had not been educated up to the State school standard now considered necessary for every dweller in town or country, but they could read and write decently; had also such knowledge of arithmetic as enabled them to keep their modest accounts. Such having been the early training of Bill's helpmate, it was a fair augury that, with luck and good conduct, they were as likely as any young couple of their age to prosper reasonably, so as eventually to acquire a competence, or even, as indeed not a few of their old friends and neighbours had done, to attain to that enviable position generally described as 'making a fortune.'

For the first few years nothing could have been more promising than the course of affairs at Chidowla or 'Appletree Flat,' as their homestead was formerly named, in consequence of the umbrageous growth of the 'angophora' in the meadow by the mountain creek, which bordered their farm. Bill stayed at home and worked steadily, until he had put in his crop. He cleared and cultivated a larger piece of ground with each succeeding year. The seasons were genial, and the rainfall, though occasionally precarious, did not, during this period, show any diminution. But annually, before the first spring month came round, Bill saddled the old mare, and leading a less valuable or perhaps half-broken young horse, packed his travelling 'swag' upon it and started off for the shearing. Jenny did not particularly like being left alone for three months or perhaps four, with no one but the children, for by this time a sturdy boy and baby girl had been added to the household. But Bill brought home such a welcome addition to the funds in the shape of the squatters' cheques, that she hid her uneasiness and discomfort from him, only hoping, as she said, that some day, if matters went on as they were going, they would be able to do without the shearing money, and Bill could afford to stop with his wife and children all the year round. That was what *she* would like.

So time went on, till after one more shearing, Bill began to think about buying the next selection, which an improvident neighbour would shortly be forced to sell, owing to his drinking habits and too great fondness for country race meetings.

The soil of the land so handily situated was better than their own, and, as an adjoining farm, could be managed without additional expense.

The 'improvements' necessary for holding it under the lenient land laws of New South Wales had been effected.

They were not particularly valuable, but they had been passed by the Inspector of Conditional Purchases, who was not too hard on a poor man, if he made his selection his '*bona fide* home and residence.' This condition Mr. Dick Donahue certainly had fulfilled as far as locating his hard-working wife Bridget and half-a-dozen bare-legged, ragged children thereon, with very little to eat sometimes, while he was acting as judge at a bush race meeting, or drinking recklessly at the public-house in the township.

So now the end had come. The place was mortgaged up to its full value with the bank at Talmorah, the manager of which had refused to advance another shilling upon it.

The storekeeper, who had a bill of sale over the furniture, horses and cows, plough, harrow, and winnowing machine, had decided to sell him up. The butcher and the baker, despairing of getting their bills paid, declined further orders. Poor Bridget had been lately feeding herself and the children on milk and potatoes, last year's bacon, and what eggs the fowls, not too well fed themselves, kindly produced.

Jenny had helped them many a time, from womanly pity. But for her, they would often have been without the 'damper' bread, which served to fill up crevices with the hungry brood—not that she expected return or payment, but as she said, 'How could I see the poor things hungry, while we have a snug home and all we can eat and drink?'

Then she would mentally compare Bill's industry with Dick's neglect, and a feeling of wifely pride would thrill her heart as she returned to her comfortable cottage and put her children, always neatly dressed, to sleep in their clean cots.

As she sat before the fire, near the trimly-swept hearth, which looked so pleasant and homely, though there was but a wooden slab chimney with a stone facing, a vision arose before her of prosperous days when they would have a ring fence round their own and the Donahues' farm—perhaps even an 'additional conditional lease,' to be freehold eventually—afterwards a flock of sheep and who knows what in the years to come.

'The Donahues, poor things, would have to sell and go away, that was certain; *they* couldn't prevent them being sold up—and, of course, Bill might as well buy it as another. The bank manager, Mr. Calthorpe, would sell the place, partly on credit, trusting Bill for the remainder, with security on both farms, because he was sober and industrious. Indeed, he told Bill so last week. What a thing it was to have a good name! When she thought of the way other women's husbands "knocked down" their money after shearing, forty and fifty pounds, even more, in a week's drunken bout, she felt that she could not be too thankful.

'Now Bill, when shearing was over, generally took a small sum in cash—just enough to see him home, and paid in the cheque for the season's shearing to his bank account. It was over sixty pounds last year, for he sold his spare horse—a thirty-shilling colt out of the pound, that he had broken in himself—to the overseer, for ten guineas, and rode home on the old mare, who, being fat and frolicsome after her spell, "carried him and his swag first-rate."

'As to the two farms, no doubt it would give them all they knew, at first, to live and pay interest. But other people could do it, and why shouldn't they? Look at the Mullers! The bark hut they lived in for the first few years is still there. They kept tools, seed potatoes, odds and ends in it now. Next, they built a snug four-roomed slab cottage, with an iron roof. That's used for the kitchen and men's room. For they've got a fine brick house, with a verandah and grand furniture, and a big orchard and more land, and a flock of sheep and a dairy and a buggy and—everything. How I should like a buggy to drive myself and the children to the township! Wouldn't it be grand? To be sure they're Germans, and it's well known they work harder and save more than us natives. But what one man and woman can do, another ought to be able for, I say!'

And here Jenny shut her mouth with a resolute expression and worked away at her needle till bedtime. Things were going on comfortably with this meritorious young couple, and Bill was getting ready to start for the annual trip 'down the river,' as it was generally described. This was a region distant three hundred miles from the agricultural district where the little homestead had been created. The 'down the river' woolsheds were larger and less strictly managed (so report said) than those of the more temperate region, which lay near the sources of the great rivers. In some of them as many as one hundred, two hundred, even three hundred thousand sheep were annually shorn. And as the fast shearers would do from a hundred to a hundred and fifty sheep per day, it may be calculated, at the rate of one pound per hundred, what a nice little cheque would be coming to every man after a season's shearing. More particularly if the weather was fine.

Bill was getting ready to start on the following morning when a man named Janus Stoate arrived, whom he knew pretty well, having more than once shorn in the same shed with him.

He was a cleverish, talkative fellow, with some ability and more assurance, qualities which attract steady-going, unimaginative men like Bill, who at once invited him to stay till the morning, when they could travel together. Stoate cheerfully assented, and on the morrow they took the road after breakfast, much to Mrs. Hardwick's annoyance, who did not care for the arrangement. For, with feminine intuition, she distrusted Janus Stoate, about whom she and her husband had had arguments.

He was a Londoner—an 'assisted' emigrant, a radical socialist, brought out at the expense of the colony. For which service he was so little grateful that he spoke disrespectfully of all the authorities, from the Governor downward, and indeed, as it seemed to her, of respectable people of every rank and condition. Now Jenny, besides being naturally an intelligent young woman, utilised her leisure hours during her husband's absence, for reading the newspapers, as well as any books she could get at. She had indeed more brains than he had, which gift she owed to an Irish grandmother. And though she did by no means attempt to rule him, her advice was always listened to and considered.

'I wish you were going with some one else,' she said with an air of vexation. 'It's strange that that Stoate should come, just on your last evening at home. I don't like him a little bit. He's just artful enough to persuade you men that he's going to do something great with this "Australian Shearers' Union" that I see so much about in the newspapers. I don't believe in him, and so I tell you, Bill!'

'I know you don't like Unions,' he answered, 'but see what they've done for the working classes! What could we shearers have done without ours?'

'Just what you did before you had anything to do with him and his Union. Do your work and get paid for it. You got your shearing money all right, didn't you? Mr. Templemore's cheques, and Mr. Dickson's and Mr. Shand's, were always paid, weren't they? How should we have got the land and this home, but for them?'

'Well, but, Jenny, we ought to think about the other workers as well as ourselves—"Every man should stand by his order," as Stoate says.'

'I don't see that at all. Charity's all very well, but we have our own business to look after and let other people mind theirs. Order, indeed! I call it disorder,—and them that work it up will have to pay for it, mark my words. You look at those children, William Hardwick, that's where you've got to give your money to, and your wife, and not a lot of gassing spouters like Janus Stoate, who don't care if their families starve, while they're drinking and smoking, talking rubbish, and thinking themselves fine fellows, and what fools you and the rest are to pay them for it.'

'Well, but the squatters are lowering the price of shearing, Jenny; we must make a stand against that, surely!'

'And suppose they do. Isn't wool falling, and sheep too? Aren't they boiling down their ewes, and selling legs of mutton for a shilling apiece? Why should they go on paying a pound a hundred when everything's down? When prices rise, shearing'll go up again, and wages too—you know we can get mutton now for a penny a pound. Doesn't that make a difference? You men seem to have no sense in you, to talk in that way!'

'Well, but what are we to do? If they go on cutting down wages, there's no saying what they'll do next.'

'Time enough to think about that when it comes. You take a fair thing, now that times are bad, it'll help them that's helped you, and when they get better, shearing and everything else will go up too. You can't get big wages out of small profits; your friends don't seem to have gumption enough to see that. I'm ashamed of you, I really am, Bill!'

'Well, I must go now—I daresay the squatters will give in, and there'll be no row at all.'

'What do you want to have a row for, I should like to know? Haven't you always been well treated and well fed, and well paid?—and now you want to turn on them that did it for you, just as if you were one of those larrikins and spielers, that come up partly for work, and more for gambling and stealing! I say it's downright ungrateful and foolish besides—and if you follow all the Union fads, mark my words, you'll live to rue the day.'

'Well, good-bye, Jenny, I can't stop any longer, you're too set up to be reasonable.'

'Good-bye, Bill, and don't be going and running risks at another man's bidding; and if you bring that man here again, as sure as my name's Jane Hardwick, I'll set the dogs on him.' And here Jenny went into the cottage, and shut the door with a bang, while Bill rode down the track to join his companion, feeling distinctly uncomfortable; the more so, as he reflected that he and Jenny had never parted in this way before.

'You've been a long time saying good-bye,' said that gentleman, with a sneering accent in his voice; 'that's the worst of bein' married, you never can follow your own opinions without a lot of barneyin' and opposition. It's a curious thing that women never seem to be on the side of progress—they're that narrow-minded, as they don't look ahead of the day's work.'

'My old woman's more given to look ahead than I am,' said Bill seriously. 'But, of course, we all know that we must stick together, if we expect to get anything out of the employers.'

'Yes, yes—by George, you're quite right,' said Stoate, as if Bill had enunciated an original and brilliant idea. 'What I and the workers want is to bring the capitalists on their knees—the labour element has never had its proper share of profits in the past. But we're going to have things different in the future. How was all the big estates put together, and them fine houses built, except by *our* labour? And what do we get after all, now the work's done? We've never had our fair share. Don't you see that?' Here he looked at Bill, who could find nothing to say but—

'I suppose not.'

'Suppose not? We've as much right to be ridin' in our buggies as the man as just passed us with that slashin' pair. Our labour made the land valuable—built the houses and put up the fences. Where do *we* come in, I ask you?'

'Well, I suppose the men that worked got their wages, didn't they?' answered Bill. 'There's been a deal of employment the last few years. I did pretty well out of a fencing contract, I know, and my mate started a big selection from his share.'

'Yes, yes, I daresay, that's where you fellers make the mistake. If you get a few pounds slung to you by these capitalists, you don't think of the other poor chaps walkin' about half starved, begging a meal here and a night's lodging there. What we ought to go in for is a co-operative national movement. That's the easiest of all. One man to find the money.'

'Is it?' Bill could not help saying, interrupting the flood of Stoate's eloquence. 'I've always found it dashed hard to find a few pounds.'

'I don't mean fellers like us; we work hard—a dashed sight too hard for all we get. I mean the regular professional capitalist, in a manner of speakin', that's got his money by buying land, when the Government oughtn't never to have sold it, if they'd had any savey, or had it left him by his father, as had robbed the people some other way. Well, he finds the money, you and I the muscle, and mark you, they can't do nothin' without *that*—and others, smartish chaps as comes from the people mostly, finds the brains.'

'And what after that?'

'That's what I'm a-coming to,' answered Stoate pompously. 'When the sheep's shorn, the fat ones sold, the wheat reaped, and the money put in the bank, we all divide fair, according to our shares. So much for interest on capital, so much for labouring work, so much for head work, so much for light, easy things like clerking, as most any fool can do.'

'That sounds pretty fair,' replied Bill, scratching his head, as he endeavoured to grasp the complex conditions of the scheme. 'But who's to boss the whole thing? There must be a boss?'

'Oh, of course, there'll be a council—elected by the people—that is of course the shareholders in each industrial, co-operative establishment; they all have votes, you know. The council will do all the bossing.'

'Oh, I see, and all share alike. One man's as good as another, I suppose.'

'Certainly, all have equal rights; every man willing to work has a right to have work found for him by the State.'

'But suppose he won't work when it *is* found for him? You and I have known plenty of coves like that.'

'Well, of course, there *is* a difference in men—some haven't the natural gift, as you may say—don't care for "hard graft," but you must remember no one'll have to work hard when labour's federated.'

'How'll the work be done, then?'

'Why, you see, every one will have to do four or six hours a day, rich and poor, young and old, from sixteen to sixty. Before that their eddication [Mr. Stoate's early environment—his father was a radical cobbler—had fixed his pronunciation of that important word inexorably], this eddication, I say (which is the great thing for a worker, and enables him to hold his own against the employers, who've always had a monopoly of it), has to be attended to. After sixty, they've to be pensioned off, not wanted to do no more work. And as Bellamy says in his *Looking Backward* (a great book, as all our chaps ought to read)—"If every one in the State worked their four hours a day, the whole work of the world could be easy done, and no one the worse for it."'

'That sounds well enough,' said Bill thoughtfully, 'but I'm afraid it wouldn't wash. A lot of chaps would be trying for the easy parts, and those that were cast for the rough and tumble wouldn't do it with a will, or only half and half. And who's to draft 'em off? The fellers elected to do it would have all the say, and if they had a down on a chap—perhaps a deal better man than themselves—they could drop him in for the lowest billets going.'

'That could all be set right in the usual way,' replied Stoate, pompously mouthing his words as if addressing an imaginary audience. 'Every member of the Association would have the right of appeal to the Grand Council.'

'And suppose they didn't side with the workin' feller—these talking chaps, as like as not, would hang together—he'd have to grin and bear it. He'd be no better than a slave. Worse than things are now. For a man can get a lawyer, and fight out his case before the P.M., and the other beaks. They're mostly fair and square—what I've seen of 'em. They've no interest one way or the other.'

'No more would the Grand Labour Council.'

'Don't know so much about that, working coves are middlin' jealous of one another. If one chap's been elected to the Council, as you call it, and another feller opposed him and got beat, there's sure to be bad blood between them, and the man that's up like enough'll want to rub it into the man that's down—and there'd be no one to see fair play like the beaks.'

'Why, you're getting to be a regular "master's man." That's not the way to talk, if you're goin' to be a Unionist.'

'Oh, I'll follow the Union,' replied Bill, 'if things are going to be fair and square, not any other way, and so I tell you. But if it's such a jolly good thing to put your money in a station and share and share alike with all the other chaps, why don't some of you Union chaps put your money together?—lots of you could raise a hundred or more if you didn't drink it. Then you could shear your own sheep, sell your own wool, and raise your own bread, meat, vegetables—everything. You could divide the profits at the end of the year, and if running a squatting station's such a thundering good thing, why you'd all make fortunes in no time. What do you say to that now?'

'Well, of course, it sounds right enough,' answered Stoate, with less than his usual readiness. 'There's a lot of things to be considered about afore you put your money into a big thing like that. You've got to get the proper sort of partners—men as you know something about, and that can be depended on for to work steady, and do what they're told.'

'Do what they're told? Why, ain't that the one thing you Union chaps are fighting the squatters about? They're not to be masters in their own woolsheds! The shearers and rouseabouts are *not* to obey the squatters' overseer, they must work as the Union's delegate tells 'em. What sort of fake d'ye call that? Suppose I'm harvestin'—my crop's not much now, but it may be, some day—d'ye mean to say I'm not to talk sharp to my own men, and say "do this" or "do that"? And a delegate walkin' up and down, makin' believe to be boss, while I'm payin' for the wages and rations, and horses and thrashing-machine, and the whole boiling, would I stand that? No! I'd kick him out of the place, and that dashed soon, I can tell you!' And here Bill's eyes began to sparkle and his fists to tighten on the reins as if he itched to 'stand up to his man,' with steady eye and watchful 'left,' ready for the first chance to 'land' his adversary.

The sun was scarcely an hour high when the wayfarers came in sight of the village-appearing group of edifices familiarly known as a 'sheep station.' The 'men's hut' came first into view—a substantial dwelling, with horizontal sawn slabs and shingled roof, a stone chimney and a dining-room. Boasting a cook, moreover, of far from ordinary rank. A superior building, in fact, to the one which the owner of the station thought good enough for himself for the first few years of his occupation of North Yalla-doora.

This was the abiding-place of the resident labourers on the station; men who received a fixed weekly wage, varying from a pound to twenty-five shillings per week, with board and lodging additional. The Australian labourer is catered for on perhaps the most liberal dietary scale in the world. He is supplied with three meals per diem, of beef or mutton of the best quality, with bread *à discrétion*, also tea (the ordinary drink of the country) in unlimited quantity, with milk and vegetables if procurable. Condiments, sauces, and preserves, if his tastes run that way, he has to pay for as extras.

They can be procured, also wearing apparel, boots, and all other necessaries, at the station store; failing that, at the 'township,' invariably found within easy distance of any large station.

Besides the 'men's hut' comes next in rank the 'shearers' hut,' dedicated to those important and (at shearing time) exclusive personages; the sheep-washers', the rouseabouts' huts, all necessary different establishments; as also the 'travellers' hut,' set apart for the nomadic labourer or 'swagman,' who sojourning but for a night is by the unwritten law of Bushland provided with bread and meat, cooking utensils, water, and firewood *gratis*.

Then, at a certain distance, the woolshed—with half an acre of roofed, battened yards and pens—the 'big house,' the stable, the horse-yard, the stock-yard, the milking-yard, with perhaps half-a-dozen additional nondescript constructions.

It may easily be imagined that such buildings, scattered and disjointed as they were, had much more the appearance of a village than of a single establishment owned, managed, and supported by one man (or one firm), and absolutely subject to his orders and interest.

'Might as well stop here to-night,' said Stoate; 'it's twenty-five mile to Coolah Creek for to-morrow, and the road heavy in places. Look at it! There's a bloomin' township to belong to one man, and *us* travellin' the country looking for work!'

'It took a lot of labour to put up all the huts and places, not to count in the shed and yards, you bet,' said his companion, who had been silent for the last half-hour, 'and many a cheque was drawed afore the last nail was drove in. I know a chap that's made a small fortune out of Mr. Templemore's contracts, and that's got a farm to show for it to-day. What's wrong with that?'

'Why, don't you see? Suppose the State had this first-rate block of country, cut it up in fair-sized farms, advanced the men the money to put up their places and crop it the first year, see what a population it would keep. Keep in comfort, too,' he continued, as he refilled his pipe and made ready for a leisurely smoke. 'Let me see, there's fifty thousand acres of freehold on this North Yalla-doora run, besides as much more leased. Divide that into nice-sized farms, that'd give us a thousand fifty-acre lots, or five 'underd 'underd-acre ones. See what a crowd of families that'd keep.'

'And suppose there come a dry season,' queried Bill rather gruffly, 'how about the families then? I've seen the sheep dyin' by hundreds on this very place—and the whole forty thousand 'd 'a died in another month if rain hadn't come. But I'm gettin' full up of this Union racket. Small farms in a dry country's foolishness. Where are we goin' to camp? Look at the grass on that flat! And I've seen it like a road.'

'It ain't bad near the creek,' said his companion. 'You can let the horses go while I go up to the overseer and get a bit of ration.'

'There's no call to do that. See that bag? My old woman's put bread and beef enough in that for a week anyhow, besides bacon, and tea, and sugar.'

'That's all right,' answered Stoate airily, 'but we may as well get fresh mutton for nothing. They always give travellers a pound or two here, and a pannikin of flour. It comes in handy for cakes.'

'Well, I'm d—d!' said Hardwick, unable to contain his wrathful astonishment. 'D'ye mean to tell me as you're a-goin' to *beg* food from this squatter here and take his charity after abusing him and all belonging to him and schemin' to ruin 'em? I call it dashed, dirty, crawling meanness, and for two pins I wouldn't travel the same side of the road with you, and so I tell you, Janus Stoate.'

There was a snaky glitter in Stoate's small, black eyes as he met for an instant the bold gaze of the Australian; but, with characteristic cunning, he turned it off with a half laugh.

'Why, Bill, what hot coffee you're a-gettin', all over a little joke like this 'ere. Now I feel as I've a right to be fed on the road when I and my feller-workers bring our labour to the door—in a manner of speakin'. We've no call to think ourselves under obligation to the squatters for their "miserable dole," as our Head Centre calls it. It's only our due when all's said and done.'

'Miserable dole,' growled Bill, now engaged in taking off his pack. 'That's a dashed fine name to give free rations, to the tune of half-a-dozen sheep a night, and a couple of bags of flour a week, which I know Tambo did last shearing. A lot of chaps going about the country askin' for work, and prayin' to God they mayn't find it—and abusin' the people that feed 'em on top of it all. I wonder the squatters don't stop feedin' travellers, and that's all about it. I would if I was boss, I know, except the old men.'

'How about the sheds and the grass when the weather gets dry?' asked Stoate, with a sidelong glance of spite.

'That's easy enough, if a chap's a d—d scoundrel; but suppose he's caught and gets five years in Berrima Gaol, he'd wish he'd acted more like a white man and less like a myall blackfellow. But stoush all this yabber. You boil the billy, while I get out the grub and hobble the horses. I feel up to a good square feed.'

So did Mr. Stoate, apparently, as he consumed slice after slice of the cold corned beef and damper which Jenny had put up neatly in Bill's 'tucker bag,' not disdaining divers hunks of 'brownie,' washed down with a couple of pints of 'billy tea,' after which he professed that he felt better, and proceeded to fill and light his pipe with deliberation.

By this time the hobbled horses had betaken themselves through the abundant pasture of the river flat, and their bells sounding faint and distant, Bill declared his intention of heading them back, in case they should try to make off towards the home they had left. He returned in half an hour, stating that they were in a bend and blocked by a horseshoe lagoon.

Both men addressed themselves to the task of putting up the small tent which Bill carried, and bestowed their swags therein, after which Mr. Stoate proposed that they should go over to the men's hut, and have a bit of a yarn before they turned in.

Bill remarked that they had to be up at daylight, but supposed that an hour wouldn't matter. So the wayfarers strolled over to a long building, not far from the creek bank, which they entered without ceremony. They found themselves in the presence of about twenty men, in the ordinary dress of the station hand, viz. tweed or moleskin trousers and Crimean shirt. Some had coats, but the majority were in their shirt sleeves. There were mostly of ages between twenty and forty, differing in nationality, speech, and occupation.

England, Ireland, Scotland, and Australia were represented. A Frenchman, two Germans, a coloured man (American), besides a tall, well-made Australian half-caste, who spoke much the same English as the others, but had a softer voice, with rather slower intonation.

At one end of the large room was an ample fireplace, with a glowing wood fire, around which several men were sitting or standing, mostly smoking. Others were seated at the long, solid dining-table reading, for in one corner stood some fairly well-filled bookshelves. One man was writing a letter.

A few were lying in their bunks, rows of which were on either side of the room. A certain amount of quiet conversation was going on. There was no loud talking, swearing, or rude behaviour of any sort, and in spite of the bare walls and plain surroundings an air of comfort pervaded the whole.

Stoate was greeted by several of the younger men, one of whom was disposed to be facetious, as he exclaimed—

'Hulloa, my noble agitator, what brings you here? Goin' to call out the shearers, and play the devil generally, eh? You've come to the wrong shop at North Yalla-doora—we're all steady-going coves here.'

'I suppose you're game to stand up for your rights, Joe Brace, and not afraid of getting your wages raised, if the Union does that for you?'

'*If* it does,' rejoined Joe sarcastically; 'and who's to go bail for that, I'd like to know? You and your crowd haven't done any great things so far, except make bad blood between masters and men—when everything was peace and goodwill before, as the parson says.'

'Well—what's that? Yer can't get nothin' in the world without fightin' for it—I reckon we're going to have a bit of war for a change. Yes, *war,* and a dashed good thing too, when men have to take orders from their feller-men, and be worked like slaves into the bargain.'

'Brayvo, Janus, old man!' replied the other, with mock approval. 'I see what it's come to. You're to be a delegate with a pot hat and a watch-chain, and get four pound a week for gassin', while us fools of fellers does the hard graft. That's your dart, to sit alongside of Barraker and the rest of the people's try-bunes—ain't them the blokes that stands up and says, like Ben Willett, as we're trod on, and starved, and treated worse than nigger slaves?'

'So you are, if you only knew it. Look at all this here country-side in the hands of two or three men, as sucks your blood, and fattens on it!'

'The boss here ain't too fat, if that's what's the matter, and we're not a very hungry-lookin' crowd, boys,' said the speaker, looking round. 'We've got good wages, good food, a book or two to read, and a table to write our letters at. You've been loafin' in Melbourne, Janus, and got oppressed there—spent all your money, forgot to buy a decent rig-out (them's last year's boots as you have on), come on the roads to beg from station to station, and abuse them as feeds you, after your belly's full. What do you say, Paddy?'

The man whom he addressed folded up the sheet upon which he had been writing, and rising from the form on which he sat, stood before the fire, displaying an athletic figure, and determined countenance, lighted up by a pair of glancing blue eyes, which proclaimed his nationality.

'I say that this strike business is all d—d rot, run by a lot of sneaks for their own ends. *They're* the vermin that fatten on the working-men, that are fools enough to believe their rubbish—not the squatters, who've mostly worked hard for what they've made, and spent it free enough, more power to them! Where's there a man on North Yalla-doora that's got anything to complain of? We're well paid, well fed, well cooked for, eh, Jack? and as comfortable in our way as the boss is in his. More indeed, for we've got a shingled roof, and his is box-bark. The travellers' hut's shingled, so is the rouseabouts'. He's never had time to have his own place done up, though he lives like a gentleman, as we all know.'

'Yer 'arf a gentleman yerself, ain't yer, *Mister* O'Kelly?' replied Stoate sneeringly. 'No wonder yer don't take no interest in the workers—the men that makes the wealth of this country, and every other. Yer the makin's of a first-class "scab," and if the chaps here was of my mind you'd be put out of every hut on the river.' Before the last word was fully out, O'Kelly made a couple of steps forward with so vengeful a glare in his blue eyes that Stoate involuntarily drew back—with such haste also, that he trod on the foot of a man behind him and nearly fell backward.

'You infernal scoundrel!' he cried; 'dare to take my name into your ugly mouth again, and I'll kick you from here to the woolshed, and drown you in the wash-pen afterwards. I've done a man's work in Australia for the last five years, though I wasn't brought up to it, as some of you know. I've nothing to say against the men who gave me honest pay for honest work, and whose salt I've eaten. But skulking crawlers like you are ruining the country. You're worse than a dingo—*he* don't beg. You come here and whine for food, and then try to bite the hand that feeds you. Didn't I see you at the store to-night, waiting for grub, like the other travellers?'

'No, yer didn't then,' snarled Stoate.

'Well, I have before this, and more than once. I expect you're loafing on your mate, who's a decent fellow, and the sooner he parts company with a hound like you, the better. But this is our hut, and out you go, or I will, and that's the long and short of it. Come on, Joe!'

'The public's not on for a sermon to-night, Janus, old man,' said the young fellow before mentioned. 'Paddy's got his monkey up, and it'll be bloody wars if you don't clear. Yer mate's a cove as we'd like to spend the evenin' with, but the votin's agin yer, Janus, it raly is.'

'I came in with Stoate,' said Bill, 'and in course I'm here to see it out with him, man to man. But this is your hut, and not ours, mate, so we'd better get back to our camp—good-night all!'

CHAPTER II

The sun-rays were slowly irradiating 'the level waste, the rounded grey' which accurately described the landscape, in the lower Riverina, which our travellers had reached after a fortnight's travel, and where the large and pastorally famous sheep station of Tandāra had been constructed. Far as the eye could range was an unbroken expanse of sea-like plain, covered at this spring time of year with profuse vegetation—the monotony being occasionally relieved by clumps of the peculiar timber growing only amid the vast levels watered by the Darling. The wilga, the boree, and the mogil copses were in shape, outline, and area so curiously alike, that the lost wanderer proverbially found difficulty in fixing upon any particular clump as a landmark. Once strayed from the faint irregular track, often the only road between stations thirty or forty miles apart— once confused as to the compass bearings, and how little hope was there for the wayfarer, especially if weary, thirsty, and on foot! The clump of mogil or wilga trees, which he had toiled so many a mile in the burning afternoon to reach, was the facsimile of the one left, was it that morning or the one before? More than once had he, by walking in a circle, and making for apparently 'creek timber' at variance with his original course, found himself at the *same clump*, verified by his own tracks, and the ashes of his small fire, as the one which he had left forty-eight hours ago.

Reckless and desperate, he takes the course again, feeling weaker by two days' hard walking—footsore, hungry—above all, *thirsty*, to the verge of delirium. Let us hope that he falls in with a belated boundary rider who shows him an endless-seeming wire fence, which he commands him to follow, till he meets the jackaroo sent with a water-bag to meet him. If this good angel (not otherwise angelic-seeming) 'drops across' him, well and good; if not so, or he does not 'cut the tracks' of a station team, or the lonely mailman going a back road, God help him! Soon will the crows gathering expectant round a pair of eagles, telegraph to the sharp-eyed scouts of the wilderness that they may ride over and see the dried-up, wasted similitude of what *was* once a man.

No such tragedy was likely to be enacted in the case of our two shearers. They were fairly mounted. They had food and water to spare. Bill was an experienced bushman, and both men had been along this track before. So they followed the winding trail traced faintly on the broad green sheet of spring herbage, sometimes almost invisible—or wholly so, where an old sheep camp had erased the hoof-or wheel-marks—turning to the right or the left with confident accuracy, until they 'picked up' the course again. Wading girth-deep through the subsidiary watercourses—billabongs, cowalls, and such—bank high in this year of unusual rain and plenty (they are synonymous in riverine Australia, 'arida nutrix'), and scaring the water-fowl, which floated or flew in countless flocks.

That gigantic crane, the brolgan (or native companion), danced his quadrille in front of them, 'advance, retire, flap wing, and set to partner,' before he sailed away to a region unfrequented by the peaceful-seeming but dangerous intruder. Crimson-winged, French grey galah parrots fluttered around them in companies, never very far out of shot; the small speckled doves, loveliest of the columba tribes, rose whirring in bevies, while the

swift-footed 'emu' over the waste

Speeds like a horseman that travels in haste.

To the inexperienced European traveller beholding this region for the first time, all-ignorant of the reverse side of the shield, what a pastoral paradise it would have seemed! Concealed from his vision the dread spectres of Famine, Death, Ruin, and Despair, which the shutting-up of the windows of Heaven for a season, has power to summon thereon.

This was a good year, however, in pastoral parlance. Thousands of lambs born in the autumnal months of April and May were now skipping, fat and frolicsome, by the sides of the ewes, in the immense untended flocks. They had been but recently marked and numbered, the latter arithmetical conclusion being obtained by the accurate if primitive method of counting the heaps of severed tails, which modern sheep-farming exacts from the bleeding innocents. The percentage ranged from ninety to nearly a hundred, an almost abnormally favourable result.

How different from the famine years of a past decade, still fresh in men's minds, when every lamb was killed as soon as born 'to save its mother's life,' and in many stations one-half of the ewes died also, from sheer starvation; when immense migratory flocks, like those of the 'mesta' of their Spanish ancestors, swept over the land, destroying, locust-like, every green thing (and dry, too, for that matter), steering towards the mountain plateaux, which boast green grass and rill-melodies, the long relentless summer through—that summer which, on lower levels, had slain even the wild creatures of the forest and plain, inured from countless ages to the deadly droughts of their Austral home.

When the kangaroos by the thousand die,

It's rough on the travelling sheep,

as 'Banjo' sings.

This station, when reached, presented a different appearance from North Yalla-doora. The prairie-like plain, far as the eye could reach, was bisected by a wide and turbid stream, flowing between banks, now low and partly submerged, now lofty and precipitous; occasionally overhanging as if cut away by the angry waters, in one of the foaming floods which, from time to time, alternated with seasons when the shallow stream trickled feebly over the rock-bars in the river-bed.

The buildings were large, but less complete in appearance than those of Yalla-doora. An air of feverish energy pervaded the whole establishment, which seemed to denote that time was more valued than finish, for the pressing work in hand. The windings of the river could be distinctly marked by the size of the great eucalypts which fringed the banks, refusing to grow away from its waters. How often had they been hailed with joy by the weary wayfarer, athirst even unto death, who knows that his trials are over, when from afar he sights the 'river timber.' And now, the signs of the campaign were visible. Men rode in at speed from distant parts of the immense area known as Tandara 'run.' From the far horizon, came nearer and yet nearer the lines of unladen waggons, with long teams of lagging horses or even bullocks, from twelve to twenty in number.

Far from fat and well-liking were these necessary beasts of draught, but sure to leave the station frolicsome and obese after a few weeks' depasturing upon the giant herbage which for a hundred leagues in every direction waved in vast meads like ripening corn. An assemblage of tents and hastily constructed shelters on a 'point' of the river proclaims the 'camp' or temporary abode of the expectant shearers and rouseabouts, wool-pressers, ordinary hands, and general utility men, upon every large run at shearing time, but more especially on so exceptionally important a property as that of Tandara.

'By George! there's a big roll up on Steamer Point this time,' said Bill. 'I've shorn here twice, and never seen as many afore. There won't be stands for half of 'em when the roll's called.'

'No more there will,' said Stoate, as he looked in the direction of the populous camp, where much talk and argument seemed to be going on. 'And them that wrote and got their names put down months back won't have a rosy time of it neither.'

'Why not?' queried Bill. 'Ain't they done right to come and shear when they promised last year, and got the cove to keep places for them?'

'Oh, I didn't mean that, though I don't hold, mind you, with taking places such a dashed long time before shearin's on. It's hard on a chap, when he comes to a shed after travellin' three or four 'underd mile, to be told that all the stands is took up. But there'll be a big row all the same.'

'How's that?'

'Why, Drench the delegate told me, the last place we stopped at, that orders had come up that if the boss wouldn't give in to the Shearers' Union agreement the men were to be called off the board.'

'Hunter won't stand it,' said Bill. 'You take my word. He's always been a good employer; no man can deny that. Good wages, good rations, and pays cash on the nail when the men want it. Don't even give cheques, and that blocks the publican, because a chap can pay as he goes, and needn't hand his cheque over the bar counter. But I know what he'll say to the delegate, or any other man that tells him he's not to be boss in his own shed.'

'What'll that be?' asked Stoate, with a sidelong look, half of curiosity, half of concealed malice.

'He'll tell 'em to go to hell and mind their own business, and leave him to look after his; that he'll see the Union and every one connected with it d—d first before he'll give up the right to manage his own property in his own way.'

'We'll show him different—that is, the Union will,' said Stoate, correcting himself hastily. '*His* property! Who made it? who dug the tanks and put up the fences, and shepherded the sheep afore they was paddocked? and built the blooming shed, as is an emblem of tyranny, to my thinking—when every man ought to have his five 'underd or a thousand ewes of his own, and a neat little place to shear 'em in? *His property!* I say it's *our* property. *We* made it—with the labour of our 'ands—and we ought to have the biggest say in the managin' of it.'

'What about buyin' the sheep and cattle, and the horses, and the payin' of wages this year?' said Bill. 'Suppose they come o' theirselves, "kinder growed," as the nigger gal says in that book about slavery in America, as Jenny read out to me last winter.'

'Wages be hanged!' retorted the disciple of Henry George and Dellamy. 'Our labour makes the fund out of which they pays their bloomin' *wages*, as they call 'em—infernal skinflints, as they are. It's dashed easy for them as gets the profits of our hard earnin's to dribble a trifle back, hardly enough to keep us in workin' order, like them team 'orses as is just turned out—a bite of chaff, and that's about all.'

'Well, only for the chaff, they'd be deaders the first dry season—down from weakness for a week or two, with their eyes picked out by the crows, and the ants eatin' 'em alive. I've seen the wild "brumbies" like that. I expect *they* ought to go on strike for stable keep, and three feeds of oats a day?'

'Men and 'orses is different—you can't compare 'em, in the way of their rights.'

'No; I know you can't,' answered Bill. 'The horses are a dashed sight the straightest crowd of the two. Howsomever, we shan't agree on them points, if we talk till Christmas. You take your way, and I'll take mine. But look here, Stoate, if there's goin' to be any of this burnin' and smashin' racket, as I've heard tell of, I'm *not on*. Mind that—don't you make any mistake! I've a bit of property of my own, as I've worked hard for, and I'm not goin' to hurt another man's savin's, Union or no Union, for all the Labour delegates in Australia, and so I tell you.'

Stoate did not speak for a few moments, then his eyes once more assumed the covert look of malice which they had worn before, as he said slowly—

'That means that you're not game to stand up for the rights of your horder, and you'll act the spy on the men as does.'

Bill's grey eyes blazed out with so sudden a light, as he made a half movement to jump off his horse, that Stoate involuntarily tightened his rein, and touched his leg-weary steed with the one spur of which he made constant use. But Bill resumed his saddle seat, and putting strong constraint on himself, replied: 'I'm that game as I'll give you a crack on the "point," as 'll stop your blowin' for a bit, if you'll get down and put your hands up. You're a light weight, and not very fit, or I'd knock some of the gas out'n yer now if you'd stand up to me. Not as you would—you're a deal better at talkin' than fightin', let alone workin'. But you and me's mates no more, mind that. You clear out with your moke, and make your own camp, and don't you come anigh me never again, or I'll give you what for, in a style you'll remember till the shearin' after next.' And so saying, Bill touched up his horse, and went off at a hand gallop, with his pack-horse—which by this time had learned to follow his companion steed—after him.

Mr. Stoate regarded this action on the part of his whilom companion with baleful eye and resentful feeling, which at length found vent in these memorable words—

'You're very flash, Bill Hardwick, with your fresh 'oss and yer packer. S'pose you think you've left me in a hole, all for a few words on these blarsted, hungry, grinding squatters; but I've seen better coves'n you straightened afore to-day. And by——! I'll be even with yer before the year's out, as sure as my name's Janus Stoate!'

After which pious resolve, Mr. Stoate jogged sullenly onward to the head station, where his sense of the dignity of labour did not prevent him from joining a crowd of men, who were in turn receiving the ordinary bush dole—viz. a pound or two of fresh beef or mutton, in addition to a pint pannikin of flour. As there were at least forty or fifty men who received these components of two substantial meals— supper and breakfast—it may be guessed what a daily contribution the squatter was required to make toward the support of the nomadic labourer of the period.

With respect to that universally recognised Australian institution, the 'travellers' hut,' to which Mr. Stoate betook himself, on receiving his free supper and breakfast materials, an explanation may not be out of place. In the good old times, 'before the war,' in the pre-union days, and when owing to the smaller size of pastoral properties the hands required were necessarily fewer, the chance labourer was made free of the 'men's hut.' In those Arcadian days the men's cook prepared his meals, and he sat at meat with the permanent employés.

This was all very well, when one or two casual guests at the outside were wont to arrive in an evening. But when, in consequence of the growth of population, and the increase of stock, the units were turned into scores, with a possibility of hundreds, the free hospitality had to be restricted.

Complaints were made by the permanent hands that the pilgrim was in the habit of picking up unconsidered trifles, when the men had gone to work after breakfast, and absconding with the same. The cook, too, expostulated, inasmuch as the 'traveller,' after availing himself copiously of the meals set before him, generally took the precaution of loading himself with 'cooked food' sufficient for the next day or two, whereby he, the cook, was kept baking and boiling all day and half the night, in addition to his ordinary work.

For some or all of these reasons, the 'travellers' hut' was decided upon. A roomy and substantial structure, placed near the creek or dam, as the case might be, at a certain distance from the other buildings, to which all future travellers not being gentlefolk, coming with introductions to the overseer's quarters, or 'the big house,' were relegated. 'Bunks' or sleeping-places, a table, and stools were mostly provided; also a load of firewood, an axe, a frying-pan, bucket, and iron pot.

Wayfarers henceforth came under the obligation to cook for themselves. The frying of chops, the boiling of beef and the baking of cakes—operations, with which every bushman is familiar, not being considered to be hardships worth speaking of. The stock of firewood was kept up, it being found that, in default, the uninvited guests felt no delicacy in burning the interior fittings, or even the doors and window frames. To this sanctuary, Mr. Stoate, in place of his former comfortable camp with Hardwick, was fain to betake himself. It was half a mile 'down the creek,' and he cursed freely at being told by the overseer that he must turn out his horse in the 'strangers' paddock,' another half-mile farther, and on no account to put him into the homestead horse-paddock.

'I'm not going to have all the feed ate up that I've saved for the station horses,' said that functionary, in decided tones, 'and so I tell you. You shearers and rouseabouts think it's nothing, I suppose, to find grass for a hundred or two horses, and a mob of bullocks big enough to stock a small run. But you'll have to pay for your grass one of these fine days, if you don't mind your eye.'

'D'ye think a man's to walk all over the bloomin' bush, lookin' for work and carrying oats and hay with him, if he's got a moke?' growled Stoate. 'The squatters have got all the blessed country, and they grudge a pore man a mouthful of food, and every blade of grass his horse eats.'

'A poor man!' said the overseer. 'What sort of a poor man d'ye call yourself, Stoate? Your cheque last year, what with fencing and shearing, was over forty pounds for three months' work. You've neither wife, chick nor child (not in this country, anyhow). What have you done with your money? Spent it in town; now you come up here crawling and begging for the bread you eat, and doing all the harm you can to the men you're living on. Why don't you keep a pound or two for the road, like Bill Hardwick and other chaps? Then you needn't be beholden to any one; and if you like to talk rot to the men that are fools enough to trust you, that's their look-out. But to come here and to every station along the river begging for food and trying to harm the men you're living on is mean, d—d mean, and treacherous to boot. If the boss was of my way of thinking, he'd never let you inside a shed of his, or pay you another pound for shearing, and now you know my mind,—take your grub.'

And then Mr. Macdonald, an athletic Australian Scot, who towered above the short though wiry Londoner as does a mastiff above a lurcher, poured the pannikin of flour into the 'tucker bag' which Stoate held out, and cutting off a lump of fat mutton tossed it contemptuously at him.

Stoate caught the meat before it fell, and looked at the overseer with evil passions writ plain in his sullen face and snaky eye, as he said: 'You might come to be sorry for this some day, boss, big as you are!'

'Yes, you sneaking hound, I know what that means. But I've got old Harry Bower (who used to shepherd here long ago, before he turned bushranger) as night-watchman at the shed, in case some of you dogs that disgrace the Shearers' Union take a fancy to light it up. He was a *man* when he took to the bush. *You'd* do it and fellows like you, only you haven't the pluck. He's got a double-barrelled gun, and swears by his God he'll use it if he catches any curs sneaking about the shed after dark. The grass is too green to burn for a month or two, but if I come across you near a bush fire, after shearing, I'll shoot you like a crow. So take that with you—and do your worst.'

Mr. Macdonald, though a born Australian, had inherited, it will be seen, the characteristic 'perfervidum ingenium.'

It seemed imprudent of him to speak so openly before the crowd of shearers and '*bona-fide* travellers,' so called. But a bold, declared policy is sometimes more diplomatic than a halting, opportunist one.

The men knew that war was declared, given certain acts of aggression or intimidation on their part. Severe sentences would unquestionably follow—if convictions were secured before the courts. On the whole, though they did not fear him, they respected him more for his openness and decided action.

'He's a *man* that hits out straight from the shoulder,' said one young fellow. 'I like that sort. You know where you have 'em. I don't hold with all this Union racket. It does more harm than good, to my mind. The most of these delegates is reg'lar blatherskites, as I wouldn't trust to carry a pound note across the street. Pretty coves to make laws for the likes of us.'

'I'm dashed sorry I ever had any truck with this Union crowd,' said his mate, as they walked away. 'I'd never no call to complain, as I know. If I didn't like a man's ways in his shed, I didn't shear there. There's plenty more. I don't fancy free men like us shearers bein' under one man's thumb, and him lookin' out for himself all the time. It's too much of the monkey for me, and I'm not goin' to stand it after this season, no matter what comes of it.'

The minor troubles having been surmounted, the roll-call read over, the rouseabouts settled and contented—each man in receipt of twenty-five shillings per week, with everything found on a scale of liberality, not to say profuseness, huts, cooks, wood and water, beef and mutton, tea and sugar, vegetables—everything reasonable and unreasonable, in fact, that the heart of bushman could desire.

The shearers, in number nearly a hundred, were apparently placated by being allowed to shear for the first time at Tandara under 'Union Rules,' a copy of which was posted up in a prominent part of the shed, setting forth that on certain points of dispute, if such should arise, the Delegate, that important, dignified personage, should have the power of joint decision with the shed manager. Wool had gone down nearly one-half in price, fat sheep as much or more; but holding to a modern doctrine that wages were not to be regulated by profits, and that Labour and not Capital provided the wage-fund, the same rate of payment per hundred sheep as was paid in more prosperous times had been exacted by the shearers' representatives. This was agreed to under protest, though considered inequitable by the proprietors of North Yalla-doora and other representative sheds as the lesser evil, compared with that of a delayed shearing and perhaps ruined wool clip. A truly serious matter.

For the same reason the Union Rules had been accepted by several proprietors, though much against the grain, and the woolshed ticketed for the first time as a 'Union Shed.' This was done under the impression that a feeling of loyalty to the principles which professed to guide the Shearers' Union would ensure steady and continuous work.

It was a concession to expediency, unwillingly made by Mr. Hunter and others at the last moment, in the hope of 'getting the shearing over quickly'—a matter involving great gain or loss. The latter, in this particular era of low prices of wool and stock of all kinds, cattle and horses, as well as sheep, approaching the margin of ruin, ominously close. 'If the fellows shear decently and behave themselves, I don't care what they stick up in the shed, or what they call their confounded Union. They shore well enough for me and Anderson last year, so I shall go on with them as long as they treat me well. You might as well do so, too.'

This had been the reasoning of Mr. M'Andrew, one of Mr. Hunter's neighbours, a shrewd, somewhat self-seeking man of the world. And it had a savour of argument about it. 'What did it matter,' he had said, 'how other squatters looked at the question? All they had to think of was to get their own work properly done, and let every man mind his own business. He was not sure that the Pastoral Association did much good. It only set the men and masters more at odds with each other. A great deal of this ill-feeling and strike had been brought on by such proprietors as old Jackson, M'Slaney, and Pigdon. Men notoriously hard and grasping in their dealings with their employés—cutting down wages, the price of shearing and contract bush work, in every way possible; feeding, housing, and paying their people badly, while charging exorbitant prices for necessaries—flour, meat, shears, tobacco—all things, in fact, which they could not carry with them and were bound to buy from the station store. These pastoralists were primarily responsible for the dissatisfaction which had led to the strikes and rioting. For his part, as he had always acted fairly and squarely with his men, as everybody knew, it was not to be expected that he should be compelled to pay up for a contest which he had no share in bringing on.'

This had seemed fair reasoning to that class of men who are glad of any excuse to avoid paying cash out of pocket and to the avowal of a decided policy. But there were other squatters equally averse to unnecessary outlay, who, possessing more forecast and logical acumen, refused on principle to make terms with the shearers' or any other Union. They had stated their grounds of dissent from the policy of opportunism, and, what was more important, acted upon them with courage and consistency.

'This station,' said Archibald Douglas Kinross, 'chiefly freehold land, with the sheep depasturing thereon, is *my* property, as the law stands at present. And I claim the right of every Briton to manage his own affairs in his own way. To employ persons to do my work—*my* work, you understand, not any one else's—as I shall choose, in my own way and after my own taste. If any section of workmen does not wish to work for me, they are at liberty not to do so. I leave them absolute freedom in that respect; but if they accept my pay and my employment, they must do my work *as I choose*—not as *they* choose—all socialistic sophistry notwithstanding.

'Australia still contains men willing to work for high wages and good food, and to do what they are told by a fair employer, and if I am threatened or my property injured by lawless ill-disposed persons, I shall appeal to that statute under which law and order have hitherto, in Australia, been vindicated. Moreover I, Archie Kinross, am *not* going to place myself under the heel of any body of men calling themselves by one name or another. Once concede Trade Unions their right to coerce the individual, and farewell to that freedom which has so long been the Briton's boast.

'Every man who had the misfortune to acquire or inherit property would, as the so-called Unions gained power by cowardly subservience or mistaken reasoning, be at the mercy of an irresponsible, ignorant, perhaps more or less unprincipled committee, anxious to blackmail those more fortunately placed than themselves.

'They would be told how many servants they were to employ, and what they were to pay them; feed, clothe, and otherwise provide for them. Not improbably, other concessions would be gradually exacted. The whole result being reached in a state of modified communism, certain to end in bloodshed and revolution. A social upheaval, which all history tells us is the invariable precursor of a military despotism.'

After ever so much trouble, worry and anxiety, arising from the offensively independent and even obstructive attitude of the shearers at all the sheds in the Lower Darling and elsewhere in New South Wales, a start was made at Tandara.

Jack Macdonald, bitterly aggrieved that his employers should have given in, was almost out of his mind with the irritating, puerile demands and objections which he had to meet.

'In old days he would have knocked down the ringleader, and told the sympathisers to "go to the devil"—that they need never show up at this shed or station again. Never should they get a pound of mutton or a pannikin of flour from the store, if they were dying of hunger; that they were ungrateful dogs, and here—at Tandara of all places, known for the most liberal station in the whole blooming district for pay and rations, where useless old hands were pensioned and kept on at make-believe work, when no one else would have had them on the place; where more expensive improvements—huts, fencing, tanks, wells, and stock-yards—had been made and put up, than on any station from the Queensland border to the sea. And now, what had come of it all?

'Where was the gratitude of the working-man, who, with his fellows, had been fed, lodged, and supported in good seasons and bad—when wool was down and money was scarce, and half the squatters on the verge of ruin? When the shed was down with influenza last year, didn't the wife and daughters of the "boss," who happened to be staying over shearing that year, make jelly, sago puddings and cakes, all sorts of blooming luxuries for the men that were going to die (by their own account), and couldn't hold their heads up?

'And now, because labour was scarce, owing to the Coolgardie goldfield having broken out, and the season coming on early, with the burr and grass seeds ripening every day, they must try and ruin their best friends, the squatters—threatening to strike for this and that—faulting the meat, the bread, the sugar, the tea, every mortal thing (far better than ever they'd been used to), and all at the bidding of a fellow like Stead, a man that had been educated at the expense of the State, people putting their hands in their pockets to pay for his schooling. And this is the first use he makes of it. It was enough to make a man feel ashamed of the colony he was born in, ashamed of being an Australian native, enough to make him clear out to South Africa, where the Boers and blackfellows were said to be no great things, but couldn't be such sneaks and dogs and thieves as his countrymen here.'

Jack Macdonald repeated this unreserved statement of opinion so often, for the benefit of all whom it might concern, that he began to know it by heart, and half thought of standing for the district, when the next election came round. However, the men liked him, and didn't mind his hard words, knowing that they held the key of the position, and that he was powerless if he wanted his sheep shorn. He couldn't afford to kick them out, however much he might wish so to do. All the sheds in the district were short of men, and if the shearers left in a body, the year's clip would suffer ruinous loss and injury. So they turned up their noses at the beautiful, fat, well-cooked mutton,—said 'they wanted more chops.' To which Macdonald sarcastically replied 'that he supposed they must grow a new breed of sheep, *all chops*.' In spite of their *five* meals a day, early breakfast, tea and 'brownie' at eleven o'clock, dinner at one, afternoon tea at four o'clock, and supper at half-past six, they were not satisfied, and, indeed, would not have gone without a second supper at 9 P.M. if the cook had not refused point-blank, and being a fighting man of some eminence, invited the deputation to 'step outside and put up their hands,' one after the other.

However, as before mentioned, a start *was* made, and though the quality of shearing was no great things, and Mr. Stoate, duly elected Shearers' Delegate, produced his appointment and walked up and down the shed, with great dignity, carefully ignoring Macdonald, and ostentatiously writing or telegraphing to W. Stead, Esq., President of the A.S.U., Wagga Wagga,[1] N.S. Wales, some kind of progress was made, and the super's face began to lose its saturnine expression. The weather, which in the early days of spring had been showery and unfavourable, changed for the better, and the heaviest of the flocks having been shorn, 'big tallies'—a hundred and thirty, and even one hundred and fifty or sixty—began to be made.

1. Pronounced 'Waūgăh Waūgăh.'

The discontented shearers even, whose minds had been unsettled by specious, communistic talk, prophesying a general distribution of property among the wage-earners, according to the gospel of Bellamy, commenced to be more or less satisfied. Visions of the big cheque, to which each man was adding now (prospectively) at the rate of from a pound to thirty-five shillings *a day*, commenced to float in the air. All was comparative peace and joy. Macdonald, it is true, had a trifling altercation with Mr. Janus Stoate one Friday afternoon, during which the last-named gentleman received a telegram, which he put into his pocket, after reading it, with a sneering smile. 'You'll know directly who's master on this floor—you, the hired servant of a capitalist, as is livin' on the blood of these pore ignorant chaps; or me, that's been elected by the workers of the land to see as they gets justice from their grindin' employers.'

Macdonald made one step towards the insolent underling, as might the second mate of a north sea whale-ship, if cook or fo'c's'le hand dared withstand him, while the wrathful glitter in his eye caused the offender to alter his tone. But the thought of the shearing, now three-parts through, being delayed on his account, was even a stronger controlling force.

Halting, with an effort, he glared for a few seconds at the contemptible creature, that yet had such power of annoyance, as if he could crush him with his heel. Then with studiously calm and measured tones, he said: 'You'd do great things if you were able, Mr. Delegate Stoate. If I had my way, I'd have you shot and nailed up on a barn door, as they do your namesakes in the old country. That's the only way to treat varmint, and it's a pity it isn't done here.'

The man received this little compliment with an attempt at cynical self-possession, which his shifty, malignant gaze belied, as the small eyes gleamed with reptilian malice. 'I'll learn yer,' he hissed out, 'to talk to the people's chyce as if he was the dirt under yer feet.' 'Men of the Australian Shearers' Union,' he said, raising his voice to a shrill cry, 'listen to me, and drop them shears — every man Jack of yer. D'ye know what's in this bloomin' tallagram? A strike's ordered. D'ye hear? — a *strike*! Here's the wire from the Head Centre at Wagga.

"'By order of the President and Council of the Australian Shearers' Union. Every shed in the Darling district, Union or non-Union, is hereby commanded to come out and stop working *instantly* on receiving this notice from the Delegate of the Branch, under penalty of being reported to the Council of the Union at Headquarters.

Signed by me, W. STEAD,

At Wagga Wagga, this 30th September 189-.'"

CHAPTER III

This was a bombshell with a vengeance. The anarchist, who threw it metaphorically, would have had no scruples — except those of personal apprehension — in casting a dynamite duplicate on the shearing floor. A sudden confusion filled the shed. Murmurs and sullen rejoinders were made, as the more prudent division of the men recognised that their shearing cheques, the outcome of weeks of hard work, were doomed to delay, perhaps to forfeiture. Some openly withstood the triumphant delegate, others, less impulsive, were disposed to temporise, while 'I thought this was a Union shed' remarked, with slow impressiveness, a gigantic native, considerably over six feet in height, whose wiry, muscular frame and tremendous reach stamped him as one of the 'ringers' of the shed. 'Ain't the Union Rules put up there?' pointing to the copy ostentatiously affixed at the end of the shed for reference. 'What's this darned foolishness, stoppin' men that's only a week's work between them and a big cheque?'

'You can read and write, I suppose,' replied Mr. Stoate contemptuously. ('Better nor you,' murmured a young fellow just within earshot.) 'Is them words on the telegram, what I told the men of this shed, and are you thereby ordered to come out, or are you not? That's what I want to know. Are you a-goin' to defy the Union? Think a bit afore you chance that and turn "scab."'

'I'm goin' to think a bit—just so,—and I hope you other chaps'll do the same, and not rush into law, like a bull at a gate, and lose your money, because of any second fiddle in the land. As to being a "scab," Delegate Stoate, I'm no more one than you are, perhaps not as much, if the truth's told. But don't you say that to me again, or I'll pitch you through one of them skylights, with one hand too.' And here the giant stretched forward his enormous fore-arm, and looking upward to the skylight in the roof of the woolshed, made as though there would be no unusual difficulty in the feat. 'Show me that telegram, please; this step wants consideration.'

'Ain't you goin' to obey the Union?' demanded Stoate with a great assumption of dignity. 'P'raps you ain't aweer, men, as this is a serious act of disobedience, which I shall report accordin'.'

'That's all very well,' answered the dissenter, whose unusual height, as he towered above his fellows, seemed to give him a certain title to leadership. 'I'm as good a Unionist as any man here; but I see no points in chuckin' away our money and hurtin' an employer who's been fair and square with us. Where's he gone against our rules? I ask you all. Isn't the rules put up at the end of the shed, all ship-shape and reg'lar? Didn't we stop shearin' for two days last week, and the weather fine, because the delegate here said the wool was damp? I didn't feel no damp, nor my mate neither, and we lost two dashed good days' work—a couple of pounds each all round. Now, I don't want to go dead against the Union, though I can't see the fun of losin' a goodish cheque, and, as I say, hurtin' a gentleman as never did any man here a bad turn. Let's try a middle course. Suppose we pick a man as we all can trust, and send him to Wagga. He can interview the Head Centre there, and *make sure*, afore we chuck away our stuff, whether every Union shed's bound to come out, or whether, under partic'lar circumstances like this here, we can't *cut out the shed* afore we go. I move a resolution to that effect.'

'And I second it,' said Bill Hardwick. 'I want to take my money home to my old woman and the kids; I've got a lot to do with it this season, and so, I daresay, have most of you, chaps. I don't see no sense in clearin' out now, when we've got fifty or sixty pound a man, to take and goin' off with neither money nor grub. Of course, we can *wait* to be paid out of Union funds, but we know what *that* means. Those that votes for Jim Stanford's motion, and fair play, hold up your hands.'

The scene that followed was hard to describe. A forest of hands was held up, while there rose a babel of voices, some laying down the law, others expressing a doubt of the prudence of flouting the mysterious powers of the A.S.U., in the midst of which Mr. Stoate, standing upon the wool table, vainly attempted to make himself heard.

The controversy continued until the dinner-bell rang, by which time it was clear that the sense of the meeting was overwhelmingly in favour of Stanford's amendment.

So, in spite of Stoate's threats and envious malice, a steady-going, middle-aged shearer of known probity and experience was chosen and despatched to Narandera, *en route* for Wagga Wagga, for further instructions. In the meantime, it was agreed to go on with the shearing, to which the men addressed themselves with such energy and determination, that when the knock-off evening bell sounded, the tallies were larger than on any preceding afternoon of the week. Jack Macdonald was delighted, though he refrained from open commendation, as he noticed that all the fast shearers made a point of shearing carefully and giving no room for disapprobation on his part.

Mr. Stoate viewed the whole proceedings with unconcealed disgust, and talked big about taking down the names of every man in the shed, and so reporting them that they would never get another 'stand' in a Union shed. He found, however, that except among the young, unmarried men, and a few reckless spendthrifts, who were carried away by the specious ideas at that time freely ventilated, he had little influence.

Stanford and Hardwick were noted men—honest, hard-working, and respected as 'ringers,' and as such, leaders in their profession. As Stanford bent his long back, and lifted out a fresh sheep every few minutes from the pen, with as much apparent ease as if the big, struggling seventy pound wether had been a rabbit, a feeling of industrial emulation seemed to pervade the great shed, and each man 'shore for his life,' as old Billy Day expressed it—'and that dashed neat and careful, as if there was a hundred pound prize at next Wagga Show hangin' to it.'

'Wait till George Greenwell comes back,' said Stoate—'and he ought to be here inside of eight days, as he can get the rail from Narandera—and see what you'll have to say, then.'

Of course, telegrams had been sent, and arrived with reiterated command from the Napoleon at Wagga Wagga—to lay down their arms, or rather their shears, as ordered.

And this was the crowning injustice and treachery of the ukase—that all the *Union* sheds in New South Wales, where the proprietors had surrendered their independence, and pocketed their pride, at the bidding of expediency, were penalised. Those squatters who 'bowed not the knee to Baal,' and fought out the contest, with sheds half full of 'learners,' and strangers from other colonies, brought over by the Pastoral Association, as well as the free shearers, who, intimidated by the Union guerillas, were often injured and hindered as to their lawful work, were now in a far better position. They were able to laugh at the surrendering squatters.

'You have given in,' said they; 'sacrificed principle and set a bad example for the sake of getting quickly through this season's shearing. You betrayed your pastoral comrades, and are *now betrayed by the Union*; you are left in the lurch. Serve you right!'

So, 'deserted in their utmost need,' with half-shorn sheep, and no hope of fresh men—as the non-Union sheds had secured most of the available labour—they were in a pitiable condition, neither help nor sympathy being procurable; while many of the free sheds were shearing steadily and comfortably, with a 'full board.'

In seven days, Mr. Greenwell was expected to appear. He could ride to Narandera in three days; twenty-four hours would take him to Wagga Wagga, after stopping for the night at Junee Junction. This was far and away the finest railway station in New South Wales, perhaps in Australia, having not only an imposing structure connected with the railway proper, but a very fine hotel, erected by the Government of New South Wales, liberally managed and expensively furnished.

There, the railway passenger could spend the night, or a week, if he so decided, being sure that he would be called at the proper time, either by night or day, to be despatched on his journey in an enviable and Christian state of mind.

The days passed on at Tandara, the week was nearly over. Such quick and clean shearing had never been done there before. The last day of the allotted time approached. Greenwell had not arrived, but surely he would turn up on the morrow.

Stoate was uneasily anxious. He hinted at treachery. But Greenwell, a regular, downright 'white man,' could not be 'got at.' Every one scoffed at the idea. One of the rouseabouts, who had known better times, hummed the refrain of 'Mariana in the moated grange': 'He cometh not, she said.' Worst of all, from Stoate's point of view, the shearing would be finished in two more days. The shed would then be paid off—shearers, pressers, rouseabouts, the cook and his mate, everybody down to the tar-boy. If their emissary didn't come before then, he might just as well not come at all. The 'might, majesty, and dominion' of the Australian Shearers' Union, with 20,000 members in all the colonies, which had aimed at one great 'Australian Labourers' Union' in town and country, would be set at nought. They had planned the inclusion of every worker—that is, muscle-worker, for brains didn't count—from the ship's cook of the coaster to the boundary rider on the Lower Darling or the Red Barcoo; from the gas-stoker in Melbourne or Sydney, where they hoped to plunge the cities into darkness, to the stock-rider, behind his drove of Queensland bullocks; and the back-block carrier, with his waggon and team of fourteen unshod Clydesdales or Suffolks.

And now, in the case of the Tandara shed, one of the best known and oldest stations on the Darling, this campaign against capital was to end in defeat and disappointment.

Stoate groaned in despair, as the eighth day arrived and no messenger. For the last forty-eight hours he had been looking anxiously for the cloud of dust at the end of the long, straight road across the endless plain, which heralded the approach of team, coach, or horseman.

As if to aggravate the Strike leaders, and all connected with that beneficent institution, the weather had been miraculously fine. No spring storms had come out of the cloudless sky, not so much as a 'Darling River shower'—four drops upon five acres,' in the vernacular—had sprinkled the red dust of the plain, to give the delegate the excuse to declare the sheep too wet to shear, and so lose a day. Nothing, in fact, happened. And on the noontide hour of the fourth day succeeding the week, Tandara shed 'cut out.' The 'cobbler,' the last sheep—a bad one to shear, and so considerately left for 'some one else,' by every man who picked out of the large middle pen—was lifted aloft by Stanford, amid the jeers of the men, now preparing with stiff backs and aching sinews to surrender their task for a full week at any rate, before they 'struck' the next shed, lower down the river.

'I could shear him,' said he, regarding the closely wrinkled 'boardy' fleece, 'if he was covered with bloomin' pin-wire. My word! isn't it a pity that Greenwell didn't turn up afore? Eh, Mr. Delegate? D'ye think the Union'll guillotine us, same as they did chaps at the French Revolution? I'm off to Launceston in case of accidents. My cheque'll keep me for the rest of the summer, in a country that *is* a country—not a God-forsaken dust-heap like this.' Thus speaking, and shearing all the while, with punctilious precision, Mr. Stanford trimmed the 'cobbler' with a great affectation of anxiety, and dismissing him down the shoot of the pen with a harmless kick, said, 'Good-bye, and God bless you, old man; you make eighty-nine—not a bad forenoon's work.'

'Come along, men, down to the office,' said Macdonald, 'your money's ready for you—the storekeeper and I were up pretty nigh all night getting the accounts made out. You'll enjoy your dinners all the better for having your money in your pockets. The rouseabouts and shed hands can come in the afternoon. They won't want to leave before morning.'

'Who's that coming along the Wagga road on a grey horse?' said a sharp-eyed young shearer. 'By Jing! I believe it's Greenwell. Whatever can have kep' him, Mr. Stoate?'

'Never mind him,' said Macdonald. 'John Anderson, this is your account; look it over. £45:10:6. You'll take a cheque; here it is—sign the book. I'll take you all by the alphabet.'

As the men stood round the little room at the side of the big store, that served for the station office, the traveller on the grey horse rode slowly towards them.

The men were in a merry humour. Their keen eyes had recognised horse and rider afar off. It *was* the messenger who had so signally failed in coming up to time. He was received with a storm of ironical cheers and derisive exclamations.

'Halloa, George—where yer been? To Sydney and back? Got warrants for us all? To think as we should ha' cut out, and you on the road with an order from the Head Centre in your pocket! Come along, Mr. Delegate, and talk straight to him.'

These and the like specimens of humorous conversation were shouted at the unlucky emissary, who, as he came up and wearily dismounted, evidently knew that an explanation would be demanded of him.

Stoate walked out with a solemn and dignified air to meet him. 'Well done, Mr. Delegate, give it to him from the shoulder. He's a jolly telegraph, ain't he? Why, Joe Kearney the sprinter could have *run* all the way and beat him, hands down.'

'Will you oblige me by statin' the cause of your delay on a mission of importance to the Union and your feller-workers?'

'Now then, George, speak up—give us the straight griffin. What was it? Honour bright; did yer join a circus? Was there a good-looking girl in the way? And you a married man. For shame of you!'

Between the awful visage of Mr. Stoate and the running fire of chaff from his mates, Greenwell looked rather nonplussed.

However, girding himself for the contest, he mustered up courage, and thus delivered himself.

'Well, boys, the long and short of it is, I was took ill at Junee, on the return journey, and after stayin' a day, just as I was startin' back, some old mates of mine, as had just cut out at Hangin' Rock, come along, and—well, the truth's the truth, we all got on a bit of a spree. Now the murder's out, and you can make the best of it. I don't see as there's anything broke, so far.'

'Anything broke,' retorted Stoate indignantly. 'Hasn't the shed been cut out, in direct disobedience of orders, and the Union treated with contempt?'

'We're just gettin' our cheques,' called out a young fellow at the back of the crowd. 'Jolly awkward, ain't it? But I'll get over it, and so'll Dick Dawson.'

When the weighty matter of the payment was over, and the men were finishing their 'wash and brush up,' getting up their horses and settling their packs, one of the older men approached Stanford, who was quietly proceeding with his preparations, and thus addressed him—

'Now, Jim, you knowed that chap afore, didn't yer? Hadn't yer no notion as he might get on a "tear," with money in his pocket, and half nothin' to do like?'

Mr. Stanford made no verbal answer, but drawing himself up to the full height of his exalted stature, looked down into the interrogator's face, with an expression of great solemnity. It is just possible that he may have observed a slight deflection in the corner of his left eye, as he relaxed the severity of his countenance, while he observed resignedly, 'Well, it might have been worse; I've got the boss's cheque for £57:14s., and a few notes for the road in my pocket, this blessed minute.'

'Mine's a shade more'n that,' replied 'Long Jim,' with deliberation. '"All's well that ends well" 's a good motter. I've done enough for this season, I reckon. I had a fairish fencing contract in the winter. It'll be time enough to think about the "dignity of labour" and the "ethics of war" (wasn't that what the Head Centre called 'em?) afore next shearin' comes round. I'm off to a cooler shop across the Straits.'

The shearing at Tandara having ended satisfactorily to the shearer, the sheep-washers, the rouseabouts, the boundary riders, the overseers, to every one connected with the establishment in fact, from the 'ringer' to the tar-boy, all of whose wages and accounts were paid up to the last hour of the last day, in fact to every one except Mr. Janus Stoate, whose remuneration was in the future, a great silence commenced to settle down upon the place so lately resounding with the 'language used, and the clamour of men and dogs.' The high-piled waggons, drawn by bullock teams of from twelve to twenty, and horse teams of nearly the same number, had rolled away. The shed labourers had walked off with swags on their backs. The shearers, many of whom had two horses, poor in condition when they came, but now sleek and spirited, had ridden off with money in both pockets, full of glee and playful as schoolboys. The great shed, empty save for a few bales of sheepskins, was carefully locked up, as were also the shearers' and the other huts. Even Bower, the grim night-guardian of the woolshed, liberally remunerated, had left for Melbourne by Cobb and Co.'s coach. There, among other recreations and city joys, he betook himself to the Wax-works in Bourke Street.

As with hair and beard trimmed, newly apparelled from top to toe, he wandered around, looking at the effigies of former friends and acquaintances, now, alas, cut off in their prime, or immersed in the dungeon of the period for such venial irregularities as burglary, highway robbery, manslaughter, and the like, his gaze became fixed, his footsteps arrested. He stands before the waxen, life-like presentment of a grizzled elderly man, in rough bush habiliments, his hat a ruin, his clothes ragged and torn, his boots disreputable. A double-barrelled gun rests on his shoulder, while above his head is a placard, on which in large letters could seen by the staring spectator—

'HARRY BOWER, THE CELEBRATED BUSHRANGER.'

Cut to the heart, not so much by the heartless publicity of the affair as by the disgraceful attempt to brand him as a dirty disreputable-*looking* individual, he glared angrily at his simulacrum. 'And me that was always so tasty in my dress,' he muttered. So saying, he seized the hapless figure by the arm, and dragging it along with wrathful vehemence, made for the door.

'Oh, Mr. Bower, Mr. Bower!' cried the proprietress, 'ye'll ruin him—I mane yerself. Sure ye wouldn't go to injure a poor widdy woman, and all the people sayin' it's your dead imidge.'

'Imidge of me, is it?' shouted Bower, the furious, ungovernable temper of the 'long sentence convict' breaking out. 'I'll tache ye to make a laughing-stock of Harry Bower, this day. Ye might have dressed me dacent, while ye wor about it.'

So saying, he dragged the inanimate malefactor through the door, and casting him down upon the Bourke Street pavement, commenced to kick him to pieces, to the great astonishment of the crowd which speedily gathered around him. A rumour had started that 'Bower the bushranger was killing a man outside the Wax-works,' and before many minutes the street was blocked with men, women, and children, lured to the spot by the expectation of seeing a real live bushranger in the exercise of his bloodthirsty vocation.

A few minutes later—having dissevered several vital portions of the 'Frankenstein' individual, and, like Artemus Ward's enthusiastic Bible Christian, who 'caved Judassis' head in,' more or less demolished the victim—Mr. Bower, desisting, stalked moodily up the street, his peculiar reputation not leading any one to volunteer pursuit. There was no constable in sight, so the Mrs. Jarley of the establishment was left to her lamentations, and the dubious satisfaction of a remedy by civil process.

Next day, below startling headlines, similar paragraphs appeared in the leading journals.

'AN EX-BUSHRANGER.

'Assault with intent to do grievous bodily harm.

'About three o'clock yesterday afternoon, such denizens of Bourke Street as were passing Mrs. Dooley's interesting collection of Wax-works were alarmed by the spectacle of an aged man of athletic proportions, who had assaulted an individual of similar age and appearance; had thrown him down on the pavement, and was savagely kicking him about the head and the body, indeed it was feared—such was the fury of his gestures—that he was actually trampling the unfortunate victim of his rage to death. None dared to interfere, every one appeared paralysed; but after one or two public-spirited individuals had started for the Swanston Street police station, an adventurous bystander called out, 'Why, it's a wax figure.'

Though a shout of laughter greeted the announcement, no one cared to remonstrate with the hero of so many legends—the man who, long outlawed, and captured after a desperate resistance, had barely escaped the gallows for the manslaughter of the warders of the hulk *President* in a frustrated plot for escape—the dreaded bushranger, Henry Bower. We have since learned that this attempt at *felo de se* (in wax)—for the injured individual turned out to be a fairly correct likeness of himself—can only be proceeded for as a debt, which Bower in his cooler moments will not be averse to liquidating, he having returned from the bush with a reasonably large cheque, earned in the service of an old employer, who gave him a berth at a couple of pounds a week as night-watchman of his woolshed. In these times of disturbance and incendiary troubles, most of our readers will concur with our opinion, that old Harry Bower, with his double-barrel, not swayed by frivolous objection to bloodshed, was, in such a position of trust, "the right man in the right place."'

When the shearers took their cash or cheques as each elected, and departed, splitting into small parties, on different routes, division of opinion took place likewise. Bill Hardwick openly declared his intention, as did several others, to 'cut the Shearers' Union' and go 'on their own' for the future. 'I've had enough of this Union racket,' said he, as, lighting his pipe, and jogging off with his two fat horses, saddled and packed, he prepared to take the 'down river' road. 'I don't see no points in being bossed by chaps like this Stead, and callin' theirselves chairmen and presidents, and what not—fellers as have done dashed little but blather this years and years. They've turned dog on the squatters as trusted 'em and "went Union," and deuced near done us out of six weeks' hard graft at this very shed. We've got our cash, boys; that'll carry us on for a bit. But suppose we'd turned out when that galoot at Wagga wanted us to, where should we be now? Travellin' the country without a shillin' in our pockets, our shearin' money forfeited by the next police magistrate (and serve us right, too, for bein' such bally fools), and summonses and warrants out against every man on the board. I'm full of Mr. Head Centre at Wagga, with his top hat, and gold chain, and his billiards, as our money goes to pay for. But he won't get none of mine to monkey with, nor you either, Janus Stoate, and so you may tell him next time you wire.'

'I'll report your language to the Union secretary, William Hardwick, never fear,' replied Stoate, fixing his snaky eye upon him. 'You'll soon know which is the strongest—you or the Association, as protects the workers' interests. So I warn you, and all others as is fools enough to stand by you.'

'That'll do, Mr. Delegate,' said Bill; 'don't you go to bully me. Say another word, and I'll give you a smack or two, that'll make a better yarn when you're touching up the tell-tale business for the Head Centre. I'm off to Moorara, where there's 300,000 sheep to shear, and a board only half full. Who's comin' my way?'

There had been a hum of approbation when Bill finished his humble oratorical effort, after which a dozen of the best and fastest shearers announced their intention to go with him, to the wrath and despair of Mr. Stoate.

'I'll be even with you, Bill Hardwick,' he yelled, 'and you too, Johnny Jones—see if I don't. You'll get no stands from us this year, nor next either.'

A hundred and fifty miles below Tandara. A red-walled promontory overlooking the Darling, in this year a broad, majestic stream, with anabranches of equal breadth and volume running out for many a mile, where the river steamers took their course, cutting off corners, and, because of the depth of water in this most bountiful season, almost indifferent to obstacles. Here stood the great Head Station of Moorara. Miles of fencing of substantial character surrounded it on all sides. There was none of the ordinary carelessness as to finish, popularly supposed to be characteristic of back-block stations 'a thousand miles from everywhere,' as had been said descriptively by an imaginative tourist. On the contrary, every hut, paling, fence, gate, wall, and roof in that immense holding was in what old-fashioned English country people called 'apple-pie order.'

Everything was mended and kept right, up to date. Six carpenters and three blacksmiths lived on the premises all the year round.

There was no waiting until that pastoral millennium 'after shearing' arrived. Everything was done at once, and done well. The 'stitch in time' was an article of the faith at Moorara, and, as such, religiously observed. If any superficial judging tourist, observing these things, ventured to remark that such improvements must have cost a mint of money, or to hint a doubt whether such a place 'paid,' he was frowned down at once and haughtily reminded that this was Moorara, the property of the Hon. Mr. M'Cormack, whose sheep shorn last year (this was *one* of his long list of stations) would total up to over a million!

Just calculate what so many fleeces come to, the average weight being eight or nine pounds, and the value per head *rarely* under as many shillings. Then, of course, there are the other stations, carrying six hundred thousand high-class merino sheep!

Now the woolshed to which Bill and his ten or twelve companions were bound was one of which the owner had 'stood out' from the first against the tyranny of the Shearers' Union.

As Bill and his companions journeyed down the river, rumour reached them of serious developments of the Great Strike. This protest against the alleged dictation of Capital had reached its culminating stage. The o'er-vaulting ambition of the State-school educated Mr. Stead, the originator and prime mover of the Civil War, which was now fully recognised, had struck a blow at the State itself—that State under which he had been bred and nurtured, fed, protected, and presented with a 'free, compulsory, and secular education.' He had justified the forebodings of old-fashioned Conservatives, who had always doubted the wisdom of educating the labouring classes at the expense of the ratepayers, of breeding up an army of enemies to Capital and to the settled order of the Government.

And now the long-threatened result *had* come to pass—a revolt against order and good government, a deliberate attempt to subvert the Constitution under the specious guise of federated labour. It had commenced with a quarrel between the cook's mate of a coasting steamer and the so-called 'delegate' of the crew, spreading with portentous rapidity, like the bush-fires of the land, until it enveloped the stock-riders of the Paroo and the teamsters of 'the Gulf.' It menaced life and property. It attempted to plunge cities into darkness by 'calling out' the gas-stokers. It essayed to paralyse commerce by intimidating the carriers, whom it forbade to convey the wool—the staple Australian export—to the wharves, by restraining the wharf labourers from loading the vessels.

But, in these two instances, the common-sense of the city populations came to the rescue. The young men of the learned professions, of the upper classes—in the true sense of the word—came out to play a man's part in the interests of law and order. They manned the gas-works, and, amid furnace-heat and grime, provided the necessary labour, all unused as they were to toil under such conditions. The cities were *not* wrapped in darkness, and the streets were *not* made ready for the spoil by the burglar, the garrotter, and the thief. A line of wool teams was driven down the principal street of Sydney by barristers and bankers, by clerks and merchants, chiefly young men, high-couraged and athletic. But on the foremost waggon, high-seated behind his four-horse team, which he tooled with practised ease, might be recognised the leonine visage and abundant beard of Winston Darling, the Explorer, the Pioneer Squatter, the well-known Pastoral Leader and Ruler of the Waste.

The streets were crowded with yelling, blaspheming, riotous Unionists, with difficulty kept within bounds by a strong body of police.

Stones were thrown, and foul epithets freely used. But though one youthful driver had his head cut open, no further damage was done. And the wool was safely conveyed to the wharves and shipped in spite of the threatening demeanour of the assembled thousands.

These amateurs, native-born Australian gentlefolk, worked for weeks, from six to six, in many instances galling the hands, which were wholly unused to such rude treatment. But they kept at it till the stubborn conflict subsided, and not till then did they fall out of the ranks of the 'muscle-workers,' who in this and other instances have arrogated to themselves the title of the *only workers* in this complex and many-sided body politic.

This demonstration was chiefly confined to the seaports. When, however, the Ministry was sufficiently strong to call out the

Volunteer regiments, their disciplined action gained control of the disorderly mobs, and order was regained, without discouraging delay.

But in the bush, far from help, police or military protection, matters were far otherwise. Lonely stations were terrorised. Large camps of armed and apparently desperate men were formed, who intimidated those non-Union shearers and bush labourers who neither conformed to their rules nor submitted to their dictation.

They were in many cases captured, so to speak, assaulted, maltreated, and illegally restrained from following their lawful occupation. The carriers' horses or bullocks were driven away or slaughtered, their waggons, in some instances, burned.

These outrages were directed against men and their employers who had dared to be independent, to exercise the right of free Britons to manage their own affairs and their own property.

It may easily be imagined how bodies of two or three hundred men, well armed and mounted, could terrorise a thinly-populated country. Specific acts of incendiarism and other offences against property were frequent. Woolsheds were burned with their contents, sometimes to the value of thousands of pounds; fences were cut and demolished; bridges and telegraph lines destroyed; in short, no lawless action which could result in expense and loss to the pastoralist, or those of the labourers who defied the New Tyranny, was omitted.

CHAPTER IV

Some explanation of the Great Australian Strike of 1890, which lasted in more or less virulence and intensity until 1895, producing widespread damage and ruinous loss, may not here be out of place.

This important industrial conflict exhibited the nearest approach to civil war which Australia has known. It originated, as did certain historical revolutions and mutinies, from an occurrence ludicrously insignificant compared with the magnitude of the results and the widespread disasters involved.

A fireman was discharged by the captain of a coasting steamer belonging to the Tasmanian Steam Navigation Company, whereupon the Seamen's Union took up the matter, the man being their 'delegate,' and demanded his reinstatement.

He had been 'victimised,' they asserted, by the chief steward, who must be dismissed or the fireman reinstated. The Cooks' and Stewards' Union, in the interests of the chief steward, held an inquiry, in conjunction with the Seamen's Union, to which the fireman belonged. The result failed to substantiate any charge against the chief steward. But the Seamen's Union decided to hold the captain responsible, threatening to take the crew out of the ship. No inquiry was asked of the owners.

About a month after the threat the crew gave notice, and were paid off. The captain had received the following letter:—

'SEAMEN'S UNION OFFICE,

SYDNEY, *July 1890.*

'Captain — —, Steamer — —.

'DEAR SIR—We are instructed by the members of the above Society to state that we intend to have our delegate — — reinstated on board. If he is not reinstated by the return of the ship to Sydney, the crew will be given twenty-four hours' notice.

'We intend to protect our members from being victimised (*sic*) by chief stewards and others, and intend at all hazards to have him reinstated.—I remain, yours truly,

'THE PRESIDENT AND ACTING SECRETARY.'

'SYDNEY, *6th July 1890.*

'The Acting Secretary.

'SIR—With regard to your letter as to the discharge of a fireman from the steamer *Corinna*, the captain informs me that the chief steward had nothing whatever to do with the discharge. The fireman made no complaint about his food. He was discharged in the Company's interests, but there is no objection to his joining any other of the

Company's vessels. The captain also was not aware that he was a delegate, and had nothing to do with his discharge. It seems strange that men should leave the Company without explanation, while the Company is denied the same right.—I remain, etc.'

Now, what in the world had the colliers of Newcastle, N.S.W., to do with the injustice or otherwise meted out to the fireman through that powerful and distinguished official, the ship's cook, or even by the chief steward? Such would be the common-sense view of any ordinary person, especially if he had been reared in the belief that 'mind your own business' was a maxim of weight and authority, verified by the lore of ages. Not so thought the leaders of the mining community. A fatal fascination appeared to have actuated one and all under the influence of a false and specious principle.

No sooner had the steamer arrived at the Agricultural Association's wharf desiring a cargo of coal than the miners 'came out' of the Sea Pit, at that time in full work. Then the Northern Colliery owners, justly indignant at this breach of agreement, stopped work at all the pits under their control. Fourteen days' notice should have been given by the miners, on the terms of their agreement.

There was no grievance between master and man, and yet at the bidding of an outside person the miners abandoned their work without notice.

The Unionist shearers, at the instigation of their dictator, hasted to join the revolt. They commenced to formulate an agreement imposing higher pay, shorter hours, the supervision of sheds by workmen appointed by themselves, the deposition of the rule of the employer over his own work, as to his own property, in his own woolshed.

Then the employers, up to that time slow to move and more or less disunited, saw that the time had come for them to combine against the tyranny of a communistic organisation. The Shearers' Union, however, as represented by their president, thought it improper of other people to form Unions. They began to threaten as follows:—

'Should the employers maintain their present attitude, the trades' organisation will be compelled to use *every means* to win their cause, methods which at present they have avoided.

'For instance, they could call out *all the shearers* (sic), and at one blow cause widespread disaster. [This they did later on, including those who, in reliance on their promises, were shearing under Union Rules.] The effects of such a step would be to paralyse the whole industry of the colony. In Victoria, shearing is only just commencing. In New South Wales it is barely half over. At the Labour Conference in Sydney it was decided that the Western miners be called out next day. This meant cutting off the sole remaining coal supply of the colony. Decided also that all the shearers, rouseabouts, and carriers be called out. Instructions sent accordingly.

'In New South Wales alone this will affect 22,000 shearers, 15,000 rouseabouts, 10,000 carriers also, together with all affiliated trades, such as butchers, bakers, grocers, and compositors. Whether the railway men will be included cannot be now ascertained.'

As a sample of the class of arguments used to set class against class, and to inflame the minds of the bush labourers against their employers, the following circular, signed by the leaders, and privately distributed, may serve as a specimen. It was headed:—

AN APPEAL TO STATION LABOURERS.

'A shed labourer's lot is not a happy one. To work all hours and to endure all manner of privations. To work hard for a miserable starvation wage. A victim of capitalistic greed and tyranny. Suffering *worse treatment than the negro slaves* of the Southern States of America. The reason for this being that they have had no means of protection. Let them unite. Let them be men, free men, and have a voice in the settlement of the terms at which they shall sell their labour.

'The rights of the labourers will then be recognised. Capital will no longer have Labour by the throat. The mighty heritage of a glorious independence is in their grasp.

'Let them rise above the bondage of capital, and be a unit in that which will make one powerful whole—the General Woolshed Labourers' Union of Australia!'

That this sort of language was calculated to arouse the passions and heighten the prejudices of uneducated men may well be conceded. The ludicrous comparison with the 'wrongs of slaves' in the Southern States of America might raise a smile, had not reports of outrages, unhappily but too well authenticated, followed this and similar proclamations.

However, the Employers' Union and the Pastoral Association were not minded to submit tamely to the oppression of a 'jacquerie,' however arrogant, as the following extract from a metropolitan journal, under date 22nd September 1890, will show:—

'In Sydney that picturesque procession of lorries, loaded with non-Union wool, and driven by leading merchants and squatters, will once more betake itself through the streets, and may be the signal of actual civil war. These waggons, with their unaccustomed drivers, embody in a dramatic shape that aspect of the strike in which the Unionists have morally the weakest case. The shearers have undertaken to make Unionism *compulsory* at one stroke, in every woolshed in Australia, by the tyrannical process of forbidding every bale of wool shorn by non-Unionists to reach a market. Why must merchants and squatters, at the risk of their lives, drive these particular bales of wool to the wharf? We frankly hope that the wool "boycott" will break down hopelessly, ignobly. All reasonable men are against this fatal blunder of the Unionists.'

Commencing in 1890 among men 'who go down to the sea in ships,' the revolt against employment and authority spread among 'all sorts and conditions of men' dwelling in the continent of Australia. All trades and occupations by which the muscle-workers of the land, falsely assumed to be the only labourers worthy of the name of 'working-men,' were attempted to be captured and absorbed. To account for the readiness with which the new gospel of labour was accepted, it must be borne in mind that many of the better-educated labourers and mechanics had been for years supplied by their leaders with so-called socialistic literature. They had in a sense sat at the feet of apostles of the school of Henry George and Mr. Bellamy.

The former was convinced that all the 'riddles of the painful earth' might be solved by the taxation and gradual confiscation of land; this plausible-appearing policy would remove all the oppressions and exactions under which the excellent of the earth had so long groaned. Mr. Bellamy's method of procuring universal happiness, solvency, and contentment was simple and comprehensive. Every adult was to be compelled to labour for four hours of the day—no one to be permitted to work for *more* than this very reasonable, recreational period. Every one to be pensioned when he or she reached the age of sixty.

By this happy apportionment of the primeval curse, every one would be obliged to furnish a sufficient quantity of labour to provide for his own and other people's wants.

No one would be expected to do a full day's work—always unpopular as a task, and suspected to be unwholesome.

Dining and Music Halls, an artistic atmosphere, with all mental and physical luxuries, to be provided by the State, in exchange for Labour Coupons of specified value.

It cannot be doubted that speculative theories of this nature, proposals for minimising labour and dividing the wealth, accumulated by the industry and thrift of ages, among individuals who had neither worked nor saved for its maintenance, had a wide-reaching influence for evil among the members of the Labour Unions. Dazzled by alluring statements, they were ready to adopt the wildest enterprises, founded on delusive principles and untried experiments.

Perhaps the most important of the Utopian projects, which at the close of the conflict found favour in the eyes of the Unionists, was that of a Communistic settlement in Paraguay, to which the leader, an Americanised North Briton, gave the name of New Australia. This was to be somewhat on the lines of the settlement so delicately satirised by Hawthorne in the *Blithedale Romance*.

It was decided by a caucus of certain wise men of the Union that a country where the dietary scale for working-men was the most liberal in the world, the hours of work the *shortest*, the pay the highest, the climate the most genial, the franchise the most liberal, was not adapted for British labourers. It was accordingly agreed to establish a co-operative community in a foreign land, where brotherly love and the unselfish partition of the necessaries of life might exhibit to an admiring world an ideal State, free from the grasping employer and the callous capitalist. This modern Utopia they proposed to call New Australia. Money not being so scarce among Australian labourers as, from the tremendous denunciations of their leader, which freely compared them to negro slaves (only worse paid, fed, and driven), might have been supposed, they were expected to pay sixty pounds each towards the charter and freight of a suitable vessel.

This notable plan they carried out. One man indeed sold a cottage in a country town for £400, and putting the cash into the common fund, sailed away for South America amid great jubilation from the Radical press and Labour organs; thankful, however, before long to work his passage back to England.

Hope and Mr. W. G. Spence told a flattering tale before experience came to the audit. A tract was found in the Paraguayan Chaco—'234,000 acres, well watered and timbered—splendid land,' thus described in the New Australia newspaper, the journal of the New Co-operative Settlement Association, Wagga, New South Wales, 28th January 1892.

In September 1893 two hundred and sixty New Australians arrived to take possession of the Promised Land. Even on board ship differences of opinion arose. In December there was a notable desertion. The 'five-meal, meat-fed men' doubtless thought sadly of poor 'Old Australia,' where they had no dictator and few privations, save those irreparable from high wages and good food. They missed many things for which they had been the reverse of thankful, when supplied gratis. They even missed the police and the magistrate. One man at any rate did, who was thrashed for impertinence, and could not so much as take out a summons for assault. They must have gasped when they saw, in their own journal, in answer to questions—'A. K. If you didn't like it, you could leave. The equal annual yearly division of wealth production would enable you to ship back to Australia, if you wanted to.' Many wanted to, but the Dictator's reply, slightly altered from that of Mr. Mawworm in *The Serious Family*, was—'We deeply sympathise, but we *never* refund.' As to how the deserters got to Buenos Ayres, on their way 'home,' doubtless many tales of adventure could be told. The equal partition did not work out well. No one had a right to anything, apparently— milk for a sick child—a razor—any trifling personal possession, when all had a right to everything. The dissatisfaction deepened to despair. The 'rest is silence.' Migration to the 'Gran Chaco' is played out.

The Shearers' Strike drifted into the Shearers' War. Not vigorously dealt with at the beginning by the Government of any colony, it emboldened the agitators, who called themselves tribunes of the people, to suggest bolder assaults upon the law, to carry out yet more dangerous disturbances of the public peace.

The specious process of 'picketing'—an illegal practice involving insult and intimidation, under the transparent guise of 'persuasion'—was tacitly permitted. Becoming habituated to the assembling in force, armed and drilled in military fashion, it was patent to the lowest intelligence that the Government, if worthy of the name, must confront these menacing and illegal levies.

The tardy Executives, which had watched the ill-usage of free citizens, the burning of woolsheds, the killing of stock, with apparent apathy, now became alarmed and ordered out the Volunteer regiments. Directly a disciplined contingent, properly armed and officered, took the field, the pseudo-guerillas disbanded and disappeared. If prompt measures had been taken at the start, years of demoralisation and damage, loss of wages, and ruin of property would have been saved both to employers and workmen.

Such a disgraceful incident as that reported from Bowen Downs in July 1895 might never have occurred.

'A private message states that *two attempts* have been made within three days to poison free shearers here. On the first occasion eight men were poisoned; on the second, forty-nine.'

A Barcaldine telegram states: 'Forty-nine fresh cases reported from Bowen Downs. Strychnine suspected to have been put into the meat and sago pudding used by the men. A letter received states that the scenes in the shed at Bowen Downs were beyond description. The men, contorted with agony, lying about in all shapes. One man named Thomas has since died. He is not known in the district. Name probably an assumed one. Richardson, one of five brothers, said to be very bad; also Christie Schultz; a second death expected.

'Bowen Downs was managed by Mr. Fraser for a Scottish Investment Company. It is expected that 250,000 sheep will be shorn there this year. Sharing in the "strike troubles" last year (1894), the sheep were shorn by free labourers and some Unionists.

'They followed the example of Howe and others on the Barcoo run, and went to work in defiance of the Union mandate. This year many of the same men returned to the station to shear.

'The authorities had previous information that poisoning was likely to be resorted to on some stations. The Aramac and Mutta-burra police are at the station. No evidence was attainable against the authors of this cowardly crime, resulting in one murder at least, and the possible death of a score or more of their fellow-workmen. It is significant, however, as against the theory of *accident*, that the injured men, well-nigh sick unto death, were *free shearers*.

'It is notorious that elaborate preparations have been made for committing further outrages on property, and violence on persons. Hitherto the Government has erred on the side of insufficient precaution and protection to loyal subjects.

'Violence and intimidation, on the other hand, have been approved by the Labour Federations. A demand is made by them that employers should not be allowed the right to employ any but Union men, on Union terms. Such an edict is inadmissible in a free country. So Sir Samuel Griffith, C.J., of Queensland, stated the case.

'The Moreton Mounted Infantry left by the Wodonga for the seat of the disturbance. In consequence of further outrages by the so-called Labour organisations, one of which was the shooting of a team of working bullocks, eleven in number, belonging to a non-Union carrier, Colonel French has been sent to the north with a force of 130 men, having also a field-piece and a Gatling gun. The Union leaders had boasted of the wreck and ruin of squatting property which would follow the strike.'

In the second year of the revolt a special parade of the Queensland Mounted Infantry was ordered. They were ready to a man. In view of the outrages already committed, and the justifiable expectation of more to follow, military protection was manifestly needed. This drew forth a pathetic remonstrance from the 'General Secretary of the Australian Labour Federation.' He was virtuously indignant at the whole force of the Government being 'strained to subjugate the wage-earners of the central district, under the dictation of capitalistic organisations.' It was emphasised that 'the Australian Labour Federation's steady influence had always been used to substitute peaceful agitation and moderation for needless suspension of industry. The Government is urged to use its influence to induce organised capitalism to meet organised labour in the conference.'

The high official so addressed replied: 'The Government is merely endeavouring to maintain law and order; to punish disorder, violence, and crime. The existing state of matters is misrepresented by the Labour organs.'

As might have been expected, manslaughter and arson, if not murder and spoliation, *did* result from this and similar teachings. Some of these crimes were undetected, others were partially expiated by imprisonment; while in more instances the wire-pullers—the deliberate and wilful offenders against the law of the land—escaped punishment. But when the burning of the *Dundonald* took place, with the capture of free labourers by disguised men, the tardy action of the Executive was accelerated. That the apprehensions of the dwellers in the pastoral districts, and their appeals to the Government of the day in the first years of the strike, were not without foundation, an extract from a letter taken, among others, from the person of an arrested 'labour organiser,' affords convincing proof.

'QUEENSLAND LABOUR UNION, MARANOA BRANCH,

'ROMA, *10th March 1891.*

'DEAR GEORGE—It is a mistake collecting our men at the terminus of the railway. Better to split them up in bodies of a hundred and fifty each. One lot to stop at Clermont, another at Tambo; others at outside stations, such as Bowen Downs, Ayrshire Downs, Richmond Downs, Maneroo, West-lands, Northampton, and Malvern Hills. Say a hundred and fifty at Maranoa, same below St. George. Every station that a hundred and fifty men came to would demand police protection from the Government. Then, if you wanted to make a grand coup, send mounted messengers round and have all your forces concentrated, away from railways if possible, and force the running by putting *a little more devil* into the fight. They will have no railways to cart the Gatling guns and Nordenfeldts about.—Yours, etc.

NED — —.'

Such were the missives which passed between the 'labour organisers' and their 'brother officers.' Small wonder that the rank and file were stirred up to deeds of wrong and outrage, stopping short by accident, or almost miracle, of the 'red fool-fury of the Seine.' Imagine the anxiety and apprehension at the lonely station, miles way from help, with a hundred and fifty horsemen, armed and threatening, arriving perhaps at midnight—the terror of the women, the mingled wrath and despair of the men. And the temperate suggestion of the labour organiser to 'put a little more devil into the fight, to force the running!'

Doubtless it would, but not quite in the manner which this calculating criminal intended. Such a wave of righteous indignation would have been evoked from the ordinarily apathetic surface of Australian politics, that the culprits and their cowardly advisers would have been swept from the face of the earth.

If it be doubted for a moment whether the serious acts of violence and outrage alluded to were actually committed, or, as was unblushingly asserted by the so-called democratic organs, invented, exaggerated, or—most ludicrous attempt at deception of all—got up by *capitalists and squatters* for the purpose of throwing *discredit upon Unionists*, let a list of acts perpetrated in deliberate defiance of the law of the land be produced in evidence.

The Dagworth woolshed had seven armed men on watch, as the Unionists had threatened to burn it. Among them were the Messrs. Macpherson, owners of the station. When the bushranger Morgan was killed at Pechelbah, in their father's time, they hardly expected to have to defend Dagworth against a lawless band humorously describing themselves as Union Shearers.

In spite of their defensive operations, a ruffian crawled through and set fire to the valuable building, which was totally consumed.

They were armed, and shots were freely interchanged. One Unionist found dead was believed to be one of the attacking party.

The 'Shearers' War' languished for a time, but was still smouldering three years afterwards, as on the 4th of August 1894 the Cambridge Downs woolshed was burnt. This was a very expensive building, in keeping with the size and value of the station, where artesian bores had been put down, and artificial lakes filled from the subterranean water-flow. Money had been liberally, lavishly spent in these and other well-considered improvements, aids to the working of the great industrial enterprise evolved from the brain of one man, and having supported hundreds of labourers and artisans for years past. In the great solitudes where the emu and kangaroo or the roving cattle herds alone found sustenance, the blacksmith's forge now glowed, the carpenter's hammer rang, the ploughman walked afield beside his team, the 'lowing herd wound slowly o'er the lea,' recalling to many an exiled Briton his village home.

The 'big house,' the squire-proprietor's abode, rose, garden-and grove-encircled, amid the cottages and humbler homes which it protected—a mansion in close resemblance, allowing for altered conditions and more spacious surroundings, to homes of the Motherland, which all loved so well. At what cost of head and hand, of toil, and danger, and hardship, ay, even of blood, let the headstones in the little shaded graveyard tell! And now, when long years, the best years ot early manhood, had been expended freely, ungrudgingly in the conflict with Nature, was the workman, the junior partner in the enterprise, well paid, well fed and housed during the doubtful campaign, the loss of which could smite to ruin the senior, to lay his rash destroying hand upon the beneficent structure he had helped to raise?

Pulling down in suicidal mania, at the bidding of a secret caucus, the industrial temple, which so surely would whelm him and his fellows in its ruins!

Ayrshire Downs woolshed followed suit. At Murweh, the roll of shearers was about to be called, and fifty thousand sheep were ready for the shears, when it was set on fire and burned—all the preparations for shearing rendered useless. A makeshift woolshed would probably be run up, which meant loss of time—hasty indifferent work, a few thousand pounds loss and damage inevitable. At Combe-Marten a station hand was shot, and several prisoners committed to take their trial at Rockhampton. The woolshed at Errangalla was burned to the ground.

The Netallie shed, with eighty thousand sheep in readiness, was attempted to be set on fire—kerosene having been profusely exhibited for the purpose—but, with all the goodwill (or rather bad) in the world, the plot miscarried. After a riot at Netallie a large force of Unionists attempted, but failed, to abduct the free labourers.

At Grasmere woolshed the police were compelled to use firearms. Shortly before 9 P.M. a hundred Unionists came to Grasmere, and gathered at the men's huts, saying that they were armed and determined to bring out the free labourers. Sergeant M'Donagh said they could not be allowed to do so. He was felled to the ground, and the door of the free labourers' hut smashed in with a battering-ram. Shots were exchanged between the police and the Unionists. Two of the latter were wounded. One free labourer fired with a revolver. The attacking party then retired, taking the wounded men with them.

The police overtook them, and, taking charge of the wounded men, conveyed them to Wilcannia Hospital in a buggy. One was shot in the left breast; the other near the same spot. The bullet travelled to the back, near the spine. From the size of the bullet it would appear to have been fired by a free labourer, the police navy revolvers carrying a larger bullet.

Unaware of the extreme length to which 'the ethics of war' (to use a phrase grandiloquently applied in one of Mr. Stead's harangues) had been pushed, Bill Hardwick and his comrades rode gay and unheeding 'down the river.'

They were within a dozen miles of Moorara, and had travelled late in order to get to the station that evening, as shearing had commenced. An unwonted sight presented itself. Before them lay a large encampment, from which many voices made themselves heard, and around which were fires in all directions. 'Hulloa!' said one of the men, 'what's all this? Have they moved the station up, or what is it? Have the men got to camp here because of the grass, and ride to Moorara and back, like boys going to school?'

'By Jove! it's a Union Camp,' said Bill; 'we'd better look out. They're a rough lot here by all accounts. They might go for us if they hear we've dropped the A.S.U.—for a bit.'

'I don't see as they can do much,' said a grey-haired man, one of the best shearers in the shed. 'We've come last from a Union shed. We've no call to say more nor that till we get to Moorara.'

'That's all right,' said a younger man, who, like Hardwick, was a selector on the Upper Waters, 'but that sweep Janus Stoate might have wired to the delegate here and put us away. Anyhow, we'll soon see.'

'Who goes there?' suddenly demanded a voice from the pine scrub. 'Who are you, and where from?'

'Who are you, if it comes to that?' answered Bill. 'Is this here an army, and are you goin' to take the bloomin' country, that a man can't ride down the river on his own business?'

'We'll soon learn yer,' said the man who had challenged. 'Where are yer from last?'

'From Tandara. It's a Union shed, I believe, and we shore under Union Rules.'

'We know all about that. What's yer name—is it William Hardwick?'

'I never was called anything else,' answered Bill, who, now that he had got his monkey up (as he would have said), cared for nothing and nobody.

'Well, yer accused by the delegate, as was in charge of that shed, of disobedience of orders; also of conspiring to bring the Union into contempt, and of being on the way, with others, to shear at a non-Union shed against the interests of the Australian Workers' Federated Union. What d'ye say in reply to the charge?'

'Go to the devil,' said Bill, at the same time spurring his horse. But the strange man jumped at his bridle-rein, and though Bill got in a right-hander, before he could get loose, armed men broke out of the pine clump, and, rifle in hand, forced the party to dismount.

'Tie their hands,' said the leader. 'We'll show the bally "scabs" what it is to pal in with the squatters, as have ground down the workers long enough. March 'em up to the camp and bring 'em afore the Committee.'

'This is a jolly fine state of things,' said one of the younger men of Bill's party. 'I used to believe this was a free country. One would think we was horse-stealers or bushrangers. Are ye goin' to hang us, mate?'

'You hold yer gab, youngster, or it'll be the worse for you. We'll straighten yer a bit, afore yer goes shearin' again in the wrong shed,' said a man behind him, sourly, at the same time giving him a blow on the back with the butt-end of a rifle.

'By——! if my hands was loose, I'd give yer something to remember Dan Doolan by, yer cowardly, sneakin', underhand dog, crawlin' after fellers like Stoate, keepin' honest men out o' work, and spendin' it on spoutin' loafers. Well, we'll see who comes out on top, anyhow,' upon which Mr. Dan Doolan relapsed into silence—being 'full up,' as he would have expressed it, of 'Government of the people, by the people, for the people,' in its logical outcome.

Arrived at the camp, they were surrounded by a crowd of men, looking less like workmen of any kind than an array of freebooters. Nearly all had arms. Others had apparently put them by for the night. They affected a raffish, semi-military rig, and evidently regarded themselves as revolutionists; which, in point of fact, they were. Not as yet, perhaps, ripe for a policy of plunder and bloodshed, but within measurable distance of it—needing but an accidental contest with the police or a well-defended station (and there were such) to be irrevocably committed to it.

A great show of form and ceremony was aimed at, as Bill and his companions in captivity were brought before half-a-dozen serious-looking individuals, seated before a table outside of a tent of larger than average size. One man was in the centre, and was addressed as Mr. President.

'Have you brought the suspected individuals, mentioned in the communication received by the Committee this morning, before us?'

'Yes, Mr. President. Here they are. We found them close by the camp, a-ridin' towards Moorara.'

'What are their names?'

The apprehending personage read out from a telegraph form the names of William Hardwick, Daniel Doolan, George Bond, Donald MacCallum, James Atkins, Joseph Warner, John Stevens, Cyrus Cable, Thomas Hyland, John Jones, William Murphy, Jacob Dawson, and Martin Hannigan.

'You stand charged with obstructing the work of the Delegate of the A.S.U. at Tandara, and disobeying an order to come out, sent by the duly authorised Vice-President at Wagga Wagga. How do you plead?'

'Is this a bally Supreme Court?' inquired Bill. 'What are we to plead for? I never signed no agreement to obey a pair of loafers like Stoate and Stead. I've seen one of 'em beg rations from a squatter, layin' by to do him all the harm in his power, and the other tried his best to take their money out of the pockets of hard-working men at Tandara. You may talk till you're black in the face, I'm not goin' to play at court work, for you or any other blatherskite, and so I tell you.'

'Remove these men to the lock-up hut, and place a sentry before the door,' said the chairman, with dignity.

So Bill and Co. were hauled off, and bundled into a small hut, where they spent the night without food or bedding.

Their swags had been considerately taken care of, and their horses turned out among the camp herd for the night. This done, they listened to the order given to the sentry to shoot any man that attempted to come out; and much musing upon the strange condition in which they found themselves in their native country, spent the night in a most unpleasant state of discomfort.

As for the *corps d'armee*—as they, no doubt, considered themselves to be—they were more jovial and self-contained.

Songs and recitations were given, apparently met with admiration and applause. Rifles and revolvers were discharged, as well to have the loading replaced as to inform any employés of the adjoining station that the camp was armed, and considered itself to be an independent, well-provided contingent. Orations were made by speakers filled with detestation of the tyranny of the squatter, and the malignant nature of all Capital, except when diverted into the pocket of the virtuous (and muscular) working-man.

Hints were thrown out, not too closely veiled, of the retribution in store for those treacherous enemies of the working-man, who, instead of supporting him, like brothers, against the curse of Capital, presumed to have opinions of their own, and exercised the right of private judgment even against the interests of their own *Order*—this was a great word with them. Dark suggestions were made with regard to a cargo of free labourers (otherwise 'scabs' or blacklegs) now coming down river in a steamboat. They were to be met and 'dealt with,' after what fashion the speakers did not as yet enlighten their hearers.

When the wire-pullers of the Australian Shearers' Union had converted or terrorised the labourers of the land to such an extent that employers were met at every turn by exorbitant demands, or impossible regulations, it became necessary to form a Pastoral Association to oppose the tyranny. For it was evident that unless united action was taken they would be no longer permitted to manage their own affairs.

The work and wages connected with an immense export, with a property to the value of hundreds of millions sterling, were to be regulated by irresponsible impecunious agents, chosen by a plebiscite of labourers naturally unfitted for the direction of affairs involving important national issues.

Some idea of the magnitude of the interests involved may be gathered if it is considered that the cost of management of the vast flock of sheep depastured on the freehold and Crown lands of the colonies necessitates the paying away annually not less than £10,000,000 sterling, most of which is expended for wages, for shearing, and for stores. Shearing, which lasts for a considerable period of each year, finds employment for 25,000 shearers, and the extra hands required in connection with this work may be put up at 10,000 to 12,000.

The following figures tend to further explanation of the position:— Value of freehold land on which stock is depastured, £200,000,000 sterling; value of sheep and plant, £100,000,000 sterling. The income from the properties is, as nearly as possible—from wool, say £22,000,000, from surplus stock £5,250,000, and stock £27,250,000.

The outgoings will be—for wages, carriage, stores, £10,000,000; interest on £300,000,000 capital at 5¾ per cent, £17,250,000; total outgoing, £27,250,000. The returns are comparatively small, taking the whole of the population together.

The frequent droughts, causing the loss of millions of sheep, with other ills and ailments fatal to stock, have not been taken into the calculation. The properties as a whole will bear no increase in cost of management.

Another reason which actuated the employers, pastoralists, merchants, and others connected with the pastoral industry, was that the sudden withdrawal of their labourers was attended with greater loss and expense than, say, in the case of mines or shipping. The mines could be closed, the ships laid up. Expenditure on the part of owners would then cease until the strike was ended. But, on the far back stations, wells had to be worked, wood carted for machinery, edible shrubs cut for starving sheep, in default of which *immediate loss* of stock to a very great extent would take place.

CHAPTER V

One of the methods which the Pastoralists were compelled to use to defeat the attempted domination of the Shearers' Union was to import free labour: men who were contented to work for high wages and abundant food; to obey those who paid, lodged, and fed them well. It may here be stated that the fare in shearing time, provided for the shearers, the station hands, and the supernumerary labourers, was such as might well be considered not only sufficing and wholesome, but luxurious, in any other part of the world. Three principal meals a day, consisting of beef or mutton, good wheaten bread, pudding, vegetables when procurable; three minor repasts of scones and cakes, with tea *ad libitum*; the whole well cooked, of good quality, with no limitation as to quantity. Where is the rural labourer in Europe similarly provided?

Agencies were established in the principal towns of the colonies. Men were hired and forwarded to such stations as were in need. The cost of transit was paid by the associated employers. They were forwarded by rail, by coach, on horseback, or by steamer, as such transit was available. An unfair, even illegal system of intimidation, under the specious name of 'picketing,' to prevent the men thus engaged from following their lawful occupation, came into vogue. Unionists were stationed along roads or near stations, nominally to 'persuade' the free labourers not to fulfil their agreements, but, in reality, to threaten and abuse, not infrequently with brutal violence to assault and ill-treat the nonconformists.

The majority of the Unionists were well-intentioned men, led away by specious demagogues; but among them were lawless ruffians, who, ignorantly prejudiced against their superiors and even their equals, who had risen in life by the exercise of industry and thrift, were capable of any villainy, not even stopping short of arson and bloodshed. Up to this time the Ministry of the day had been tardy and over-cautious, both in the protection of property and in the punishment of a criminal crew. But they were gradually coming to a determination to stop such disorders summarily. The strong arm of the law was invoked to that intent. For too frequently had peaceable workmen, under the ban of the Unionist tyranny, been captured, ill-treated, robbed, and temporarily deprived of their liberty.

Grown bold by previous toleration, the Union Camp by Moorara had determined to make an example of this particular steamer, with her load of free shearers and rouseabouts—to teach them what the penalty was of withstanding the Australian Shearers' Union and bringing a load of blacklegs past their very camp.

It was nearly midnight when a scout galloped in to announce that the *Dundonald* was within half a mile of the camp, on her way down river with fifty free labourers on board.

'By the God of Heaven,' shouted a dissolute-looking shearer, 'we'll give them a lesson to-night, if we never do it again. I know the agent well—a d—d infernal swell, who looks upon working-men as dogs, and talks to them like the dirt under his feet. I told him I'd meet him some day, and that day's come.'

'Come along, lads,' shouts an evil-faced larrikin from a city lane; 'let's give it 'em hot. We'll burn their bloomin' boat, and have roast blackleg for breakfast.'

'You'd as well mind your eye, my lad,' said a slow-speaking, steady-going Sydney-sider, from Campbelltown. 'Seth Dannaker's the skipper of this boat—I can hear her paddles now, and he'll shoot straight if you meddle with his loadin'. You're not the sort to face Seth's pea-rifle, 'nless yer got a fairish big tree in front of yer.'

Upon this discouraging statement, the product of 'a city's smoke and steam'—under-sized, untended from childhood, grown to manhood, untaught save in precocious villainy—slunk into the background, while from the centre of a group emerged the man who had posed as the 'President of the Council,' and thus addressed the crowding shearers:—

'Bring out Bill Hardwick and them other "scabs." We'll have 'em in front when the shootin' begins. It'll do 'em good to feel what their friends' tyranny's brought the people to.'

The sentry was directed to quit his post, and a score of eager hands competed for the privilege of dragging out the weary, famished men, and rushing with them to the river-bank, while with slow, reverberating strokes the measured beat of the paddles was heard, as the dimly-lighted hull of the steamer showed amid the ebon darkness—the throbbing of her overpowered engines sounding like the heart-beats of some monstrous creature, slow-emerging from the channels of a prehistoric morass.

'Boat ahoy!' shouted the President, with an accent telling of a seaman's experiences. 'Heave to, and let us have a look at your passenger list.'

'Who the hell are you, anyway?' was returned in answer—the intonation confirming the Sydney-sider's information. 'What's my passenger list to you? I'm bound to Moorara, and the men on board hev' their passage paid—that's all I've to look to. Full steam ahead!'

A derisive laugh was the only answer from the river-bank. But the skipper's complacency was of short duration, as a violent shock almost dislodged him from the bridge, and made every bit of loose timber, or unsecured deck cargo, rock and rattle again. The *Dundonald* had gone full speed against a wire rope, or rather against two twisted together, which had been feloniously taken from a punt higher up the river, because the misguided lessee had carried across free labourers.

A yell of exultation burst from the excited crowd, now fully determined to board the obnoxious steamer, while a voice from their midst, after commanding silence, called out, 'Steamer ahoy!'

'Well, what is it? What do you want, stopping me on a voyage? You'd as well take care; I'm a quiet man, but a bad one to meddle with.'

'We want those infernal traitors you've got aboard.'

'And suppose I won't give up my passengers?'

'Then we'll burn yer bloomin' boat, and roast them and you along with it. Don't yer make no mistake.'

'Then you'd better come and do it.'

At this defiance, a chorus of yells and execrations ascended through the warm, still air, as a hundred men dashed into the tepid waters of the smooth stream, the slow current of which hardly sufficed to bear them below the steamer's hull. Like a swarm of Malay pirates, they clambered on the low rail of the half barge, half steamer, which had done her share in carrying the wool-crop of the limitless levels so many times to the sea. But her last voyage had come. The crew stubbornly resisted. Many a man fell backward, half stunned by blows from marline-spikes and gun-stocks—though as yet only a few shots were fired—and more than one of the rioters narrowly escaped death by drowning. But the 'free labourers,' disordered by the suddenness of the onslaught, fought but half-heartedly. Outnumbered by ten to one, they were driven back, foot by foot, till they were forced aft, almost to the rail, before the skipper yielded.

A few shots had been fired from the bank before the charge through the water was made, in the pious hope of hitting the captain or one of the crew; better still, a free labourer. They were promptly returned, and one of the men nearest the leader fell, shot through the body. But at that moment the leader's strident voice was heard. 'Stop firin'; I'll shoot the next man that holds up a gun. Let's catch 'em alive and deal with 'em and their blasted boat afterwards. There's enough of yer to eat 'em!'

When the surrender was imminent, the skipper had one of the boats lowered—a broad-beamed, serviceable, barge-like affair, in which great loads had been conveyed in the flooded seasons—and putting a white cloth on to the end of his rifle-barrel, called for a parley. It was granted.

'See here, yer darned pirates! I want a word or two. There's a ton of powder on board, and the man you wounded with your cowardly first shoot is sitting on a chair beside a coil of fuse, with a sperm candle and a box of matches. It's a sure thing he won't live, and he don't love the men that took his life, foul and coward-like. I'm to fire this revolver twice for a signal, and next minute we'll all go to hell together, sociable like. Jump into the boat, men, and take your guns, some grub, and a tarpaulin. Those that like may stay with me—I stop with the ship.'

If there's anything that undisciplined men fear, it is an explosion of gunpowder. They did not know for certain whether there was any on board. But if there was, there was no time to lose. A panic seized them, one and all. The crew descended into the boat in good order, obeying the captain's commands. His cool, decided voice imposed upon the rioters. They tumbled into the river by scores—knocking over their comrades and even striking them, like men in a sinking vessel, under the influence of fear—until the last man had reached the bank, when they even ran some distance in their terror before they could rid themselves of the fear of hearing *too late* the thunderous roar of the explosion, and being hurled into eternity in an instant.

The free labourers, on the other hand, from having assisted in the navigation of the steamer in her slow voyage from Echuca, had made themselves acquainted with every nook and cranny and pound of cargo on the boat. They knew that there was no magazine, nor any powder, and, divining the captain's ruse, made for the opposite bank with all convenient speed. Those who could swim, lost no time; and those who could not, escaped into the bush, undisturbed by the privateering crowd that had been so valorous a few minutes before.

When the boat returned and not before, the captain descended with deliberation, remarking, 'Now, lads, we've got a clear track before us. There ain't no powder, there ain't no wounded man, and I reckon them long-shore skunks will find themselves in an all-fired mess when the police come. There's a big body of 'em only ten miles from here, at Moorara Station. We'll just make camp and have a snack—some of us want it pretty bad. We'll build fires to warm those that's wet—wood's plenty. Leave 'em burning and make down river so's to warn the police under Colonel Elliot. The Union army won't cross before morning, for fear of the old tub blowing up and making a scatteration among 'em.'

The programme was carried out. The night was of Egyptian darkness. Supper was hastily disposed of. The fires were freshly made up, and shortly afterwards the whole contingent took the down-river road and by daylight were miles away from the scene of the encounter.

The unusually large body of police which had been ordered up by the Government, to join with another force on the Darling, had made rendezvous at Moorara, having heard from a scout that mischief, rather above the ordinary limit, was being enacted near Poliah. When, next morning, the captain and crew of the *Dundonald*, with the greater portion of the free labourers, arrived, a strong sensation was aroused. This was an unparalleled outrage, and, if unchecked, meant the commencement of *Civil War*, plain and undisguised.

What horrors might follow! A guerilla band, with its attendant crimes—murder, pillage, outrage! Such a band of reckless desperadoes, armed and mounted, like a regiment of irregular horse, was sufficient to terrorise the country; gathering on the march, till every criminal in the land that could steal a horse and a gun would be added to their ranks in a surprisingly short time.

Once launched on such a campaign of crime, the country would be ravaged before a military force could be organised. The proverbial snowball may be arrested at the first movement, but after gathering velocity, it descends the mountain-side with the force and fury of the avalanche.

The colonel in command of the Volunteers was a soldier to whom border raids in wild lands, with a wilder foe, was not unfamiliar. 'Boot and saddle' was sounded. Without a moment's unnecessary delay, the troop was in full marching order along the 'river road,' a well-marked trail, heading for Poliah.

The night was still dark, but comparatively cool. No inconvenience was felt as the men trotted briskly along and joked as to the sort of battle in which they would engage.

'Bless yer, they won't fight, not if there was another thousand of 'em,' said a grizzled sergeant, 'and every man with the newest arm invented. I've seen mobs afore. Men as ain't drilled and disciplined never stands a charge.'

'They've got rifles and revolvers, I know,' said a younger man, 'and they can shoot pretty straight, some of 'em. Suppose they keep open order, and pepper us at long range? What's to keep 'em from droppin' us that way, from cover, and then makin' a rush?'

'There's nothin' to keep 'em, *only they won't do it*,' replied the sergeant oracularly. 'They know the law's agin' 'em, which means a lot in Australia—so far. Besides that, they've never faced a charge, or don't know what it's like to stiffen up in line. You'll see how they'll cut it when they hear the colonel give the word, not to mention the bugle-call. Why, what the devil——?'

Then the sergeant, ending his sentence abruptly, almost halted, as a column of flame rose through the night air, sending up tongues of flame and red banners through the darkness which precedes the dawn.

'D—d if they haven't burned the bloomin' steamer!' quoth he. 'What next, I'd like to know? This country's going to the devil. I always thought it was a mistake sending our old regiment away.'

'Halt!' suddenly rang out in the clear, strong tones of the colonel—the voice of a man who had seen service and bore the tokens of it in a tulwar slash and a couple of bullet wounds. 'These fellows have set fire to the steamer, and of course she will burn to the water's edge. They will hardly make a fight of it though. In case they do, sergeant, take twenty men and skirt round so as to intercept their left wing. I'll do myself the honour to lead the charge on their main body, always supposing they wait for us to come up.'

The character of the resistance offered proved the sergeant's estimate to be absolutely correct. A few dropping shots were heard before the police came up, but when the rioters saw the steady advance of a hundred mounted men—an imposing cavalry force for Australia—saw Colonel Elliot, who rode at their head with his sword drawn, heard the clanking of the steel scabbards and the colonel's stern command, 'Charge!' they wavered and broke rank in all directions.

'Arrest every man on the river-bank with firearms in his hands,' roared the colonel. The sergeant, with a dozen of his smartest troopers, had each their man in custody a few seconds after the order was given—Bill Hardwick among the rest, who was fated to illustrate the cost of being found among evil-doers. One man alone made a desperate resistance, but after a crack from the butt-end of a carbine, he accepted his defeat sullenly. By the time his capture was complete, so was the rout of the rebel array. Hardly a man was to be seen, while the retreating body of highly irregular horse sounded like a break-out from a stock-yard.

Matters had reached the stage when the stokers at the Gas Works were 'called out,' and the city of Melbourne threatened with total darkness after 6 P.M.

Then a volunteer corps of Mounted Rifles was summoned from the country. The city was saved from a disgraceful panic—perhaps from worse things. The Unionist mob quailed at the sight of the well-mounted, armed, and disciplined body of cavalry, whose leader showed no disposition to mince matters, and whose hardy troopers had apparently no democratic doubts which the word 'Charge!' could not dispel.

At the deserted Gas Works, aristocratic stokers kept the indispensable flame alight until the repentant, out-colonelled artisans returned to their work.

This was the crisis of the struggle—the turning-point of the fight; as far as the element of force was concerned, the battle was over. It showed, that with proper firmness, which should have been exhibited at the outset, the result is ever the same. The forces of the State, with law and justice behind them, must overawe any undisciplined body of men attempting to terrorise the body politic in defence of fancied rights or the redress of imaginary wrongs.

The rioting in the cities of Melbourne and Sydney was promptly abated when the citizen cavalry, 'armed and accoutred proper,' clanked along Collins Street in Melbourne, while Winston Darling led the sons of his old friends and schoolfellows, who drove the high-piled wool waggons in procession down George Street in Sydney to the Darling Harbour Warehouses.

Much was threatened as to the latter demonstration, by blatant demagogues, who described it as 'a challenge; an insult to labour.' It was a challenge, doubtless—a reminder that Old New South Wales, with the founders of the Pastoral Industry—that great export now reaching the value of three hundred millions sterling—was not to be tyrannised over by a misguided mob, swayed by self-seeking, irresponsible agitators.

No doubt can exist in the minds of impartial observers that if the Ministries of the different colonies over which this wave of industrial warfare passed, in the years following 1891, had acted with promptness and decision at the outset, the heavy losses and destructive damage which followed might have been averted.

But the labour vote was strong—was believed, indeed, to be more powerful than it proved to be when tested. And the legislatures elected by universal suffrage were, in consequence, slow to declare war against the enemies of law and order.

They temporised, they hesitated to take strong measures. They tacitly condoned acts of violence and disorder. They permitted 'picketing,' a grossly unfair, even illegal (see Justice Bramwell's ruling) form of intimidation, employed to terrorise the free labourers.

The natural results followed. Woolsheds were burned, notably the Ayrshire Downs; the Cambridge Downs shed, 4th August 1894; Murweh, with 50,000 sheep to be shorn—roll to be called that day. Fences were cut, bridges sawn through, stock were injured, squatters and free labourers were assaulted or grossly reviled.

Everything in the way of ruffianism and disorder short of civil war was practised, apparently from one end of Australia to the other, before the Executive saw fit to intervene to check the excesses of the lawless forces which, well armed and mounted, harassed the once peaceful, pastoral Arcadia.

At length the situation became intolerable; the governing powers, with the choice before them of restraining bands of *condottieri* or abdicating their functions, woke up.

It was high time. From the 'Never Never' country in remotest Queensland, from the fabled land 'where the pelican builds her nest' to the great Riverina levels of New South Wales, from the highlands of the Upper Murray and the Snowy River to the silver mines of the Barrier, a movement arose, which called itself Industrial Unionism, but which really meant rebellion and anarchy.

It was rebellion against all previously-accepted ideas of government. If carried out, it would have subverted social and financial arrangements. It would have delivered over the accumulated treasure of 'wealth and knowledge and arts,' garnered by the thrift, industry, and intelligence of bygone generations, to one section of the workers of the land—the most numerous certainly, but incontestably the least intelligent—to be wasted in a brief and ignoble scramble.

The list of outrages, unchecked and unpunished, during this period, makes painful reading for the lover of his country.

A distinguished and patriotic member of the 'Australian Natives' Association,' in one of his addresses before that body, declared 'that, for the first time in his life, he felt ashamed of his native country.' That feeling was shared by many of his compatriots, as day after day the telegrams of the leading journals added another to the list of woolsheds deliberately set on fire, of others defended by armed men—sometimes, indeed, unsuccessfully.

When the directors of the Proprietary Silver Mine at Broken Hill saw fit to diminish the number of miners, for which there was not sufficient employment, it was beleaguered by an armed and threatening crowd of five thousand men. A real siege was enacted. No one was allowed to pass the lines without a passport from the so-called President of the Miners' Committee.

For three days and nights, as the Stipendiary Magistrate stated (he was sent up specially by the New South Wales Government, trusting in his lengthened experience and proved capacity), the inmates of the mine-works sat with arms in their hands, and without changing their clothes, hourly expectant of a rush from the excited crowd.

The crisis was, however, tided over without bloodshed, chiefly owing, in the words of a leading metropolitan journal, to the 'admirable firmness and discretion' displayed by the official referred to—now, alas! no more. He died in harness, fulfilling his arduous and responsible duties to the last, with a record of half a century of official service in positions of high responsibility, without a reflection in all that time having been cast upon his integrity, his courage, or his capacity.

More decisive action was taken, and was compelled to be taken, in Queensland than in the other colonies.

There, owing to the enormous areas necessarily occupied by the Pastoralists, the immense distances separating the holdings from each other, and, perhaps, the heterogeneous nature of the labour element, the acts of lawlessness became more serious and menacing. A military organisation was therefore found to be necessary. Volunteers were enrolled. Large bodies of these troops and of an armed constabulary force were mobilised, and many of the incidental features of a civil war were displayed to a population that had rarely seen firearms discharged in anger.

The nomadic population had been largely recruited from the criminals of other colonies, who, fleeing from justice, were notoriously in the habit of crossing the Queensland border, and evading a too searching inquiry.

These were outlaws in the worst sense of the word; desperate and degraded, conversant with undetected crime, and always willing to join in the quasi-industrial revolts, unfortunately of everyday occurrence.

In these, bloodshed was barely avoided, while hand-to-hand fights, inflicting grievous bodily injury, were only too common.

CHAPTER VI

After the burning of the *Dundonald*, a score of the rioters had been arrested and imprisoned. But owing to the confusion of the *mêlée* and the prompt dispersion of the Unionists it had been found difficult to procure the necessary identification and direct evidence of criminality. Thus, after some weeks of imprisonment, all were discharged except six prisoners, among whom, unfortunately for himself and his family, was that notorious malefactor, William Hardwick. Fate, in his case, would appear to have leaned to the wrong side!

His appearance and manner had so favourably impressed the Bench of Magistrates, before whom, after several remands, he and his fellow-prisoners had been brought, that they were on the point of discharging him, when Janus Stoate was tendered by the Sub-Inspector of Police in charge of the case as a material witness for the Crown. He had kept in the background after he saw the affair well started, taking care to be heard protesting against violence on the part of the Unionists. Having been sworn, he admitted his connection with them, to the extent of belonging to the camp and having acted as a delegate, appointed by the Council of the Australian Shearers' Union. He had worked last at Tandara woolshed. At that station the men had completed their contract and been paid off in the usual way. He as delegate had received notice from the President of the Union to call out the shearers before shearing was concluded. They declined, temporarily, and a messenger, elected by the men, was sent to Wagga Wagga for further instructions.

Before he returned, the shed had 'cut out'—finished shearing, that is. He could not say he approved of the arrangement, but was glad that the contract was completed and all settled amicably. He was an upholder of passive resistance, and could bring witnesses to prove that he dissuaded the men from violence.

'Did he know the defendant, William Hardwick?'

'Yes, very well—he was sorry to see him in this position.'

'Had he seen him inciting or assisting the men who were concerned in the burning of the steamer?'

'No, he could not say that he had, but——'

The witness was urged to explain, which he did, apparently with unwillingness.

'He had seen him standing by the river-bank, with a gun in his hand.'

'Did he discharge the gun?'

'Yes, he did; he saw him put the gun to his shoulder and fire.'

'Was it directed at any one of the crew of the *Dundonald*?'

'He could not say that. The night was dark—just before daylight. He fired at or near somebody, that was all he could say.'

'That will do.'

Another Unionist witness was brought forward. This man was actuated by a revengeful spirit towards the free labourers, and especially towards those shearers that had opposed the Union. He therefore gave damaging evidence against Bill and his companions. He swore that he had seen Hardwick—that was his name, he believed—anyway he was the 'blackleg' now before the Court— loading and firing, like some of the camp men.

He was warned not to use the expression 'blackleg,' as it was disrespectful to the Court. Such conduct might lead to his being committed for contempt of Court and imprisoned.

The witness had 'done time' in another colony, been before a Court more than once or twice probably. He laughed impudently, saying, 'He didn't mean no offence, but it was 'ard on a man, as was true to his fellow-workers, to keep his tongue off such sneaks.'

This was one of the cases where a magistrate, not being able to deal effectively with a witness, will take as little offence as possible, so as to get him out of the box and have done with him. In a city or county town such a man would be sent to gaol for twenty-four hours, for contempt of Court, to appear next morning in a chastened frame of mind. But as the fire-raisers were to be committed for trial and forwarded under escort to the Circuit Court at Wagga Wagga, nothing would be gained by delaying the whole affair for the purpose of punishing a single witness.

So poor Bill, being asked by the magistrate what he had to say in his defence, made a bungling job of it, as many an innocent man, under the circumstances, has done before, and will again.

'He could only state, that though seen among the Unionist rioters, he was there under compulsion; that he and his mates, who had come from Tandara, had determined, after seeing the unfair way in which the sheds that "shore Union" had been ordered out, to cut loose from the tyranny. But they had been captured by the rioters at Moorara; made to carry arms and stand in front, where they were nearly being shot. As God was his Judge, he never fired a shot or meant to fire one. He would far rather have emptied his gun at the fellows who had robbed and ill-treated him—for his horses, saddles, and swag were "put away," he believed, his cheque and loose money were gone, and he had nothing but what he stood up in. What call had he to hurt the boat, or any one aboard her? It was the other way on. The witnesses had perjured themselves, particularly Janus Stoate, who had eaten his bread and borrowed money from him in times past, and now was swearing falsely, to ruin him, and rob his wife and children of their home. He had no more to say.'

Unluckily for poor Bill, several of the accused, who *were* guilty, had made substantially the same defence. They were proved, by the evidence of the crew of the *Dundonald* and the police, to have been actively aiding and abetting in the outrage. One, indeed, who tried to look virtuous and made a plausible speech, had been seen pouring kerosene over the doomed steamer, preparatory to her being set on fire.

This prejudiced the Bench against all defences of the same nature as Bill's. He might, of course, have called on his mates, who had left the Tandara shed with him, resolving to sever all connection with the Union. They would, of course, have been able to corroborate his story, and have ensured his discharge. But, here again, Fate (or else blind Chance, which she too often resembles) was against him. 'Fortune's my foe,' he might have quoted, with reason, had such literary *morceaux* been in his line.

One of the shearers from Tandara, being a smart bushman, had escaped, in the uncertain light and confusion of the *mêlée*, and discovering the horses of the party, feeding by themselves, in an angle of the station fence, caught the quietest of the lot, annexed a stray halter, and ran them into a yard. He then returned to the insurgents, and mingling with the crowd, managed to warn his comrades, except Bill, who was wedged in between two armed men, with another at his back, by special instruction of Stoate. Leaving unostentatiously, they escaped notice, and providing themselves with saddles and bridles from the numbers which lay on the ground outside of tents, or on horizontal limbs of trees, departed quietly, and by sundown were many a mile away on the road to the next non-Union station. They would not have abandoned their companion had they the least idea of what he was likely to undergo at the hands of the law; but the last thought that could have entered into their heads would be that *he* was liable to arrest and trial in connection with the burning of the steamer. So, believing that they might run serious risk by remaining among the excited, dangerous crowd, at the same time being powerless to do him any good, they decided to clear off.

As there was sworn evidence to incriminate him without available witnesses to testify in his favour, the Bench had no alternative but to commit William Hardwick for trial at the next ensuing Assize Court, to be holden at Wagga Wagga. Thither, with the other prisoners, ruffians with whom he could neither sympathise nor associate, was poor Bill, manacled and despairing, sent off in the up-river coach, a prey to anxiety and despondent imaginings.

What would be Jenny's feelings when she saw in an extract from the *Wilcannia Watchman*, too faithfully copied into the *Talmorah Advertiser*:—

'OUTRAGE BY UNIONISTS.

'Burning of the "Dundonald."

'Arrest and trial before the Bench of Magistrates at Tolarno. William Hardwick, John Jones, J. Abershaw, T. Murphy, and others, committed for trial at next Assize Court. Severe sentences may be looked for.'

Jenny's distress at this announcement may be imagined. She had not heard from Bill since he left Tandara, at which time he had written in good spirits, mentioning the amount of his cheque, and his resolution to cut loose from the Shearers' Union (which he was sorry he ever joined), and more particularly from Stoate and all his works.

'It's that villain, and no one else,' cried poor Jenny. 'I knew he'd do Bill a mischief before he'd done with him—a regular snake in the grass. I'd like to have a crack at him with a roping pole. He's worked round poor Bill, some road or other, who's that soft and straightforward, as any man could talk him over—and yet I wonder, after what he wrote——'

And here Jenny took Bill's last letter out of her homely treasure-chest, read it once more and cried over it, after which she dried her eyes and changed her dress, preparatory to seeking counsel of Mr. Calthorpe, the banker in the township. This gentleman received her sympathetically, and heard all she had to say, before giving an opinion.

In small and remote centres of population such as Talmorah the bank manager is, even more than the clergyman or the doctor, the 'guide, philosopher, and friend' of the humbler classes, whom he chiefly advises for their good, and, in moderation, aids pecuniarily, if he can do so, with safety to the bank. He is often young, but, from a wider than ordinary outlook on men and affairs, endowed with discretion beyond his years. For Jenny and her husband he had a genuine liking and respect, based chiefly on his knowledge of character, but partly on the creditable state of Bill's bank account.

'It's a bad business, Mrs. Hardwick,' he said, when Jenny had concluded her story in a fit of weeping, which she could not restrain. 'And Bill's the last man I should have expected to be mixed up with this affair. It's wonderful what harm this strike business is doing all over Australia. However, it's no use thinking of that. The question is, how to help your husband out of the trouble, now he's in it. He's only committed now—which doesn't go for much. It's the trial before the Judge and Jury we have to look to.'

Here Mr. Calthorpe took down a file of newspapers and looked through them. 'Yes, I thought so; to be tried at next ensuing Assize Court at Wagga. You'd like him to have a lawyer to defend him, wouldn't you?'

'Of course I would,' replied the loyal wife. 'We've worked hard for our bit of money, but I'd spend the last shilling of it before Bill should go to gaol.'

'Quite right. Bill's man enough to make more—his liberty's the main thing. Well, I'll send a letter by this night's mail to the Manager of our bank at Wagga and ask him to see Mr. Biddulph, the solicitor—I was stationed there years ago—and *he'll* get him off if any one can. Money is wanted, though, to pay witnesses' expenses—you must be prepared for that.'

'Whatever's wanted, let him have, in God's name,' Jenny cried recklessly. 'You know Bill's good for it, sir, and I've butter-money saved up of my own. Bill always let me keep that. I've got it in this bag. It will do to begin with.'

'Never mind that,' said the banker, good-humouredly. 'I have your deeds, you know, and the balance is on the right side of your account. So don't be down-hearted, and I'll let you know as soon as I hear from Biddulph. Good-bye, and keep up your spirits; fretting won't do you any good, or Bill either. All right, Mr. Mason,' he said, as his assistant, after knocking, looked in at the door; 'tell Mr. Thornhill I can see him in a minute.'

'I'll never forget your kindness,' said Jenny, as she shook hands warmly with the friend in need. 'You'll let me know directly you hear anything.'

'You may depend on that. Good-bye till Saturday; the up-river mail will be in then.' As she passed out, a stoutish, middle-aged man came in.

'Morning, Calthorpe. Comforting the widow or the orphan? Saw she was in trouble.'

'Deuced hard lines,' said the Manager gravely. 'Very decent people — selectors at Chidowla, near Curra Creek. Her husband's got into trouble — committed for trial about that burning of the *Dundonald*.'

'Serve him right, too. Those Union fellows are playing the deuce all over the country. If they're not stopped there's no saying what they'll do next. The country's going to the devil. The Government won't act with decision, while property is being destroyed and life menaced every day. I don't blame the men so much; it's these rascally agitators that ought to suffer, and they mostly get out of it.'

'I'll never believe that Bill Hardwick went in for the steamer-burning business,' said the banker, 'though he seems to have got mixed up with it somehow. There's some cur working it, I'm sure. He's got a decent stake in the country himself. He'd never risk losing his farm and the money that he's saved. I won't believe it till it's proved.'

'But he must have been with those Union fellows or they couldn't have arrested him,' answered the squatter. 'What was he doing in a Union Camp? Comes of keeping bad company, you see. I'm sorry for his wife — she seems a good sort; but if a man takes up with such people, he must pay the penalty.'

And then the Manager went keenly into his client's business, removing all thought of Bill's hard luck and Jenny's sad face from his mental vision. But after his day's work was done, and his books duly posted up, as he took his usual walk round the outskirts of the township, the 'case of William Hardwick, charged with arson in the matter of the steamer *Dundonald*,' recurred again and again with almost painful iteration.

'Must be a put-up job!' he ejaculated, as he turned towards the unpretending four-roomed cottage which served him for dwelling-place, office, and treasure-house. His clerk and assistant, a young fellow of twenty, in training for higher posts when the years of discretion had arrived, slept there with him.

But both took their meals in the best hotel of the township (there were only two)—a more interesting way of managing the commissariat than house-keeping where servants were scarce, as well as presenting distinct advantages from the cooking side. It may be added that they were never absent from the bank at the same time.

In addition to the convenience of the latter arrangement a country banker in Australia finds his account in a general suavity of demeanour. Bits of information then fall in his way, which a less cordial manner would not have attracted.

At the ordinary table of the Teamsters' Arms, Talmorah, being a great 'carrying centre,' all sorts and conditions of men were represented. Not that the partially renovated swagman or bullock-driver sat at meat with the correctly attired squatter, station-manager, or commercial traveller. Such is not the fashion in rural Australia. Meals, except in case of illness, are not served in private rooms—a limited staff of servants forbidding such luxury. But a second table is provided, of which the lower tariff practically effects a separation between the socially unequal sections. If not, a hint is never wanting from the prudent but decisive landlord.

At the bar counter, however, a nearer approach to democratic equality is reached; and it was here that Mr. Calthorpe caught a few words that decided him to ask for a glass of beer, while a rather heated argument was being carried on.

'Heard about Bill Hardwick fallin' in, over that steamer-burnin' racket?' queried a sunburnt teamster, whose dust-enveloped garb and beard proclaimed a long and wearisome trail.

'We all heard of it,' answered the man addressed—an agricultural-appearing person, not so distinctively 'back-block' in appearance as the first speaker—'and we're dashed sorry it's true in this quarter. Bill's a neighbour of mine, and a straighter chap never stepped. I don't hold with that sort of foolishness that the Union's been carryin' on lately. I joined 'em and so did Bill, and I'd be as well pleased I hadn't now, and so'd he I reckon. But as for him helpin' to burn a steamer, I'd just as soon believe he'd stick up this bank.'

'Banks is one thing and Union leaders is another,' decided the man from the waste, finishing a portentous 'long sleever.' 'But a chap's fool enough to go with his crowd now and again; he don't care about being ticketed as a "blackleg." Why shouldn't Bill do it as well as another?'

'Because he's the wrong sort; he's married and has a couple of kids. His wife's a hard-working, savin' kind of woman as ever you see—always at it from daylight to dark. Besides, he's lookin' to go in for another selection. That's not the sort of chap that goes burnin' sheds and steamers. It's a bloomin' plant, I'll take my oath.'

'That's your notion, is it?' quoth the teamster, who, having imbibed as much colonial beer as would have half-drowned a smaller and less desiccated man, was disposed to be confidential. 'I wouldn't say as you're far out. I was comin' by Quambone with Bangate wool—forty-five bales of greasy—it's now onloadin', and I'd a yarn with a chap that was in the Union Camp at Moorara. He kep' as far back as he could, and cleared out first chance. Of course they was all mixed up when the firin' came, and some of 'em, as hadn't wanted to go too far, took their chance to cut it. But afore he went, he heard Stoate ('you know him?'—the listener nodded) tell another of the "committy," as they called theirselves, "that he'd fix up Bill Hardwick if it come to a trial—if any man had to do a stretch over it, *he'd* not get off."

'"How'll you work that?" says the other cove. "He's never gone solid along of us; and now he'll be dead agen Unionism, and no wonder. He told some one this morning he'd lost his shearing cheque."'

'So that's the way they nobbled him,' said his hearer. 'Infernal bloomin' scoundrels to swear a man's liberty away. Bill's got a friend or two yet, though, and money in the bank, though some of them spoutin' loafers has his cheque in their pockets. So long.'

The gaunt, sun-baked teamster departed to turn out his bullocks, and generally recreate after his journey, deferring till the morrow the pleasant process of receiving his cheque for carriage and safe delivery of his valuable load—over five hundred pounds' worth of merino wool.

But Mr. Calthorpe, the banker, who, without listening to the whole conversation, had caught Bill's name occasionally, touched Donahue's arm (for that perfunctory agriculturist it was) as he turned reluctantly homeward, and questioned him concerning his late acquaintance's words.

Nothing loath, indeed gratified with the chance of placating the local potentate who wielded the power of life and death (financially) over him and others, he cheerfully disclosed all that he had heard, being, moreover, a good-natured, obliging sort of fellow, as indeed thriftless persons often are.

'Now, look here, Donahue!' said the great man. 'I've a liking for Hardwick, whom I've always found a steady and industrious chap, that it's a pleasure to help. Some men are not built that way, Dick'— here he looked Donahue squarely in the face. 'They idle their time, and spend the money drinking and horse-racing that ought to go to paying their debts and keeping the wife and children.' Mr. Donahue looked embarrassed, and gazed into the distance. 'But I want your help to take this business out of winding, and if you'll work with me, I *might*—I don't say I will, mind you—recommend the Bank to give you time to pay off the arrears on your selection.'

Dick Donahue, whose cheerful demeanour covered an aching heart and remorseful feelings whenever he thought of the possibility of the family losing their home because of his want of steady industry, turned round, almost with the tears in his eyes, as he said, not without a touch of natural dignity—

'Mr. Calthorpe, I'd do what I could for Bill, who's a better man than myself, with all the veins of my heart—as poor old father used to say—and ask no return in the world; and for Jenny Hardwick, who's been a good head to Biddy and the children (more shame for me that they wanted help), I'd risk my life any day. And if you think well of givin' me more time to pay up, I've got a fencing contract from Mr. Dickson, after the New Year, and I'll never touch a drop till it's finished, and give you an order on him for the lot.'

'All right, Dick, we can arrange that; you work like a man and do your duty to your family, and you'll find a friend in me.' He held out his hand, which the repentant prodigal shook fervently, and turned away without another word.

Nothing more was said on that day, but in the following week Richard Donahue, fairly well turned out, and riding a horse 'fit to go for a man's life,' as he expressed it, started 'down river,' leaving Mrs. Bridget in a state of mind very different from that with which she ordinarily regarded her husband's absence from home 'on business,' always uncertain as to return and rarely satisfactory as to remuneration.

CHAPTER VII

The inland town of Wagga Wagga, in New South Wales, historically celebrated as the dwelling-place of the Tichborne Claimant, where that lapsed scion of the aristocracy followed the indispensable but not socially eminent occupation of butcher, was, if not *en fête*, pardonably excited at the arrival of the Judge and officers of the Assize Court to be holden on the morrow.

This traditional spectacle—almost as interesting as the Annual Race Meeting or the Agricultural Show—was afforded to the inhabitants at half-yearly intervals. The curiosity aroused by these unfamiliar personages, before whom were decided the issues of freedom or imprisonment, life or death, was concentrated and intense. The Judge who presided, the Bar, the Deputy Sheriff, the Crown Prosecutor, the Associate, were objects of admiration to the denizens of a city three hundred miles from a metropolis—chiefly ignorant of other than rural life, and to whom the ocean itself was almost unknown. To the jurymen, culled from the town dwellers and the surrounding farms, the summons to aid in the administration of justice was a memorable solemnity.

The compulsory withdrawal from their ordinary avocations was fully compensated by urban pleasures, and doubtless aided their intelligent comprehension of the laws of the land.

Among the townspeople a certain amount of social festivity was deemed appropriate to the occasion.

It may therefore be imagined that among the young men and maidens the infrequent procession of the Judge's carriage, escorted by the Superintendent of Police and half-a-dozen troopers, well armed, mounted, and accurately turned out, created a thrill of pleasurable anticipation.

These feelings were heightened by the fact that Wagga (as, for convenience, the thriving town on the Murrumbidgee River was chiefly designated) stood at the edge of a vast pastoral district, being also bounded by one of the finest agricultural regions of Australia.

The cases to be tried at this sitting of the Court concerned as well the great pastoral interest as the army of labourers, to whom that interest paid in wages not less than ten millions sterling annually.

Punctually as the Post-office clock struck ten, the Court House was filled, great anxiety being shown to behold the six prisoners, who were marched from the gaol and placed in the dock, a forbidding-looking, iron-railed enclosure with a narrow wooden seat. On this some promptly sat down, while others stood up and gazed around with a well-acted look of indifference. Bill Hardwick had never been in such a place before, and the thought of what Jenny's feelings would be if she had seen him there nearly broke his heart. He sat with his head covered with his hands—the picture of misery and despair. He knew that he was to be defended—indeed had been closely questioned long before the day of trial about his conduct on the eventful morning of the burning of the *Dundonald*.

He had asserted his innocence in moving terms, such as even touched the heart of the solicitor, hardened as he was by long acquaintance with desperate criminals as well as cases where plaintiffs, witnesses, and defendants all seemed to be leagued in one striking exhibition of false swearing and prevarication calculated to defeat the ends of justice.

'That's all right,' said the lawyer, 'and I believe every word you've said, Bill, and deuced hard lines it is—not that I believe defendants generally, on their oath or otherwise. But you're a different sort, and it's a monstrous thing that you should have to spend your hard-earned money on lawyers and witnesses to defend yourself from a false charge. But what we've got to look to, is to make the Judge and jury believe you. These d—d scoundrels that were on for burning the boat, saw you with a gun in your hand while the affair was going on, and will swear to that, back and edge. Your friend Stoate, who isn't here yet, but will be up in time for the trial, will clinch the nail, and he can bring the constable to back him up, who saw you holding a gun. He doesn't say more than that, but it goes to corroborate. The jury must go by sworn evidence. There's only your own statement, which won't weigh against deponents, who've apparently nothing to gain on the other side.'

'It's all the spite of that hound Stoate,' cried out Bill passionately. 'He was crabbed for my belittling him in the Tandara shed. He's put those Unionists up to ruining me, and I'll break his neck when I get out, if I have to swing for it.'

'No, you won't, Bill! If you get a sentence, which I hope you won't, when you come out you'll be so jolly glad to find yourself free, that you won't want to go back even for revenge. But never mind that for the present; we must look things in the face. It's a thousand pities you couldn't get some of those chaps that were driven into the hut along with you, by the Unionists, the first night. Any idea where they've gone? Know their names?'

'They went down the river, I heard say. They're hundreds of miles away by this time. What's the use of knowing their names?'

'That's my business. It's wonderful how people turn up sometimes. Come, out with their names—where they came from—all you know about them.'

Thus adjured, Bill gave their names and a sketch of personal appearance, home address, and so on. 'All of them were natives, and some of them, when they were at home, which was not often, had selections in the same district.' This being done, Mr. Biddulph folded up the paper, and left Bill to his reflections, telling him that he could do nothing more for him at present, but to 'keep up his pecker,' and not to think the race was over till the numbers were up.

This quasi-encouragement, however, availed him but little. 'He had lost his shearing cheque; and here was money,' he sadly thought, 'being spent like water, to prove him innocent of a crime for which he never should have been charged. His wife would be nearly killed with anxiety, besides being made aware that they could not now think of buying Donahue's or any other selection. How everything had gone wrong since he rode away from home that morning with Stoate (infernal, blasted traitor that he was!), and had been going from bad to worse ever since. It was against Jenny's advice that he joined the Union. She had a knack of being right, though she was not much of a talker. Another time—but when would that be?'

So Bill—'a hunter of the hills,' more or less, as was the Prisoner of Chillon—had to pass the weary hours until the day of trial, and he could exchange the confinement of the gaol for the expansive scenery of the dock—restricted as to space, certainly, but having an outlook upon the world, and a sort of companionship in the crowd of spectators, lawyers, and witnesses, finishing up with the Judge.

At this judicial potentate Bill looked long and wistfully. He had an idea that a Judge was a ruthless administrator of hard laws, with a fixed prejudice against working-men who presumed to do anything illegal, or in fact to trouble themselves about anything but their work and wages. However, he could not fail to see in this Judge a mild, serious, patient gentleman, showing greater anxiety to understand the facts of the case than to inflict sentences. Still, he was only partly reassured. Might he not be one of those benevolent-seeming ones— he had heard of such—who would talk sweetly to the prisoner, reminding him of the happy days of childhood, and his, perhaps, exemplary conduct when he used to attend Sunday School—trust that he intended to lead a new life, and then paralyse him with a ten years' sentence, hard labour, and two days' solitary in each month?

He did not know what to expect. Wasn't there Pat Macarthy, who got three years for assault with intent to commit grievous bodily harm (certainly he more than half killed the other man)? Well, his wife worked his farm, and slaved away the whole time, denying herself almost decent clothes to wear. At the end of his term, he came out to find her hopelessly insane; she had been taken to the Lunatic Asylum only the week before.

Bill hardly thought that Jenny would go 'off her head,' in the popular sense. It was too level and well-balanced. But if he was sentenced to three or five years more of this infernal, hopeless, caged-in existence, he expected *he* would.

The prisoners that he had watched in the exercise yard didn't seem to mind it so much. But they were old and worn-out; had nothing much to wish themselves outside for. Others did not look as if they had worked much in their lives—had indeed 'done time' more than once, as the slang phrase went, content to loll on the benches in the exercise yard and talk to their fellow-convicts—not always after an improving fashion. But to *him* it would be a living death. Up and out every morning of his life at or before daylight,—hard at work at the thousand-and-one-tasks of a farm until it was too dark to tell an axe from a spade,—how *could* he endure this cruel deprivation of all that made life worth living?

Fortunately for him, in one sense, the day of his trial was absolutely perfect as to weather. Bright and warm—it was late December—the sky unflecked by a single cloud. But there was a cool, sea wind, which, wandering up from the distant coast, set every human creature (not in sickness, sorrow, or 'hard bound in misery and iron'), aglow with the joy of living. It raised the spirits even of that plaything of destiny known among men as William Hardwick, so that as the whispering breeze stole through the open windows of the Court he held up his dejected head and felt almost like a man again.

The proceedings commenced, the jury had been impanelled. The Crown Prosecutor threw back his gown, and fixing his eyes on the Judge's impassive countenance opened the case.

'May it please your Honour, you will pardon me perhaps if, before calling witnesses, I sketch briefly the state of affairs which, more or less connected with the strike of 1891, has developed into a condition of matters perilous to life and property, and altogether without precedent in Australia.

'From a determination on the part of the seamen on coasting steamers to refuse work unless certain privileges were granted to them by the owners, a commencement was made of the most widespread, important, and, in its effects, the most disastrous strike ever known in Australia. Into the question of the adequacy or otherwise of the wage claimed, it is not my intention to enter.

'The consequences, however, of the refusal of these seamen and others to continue at work except under certain conditions, were far-reaching, and such as could not have been reasonably anticipated. The revolt, as it was called by the leaders of the movement, spread from sea to land, and throughout all kinds and conditions of labourers, with startling rapidity.

'Many of these bodies of workmen could not have been thought to have been concerned with the original dissentients, by any process of reasoning. But by the leaders of the rebellion—for such it may truly be designated—the opportunity was deemed favourable for the promulgation of what are known as communistic or socialistic doctrines. More especially was this observable in the conduct of a large body of workmen, members of the Australian Shearers' Union. Guided by ambitious individuals of moderate education but considerable shrewdness, not wholly unmingled with cunning, the shearers, and indeed the whole body of labourers connected with the great wool export, had been misled. They were asked to believe that a conspiracy existed on the part of the representatives of capital, whether merchants, bankers, or landholders—indeed of all employers, whether private individuals or incorporated companies—to defraud the labourer of his hire.

'Inflamed by seditious pamphlets and utterances, shearers and others banded themselves together for the purpose of intimidating all workmen who were unwilling to be guided by the autocratic Unions, and arranged on their own terms with employers.

'Not only did they, by "picketing,"—an alleged method of moral suasion, but in reality a policy of insult, annoyance, and obstruction,—forcibly prevent other workmen from following their lawful occupations, but they commenced to destroy the property of the pastoral tenants, believed to be opposed to Union despotism. As a specimen of the inflammatory language used, perhaps your Honour will permit me to read an extract from a paper published in the (alleged) interest of the working classes.'

His Honour 'thought that however such extracts might indicate a tendency on the part of certain sections of workmen to engage in acts of violence causing injury to property,—a most lamentable state of feeling, in his opinion,—yet the Court was directly concerned to-day with only specific evidence as to the complicity of the prisoners in the crime of arson on which they were arraigned. He thought the extract at this stage irrelevant.'

'After drawing the attention of your Honour and the jury to the seditious, dishonest statements referred to, I will briefly refer to the lamentable list of outrages upon property, not stopping short indeed of personal violence and grievous bodily injury.

'Matters have reached such a pitch that a state of civil war may be said to have commenced. If not only the country but the towns and cities of Australia are not to be theatres of bloodshed, outrage, and incendiary flames, from which, by the mercy of Providence, Australia has up to this period been preserved, the law in its majesty must step in, and adequately punish the actors in the flagrant criminality as to which I have to address your Honour this day.'

The prisoners, having been duly arraigned, with one accord pleaded not guilty. The last name was that of William Hardwick. Just before his name was called, room was made in the crowded Court and a seat provided by the Sergeant of Police for a woman with two children, whose travel-worn appearance denoted recent arrival.

Bill turned his head, and in that fragment of time recognised Jenny with their little boy and girl. His name had to be repeated a second time. Then he drew himself up, squared his shoulders, and looking straight at the Judge, said 'Not Guilty' in a voice which sounded throughout the Court, and if it had not the ring of truth, was a marvellous imitation.

Poor Jenny, who had preserved a strained, fixed look of composure, broke down at this juncture. The sight of her husband, standing in the dock with men of crime-hardened and to her eyes of guilty appearance—one of whom, indeed, wore leg-irons, which clanked as he moved—overcame all attempts at self-possession. Her sobs were audible through the whole Court.

'Wife of the prisoner, your Honour,' explained the sergeant. 'Just off the coach; been travelling twenty hours without rest or sleep.'

'Had she not better stay in the witnesses' room?' suggested the Judge sympathetically. 'Refreshment can be brought to her there.'

But Jenny, though temporarily overcome, was not the woman to give in at such a time. Wiping her eyes, 'I've come a long way, if you please, your Honour,' she said, 'to hear my man tried on a false charge, if ever there was one; and I hope you'll let me see it out. I'll not disturb the Court again.'

It was a piteous spectacle.

Little Billy Hardwick, a precocious, resolute youngster 'rising five,' looked for a while with much gravity at his father, and then said, 'Is this a church, mother? Why doesn't father come out of that pew?'

Jenny was nearly overcome by this fresh assault on her sympathies, but accentuating her order by a shake, replied, *sotto voce*, 'It's not a church, Billy; but you mustn't talk, or else a policeman will lock you up in prison.' The child had heard of prisons, where bad people were locked up, even in Talmorah, where the primitive structure was, in his little mind, associated with the constable's children, who used to play therein when the cells were empty. He would have liked further explanation, but he read the signs in his mother's set face and closed lips, and spoke no more; while the little girl, holding on to her mother's gown, mingled her tears with those of her parent. Jenny Hardwick was 'not much in the crying line,' as an early friend had said of her, and was besides possessed of an unusual share of physical courage as well as of strength of mind. So, when she had hastily dried her eyes, she gave every indication of being as good as her word.

'Call the first witness,' said the Crown Prosecutor, anxious to get to work. This proved to be the Captain of Volunteers, who marched into the box accordingly.

'Your name is Gilbert Elliot, formerly of the 60th Regiment, now commanding a mounted Volunteer force. Were you at Moorara on the Darling on the 28th of August 1894?'

'I was.'

'Please to state what you did and what you saw then.'

'When the troop reached Poliah, at the date mentioned, I saw the steamer *Dundonald* floating down the river. She was on fire and burning fiercely. Apparently no one was on board. There was a large camp of armed men—several hundreds—whom I concluded to be Union shearers. They were yelling and shouting out that they had just burned the —— boat and would roast the crew and captain for bringing up "blacklegs." I called upon them to disperse, and as they made a show of resistance I ordered my men to charge. They commenced to retreat and disperse, upon which I caused all the men to be arrested who had arms in their hands, and who were pointed out to me as having fired at the crew of the steamer or having set fire to the vessel.'

'Do you recognise the prisoners before the Court?'

'Yes; all of them.'

'Your Honour, I appear for prisoner William Hardwick,' said a shrewd, alert-looking person, who had just then bustled into the Court and appeared to be well known to the legal section. 'May I ask to have the captain's evidence read over to me? Ordinarily I should not think of troubling your Honour or delaying the business of the Court; but I have travelled from Harden, and, being delayed on the road, have only this moment arrived.'

'Under the circumstances, Mr. Biddulph, the evidence of Captain Elliot may be read over from my notes.' This was done.

The witness's evidence was proceeded with.

'Was there any show of resistance by the men assembled in the camp?'

'There was a movement as if they were disposed to fight. They outnumbered my troopers more than six to one, but at the first charge they wavered and dispersed. They made no opposition to my arresting the prisoners before the Court. One of them, the one now in irons, made a desperate resistance, but was not supported.'

'Now, Captain Elliot,' said Mr. Biddulph, 'will you look at the prisoner at this end of the dock; do you remember him?'

'Perfectly. He had a rifle in his hand when I ordered him to be arrested.'

'Did he resist?'

'No.'

'Did he say anything? If so, what was it?'

'He said, "I'm not here of my own free-will. I've been robbed and ill-treated by these men. I was forced to carry this gun. You can see that it has not been discharged. My mates (there are several of them) can prove that." I asked him where they were. He said he did not know.'

'Then you had him arrested, though he disclaimed taking any part in the unlawful proceedings? Did you not believe him?'

'I did not. As it happened, other prisoners made substantially the same defence who had been seen firing their guns just as we rode up.'

'That will do, captain.'

The next witness was called.

'My name is Humphrey Bolton. I am a Sergeant of Volunteers, and came up from Moorara by a forced march as soon as we heard that the steamer was burnt. When we struck the camp there were six or seven hundred men, most of them armed. They appeared very excited. I saw the steamer drifting down the river. She was on fire. I saw a barge with a number of men in it. I noticed the Unionists standing on the bank of the river and firing from time to time in the direction of the barge. The men in the barge were bending down and lying in the bottom as if afraid of being hit. I did not hear of any of them being hurt; a few shots were fired back, and one man in the camp was wounded.'

'What happened next?' said the Crown Prosecutor.

'Captain Elliot ordered me to capture all men on the river-bank who had arms in their hands. The six prisoners before the Court and about a dozen others were taken in charge accordingly.'

'Did the crowd resist their capture?'

'They made a show of it at first, but as soon as we charged, they gave way and cleared off in all directions.'

'Now, sergeant,' said Mr. Biddulph, 'look at the prisoner William Hardwick. Had he arms?'

'He was carrying a gun.'

'Did you see him fire it?'

'No.'

'Did you examine it, when he said it had not been fired?'

'Yes, the captain ordered me to do so; it had not been fired recently.'

'Wasn't that proof that he was speaking the truth?'

'How could I tell? He might have been going to fire, or picked up one that had not been used. Besides, my officer told me to arrest him, and, of course, I obeyed orders. He was in company with men who had just committed a felony, at any rate.'

'I see—evil communications. You may go down, sergeant.'

The next witness was the captain of the *Dundonald*.

'My name is Seth Dannaker, Master Mariner, out of Boston, U.S.A. I was lately in command of the steamer *Dundonald*—now at the bottom of the river Darling. I had come from Pooncarrie, carrying forty-five free labourers, last Saturday, without obstruction or disturbance. I took wood on board, and tied up, with swamp all round, a little below Poliah. We heard that a large camp of Unionists were waiting to attack us there; they had wire ropes across the river. We had steam up all night and a watch was kept. About four o'clock A.M. a mob of disguised men rushed on board the boat, and took possession of her. They knocked me about, and put me and the crew on board the barge, now moored at Moorara. They afterwards set the *Dundonald* on fire. She drifted down the river, and finally sank. They took possession of the free labourers, and counted them. They had guns and revolvers, threatening to shoot me and all who resisted them. I have lost all my personal effects, including money. I thought this was a free country; now I know it isn't.'

Cross-examined by Mr. Carter, appearing for the prisoners—with the exception of William Hardwick.

'You say you were threatened by one or more of the Unionists. Can you recognise any of the prisoners now before the Court?'

'Yes; the man in irons. I was told his name was Abershaw. He put a revolver to my head, swearing he would shoot me if I resisted; also that he would burn the b——y steamer, and roast me and the Agent of the Employers' Association for bringing up blacklegs.'

'Was he sober?'

'I cannot say. He was much excited, and more like a madman than any one in his senses. Two or three men struck me. I cannot identify any other prisoners. I had left my revolver in the cabin, or I should have shot some of them.'

'Did you see any persons firing at the vessel or crew?'

'Yes; there was a line of men on the bank firing with rifles at the crew. They wounded two of them. I cannot identify any of them.'

Cross-examined by Mr. Biddulph.

'Will you look at the man in the corner of the dock nearest to you? Did you see him firing or carrying a gun?'

'I never saw him at all, to my knowledge. Of course there was confusion.'

Next witness. 'My name is James Davidson. I am the Agent of the Employers' Association. On or about the 28th August 1894, I came up in the *Dundonald* in charge of free labourers (forty-five) to a spot near Poliah. The police had been sent for from Tolarno. We had heard of the Unionists intending to obstruct the boat, and so kept watch above and below. Next morning, just before daylight, a number of men rushed on board. One of them pointed a gun at the man who tried to set the boat free, threatening to kill him if he moved. They went into the wheel-house, and struck the captain; I heard them tell him they would kill him and burn the boat. He was knocked about badly. I got a few blows before the leaders got the men quiet. Then they started getting my men out.'

By the Crown Prosecutor. 'Whom do you mean by your men?'

'The free labourers.'

'Did they resist, or go quietly?'

'Some went quietly—others resisted, and were thrown overboard. A few were only in their shirts, as they had not had time to dress. They were then set up in a line and counted, to see if they were all there. A guard was put over them.'

'Was the guard armed?'

'Yes. Another gang was busy unloosing the steamer, and preparing her for the fire. They smashed in the cabins and stole everything. Nothing escaped them when they began to pillage. I lost my portmanteau, clothes, and money. Everything was taken out of my cabin, leaving me nothing but the clothes I had on.'

'Were the Unionists much excited?'

'Excited?—raving mad, I should call it. We were lucky to get off with our lives. Fortunately, few persons were injured. We received every attention when we got to Moorara. There is a large Union Camp at Tolarno. They have given out that they intend to burn two more steamers, for carrying free labourers.'

'Do you identify the prisoners in the dock?'

'Two of them. The man in irons struck the captain, and said he would burn the boat and roast him alive. The one with the large beard was the one who said he would shoot the man who was unloosing the cable. The others I have no knowledge of.'

By Mr. Carter. 'Did you see the prisoner William Hardwick—the one at this end of the dock?'

'Not that I am aware of.'

'You said you lost some money?'

'Yes, ten or twelve pounds; it was in a purse in my portmanteau. I had to draw on the Association for a few pounds, as I was left penniless and without a change of wearing apparel.'

'I suppose that was a form of "picketing," in accordance with the "ethics of war."'

'"Pickpocketing," I should call it.'

'One moment, Mr. Davidson,' interposed Mr. Biddulph, as the Agent turned to leave the witness-box. 'Did you see the prisoner at this end of the dock, carrying a gun or in any way joining in this creditable work?'

'I never saw him at all.'

'That will do.'

'Call Janus Stoate, witness for the Crown.'

As his name was mentioned, Bill turned his head towards the door where the witnesses came in, with a look of murderous hate, such as no man had ever seen before on his good-natured countenance.

Jenny, as she looked anxiously towards the dock, hardly knew him. By that door was to walk in the man who had eaten many a time at his humble but plentiful table, and in return had treacherously denounced him, ruined his character, helped to deprive him of his hard-earned wages, gone near to render his children paupers, and break his wife's heart. A man of his easy-going, confiding character, easily deceived, is not prone to suspicion, but when injured — outraged in his deepest, tenderest feelings — is terrible in wrath. As Bill unconsciously clenched his hands, and stared at the open door, he looked as one eager to tear his enemy limb from limb.

But the thronged Court was disappointed, and Bill's vengeance delayed, as no Janus Stoate appeared.

Mr. Biddulph, who had left the Court, now appeared in company with a mounted trooper, whose semi-military attire told of a rapid ride. He spoke in a low voice to the Sub-Inspector of Police, who thereupon proceeded to address the Judge.

'If your Honour pleases, there will be a trifling delay before this witness can give his evidence, owing to circumstances to which I cannot at present allude. As the hour for your Honour's luncheon has nearly arrived, may I suggest a short adjournment? I can assure your Honour that I make the application for sufficient reasons.'

'I am opposed,' answered the Judge, 'to adjournments in criminal cases; but on Mr. Sub-Inspector's assurance, I consent to relax my rule. Let the Court be adjourned until half-past one o'clock.'

There was a gasp of relief, half of satisfaction, half of disappointment, from the crowd as they hurried from the Court to snatch a hasty meal and ventilate their opinions.

'It's another dodge of the Government to block our workers from gettin' justice,' said one oratorical agitator, partially disguised as a working-man, and whose soft hands betrayed his immunity from recent toil. 'It's a conspiracy hatched up to block Delegate Stoate's evidence agin that blackleg Hardwick.'

'You be hanged!' said a rough-looking bushman, who had just hung his horse up to one of the posts in front of the Murrumbidgee Hotel. 'You won't have so much gab when you see Delegate Stoate, as you call *him*, before the Court, and some one as can tell the truth about him. Bill Hardwick's as honest a cove as ever walked, and he *is* a worker, and not a blatherskite as hasn't done a day's work for years, and sets on skunks like Stoate to rob honest men of their liberty. Don't you stand there gassin' afore me, or I'll knock your hat over your eyes.'

There was presumably a majority of Mr. Stoate's own persuasion around listening to the foregoing remarks, but the onlookers did not seem inclined to controvert this earnest speaker's arguments—seeing that he was distinctly an awkward customer, as he stood there, obviously in hard condition, and eager for the fray.

'See here now, boys,' said a large imposing-looking policeman, 'sure it's betther for yees to be gettin' a bit to ate and a sup of beer this hot day, than to be disputing within the hearin' of the Coort, and may be gettin' "run in" before sundown. Sure it's Misther Barker that's sittin' the good example.' Here he pointed to the agitator, who, after mumbling a few words about 'workers who didn't stand by their order,' had moved off, and was heading straight for the bar of the Murrumbidgee Hotel.

This broke up the meeting, as the Union labourers were anxious to hear the conclusion of the case, Regina *v.* Hardwick and others, and were not unobservant either of the unusually large force of police which the Resident Magistrate of Wagga Wagga, a man of proverbial courage and experience, had called up, in anticipation of any *émeute* which might arise as a result of this exciting trial. At half-past one o'clock the Judge, accompanied by the Deputy Sheriff, took his seat upon the Bench, and the Court was again formally declared open.

As the name Janus Stoate was called by the official, in a particularly clear and audible voice, every eye was turned toward the door by which the Crown witnesses entered, and that distinguished delegate walked in, closely accompanied by a senior constable.

His ordinarily assured and aggressively familiar manner had, however, deserted him; he looked, as the spectators realised, some with surprise, others with chagrin, more like a criminal than a Crown witness.

Bill's gaze was fixed upon him, but instead of homicidal fury, his whole countenance exhibited unutterable scorn, loathing, and contempt. As he turned away, he confronted the spectators and the Court officials generally, with a cheerful and gratified expression, unshared by his companions in misfortune.

Even they regarded Stoate with doubt and disfavour. Deeply suspicious and often envious of their fellow-workmen who attained parliamentary promotion, and more than that, a fixed and comfortable salary, they were skilled experts in facial expression. In the lowered eyes and depressed look of Mr. Delegate Stoate they read defeat and disaster, not improbably treachery.

'The beggar's been squared or "copped" for some bloomin' fake,' said the prisoner on the other side of the man in irons. 'He's goin' to turn dog on us, after all.'

'If I don't get a "stretch,"' growled the other, 'his blood-money won't do him no good.'

'Silence in the Court,' said the senior Sergeant, and Mr. Stoate was duly sworn.

'Your name is Janus Stoate, and you are a shearer and a bush labourer?' said the Crown Prosecutor.

'That is so, mostly go shearin' when I can get a shed.'

'Now, do you know the prisoners in the dock? Look at them well. Their names are William Stokes, Daniel Lynch, Hector O'Halloran, Samson Dawker, Jeremiah Abershaw, and William Hardwick.'

'Yes, your Honour; I've met 'em as feller workers. I don't know as I've been pusson'ly intimate with 'em — except prisoner Hardwick.'

'*He does know him*, to our sorrow, the false villain!' cried out Jenny, coming a pace forward with a child in each hand, and delivering her impeachment before any one could stop her. 'Ask him, your Honour, if he hasn't lived with us, lived *upon* us I call it, for weeks at a time — and now he's going to bear false witness and ruin the family, body and soul.'

'Is this the person who interrupted before?' said the Judge. 'Order *must* be kept in the Court. Let her be removed.' Here the Deputy Sheriff said a few words in a low tone to his Honour. 'Indeed!' said the Judge mildly. 'She must control her feelings, however. My good woman, if I hear another interruption, it will be my duty to have you removed from the Court.'

'Mrs. Hardwick,' said Biddulph, when Jenny's sobs had ceased, 'don't you make a fool of yourself, you're hurting Bill's case. I thought you had more sense. Do you want me to throw it up?'

This settled poor Jenny effectually, and humbly begging pardon, she promised amendment, and kept her word — only regarding Stoate from time to time with the expression which she had assumed at times when a native cat (*Dasyurus*) had got into her dairy.

'Were you at a place called Poliah, on the river Darling, on or about the 28th August last?'

'Yes, I was.'

'Was there a camp there of Unionist shearers?'

'There was workers of all sorts, besides shearers, rouseabouts, and labourers, also loafers.'

'Very likely; but what I want you to tell me is, were they chiefly shearers? In number, how many?'

'Well, say six or seven 'underd.'

'You acted as a delegate, I believe, under rules of the Australian Shearers' Union, at several stations during shearing?'

'I was app'inted as delegate by my feller-workers, and acted as sich on several occasions.'

'What were your duties as a delegate?'

'I 'ad to be in the shed while shearin' was goin on, to see the rules of the Australian Shearers' Union was carried out strickly, and that the men got justice.'

'In what way?'

'Well, that they wasn't done out of their pay for bad shearin', when they shore reasonable well; that they got proper food and lodgin', and wasn't made shear wet sheep, which ain't wholesome—and other things, as between employer and employee.'

'As delegate, did you go to Poliah? and did you see a steamer called the *Dundonald* on the river?'

'Yes, I did.'

'Did you see a number of men rush on board of her, and take the free labourers out of her?'

'No. I was at the back of the camp persuadin' of the men not to use no vi'lence. Then I heard a great hubbub, and guns fired. After that I saw the steamer afire and drifting down river.'

'Did you see who set it on fire?'

'No.'

'Did you see who fired the guns?'

'No; I heard the reports of 'em.'

'Did you see any men on the bank with guns in their hands?'

'Yes; a line of 'em along the river.'

'Were the prisoners now before the Court there?'

'They might have been, I can't speak positive.'

'Was the prisoner Hardwick there carrying a gun?'

'I can't be sure. He might have been. I thought I saw him, but I wasn't near him, and I can't be sure in my mind.'

'You can't be sure?' asked the Crown Prosecutor angrily. 'Didn't you swear at the Police Court at Dilga that you saw him not only holding a gun, but firing it towards the steamer? I'll read your deposition. "I saw the prisoner holding the gun produced. He appeared to have been firing it."'

'Now, Mr. Stoate, is that your signature? and how do you account for your going back on your sworn evidence? You're intelligent enough—in a way. I am at a loss to understand your conduct.'

'Well, I was a bit flurried at the time—confused like. The police came down and charged the mob, and a lot of the shearers cleared out.'

'Then you won't swear that Hardwick held the gun, or fired it?'

'No; I wasn't near enough to him to be dead certain. It was a man like him.'

'Your Honour,' said the Crown Prosecutor, 'this is a most extraordinary change of front on the part of this witness; it amounts to gross prevarication, if not something worse. I *may* have occasion to prosecute him for perjury. You may go down, sir.'

'Not yet. With your Honour's permission, I propose to cross-examine the witness,' interposed Mr. Biddulph. 'Now, Mr. Delegate Stoate, is Janus your Christian name?'

'Yes.'

'Janus, is it? Sounds more heathen than Christian; more suitable also, if I mistake not. Now, Janus Stoate, you're my witness, for the present—remember that—and I advise you to be careful what you say, for your own good, and don't "suppose" so much as you did in your answer to my learned friend. You and Hardwick were on friendly terms before shearing, and came down the river together?'

'Yes, we were friends, in a manner of speakin'.'

'Were you friends or not? Answer me, and don't fence. Have you not stayed at his house often, for more than a week at a time?'

'Yes, now and then—workers often help one another a bit. I'd 'a done the same by him if he'd 'a come along the road lookin' for work.'

'Given him house-room, and three meals a day for a week or more, I daresay. But, let me see—*have you a house?*'

'Well, not exactly. I live in Melbourne.'

'Where?'

'At a boarding-house.'

'You left his house, then, for the shearing, the last time you were there. You had board and lodging for the previous night, and came down the river to North Yalla-doora together; is that so?'

'Yes.'

'Did you say you were a delegate before the shearing began?'

'No.'

'Why not?'

'For no reason in partic'lar.'

'Did you and he have a dispute on the road, and part company before you came to North Yalla-doora?'

'Well, we had a bit of a barney, nothing much.'

'Oh! nothing much? You were at Tandara while the shearing was going on; and did he and others refuse to come out on strike when you produced a telegram from the Head Centre, or whatever you call him, at Wagga?'

'He refused to obey the order of the properly app'inted hofficer of the Australian Shearers' Union; and was disrespectful to me, pusson'ly.'

'Did you then say that you would make it hot for him at the next shed?'

'I don't remember. But I was displeased at his disloyal haction.'

'Disloyal to whom? to the Queen?'

'No, to a greater power than the Queen—to the People, as is represented by the Australian Shearers' Union.'

'Very good; keep that for your next speech. You'll find out something about the powers of Her Majesty the Queen before long.'

'Do you not think, Mr. Biddulph,' said the Judge, with much politeness, 'that you have tested this part of the cross-examination sufficiently?'

'It was necessary to prove malice, your Honour; but I will proceed to the witness's acts and deeds, which are more important. Now, Mr. Delegate, answer these few questions straightforwardly.'

'I am on my oath, Mr. Lawyer.'

'I am aware of that; I don't attach much importance to the obligation, I am sorry to say. Did you not say to the President of the Shearers' Committee, during the riot, which might have ended in murder, and did end in arson—"Send a couple of men with Bill Hardwick and put him in the front with a rifle"?'

'Nothing of the sort.'

'If it is sworn by a respectable witness that he heard you, will you still deny it?'

'Certainly I will.'

'Call Joseph Broad. (I merely call this witness to be identified, your Honour.) Did you see this man at the shearers' camp?' to Stoate.

'I saw him there, but that's all.'

'That will do, Broad; go out of Court for the present. Did you hear your President speak to him?'

'Not to my knowledge.'

'Did Lynch and another man stand on each side of Hardwick on the bank of the river, and threaten to shoot him if he didn't stop there and hold out his rifle?'

'I didn't hear them.'

'Now listen to me, and be very careful how you answer this question. Did *you* stand close behind him with a revolver and say, "Don't you move for your life"?'

'Not that I remember. We was all crushed up that close together, as the crew of the steamer fired into us, that a man couldn't tell who was next or anigh him.'

'Very probably. That will do. Stay,' as Mr. Stoate turned away, and left the witness-box with a relieved expression. 'Go into the box for a moment. How did you come here — walk or ride?'

'Rode.'

'Rode your own horse?'

'No, a police horse; I came up with Sergeant Kennedy.'

'Oh, then, he lent you a horse — very kind of him — and accompanied you here. How was that?'

'Well, I believe there was some sort of a case trumped-up against me.'

'Oh! some kind of a trumped-up case, was there? We'll hear more about that, by and by. That will do for the present, Mr. Delegate.'

The witness then left the Court, followed by the strange trooper, so closely indeed, that but for the absence of handcuffs he might have been thought to have been in custody.

'Call Sergeant Kennedy.'

John Kennedy, being duly sworn, deposed as follows: 'I am a senior Sergeant of Police, stationed at Dilga, on Cowall Creek, which runs into the Darling. I saw the last witness at Tandara Run on December the 20th instant. He was given into my custody by Mr. Macdonald, the manager, charged with wilfully and maliciously setting fire to the run. I searched him in his presence and found on him two half-crowns, a knife, a meerschaum pipe, a plug of tobacco, two sovereigns, a copy of Union Shearers' rules, a letter, and a cheque. The cheque was drawn by John Macdonald in favour of William Hardwick, dated 10th October. The amount was £55: 17s.'

When this announcement was made an audible murmur arose from the body of the Court, even a few hisses were heard, which were promptly suppressed. Bill opened his eyes in wonder and amazement, and then turned to where Jenny sat crying peacefully to herself, but not from grief. Their money had been recovered, their traitorous enemy disgraced and confounded. She, in her mind's eye, saw her home once more glorified with Bill's presence—a free, unstained man. God was merciful, and she despaired no longer of His goodness.

'You didn't observe anything in the rules of the A.S.U. as to pocketing the cash of all shearers unfriendly to the Union? No? Then you may go down.'

'I have no questions to ask this witness,' said the Crown Prosecutor, with emphasis—'at present, that is to say.'

So Mr. J. Stoate, who had departed with the trooper, was for greater safety and security lodged in the modern substitute for the dungeon of the Middle Ages, until the Judge, after the finding of the jury, should have pronounced sentence or otherwise on the *other* prisoners.

CHAPTER VIII

'Call Cyrus Cable!' for the defence. As the long-legged, bronzed Sydney-sider lounged up to the witness-box, Bill's face, which had assumed a more hopeful expression, became distinctly irradiated. For this man was one of the shearers who had travelled down with him from Tandara, and had agreed to drop all connection with the Union and its revolutionary tactics. They had both been imprisoned at Poliah; had suffered wrong and indignity at the hands of the insurgents. How had he come up from the Darling, just in the nick of time? Bill didn't know, but if he had seen Dick Donahue outside of the Court he might have guessed.

'My name's Cyrus Cable, native of Bathurst. I'm a shearer in the season; have a selection at Chidowla, this side of Tumberumba. I know some of the men in the dock; saw them at Poliah when the row was on and the steamer was burnt.'

'Will you point out any of the prisoners that you can identify?'

'Well, there's Bill Hardwick, an old mate of mine—and fellow-prisoner, if it comes to that. It's dashed hard lines on him to be scruffed and gaoled by those Union scallowags, first for not joinin' 'em, and then locked up and tried because they ill-treated him and he couldn't get away. I call that a queer sort of law.'

The witness is requested to confine himself to answering such questions as are put to him, and not to give his opinion as to the law of the land.

'Do you identify any other prisoners?'

'Yes. I saw that beauty with the hobbles on, fire his gun at the crew on the boat twice; I saw him reload. He was one of the men as hustled Bill, and the rest of our mob that came from Tandara, into the tent and set a guard on us. I took notice of him then, and can swear to him positive.'

'Was the prisoner Hardwick with the rioters?'

'Yes, like me, because he couldn't help himself. I heard the President, as he calls himself—there he is, the t'other end of the "bot" (I mean the dock, but it's so like a branding pen)—say to that Janus Stoate, him as passed the wire with our names when we left Tandara—"Put a good man on each side of Bill Hardwick, so's he can't stir, and they'll take him for a Unionist and keep pottin' at him. What fun it'll be!" and he laughed. "I'll be behind him," says Stoate, "so he won't have no chance of boltin'." That's the way it was worked to bring Bill, as straight a chap as ever sharpened shears, into this steamer-burnin' racket.'

'How was it that you and your mates left your comrade in the lurch?'

'Well, we cleared as soon as the police came. The Union men bolted in all directions and left the free labourers to mind themselves. We thought Bill was comin' after us, and never missed him till we were miles away.'

'Did you not return to rescue him?'

'No fear! We thought the police might run *us* in for "aidin' and abettin'." It was every man for himself, and the devil take the hindmost.'

The witness was reprimanded for levity, and directed not to refer to the devil unnecessarily. In cross-examination he stated that he took particular notice of the man in irons, as he had repeatedly struck him and his mates with the butt-end of his rifle. Like the other rebels, he was very brave against unarmed men, but cut it when the police showed they meant business.

'Have you not a revengeful feeling against the prisoner Abershaw, the one who is (very improperly, in my opinion) brought into the Court in leg-irons?'

'Well, I've the feelings of a man, and I don't cotton to a cowardly dog who kept rammin' the butt-end of his gun into the small of my back, when I couldn't defend myself. But I'm here to speak the truth, and to get justice for an innocent man.'

'I suppose you were told that you would be paid your expense for attending this trial?'

'I got a Crown subpœna. So did Martin.'

'Who served it to you?'

'A police constable at Toovale.'

'Was anybody with him?'

'Yes, Dick Donahue. He told me and my mate, Martin Hannigan, that Bill Hardwick was to be tried at Wagga for burnin' the *Dundonald* and shootin' at the crew. "That be hanged for a yarn!" says I. "Fancy Bill, with a farm and a wife and kids, settin' out to burn steamers and kill people! Holy Moses! Are you sure he didn't rob a church, while he was about it?" But he said it was no laughing matter, and he might get three years in gaol. So of course we come, and would have turned up if we'd had to do it on foot and pay our own expenses!'

'Of course, your Honour will note this witness's evident bias?' said the counsel for the prisoners.

'I shall take my notes in the ordinary manner,' said the Judge. 'It is not necessary for counsel to suggest points of practice to a Judge before he addresses the Court at the conclusion of the evidence.'

'Your Honour will perhaps pardon me; I thought it might have escaped your notice.'

'I trust, Mr. Carter, that *nothing* escapes my notice in an important criminal case. Let the next witness be called.'

'Martin Hannigan is your name?' said Mr. Biddulph. 'You were at Poliah Camp on the 28th of August, were you not? Do you know the prisoners before the Court?'

'Some of them. I know Bill Hardwick, and the man with the leg-irons, but not his name. Yes; I know the one with the black beard — they called him the President.'

'Who called him by that title?'

'The shearers, or rioters, or loafers, whoever they were. They were six of one and half-a-dozen of the other, if you ask me.'

'Never mind answering what you are not asked. What did you *see them do*?'

'Well — Mr. President and his mob, all armed, made Bill and me and eight or nine other chaps that came down from Tandara, prisoners of war, in a manner of speakin' — "robbery under arms" I call it, for they boned our swags, our horses, our grub, and our pack-saddles. I found the horses, when they were boltin' from the police, or we should 'a never seen 'em again; two of us had to ride bareback. I seen that gaol-bird there — he's "done time," I'll take my oath — and another man shovin' Bill Hardwick between them towards the river-bank — one of 'em was puttin' a gun into his hand — swore he'd shoot him if he didn't carry it. I saw one of 'em fire at the boat. I'd not swear he hit anybody. I heard the "President" say, "We'll burn the bally boat; that'll learn 'em to bring 'scabs' down the river." I saw the steamer blaze up after the crew and free labourers was out. Then the police came, and Martin, my mate, and I cleared for our lives. We caught our horses in a bend and rode down the river to Toovale, when we got a non-Union shed, and wired in. That's about all I know.'

By the Crown Prosecutor.

'Your name is Martin Hannigan. Are you an Irishman?'

'No, nor an Englishman either. I'm an Australian, and so was my father. What's that to do with the case?'

'I thought you were rather humorous in your evidence, that's all. The Irish are a witty race, you know.'

'So they say. I've never been there. Anythin' else you'd like to ask me?'

'Only a few questions. When were you served with a subpœna to attend this Court, and where?'

'At Toovale, on the Lower Darling. The policeman came to the shed where Cable and I were working and served us. Dick Donahue came with him, and told us that Bill Hardwick was being tried with the other men for burning the *Dundonald*.'

'Didn't you know before? That seems strange.'

'Well, we were workin' hard to make up for lost time, by this strike foolishness, and we were too dashed tired at night to go in for readin' papers, or anything but supper and a smoke.'

'I suppose Donahue told you all about Hardwick's being arrested, and you had a talk over the case—what evidence you could give, and so on.'

'He didn't say much about evidence. He knew we was there, and seen all there was to see; might have *felt* something too, if a bullet had come our way—they were flying pretty thick for a few minutes. I seen that President chap fire once, and load again.'

'And that was all that passed?'

'Yes, pretty well all; we weren't "coached," if that's what you mean.'

'You swear that you saw that man fire, and load again?'

'Yes.'

'Did you see the free labourers?'

'Yes, forty or fifty; some looked damp, as they had been chucked into the river. Some had only their shirts on. They were stood up in a line, and counted like a lot of store cattle. They cleared off like us, when the police came, and the Union fellows bolted. We passed little mobs of them makin' down the river.'

'You swear you didn't see Hardwick fire his gun?'

'It wasn't his gun, and he didn't shoot.'

The sensational part of the trial was over; other witnesses were examined for the defence. They agreed in 'swearing up' for the prisoners before the Court, always excepting for Bill Hardwick. 'The other four men had exhibited great mildness, and a desire for peace. They had not seen the captain of the *Dundonald* assaulted; they saw the steamer on fire—they didn't know how it had started burnin'—might have been from kerosene in the cargo—it often happened. There was some shooting, but the crew of the steamer fired first. They didn't see any of the prisoners firing at the boat, except William Hardwick. Would swear positive that he had a gun, and loaded, after he fired every time—yes, every time. Saw no men thrown overboard. Some of them swam ashore, but they did it of their own accord.'

These witnesses broke down under cross-examination.

The Crown Prosecutor made a brief but powerful address to the jury, pointing out discrepancies in evidence, and the manifest perjury committed by the last witnesses. He trusted the jury would not overlook their conduct, and appraise their evidence at its true value.

The counsel for the defence, a well-known barrister, made a long and impassioned appeal to the jury 'to excuse the more or less technically illegal acts, which, he admitted, could not be defended. It was, however, in the line of "rough justice," the origin of which was a long series of capitalistic tyranny and oppression. They had suffered long from inadequate payment for their skilled labour, for shearing was no ordinary muscle work which could be performed by the mere nomadic labourer of the day. It required an apprenticeship, sometimes lasting for years. It was difficult, and exhausting beyond all other bush labour, having to be performed at a high rate of speed and for long hours, unknown to the European workman. The food was of bad quality, the cooking rude. The huts in which they had to dwell, worse than stables, nearly always. They had besides to travel long distances, expensive in time lost and wayside accommodation. For all these reasons, they had come to the conclusion that the question of pay and allowances, with other matters, required reconstruction, and failing to obtain a conference with the Employers' Union—a combination of squatters, merchants, bankers, and plutocrats generally—they had used the only weapon the law allowed to the workers of Australia and had organised a *strike*.

'The labour leaders had in all cases counselled moderation and constitutional action for the redressing of their wrongs. But—and it was by none more regretted than by the labour organisers themselves—rude and undisciplined members of the Union had resorted to personal violence, and had injured the property of squatters and others, believed to be desirous of crushing Unionism. Some allowance might be made for these men. They saw their means of livelihood menaced by cargoes of free labourers, bought up like slaves by the capitalistic class. They saw their wages lowered, their industry interfered with—the bread taken out of their mouth, so to speak—by a wealthy combination, which had no sympathy for the workers of the land, who had by their labour built up this enormous wool industry, now employing armies of men and fleets of vessels.

'Were they, the creators of all this wealth, to be put off with a crust of bread and a sweating wage? No! They had been worked up to frenzy by a plutocratic invasion of their natural rights; and if they crossed the line of lawful resistance to oppression, was it to be wondered at? He trusted that his Honour, in the highly improbable event of a verdict of "guilty," would see his way to inflict a merely nominal term of imprisonment, which, he undertook to say, would act as an effective caution for the future.'

His Honour proceeded to sum up. 'In this case, the prisoners were charged with committing a certain act, distinctly a criminal offence, punishable by a term of imprisonment. He would not dilate upon the collateral results, but impress upon the jury that all they had to consider was the evidence which they had heard. Did the evidence point conclusively to the fact that the prisoners had committed the crime of arson—the burning of the steamer *Dundonald*—then and there, on the 28th of August last, on the waters of the Darling River? With the conflicting interests of the pastoral employers, and the rate of wages, or the propriety of strikes, or otherwise, they had nothing whatever to do. He would repeat, *nothing whatever to do.*

'Did they believe the evidence for the prosecution? He would take that evidence, *seriatim*, from his notes.

'First there was that of the officer of Volunteers, which was direct and circumstantial. He deposes to having seen the steamer *Dundonald* floating down the river, burning fiercely then, with apparently no one on board. He saw a large camp of armed men, who shouted out that they had burnt the steamer, and would roast the captain and crew, for bringing up blacklegs. This last expression, he was informed, meant non-Union labourers. He caused the arrest of several men with arms in their hands, pointed out to him as having fired at the crew of the vessel, or having set fire to her. Among them was the prisoner Hardwick, who had a gun in his hand.

'The next witness was the sergeant of Volunteers. He saw the burning vessel, the crowd of armed men, and also men firing in the direction of a barge containing the crew presumably. He arrested by the colonel's order the six prisoners now before the Court, as well as others. They had arms in their hands.

'Captain Dannaker of the *Dundonald* deposed to a very serious state of matters. He had as passengers forty-five free labourers. Before daylight, a band of armed, disguised men boarded the vessel—of which they took full possession. Their action was not far removed from that of pirates. They threatened with death the captain, the crew, the agent of the Employers' Union, several of whom were assaulted, and ill-used. They "looted" the steamer, to use an Indian term—smashing cabins and appropriating private property. These unlawful acts they completed by forcing the free labourers to land, compelling the crew to go into the barge, setting the steamer on fire and casting her away, after which she was observed to sink. He also saw men on the river-bank firing at the crew and passengers. He identifies Abershaw, the prisoner in irons, as the man who assaulted and threatened him. He did not notice prisoner Hardwick.

'Mr. Davidson, the agent of the Employers' Union, corroborates the foregoing evidence in all particulars. He himself was assaulted, as were the free labourers. He saw the rioters throw some of the free labourers overboard. He saw them unloosing the steamer and preparing it for burning. His clothes and money were taken out of his cabin. He identifies Abershaw, but not prisoner Hardwick. He identifies Dawker, the man with the large beard, as the "President," so called.

'The witness for the Crown, Janus Stoate, gave, in his (the Judge's) opinion, unsatisfactory evidence after the adjournment. He described himself as a shearer; also a delegate appointed by the Shearers' Union. Though present at the scene of outrage, he apparently saw no one conduct himself indiscreetly, with the exception of his friend and fellow-shearer, William Hardwick. He swears that he saw *him* load and fire a gun in the direction of the steamer. He did not see the two prisoners Abershaw and Dawker, identified by the other witnesses, say or do anything illegal. He heard the report of firearms, but could not say who used them, except in the case of Hardwick. In several respects his evidence differed from that given before the Bench of Magistrates at Dilga Court of Petty Sessions, when the prisoners were committed for trial. He admitted in cross-examination having had a quarrel with Hardwick at Tandara woolshed, and to having arrived here in custody.

'Sergeant Kennedy, of the New South Wales Police, deposes to the arrest of this witness at Tandara station, on a charge of maliciously setting fire to the grass on the run, and to finding in his pocket, when searched, a cheque drawn in favour of William Hardwick for £55: 17s., said prisoner having previously testified as to its being lost or stolen.

'He would tell the jury here that he had no confidence whatever in the evidence of the witness Stoate. He appeared to have prevaricated, and also to have been actuated by a revengeful feeling in the case of William Hardwick, though, strange to say, he was apparently without eyes or ears in the case of the other prisoners, all of whom had been positively identified as having been seen in the commission of unlawful acts. In conclusion, he would entreat the jury to examine carefully, to weigh well, the evidence in this very serious and important case, and with close adherence to the obligation of their oaths, to bring in their verdict accordingly. The Court now stands adjourned till two o'clock.'

The jury were absent more than an hour, and during that time Mr. Biddulph persuaded Jenny to have a cup of tea, and otherwise refresh herself and the children, who had outstayed their usual meal-time.

She, with difficulty, was induced to touch anything: dead to all ordinary feelings, as she described herself, until Bill's fate was decided. 'How can I think of anything else?' she exclaimed passionately to Dick Donahue, who, with unfailing optimism, tried to convince her that Bill must be let off, and next day would be with her and the children on the way to Chidowla.

'How can we tell?' said she. 'Wasn't there Jack Woodman, and the lawyers told him he must be let off on a point of law, instead of which he got three years, and he's in gaol now.'

'Ah! but that was for cattle-stealing,' replied Mr. Donahue; 'and Jack had been run in before, for duffing fats off Mount Banda — tried too, and got off by the skin of his teeth. This time he shook a selector's poddies, and the jury couldn't stand that. But Bill's innocent, as everybody knows. See what the Judge said about Stoate's evidence! I'll bet you a hat to a new bonnet that Bill's out a free man this afternoon, and that Stoate's in the dock for settin' fire to Tandara, with a six to one on chance of seem' the inside of Berrima Gaol, and those four other chaps to keep him company.'

Jenny couldn't help relaxing into a wintry smile at this reassuring prophecy. But her face assumed its wonted seriousness as she said, 'Well, Dick Donahue, you've been a staunch friend all through this trouble, and I'll never forget you and Biddy for it as long as I live, and Bill won't neither.'

'Don't be troubling yourself about that, Mrs. Hardwick,' said Donahue. 'You were a good friend to her and her children before all this racket — they would have wanted many a meal only for you. But I'm a changed man. I've some hope before me, thanks to Mr.

Calthorpe; and if Bill will go partners with me, we'll be Hardwick and Donahue, with a tidy cattle-station one day yet.'

'The Court's sitting,' called out some one, 'and the jury's agreed.' A rush was made by all interested persons and the spectators generally. Not a seat was vacant as the Court official demanded silence, and the Judge's Associate proceeded to read out the names of the jurors, who, headed by their foreman, stood in line on the floor of the Court.

'Are you agreed, Mr. Foreman, on your verdict?'

'We are.'

'How do you find?'

'We find William Stokes, Daniel Lynch, Hector O'Halloran, Samson Dawker, and Jeremiah Abershaw guilty of arson, and we find William Hardwick *not guilty*.'

The verdict of guilty was received in silence. A number of the spectators were Unionists, and though the more sensible members of the association had always been opposed to lawless proceedings, yet from a mistaken sense of comradeship they felt bound not to repudiate the acts of any of their confraternity. No doubt at the next ballot the voting would have been almost unanimous against injury to property, and such outrages as the law's slow but sure retribution has never yet failed to overtake.

But when the verdict of 'Not Guilty' was announced, there was a cheer which it tasked the stern mandate of the Deputy-Sheriff and the vigorous efforts of the police to suppress. Jenny did not hear much of it, as the fateful words had barely been pronounced when she fell as if dead. She was promptly carried out into the witnesses' room, and measures taken for her recovery. When she came to herself, Bill was bending over her, and the children, smiling amidst their tears, were holding fast to one of his hands.

Anxious as both husband and wife were to shake the Wagga dust from their feet and get away up the river to their half-deserted home, Bill's Court work was not yet concluded. He was constrained to appear again in the memorable cases of Regina *versus* Stoate, charged with arson, and the same Gracious Lady (who impersonates Nemesis on so many occasions over such a wide area of the earth's surface) *versus* Stoate, charged with 'larceny from the person.'

No sooner had the jury been dismissed, and, with the witnesses, were wending their way to the office of the Clerk of the Bench, expectant of expenses, than the Crown Prosecutor addressed his Honour, representing that only at luncheon had he received the depositions in a fresh case—he referred to that of Regina *versus* Stoate. He was aware that the cases just disposed of had been supposed to conclude the sitting, and that his Honour was expected at Narrabri the day after to-morrow; but under the peculiar circumstances, as several of the witnesses and two members of the legal profession who were concerned in the last case were to be briefed in this, he trusted that his Honour would overlook his personal discomfort, and consent to deal with this case at the present sitting of the Court.

His Honour feared that the jurors and witnesses in the heavy cases at Narrabri might suffer inconvenience by the postponement of his departure; but, as the adjourning of this case to the next Assize Court—nearly five months—would more seriously affect all concerned, and as he was opposed on principle to prisoners on committal being detained in gaol, or defendants delayed one week longer than was actually necessary, he would accede to counsel's very reasonable request.

'Let another jury be impanelled, Mr. Associate, and then adjourn the Court until ten o'clock to-morrow morning. I shall consider the evidence taken in the previous cases, and deliver the sentences at the opening of the Court. The prisoners may be removed.'

On the following morning the five prisoners were again placed in the dock, looking anxious, and more or less despondent, with the exception of Abershaw, the man in irons. He was a hardened offender, and reckless as to what might befall him in the shape of punishment. He had served terms of imprisonment in another colony. Like many criminals, he had unfortunately not taken warning by previous penalties, as it was less than a year since he had been released. He looked around with an affected contempt for his surroundings, and smiled at an occasional sympathiser in Court with unabashed defiance.

But, as the Judge commenced to address the prisoners before announcing the sentences, the look of tension on the other men's faces was painful to witness, and even *he* appeared to feel the seriousness of the situation.

'William Stokes, Daniel Lynch, Hector O'Halloran, Samson Dawker, Jeremiah Abershaw, you have been found guilty, on the clearest evidence, of a dangerous and concerted attack on society. If organisations of this kind were permitted—if lawless bodies of men, organising themselves with the discipline of a military force, were permitted to go about the country interfering with honest men—there could be no safety for any one in the community. I am gratified to find that the jury have arrived at the only conclusion rational men could arrive at in such a case, and with no more time spent in deliberation than was necessary to consider the case of each man separately. I do not suppose that, excepting the residents of the neighbourhood of Poliah and the Lower Darling region generally, people are fully aware of what has been going on there.

'I have had a tolerable knowledge of the country, but I had no idea, until I came to try this case, what a state of things existed in the locality mentioned in depositions—a state of things probably unparalleled in the history of New South Wales.

'I should not have thought it possible that six or seven hundred men could camp on a main stock route, by a navigable river, for the purpose of preventing honest men going to work, much less could capture, bind them as prisoners, and hold them as such.

'Let any one contemplate what may follow if this kind of thing is permitted. There would be an end of liberty and safety; but the law exists for the protection of all, whether high or low, in the community, and those who take part in proceedings of this kind must expect to have every man's heart hardened against them. If a man's liberty were interfered with, if his life were threatened by overwhelming numbers, he and every other honest man is entitled to protect himself by taking the lives of those who come upon him.

This, in law, is termed justifiable homicide; on the other hand, if lawless persons take life, they are guilty of murder.

'Having explained the law on intimidation, I will pass on to the circumstances more immediately surrounding the case. It is proved beyond doubt that the *Dundonald* steamer was deliberately and wilfully set on fire by the prisoners and others. If any person had perished in the flames by their act, or if, when shooting at the vessel, any of the crew or passengers had been killed, they would now be on their trial for murder.

'As it is, they have, most properly, been found guilty of arson by the jury, a crime punishable, under Victoria No. 89, section 6, with imprisonment with hard labour, and solitary confinement.

'I accordingly sentence Samson Dawker, who has been referred to as the "President," and Jeremiah Abershaw, to three years' imprisonment with hard labour, and periods of solitary confinement, both to be served in Berrima Gaol. The other prisoners do not appear to have been so actively employed in these unlawful, demoralising acts. They are therefore sentenced to two years' imprisonment only, with hard labour. I cannot conclude my remarks without stating that I fully agree with the verdict of acquittal by the jury in the case of William Hardwick, who might have been deprived of his liberty by a conspiracy of unprincipled persons, had not the jury rightly discriminated as to the manifest unreliability of the evidence against him. He therefore is enabled to leave the Court, I have pleasure in stating, without a stain upon his character.'

REGINA *v.* STOATE.

Charged with Arson.

'May it please your Honour,' said the Crown Prosecutor, 'the prisoner before the Court is charged with wilfully and maliciously setting fire to the grass of the Tandara Run. I purpose calling the arresting constable and the manager, Mr. Macdonald; also the aboriginal Daroolman, who is exceptionally intelligent. The case will not be a lengthy one. Call Senior Sergeant Kennedy.'

'My name is John Kennedy, Senior Sergeant of the New South Wales Police Force, stationed at Dilga, on the Darling. I called at Tandara station on duty. I there saw Mr. Macdonald, the manager. He remarked that there had been no rain for a month, and the grass was very dry. He requested me to accompany him a few miles on the up-river road. He mentioned that a man named Stoate had left shortly before, having been refused rations, threatening "to get square with him." He considered him a likely person to set fire to the Run, and was just going to track him up.

'I agreed, and put my black boy on the trail. After riding two or three miles, the boy pointed to the tracks leaving the road and making towards a sandhill. We rode fast, as we saw smoke rising. The aboriginal said "that one swaggie makum fire longa grass, me seeum lightem match." We saw a man kneeling down, and galloped towards him. Apparently he did not hear us coming; as he looked up he seemed surprised. The grass around him had just ignited and was burning fiercely. There was no wood near. Mr. Macdonald seized him by the arm, saying, "You scoundrel! You're a pretty sort of delegate! I thought you were up to some mischief." Prisoner seemed confused and unable to say anything. The black boy picked up a brass match-box, half full of wax matches; also a half-burned wax match. The match-box (which I produce) had J. S. scratched on one side. Prisoner declined to say anything, except that he was going to boil his billy. There was no wood, nor any trace of roadway in the vicinity. I arrested him on the charge of setting fire to the Tandara Run. He made no reply. On searching him I found the cheque referred to in my former depositions, it was drawn in favour of William Hardwick for £55: 17s., also a knife, two sovereigns, and some small articles. I conveyed him to the lock-up at Curbin, where he appeared before the Bench of Magistrates, and was committed to take his trial at the next ensuing Assize Court. We put out the fire with difficulty; if it had beat us it might have destroyed half the grass on the Run.'

John Macdonald, being sworn, states:

'I am the manager of Tandara station. I have known the prisoner, off and on, for some years, as a shearer and bush labourer. He came to me on December 20th and asked for rations. He was on foot. I said, "You had better ask the Shearers' Union to feed you, I have nothing for agitators; you tried to spoil our shearing, and now you come whining for rations." I threatened to kick him off the place.

'He went away muttering, "I'll get square with you yet." Being uneasy, I mounted my horse, and shortly afterwards the last witness and a black boy came up, and at my request accompanied me. The boy followed his track till it turned off the main road in the direction of a sandhill. As we rode nearer, a small column of smoke rose up. We found prisoner standing by the fire, which had just started. I saw the black boy pick up the box of matches (produced in Court) from under prisoner's feet. It was marked J. S., and was nearly full of wax matches. The black boy pointed to a half-burnt match, close to the tuft of grass from which the fire had started. I said, "You scoundrel! You're a pretty sort of delegate!" I saw the sergeant take the cheque (produced) for £55: 17s., payable to William Hardwick, out of his pocket. If we had been five minutes later, all the men in the country couldn't have put the fire out; it would have swept the Run.'

'What would have been the effect of that?' asked the Judge.

'We might have had to travel 100,000 sheep, which alone would have needed fifty shepherds, besides the expense of cooks and ration-carriers, with tents, provisions, and loss of sheep. Altogether it would have meant an expenditure of several thousand pounds at the very least—besides injury to the sheep.'

'Have you any questions to ask, prisoner?' said the Judge.

'None,' said Mr. Stoate. 'These witnesses are at the beck of the capitalistic class, and will swear anything.'

Richard Donahue and the black boy corroborated the previous evidence, the latter saying, 'Me seeum light when piccaninny match-box tumble down alonga that one fella tarouser.'

Being asked if he had anything to say in his defence, Mr. Stoate elected to be sworn, taking the oath with great solemnity, and making a long-winded, rambling defence, in which he abused the capitalists, the police, the bankers, and the selectors, who, he said, were all in a league with the 'plutercrats' to crush the Union workers, and grind down the faces of the poor. With regard to the cheque, he had picked it up, and intended to restore it to Hardwick. If that man swore that he never gave him or any other man authority to take care of his money, he swore what was false. It was a common custom among mates. If the jury convicted him on this trumped-up charge, which any one could see was manufactured, he would willingly suffer in the cause of his fellow-workers. But let the oppressor beware — a day of reckoning would come!

CHAPTER IX

The Court was not very full. The 'fellow-workers' to whom Stoate so often referred had made up their minds about him. Open warfare, rioting, plunder, even arson or bloodshed, in a moderate degree they would have condoned. But to be *caught in the act* of setting fire to a Run, and detected with a stolen cheque in your pocket—that cheque, too, belonging to a shearer—these were offences of mingled meanness and malignity which no Union Caucus could palliate. 'He's a disgrace to the Order; the Associated Workers disown him. The Judge'll straighten him, and it's hoped he'll give him a good "stretch" while he's about it.'

This was the prejudicial sentence. And having made up their minds that their over-cunning ex-delegate by dishonourable imprudence had played into the hands of the enemy, few of the Unionists took the trouble to attend, for the melancholy pleasure of hearing sentence passed on their late comrade and 'officer.'

So, the evidence being overwhelming, the jury found Mr. Stoate guilty, and the Judge, having drawn attention to the recklessness and revengeful feeling shown by the prisoner—not halting at the probable consequences of a crime against society, by which human life might have been endangered, if not sacrificed—sentenced him to five years' imprisonment with hard labour. He was immediately afterwards arraigned on the charge of 'stealing from the person,' and the sergeant's evidence, as well as that of Hardwick, was shortly taken. Being again found guilty, he was sentenced to two years' imprisonment—which, however, the Judge decreed to be concurrent, trusting that the longer term of incarceration might suffice for reformation. In conclusion, he again congratulated William Hardwick on the recovery of his money and his character, both of which he had so nearly lost through association with men who had banded themselves together to defy the law of the land, and to attempt illegal coercion of workmen who differed from their opinions.

Such associations often led to consequences not foreseen at the time. Many a man had cause to blame them for loss of liberty, if not life. He trusted that this lesson would be received in the way of warning, and that he and all honest working-men who had witnessed the proceedings in this Court would go home resolved to do their duty in their own station of life, not following blindly the lead of agitators, however glib of speech, who might prove as unprincipled and dangerous guides as the prisoner who had just received sentence.

No time was lost, it may be imagined, by Bill and Jenny in 'clearing,' as they expressed it, for Chidowla. The coach for Tumut held a very cheerful load when he and she, in company with Dick Donahue, who had covered himself with glory, and had a satisfactory outing as well, took their seats. Bill wished to cash his newly-found cheque, but Jenny—practical as usual—persuaded him to give it to her for transmission to Mr. Calthorpe.

'I brought down a pound or two that I'd got stowed away, and there'll be just enough to take us back without breaking the cheque. Mr. Calthorpe's stood by us, and we must do our level best to get square again, and show the bank as he knows the right people to back. I'll go bail we'll do it inside a year, if we don't have any more delegate and Union business, eh, Bill?'

'No fear!' replied Bill with emphasis. 'I'm another man now, though I won't get the feel of them handcuffs off me for a month o' Sundays. I'm goin' to be a free labour cove, to the last day of my life. And Janus Stoate's where he wanted to put me, d—n him! I hope he feels comfortable. But I'll never give the clever chaps as lives on us fools of shearers a chance to work such a sell again. Dick, old man, you stood to me like a trump. We must see if we can't go in for a partnership, when we're turned round a bit. What do you say, Jenny?'

'I say yes,' said Jenny, 'with all my heart. Biddy's milkin' those cows of ours now, or I don't know what I'd 'a done. I believe if we put both our selections into a dairy farm we could make money hand over fist. But we must have more cows; this cheque of Bill's—and Jenny slapped her pocket triumphantly—now we've got it, will buy near a dozen, and we'll soon make a show.'

Dick Donahue, for the first time in his life, found hardly anything to say. He gripped both their hands, but brought out little more than "Thank ye, thank you both! You've given me a new lease of life, and I'll—I'll keep my side up—now I've something ahead of me, or my name's not Dick Donahue. Thank God, it's a grand season, and that gives us a clear start, anyhow.'

When they arrived at Tumut—some time after dark, but all well and happy—they found Biddy awaiting them with the spring cart, which she had driven over. There were a few stumps on the road, but Bill's eyes were good, so that they got home safely and with a superior appetite for the supper which Biddy had set out for them. This they discussed with their friends, who had much to hear and tell; after which the Donahues drove away and left them to the enjoyment of their home, which looked like a palace to Bill, after his misfortunes and adventures.

They were both up, however, before sunrise next morning, and at the milking-yard, where they found everything just as it should be. In the dairy, moreover, there was a keg of butter three-parts full, which Biddy had made during their absence. Bill was thinking of going into Talmorah after breakfast, when a boy galloped up with a letter from Mr. Calthorpe, requesting him not to come in till Saturday (the day after next), as a few friends and fellow-townsmen wished to meet him at two o'clock at the Teamster's Arms to show their regret at his undeserved persecution, and to present him with an Address, expressive of the same.

'Bother it all,' said Bill, 'I wish they'd let a fellow alone. I suppose I shall have to make a speech.'

'Oh, you *must* go,' said Jenny. 'Mr. Calthorpe wants you, and we mustn't be ungrateful after all he's done for us. Besides, didn't you make one at Tandara, when the shed had cut out, after "long Jim Stanford" euchred the Head Centre at Wagga? My word, you were coming on then; next thing you'd 'a stood for Parliament, or been elected delegate, any way.'

'See here, Jenny,' replied Bill. 'I suppose I'll have to say something when they give me this Address, as they call it; but after that's over, if any one but you says a word about our "feller-workers" or "criminal capital," or any bally Union rot of that kind, I'll knock him over, as sure as my name is Bill Hardwick.'

Bill and Jenny went into Talmorah a little before twelve o'clock on Saturday morning, the former to meet his friends, and the latter to pay in the celebrated cheque to their account, and have a few words with the banker; also, to make quite sure that Bill didn't have more than a whisky or two on the auspicious occasion. When the meeting was assembled in the big room at the Teamster's Arms, they were astonished at the number of townspeople that turned up. Some, too, of the neighbouring squatters appeared, whom they only knew by name, and that Bill had never worked for. The clergyman, the priest, the opposition banker, the storekeepers, great and small, were there—in fact, everybody.

Saturday afternoon in country places is a recognised holiday, except for shop assistants; and as they have on other days of the week much leisure time on their hands, they do not object. It is a change, an excitement, and as such to be made the most of.

A long table had been laid on trestles in the 'hall' of the principal hotel, a room which had been used indifferently in the earlier days of Talmorah, when it was a struggling hamlet, for holding Divine service, police courts, and 'socials,' which included dancing, singing, recitations, and other expedients subversive of monotony.

Couples had been married there by the monthly arriving minister; prisoners sentenced to terms of imprisonment, even hanged, after depositions duly taken there and the verdict of a coroner's jury. Political meetings had been held, and on the election of a member for the district it had been used for a polling booth, so that it was well and favourably known to the inhabitants of the town and district, and no one had any difficulty in finding it. It was now more crowded than on any occasion recalled by the oldest inhabitant.

Mr. Thornhill, the principal landowner in the district, holding the position by reason of his wealth, power, and popularity, which is generally yielded to the squire in the old country, was unanimously elected chairman, and opened the proceedings.

'Ladies and gentlemen,' he commenced—'for I am pleased to see so many of the former present, as also my good friends and neighbours in the district, who have worked with me in peace and harmony for so many years—(murmur of applause)—we are met together this day to do an act of simple justice, as well as of neighbourly kindness, by welcoming back to his home and friends a man whom we have all known personally or by report as an honest, straightforward, industrious settler. A man of small means, but a son of the soil, and the head of a family. (Interjection—"No; Jenny's the boss.") (Laughter.) My friend who corrected me, doubtless with the best intentions, is aware, as I am, that a good wife is the very sheet-anchor of success in life—(cheers)—and that probably, if our friend Hardwick had taken her counsel rather than that of agitators and false friends, he would not have suffered the pecuniary loss, anxiety, and—er—inconvenience which we so deeply regret this day. (Great cheering.) However, that is past and gone; we have now a pleasurable aspect of the case to dwell upon. We congratulate our friend, Mr. William Hardwick, and his good and true wife, upon their return to their home and their neighbours, by whom they are so deservedly respected. (Immense cheering.) In this connection it should not be overlooked that the high character, the result of years of honest industry, neighbourly kindness, and upright dealing, was of signal advantage in the time of need. By it they had gained staunch friends, who stood by them in the day of adversity. Mr. Calthorpe, the manager of the Bank of Barataria, had done his best for them, and they knew what a power for good a gentleman in that position could be in a country place. (Loud cheering.) Their neighbour, Mr. Donahue, had mustered important witnesses for the defence in a manner which only a good bushman, as well as a good friend, could have accomplished, while Mrs. Donahue had personally managed the farm and the dairy in Mrs. Hardwick's absence. (Repeated bursts of cheering.) Other friends and neighbours, among whom he was proud to number himself, had helped in the matter of expense, which, as everybody knew who had anything to do with law and lawyers, was unavoidable. (Cheers and laughter.) Though here he must admit that his friend Mr. Biddulph's professional services were invaluable, and if ever he or any of his hearers got into a tight place—well, he would say no more. (Great cheering and laughter.) He would now read the Address. Mr. William Hardwick, please to stand forward.'

Here Bill advanced, looking far from confident. However, as he confronted the chairman, he held up his head and manfully faced the inevitable, while the following Address was read:—

'To Mr. William Hardwick of Chidowla Creek.

'DEAR SIR—We, the undersigned residents of Talmorah, desire to congratulate you and Mrs. Hardwick upon your return to your home and this neighbourhood, during your long residence in which you have been deservedly respected for industrious, straightforward conduct. We have sympathised with you sincerely, while regretting deeply the unmerited persecution by which you have suffered. We feel proud to think that residents of this district were chiefly instrumental in establishing your innocence, their evidence having caused his Honour, Judge Warrington, to discharge you "without a stain upon your character." We beg to tender you this address, signed by the principal inhabitants of this town and district, and to beg your acceptance of the purse of sovereigns which I now hand to you.'

Bill's self-possession failed him under this ordeal, and he nearly dropped the purse, which contained fifty sovereigns. Jenny had put her head down between her hands. This seemed to suggest to Bill that somebody was wanted to represent the family. So turning, so as to have a view of the assembled neighbours, as well as the Chairman, he managed to get out with:

'Mr. Chairman, ladies and gentlemen,—I'm no hand at a speech, as perhaps most of you know. I did make a try in the woolshed at Tandara just before the Shearers' War bust upon us. I don't deny as I might have come on a bit, with practice; might have been promoted as high as to be a Union Delegate—(laughter)—but bein' among the prisoners of war, when the naval battle of the Darling River took place, I was "blocked in my career," as the sayin' is. I found myself in gaol pretty soon after, when it was explained to me, for the first (and, I hope, the last) time, what steel bracelets were like. The next place where I had to talk was in the dock, when I made a speech with only two words in it. They was "Not Guilty." (Cheers.) I'm in for a longer one now, and then I'll shut up for good, and never want to hear another sham-shearer talk rot, or hear the gag about Unionism again, as long as I live. *I* don't join another one, no fear! (Cheers.) And now, I just want you to believe, all my old friends as have turned up to stand by us in this handsome way, and Mr. Thornhill, the Chairman (and if all squatters were like him there'd never have been a strike, or the thought of one), I hope you'll believe that Jenny and I feel your kindness to the very bottom of our hearts, and that we shall remember it to our dying day.' Here the cheering burst forth; stopped and began again, until one would have thought it never would have ended.

By this time, however, tables had been covered with an array of bottles of wine and beer, and certain viands in the shape of sandwiches, tongues, hams, rounds of beef, biscuits, and cakes of various hue and shape—all things necessary for a cold but generous collation. The corks being drawn, the sound wine and beer of the country was set flowing, when Bill's health and Jenny's were drunk with great heartiness and fervour.

The Chairman then proposed—'His friend Mr. Calthorpe, in fact, the friend of all present, as the gentleman who, by equipping Richard Donahue and sending him to find and notice witnesses for the defence, had done yeoman's service for the worthy pair they had met to honour that day.'

In the course of an effective speech in return for the toast of his health, which was enthusiastically honoured, Mr. Calthorpe stated that the directors of the bank which he had the honour to serve always supported their officers in any extra-commercial action—as he might call it—in favour of honourable constituents, such as William Hardwick and his wife. He might take this opportunity to inform them that a partnership was in train, and would probably be arranged under the style of 'Hardwick and Donahue,' as these worthy yeomen had decided to join their selections, indeed to take up additional, conditional leases and devote themselves to dairy-farming on a large scale. They hoped to secure a share of the profits of butter-making which were attracting so much attention in their district of Talmorah, for which the soil, climate, and pasture were so eminently adapted. He might inform them that he had applications in the names of each of the partners, for nine hundred and sixty acres of conditional leasehold. This, with the original selections, would form an area of two thousand five hundred and sixty acres. They would agree with him, a tidy grazing-farm on which to commence the dairying business! Furthermore, he would take this opportunity of stating that there was every prospect of a butter-factory being established in Talmorah within twelve months. He trusted that the new firm's enterprise would inaugurate, in that method, one of the most profitable labour-employing industries, by which our graziers, big and little, have ever benefited themselves and advanced the interests of the town and district at large.' (Tremendous cheering.)

When the applause had subsided, the prospective partners lost no time in getting off, Jenny being aware that all conversation after such proceedings was liable to conclude with the 'What'll you have?' query—one of the wiles of the 'insidious foe.' Bill confessed to two or three 'long-sleevers,' the day being warm and the lager beer cool; but Dick Donahue, who had 'sworn off' before the priest for two years, before he went down the Darling, had touched nothing stronger than tea. Upon reaching their homes, the whole four resumed their working clothes and busied themselves about the farms until sundown. 'We'll sleep better to-night, anyhow,' said Jenny as, after putting the children to bed, she sat by Bill while he had his after-supper smoke in the verandah. 'But we must be up at daylight; it will give us all we know to get the cows milked and breakfast over and clean things on, for church in the township. For we'll go *there*, Bill, as we've good right to do, after all that's come and gone—won't we?'

'Right you are, Jenny; seems as if we'd been took care of, somehow.'

So the old mare missed *her* Sunday holiday, and had to trot into Talmorah between the shafts of the light American waggon—the capital all-round vehicle, that in the bush answers so many different purposes; and the Donahues went to their chapel, where, no doubt, Father Flanagan congratulated them on their improved prospects, while admonishing Dick to be more regular in his 'duty' for the future.

From this time forward the fortunes of the firm of Hardwick and Donahue steadily improved and prospered. The wives and husbands were eminently suited for co-operative farm management.

Biddy could milk a third more cows in the morning than any other woman in the district, and had won more than one prize for butter at the Agricultural and Pastoral Show. Jenny was not far behind her in these industries, but in the curing of bacon and hams had rather the best of it, by the popular vote. Dick was the smarter man of the two, having, moreover, a gift of persuasive eloquence, which served the firm well in buying and selling stock; this department having been allotted to him. He was thus able to get the change and adventure which his soul loved, and as he stuck manfully to his pledge, he wasted no time, as formerly, in his attendance upon shows and auction sales.

He began to be looked up to as a solid, thriving grazier, and with hope before him, and increased comfort in his home and family, pressed forward with energy to the goal of success which he saw awaiting him. His children were well fed, well clothed, and well schooled, holding up their heads with the best of the other yeoman families.

Bill worked away with his old steadiness and perseverance, not envying the change and occasional recreation which Mr. R. Donahue came in for. 'He had had enough of that sort of thing to last him for the rest of his life. His home, with Jenny and the children [now an increasing flock], was good enough for him,' he was heard to say.

There was also a run of good seasons, which in Australia is summed up and may be exhaustively described in one word *Rain*, with a large R by all means. The grass was good; so were the crops; so were the prices of butter, cheese, and milk.

The factory at Talmorah was a substantial, well-equipped, scientific institution, the monthly cash payments from which caused the hearts of the storekeeper and the tradesmen of that rising township to sing for joy. The only persons who discussed the change from 'the good old times' with scant approval were the publicans, who observed that the farmers sent the monthly cheque for milk to their account at the Banks of Barataria or New Holland, and their orders by post to the tradespeople, instead of 'going into town like men and stopping at the hotel for a day,' whenever they sold a ton of potatoes or a load of wheat.

From such modest commencements many of the most prosperous families in New South Wales and Victoria have made their start in life. Such families not infrequently hold the title-deeds of thousands of acres of freehold land. Contented to live economically and to re-invest their annual profits, they acquire large landed estates. As magistrates and employers of labour their position year by year becomes one of greater provincial importance and legislative influence. In physique, energy, and intelligence their sons are an honour to their respective colonies, and a valued addition to the loyal subjects of the British Empire—that Empire, in whose cause they are, even as I write, sending the flower of their youthful manhood to a far-off battlefield, holding it their proudest privilege to fight shoulder to shoulder with the 'Soldiers of the Queen.'

MORGAN THE BUSHRANGER
AND OTHER STORIES

MORGAN THE BUSHRANGER

For several years the announcement 'I'm Morgan,' uttered in the drawling monotone which characterises one section of Australian-born natives, sufficed to ensure panic among ordinary travellers, and if it did not cause 'the stoutest heart to quail' in the words of the old romancers, was seldom heard without accelerated cardiac action. For the hearer then became aware, if he had not earlier realised the fact, that he was in the power of a merciless enemy of his kind—blood-stained, malignant, capricious withal, desperate too, with the knowledge that the avenger of blood was ever on his trail, that if taken alive the gallows was his doom, beyond doubt or argument. A convicted felon, who had served his sentence, he bore himself as one who had suffered wrongs and injustice from society, which he repaid with usury. Patient and wary as the Red Indian, he was ruthless in his hour of triumph as the 'wolf Apache' or the cannibal Navajo exulting with a foe, helpless at the stake.

An attempt has lately been made to rehabilitate the memory of this arch-criminal, so long the scourge and terror of the great pastoral districts lying between the Upper Murray and the Murrumbidgee rivers. We are not disposed to deny that there were individuals not wholly abandoned among the misguided outlaws who ravaged New South Wales in the 'sixties.' There was usually some rude generosity in their dealings with victims. They encountered in fair fight, and bore no ill-will to the police, who were paid to entrap and exterminate them. They were lenient to the poorer travellers, and exhibited a kind of Robin Hood gallantry on occasion. Among them were men who would have done honour to their native land under happier auspices. For, with few exceptions, they were sons of the soil. But Daniel Morgan differed from Gardiner, Hall, and Gilbert, from the Clarkes and the Peisleys, from O'Malley and Vane, from Bourke and Dunn. He differed as the wolf differs from the hound, the carrion vulture from the eagle. His cunning on all occasions equalled his malignity, his brutal cruelty, his lust for wanton bloodshed. Rarely was it, after one of his carefully-planned surprises, when he swooped down upon a defenceless station, that he abstained from injury to person or property.

He was skilful and persevering in discovering his 'enemies,' as he called them,—a not too difficult task,—for he had abettors and sympathisers, scoundrels who harboured and spied for him, as well as those who, fearing the vengeance of an unscrupulous ruffian, dared not refuse food or assistance. Those whom he suspected of giving information to the police or providing them with horses when on his trail he never forgave, often wreaking cruel vengeance on them when the opportunity came. He would reconnoitre from the hill or thicket for days beforehand. When the men of the household were absent or otherwise employed, he would suddenly appear upon the scene, to revel in the terror he created; certain to destroy valuable property, if indeed he did not imbrue his hands in blood before he quitted the spot.

It was, for the most part, his habit to 'work' as a solitary robber; he rarely had a companion, although in the encounter with Mr. Baylis, the Police Magistrate of Wagga Wagga, when that gentleman showed a noble example by bravely attacking him in his lair, it is supposed that his then companion was badly wounded. Mr. Baylis was shot through the body, but that man was never seen alive again. The popular impression was that Morgan killed him, so that he might not impede his flight or give information. The tale may not be true, but it shows the quality of his reputation.

It seems wonderful that Morgan should have been so long permitted to run the gauntlet of the police of two colonies. It may be doubted whether, in the present efficient state of the New South Wales force, any notorious outlaw would enjoy so protracted a 'reign,' as the provincial phrase goes. He had great odds in his favour. A consummate horseman like most of his class, a practical bushman and stock-rider, with a command of scouts who knew every inch of the country, and could thread at midnight every range and thicket between Marakat and the Billabong, Piney Range and Narandera, it was no ordinary task to capture the wild rider, who was met one day on the Upper Murray and the next morning among the pine forests of Walbundree. Horses, of course, cost him nothing. He had the pick of a score of studs, the surest information as to pace and endurance. In a horse-breeding district every animal showing more than ordinary speed or stoutness is known and watched by the 'duffing' fraternity, fellows who would cheerfully take to the road but for fear of Jack Ketch. It may be imagined how easily the hackney question is settled for a bushranger of name and fame, and what advantages he has over ordinary police troopers in eluding pursuit.

I was living on the Murrumbidgee during a portion of his career, in the years 1864 to 1869. He was seen several times within twenty miles of my station, and I have had more than one description from temporary captives, of his appearance and demeanour. There is not an instance on record of his having been taken by surprise, or viewed before he had been employed in reconnoitring his antagonist.

Some of his adventures were not wholly without an element of humour—although the victim well knew that the turn of a straw might change the intent, from robbery to murder. The late Mr. Alexander Burt, manager of Tubbo and Yarrabee, was riding on the plains, at a distance of ten or twelve miles from the head station, when a horseman emerged from a belt of pines. He wore a poncho, but differed in no respect from ordinary travellers. Without suspicion he rode towards the stranger. As he approached and, bushman-like, scrutinised horse and man, he observed the JP brand, and recognised the animal as one stolen from the station. A tall, powerful Scot, Mr. Burt ranged alongside of the individual in the poncho and reached over to collar him. At that moment a revolver appeared from under the poncho, and a drawling voice uttered the words 'Keep back!'

It was unsafe to try a rush, and the snake-like eye of the robber told clearly that the least motion would be the signal for pulling the trigger.

'What's yer name?' queried the stranger.

'My name is Burt.'

'Then Burt—you get off—that—horse.'

Being unarmed, he had no option but to dismount.

'Give—me—the—bridle. So—you—tried—to—take—my—horse—did—yer? I've—a—dashed—good—mind—to—shoot—yer. Now—yer—can—walk—home. I'd—advise—yer—to—make—a—straight—track.'

And with this parting injunction he rode slowly away, leading Mr. Burt's horse, while that gentleman, cursing his hard fate, had to tramp a dozen miles before relating the foregoing adventure.

At another time he surprised the Yarrabee Station, 'bailing' Mr. Waugh the overseer, Mr. Apps, and others of the employés of Mr. John Peter, but beyond placing the JP brand in the fire, and swearing he would put it on one of them, as a suitable memento, he did nothing dreadful.

At Mr. Cochran's of Widgiewa, as also at Mr. M'Laurin's of Yarra Yarra, preparations were openly made for his reception; yet, though he made various threats of vengeance, he never appeared at either place.

At Round Hill Station, near Germanton, he enacted one of his murderous pranks. Suddenly appearing in the shed at shearing time, he terrorised the assembled men, fired on, wounded and threatened the life of the manager. After calling for spirits and compelling all to drink with him, he turned to ride away, when, incensed by a careless remark, he wheeled his horse and fired his revolver at the crowd. A bullet took effect in the ankle of a young gentleman gaining shearing experience, breaking the bone, and producing intense agony. Appearing to regret the occurrence, Morgan suggested to another man to go for the doctor. Having started, Morgan followed at a gallop, and overtaking him, said with an oath, 'You're not going for the doctor—you're going for the police.' With that he shot the unfortunate young man through the body, who fell from his horse mortally wounded.

About the same time he was seen by Police Sergeant M'Ginnerty riding near the Wagga Wagga road. Having no suspicion, he galloped alongside, merely to see who he was. Without a moment's hesitation Morgan fired *through his poncho*. The bullet was but too sure—it may be noted that he rarely missed his aim—and the ill-fated officer fell to the ground in the death agony. He coolly propped up the dying man in a sitting posture, and there left him.

When it is considered that he killed two police officers, besides civilians, Chinamen, and others, and that he shot a police magistrate through the body (inflicting a wound nearly fatal, the consequences of which were suffered for years after), it will be admitted that he was one of the most formidable outlaws that ever roamed the Australian wilds.

He is said to have encountered a pastoral tenant, of large possession, whom he thus accosted—

'I—hear—you've—been—pounding—the—Piney—boys'—horses—haven't—you?'

The witness was understood to deny, or, at any rate, shade off the unpopular act.

'Piney Range,' near Walbundree, was understood to be at one time the robber's headquarters. Here he was harboured in secret, and more comfortably lodged than was guessed at by the public or the police. The 'boys' were a horse-and cattle-stealing band of rascals—now fortunately dispersed—who generally made themselves useful by misleading the police, as well as by giving him notice of hostile movements. Towards subsidising them the spoils of honest men were partially devoted.

But this did by no means satisfy the 'terrible cross-examiner.'

'You look here now! If yer don't drop it, the—very—next—time—I—come—over—I'll—shoot—yer.   For—the—matter—of—that—I—don't—know—whether—I—*won't—shoot—yer—now.*'

And as the dull eyes fastened with deadly gaze upon the captive's face—he looking meanwhile at the mouth of the levelled weapon, held in the blood-stained hand of one who at any time would rather kill a man than not—be sure Mr. Blank's feelings were far from enviable.

To one of his victims he is reported to have said—

'I—hear—you're—a—dashed—good—step-dancer. Now—let's—have—a—sample—and—do—yer—bloomin'—best—or—yer—won't—never—shake—a—leg—no—more.'

Fancy performing on the light fantastic before such a critic!

A cheerful squatter (who told me the tale) was riding through his paddocks one fine afternoon, in company with his family and a couple of young friends of the 'colonial experience' persuasion. They were driving—he riding a handsome blood filly. In advance of the buggy, he was quietly pacing through the woodland—probably thinking how well the filly was coming on in her walking, or that fat stock had touched their highest quotation—when he was aware of a man sitting motionless on his horse, under a tree.

The tree was slightly off his line, and as he approached it the strange horseman quietly rode towards him. He noted that he was haggard, and dark-complexioned, with an immense bushy beard. His long, black hair hung on his shoulders. His eyes, intensely black, were small and beady; his air sullen and forbidding. He rode closely up to the pastoralist without word or sign. Their knees had nearly touched when he drew a revolver and pointed it at his breast, so quickly that there was hardly time to realise the situation.

'Which—way—are—yer—goin'?'

'Only across the paddock,' was the answer.

'You—come—back—with—me—to—that—buggy.'

By making a slight detour, they came in front of the vehicle, the occupants of which were perfectly unsuspicious of the strange company into which the head of the house had fallen.

Then he suddenly accosted them, levelling the revolver, commanding them to stand, and directing the young gentleman who was driving to jump to the ground. He was famed for his activity, it is said, but the spring made on that occasion, at the bidding of Morgan, beat all former records. The other young gentleman, though of limited colonial experience, was not 'devoid of sense,' as he dropped two five-pound notes from his pocket into a tussock of grass, whence they were afterwards recovered.

After relieving all of their watches and loose cash, the bushranger asked the proprietor whether he had seen any police lately.

'Yes, two had passed.'

'And—you—fed—'em, I expect? I'm half—a—mind—to blow—the bloomin' wind through yer.'

'What am I to do?' queried the perplexed landholder. 'I should feed you if you came by. I can't deny them what I give to every one that passes.'

'D'ye—know—who—I—am?'

'I never met you before, but I can pretty well guess. I've never done you any harm that I know of.'

'It's—a—dashed—good—thing—yer—haven't.   What's—that—comin'—along the road?'

'The mail coach.'

'How—d'ye—know—that?'

'Well, it comes by every day about this time, and of course I know it.'

'Well—I'm—just—goin'—to—stick—it—up. Don't—yer—tell—no—one—yer—saw—me—to-day—or—it'll—be—a—blamed—sight—worse—for—yer.'

And with this precept and admonition the robber departed, to the infinite relief of all concerned. In a few minutes they heard the pistol shot with which he 'brought-to' the mail-coach.

'Blest if I seen a speck of him till he fired the revolver just over my head,' said the driver afterwards. 'I was that startled I wonder I didn't fall off the box.'

No harm was done on that occasion, save to Her Majesty's mails, and the correspondence of the lieges. My informant gathered up the strewed parcels and torn sheets into a large sack next morning, and forwarded them to the nearest post-office.

In Morgan's whole career there is not recorded one instance of even the spurious generosity which, if it did not redeem, relieved the darkness of other criminal careers. He had apparently not even the craving for companionship, which makes it a necessity with the ordinary brigand to have a 'mate' towards whom, at any rate, he is popularly supposed to exhibit that fidelity which he has forsworn towards his kind. Rarely is it known that Morgan pursued his depredations in concert with any one. He may have had confederates, harbourers he must have had, but not comrades.

He was never known to show mercy or kindness towards women. When they were present at any of his raids, he seems either to have refrained from noticing them or to have derided their fears. There is no record of his having suffered their entreaties to prevail, or to have ceased from violence and outrage at their bidding.

Subtle, savage, and solitary as those beasts of prey which have learned to prefer human flesh, and once having tasted to renounce all other, Morgan lurked amid the wilds, which he had made his home, ever ready for ruffianism or bloodshed—a fiend incarnate—permitted to carry terror and outrage into peaceful homes, until his appointed hour of doom. This was the manner of it.

MORGAN'S DEATH, TOLD BY THE MANAGER.

Peechelbah Station, on the Murray, was a big scattered place, a regular small town. There was the owner's house—a comfortable bungalow, with a verandah all round. He and his family had just come up from town. My cottage was half a mile away. I was the Manager, and could ride or drive from daylight to midnight, or indeed fight, on a pinch, with any man on that side of the country. I was to have gone up to the 'big house' to have spent the evening. But it came on to rain, so I did not go, which was just as well, as matters turned out.

I was writing in my dining-room about nine o'clock when a servant girl from the house came rushing in. 'What's the matter, Mary?' I said, as soon as I saw her face. 'Morgan's stuck up the place,' she half whispered, 'and he's in the house now. He won't let any one leave the room; swore he'd shoot them if they did. But I thought I'd creep out and let you know.'

'You're a good lass,' I said, 'and have done a good night's work, if you never did another. Now, you get back and don't let on you've been away from your cups and saucers. How does he shape?'

'Oh, pretty quiet. Says he won't harm nobody. They're all sitting on the sofa, and he's got his pistols on the table before him.' And back she went.

Here was a pretty kettle of fish! Many things had to be done, so I pulled myself together, and set about to study the proper place for the battle. It was no use trying to rush the house. There were a lot of hands at work on the place and in the men's huts. But in those days you couldn't be sure of half of them. I had a few confidential chaps about, and I intended to trust entirely to them and myself. I was a good man in those days, as I said before.

But here was Morgan in possession—one of the most desperate, bloodthirsty bushrangers that had ever 'turned out' in New South Wales or Victoria. Nothing was surer than, if we made an attempt to besiege the house, he would at once shoot Mr. M'Pherson, and his partner Mr. Telford, who happened to be there with him.

So I had to be politic or all would go wrong.

I first thought of the money. For a wonder I had four hundred pounds, in notes, in my desk. I had got them from the bank to buy land, which was to be sold that week. I didn't often do anything so foolish, you may believe, as to keep forty ten-pound notes in a desk.

The next thing, of course, was to 'plant' it. I made it into a parcel, and taking it over to the creek, hid it under the overhanging root of a tree, in a place that Mr. Morgan, unless he was a thought-reader, like the man we had staying here the other night, would not be likely to find.

This done, I sent my body-servant down to the men's hut, to tell them all to come up to my place—that I wanted to give them a glass of grog. Grog, of course, is never allowed to be kept on a station by any one but the proprietor or manager. But I used to give them a treat now and then, so they didn't think it unusual.

I mustered them in my big room and saw they were all there. Every man had his glass of whisky, as I had promised. Then I said: 'Men! There's a d—d fellow here to-night that you've often heard of— perhaps seen. His name's *Morgan*! He's stuck up the big house, with Mr. and Mrs. M'Pherson and the family. Now, listen to me. The police will be up directly. I intend to surround the house. But I don't want any of you fellows to run into danger, d'ye see? It's my order—mind that—that you all stop in here, till you have the word to come out. Antonio!' I said—he had been with me for ten years and was a determined fellow; a sailor from the Spanish main, half-Spanish, half-English, and afraid of nothing in the world—'Antonio, you stand near the door. My orders are that *no one* leaves this room to-night till I tell him. The first man that tries to do so, shoot him, and ask no questions.'

'By ——! I will,' says Antonio, showing his white teeth and a navy revolver.

The men looked queer at this; but they knew Antonio, and they knew me. They had had a glass of grog, besides, and I promised them another by and by. This pacified them; so they brought out some cards and set to at euchre and all-fours. They were safe. I had made up my mind what to do. I never intended Morgan to leave the place alive. I had sent off for the police, and among the men I could trust was a smart fellow named Quinlan, a dead shot and a steady, determined man. He had several times said what a shame it was that a fellow like Morgan should go about terrorising the whole country, and what fools and cowards people were to suffer it. He had his own gun and ammunition, and, when I told him, said he wanted nothing better than to have a slap at him.

We weren't so well off for firearms as we might have been, for I had hid a lot of loaded guns in an empty hut, ready to get hold of in case of sudden need. Confound it, if some of the boys hadn't taken them out the day before to go duck-shooting with. However, we rummaged up enough to arm the picked men, and kept watch.

It was a long, long night, but we were so excited and anxious that no one felt weary, much less inclined to sleep. Mr. Telford was in the house with Mr. M'Pherson, and he chaffed Morgan (they told me afterwards) about having his revolvers out in the presence of ladies. However, he couldn't get him to put them away. He was always most suspicious. Never gave a man a chance to close with him. He was well-behaved and civil enough in the house, and, I believe, only wished one of the young ladies to play him a tune or two on the piano. He drank spirits sparingly, and always used to call for an unopened bottle. He was afraid of being poisoned or drugged. Some of his *friends* wouldn't have minded much about that even, as there was a thousand pounds reward for his capture, alive or dead. I have good reason for thinking, however, that one or two of the 'knockabouts' would have given him 'the office,' if we hadn't got them all under hatches, as it were.

Daylight came at last. I've had many a night watching cattle in cold and wet, but none that I was so anxious to end as that. Of course I knew our man wouldn't stop till sunrise. He was too careful, and never took any risks that he could help.

And at last, by George! out he came, and walked down towards the yard where his horse was. I had pretty well considered the line he was likely to take, and was lying down, the men on each side of me, as it happened. But, cunning to the last, he made M'Pherson and Telford come out with him, one on each side, not above a yard away from him. As he passed by us we couldn't have fired without a good chance of shooting one of the other two. So we let him pass — pretty close too. However, when he'd passed Quinlan, the track turned at an angle, which brought him broadside on; it wasn't to say a very long shot, nor yet a very close one. It was a risk, too, for of course if he had been missed, the first thing he'd have done would have been to have shot M'Pherson and Telford before any one could have stopped him. But Quinlan had a fair show as he thought, and let drive, without bothering about too many things at once. That shot settled the business for good and all. His bullet struck Morgan between the shoulders and passed out near his chin. He fell, mortally wounded. In an instant he was rushed and his revolvers taken from him. He lay helpless; the spine had been touched, and he was writhing in his death agony, as better men had done before from his pistol.

The first thing he said was, 'You might have sent a fellow a challenge.' One of the men called out, 'When did you ever do it, you murdering dog?' He never spoke after that, and lived less than two hours.

The police didn't come up in time to do anything; no doubt they would have been ready to help in preventing his escape. But I was only too glad the thing had ended as it did. The news soon got abroad that this man—who had kept the border stations of two colonies in fear and trembling, so to speak, for years—was lying dead at Peechelbah. Before night there were best part of two hundred people on the place. I can't say exactly how much whisky they drank, but the station supply ran out before dark, and it was no foolish one either. 'All's well that ends well,' they say. We've had nobody since who's been such a 'terror' to settlers and travellers. But I don't want to go through such a time again as the night of Morgan's death.

HOW I BECAME A BUTCHER

I was wending my way to Melbourne with a draft of fat cattle in the spring of 1851, when the public-house talk took the unwonted flavour of gold. Gold had 'broken out,' as it was expressed, at a creek a few miles from Buninyong. Gold in lumps! Gold in bushels! All the world was there, except those who were on the road or packing up. A couple of hundred head of fat cattle were not, perhaps, the exact sort of impedimenta to go exploring with on a goldfield, but it was hard to stem the tidal wave, now rolling in unbroken line towards Ballarat. Men agreed that this was the strange new name of the strange new treasure-hold. I incontinently pined for Ballarat. I sold one-half of my drove by the way, purchased a few articles suitable for certain contingencies, and joined the procession; for it was a procession, a caravan, almost a crusade.

The weather had been wet. The roads were deep. Heavy showers, fierce gales, driving sleet made the spring days gloomy, and multiplied delays and disasters. None of these obstacles stayed the ardent pilgrims, whose faith in their golden goal was daily confirmed, stimulated ever by wild reports of luck. The variety of the wayfarers who thronged that highway, broad as the path to destruction, was striking. Sun-tanned bushmen, inured to toil, practised in emergencies, alternated with groups of townspeople, whose fresh complexions and awkward dealings with their new experience stamped them as recruits. Passengers, who had left shipboard but a week since, armed to the teeth, expectant of evil. Mercantile Jack, whose rolling gait and careless energy displayed his calling as clearly as if the name of his ship had been tattooed on his forehead. Other persons whose erect appearance and regular step hinted at pipe-clay. Carts with horses, ponies, mules, donkeys, even men and women, in their shafts. Bullock drays, heavily laden, in which the long teams at fullest stretch of strength were fairly cursed through the slough, to which the army column ahead and around had reduced the road. Bells! bells! bells! everywhere and of every note and inflexion, dog-trucks, wheel-barrows, horsemen, footmen, lent their aid to the extraordinary *mélange* of sights and sounds, mobilised *en route* for Ballarat.

Slowly, 'with painful patience,' as became experienced drovers, we skirted or traversed the pilgrim host. We drove far into the night, until we reached a sequestered camp. A few days of uneventful travelling brought us to the Buninyong Inn. This modest hostelry, amply sufficient for the ordinary traffic of the road, was now filled and overflowed by the roaring flood of wayfarers. The hostess, in daily receipt of profits which a month had not formerly accumulated, was civil but indifferent. 'I *might* get supper,' she dared say, 'but could not guarantee that meal. Her servants were worked off their legs. She wished indeed that there was another inn; she was tired to death of having to provide for such a mob.'

When I heard a licensed victualler giving vent to this unnatural wish, as I could not but regard it, I recognised the case as desperate, and capitulated. I managed to procure a meal in due time, and mingled with the crowd in hope of gaining the information of which I stood in need. My assistants were a white man and a black boy. The former was a small, wiry Englishman, formerly connected with a training stable. He called himself Ben Brace, after a famous steeplechaser which he had trained or strapped. Hard-bitten, hard-reared, mostly on straw and ashplant, as goes the nature of English stable-lads, to Ben early hours or late, foul weather or fair, fasting or feasting were much alike. Of course he drank, but he had enough of the results of the old stable discipline left to restrain himself until after the race was run. I had therefore no feeling of apprehension about his fidelity.

For the time was an exciting one, and had not been without its effects upon all hired labour, though things had not developed in that respect as fully as when a year's success had made gold as common as shells on the seashore. Then, indeed, by no rate of wages could you ensure the effective discharge of the indispensable duties of the road. When every passing traveller who spoke to your stock-riders, or requested a light for a pipe, had nuggets of gold in his pocket, 'or knowed a party as bottomed last week to the tune of £1200 a man,' it was small wonder that, valuable as their services were conceded to be, they should themselves deem them to be invaluable. Independent, insolent, and ridiculously sensitive as drovers became, it became an undertaking perilous and uncertain in the extreme to drive stock to market.

I have seen the only man (beside the proprietor) in charge of three hundred head of fat cattle confronting that sorely-tried squatter, with vinous gravity and sarcastic defiance, as thus—'You s'pose I'm a-goin' to stay out and watch these — — cattle while you're a-sittin' in the public-house eatin' your arrowroot? No. I ain't the cattle dorg. I'm a man! as good as ever you was, and you can go and drive your bloomin' cattle yerself.'

This fellow was in receipt of one pound per diem; his allegations were totally unfounded, as his master had done nearly all the work, and would have done the remainder had the instincts of a large drove of wild cattle permitted. I saw my friend's grey eyes glitter dangerously for a moment as he looked the provoking ruffian full in the face, and advanced a step; then the helplessness of his position smote him, and he made a degradingly civil answer.

I was fortunate in not being likely to be reduced to such destitution. Besides Ben, the black boy Charley Bamber was at exactly the right age to be useful. Of him I felt secure. He was a small imp whom I had once brought away from his tribe in a distant part of the country and essayed to educate and civilise. The education had progressed as far as tolerable reading and writing, a perfect mastery of that 'vulgar tongue' so extensively heard in the waste places of the earth, joined with a ready acquaintance with the Bible and the Church Catechism. He would have taken honours in any Sunday School in Britain. The civilisation, I am bound to admit, was imperfect and problematical.

But the son of the forest was quick of eye, a sure tracker, and the possessor of a kind of mariner's compass instinct which enabled him to find his way through any country, known or unknown, with ease and precision. He was a first-rate hand with all manner of cattle and horses, when freed from that unexorcised demon, his temper. It was simply fiendish. Bread and butter, shoes and stockings, the language of England and the language of kindness, had left that inheritance untouched. In his paroxysms he would throw himself upon the earth and saw away at his throat with his knife. This instrument being generally blunt, he never succeeded in severing the carotid artery. But he often looked with glaring eyes and distorted features, as if he would have liked in this manner to have settled the vexed question of his creation. Strange as it may appear, the incongruity of his knowledge with his tendencies was to him a matter of wrathful regret. Being reproached one day for bad conduct by the lady to whose untiring lessons he owed his knowledge, he exclaimed, 'I wish you'd never taught me at all. Once, I didn't know I was wicked; now I do, and I'm miserable.' The pony which he always rode, a clever, self-willed scamp like himself, once took him under the branches of a low-growing tree, scratching his face in the process. Lifting the tomahawk which he generally carried, he drove it into the withers of the poor animal. On reaching home he confessed frankly enough, as was his custom, and appeared grieved and penitent. He was sorry enough afterwards, for the fistula which supervened necessitated a tedious washing every morning with soap and water for twelve months. This attention fell to his lot with strict retributive justice, and before a cure was effected he had ample leisure to deplore his rashness. With all his faults he could be most useful when he liked. He was so clever that I could not help feeling a deep interest in him, and during the expedition which I describe he was unusually well-behaved.

Having put the cattle into a secure yard, and seen my retainers comfortably fed and housed, I betook myself to the coffee-room. This apartment was crowded with persons just about to visit, or on their return from visiting, the Wonder of the Age. The conversation was general and unreserved. I was amused at the usual conflict of opinion with regard to the duration, demerits, and destiny of the Australian goldfields.

The elderly and conservative colonists took a depressing view of this new-born irruption of bullion. 'It tended to the confusion of social ranks, to the termination of existing relations between shepherds and squatters, to democracy, demoralisation, and decay. Had other nations, the Spaniards notably, not found the possession of gold-mines in their American colonies a curse rather than a blessing? Would not the standard value of gold coin be reduced? Would not landed property be depreciated, agriculture perish, labour become a tradition, and this fair land be left a prey to ruffianly gold-seekers and unprincipled adventurers? The opposition, composed of the younger men, the 'party of progress,' with a few democrats *enragés*, scoffed at the words of wary commerce or timid capital. 'This was an Anglo-Saxon community. Capacity for self-government had ever been the proud heritage of the race. We had that sober reasoning power, energy, and innate reverence for law which enabled us to successfully administer republics, goldfields, and other complications fatal to weaker families of men. With such a people abundance of gold was not more undesirable than abundance of wheat. Glut of gold! Well, there were many ways of disposing of it. Civilisation developed the need for coin nearly as fast as it was supplied. A sovereign would be a sovereign most likely for our time. Land! The land of course would be sold, cut up into farms for industrious yeomen, and high time too.'

The destiny of our infant nation was not finally settled when I slipped out. I had mastered two facts, however, which were to me at that time more immediately interesting than the rise of nations and the fall of gold. These were the increasing yields at Ballarat, and that, as yet, the diggers were living wholly on mutton, of which they were excessively tired.

Long before daylight we were feeding our horses and taking a meal, so precautionary in its nature that (more especially in Charley's case) the question of dinner might safely be entrusted to the future. With just light enough to distinguish the white-stemmed gums which stood ghostly in the chill dawn, we left the sleeping herd of prospectors and politicians and prepared for a day of doubt and adventure.

Silent and cold, we stumbled and jogged along, something after the fashion of Lord Scamperdale going to meet the hounds in the next county, for an hour or two. Then the sun began to cheer the sodden landscape, the birds chirped, the cattle put their heads down, life's mercury rose.

We had reached the historic Yuille's Creek, upon the bank of which the great gold city now stands. Then it was like any other 'wash-up creek'—a mimic river in winter, a chain of muddy water-holes in summer. As I looked at the eager waters, yellow with the clay in solution, as if the great metal had lent the wave its own hue, I felt like Sinbad approaching the valley of diamonds, and almost expected to break my shins against lumps of gold and silver. I determined to advance and reconnoitre; so, leaving Ben and Charley to feed and cherish the cattle until my return, I put spurs to old Hope, and headed up the water at a more cheerful pace than we had known since daylight. I turned the spur of a ridge which came low upon the meadows of the streamlet. I heard a confused murmuring sound, the subdued 'voice of a vast congregation,' combined with a noise as of a multitude of steam mills. I rounded the cape, and, pulling up my horse, stared in wonder and excitement upon the strange scene which burst in suddenness upon me.

On a small meadow, and upon the slopes which rose gently from it, were massed nearly twenty thousand men. They were, with few exceptions, working more earnestly, more absorbingly, more silently than any body of labourers I had ever seen. They were delving, carrying heavy loads, filling and emptying buckets, washing the ore in thousands of cradles, which occupied every yard and foot of the creek, in which men stood waist-deep. Long streets and alleys of tents and shanties constituted a kind of township, where flaunting flags of all colours denoted stores and shops, and St. George's banner, hanging proudly unfurled, told that the majesty of the law, order, and the government was administered by Commissioners and supported by policemen.

I rode among the toilers, amid whom I soon found friends and acquaintances. On every side was evidence of the magical richness of the deposit. Nuggets were handed about with a careless confidence which denoted the easy circumstances of the owners. The famous 'Jeweller's Point' was just yielding its 'untold gold,' and one sanguine individual did not overstate the case when he assured me they were 'turning it up like potatoes.' I ascertained that, with the exception of an occasional quarter from an adjoining station, the grand army was ignorant of the taste of beef, that mutton was beginning to be accounted monotonous fare, and that he who reintroduced the diggers to steaks and sirloins would be hailed as a benefactor and paid like a governor-general.

Having ascertained that this society, in which no trade was unrepresented, contained several butchers, I presented myself to these distributors, my natural enemies. I found that the abnormal conditions among which we moved had by no means lessened our antagonism. We did battle as of old. They decried the quality of my cattle, and affected to ignore the popular necessity for beef. Thinking that I was compelled to accept their ruling, they declined to buy except at a low price. I retired full of wrath and resolve.

Had I come these many leagues to be a prey to shallow greed and cunning? Not so, by St. Hubert! Sooner than take so miserable a price for my weary days and watchful nights, I would turn butcher myself. Ha! happy thought! Why not? There was no moral declension in becoming a butcher, at least temporarily; all one's morale here was *bouleversé*. 'Tis done. 'I will turn the flank of these knaves. Henceforth I also am a butcher. Chops and steaks! No! steaks only! Families supplied. Ha! ha!'

I returned to the cattle, which I found much refreshed by the creek side. We drove them to the bank of the great Wendouree Lake, then a shallow, reedy marsh, made a brush yard, established ourselves in the lee of a huge fallen gum, and passed cheerfully enough our first night at Ballarat.

Next morning I commenced the campaign of competition with decision. I gave Charley a lecture of considerable length upon his general deportment, and the particular duties which had now devolved upon him. He was to look after or 'tail' the cattle daily by the side of the lake; to abstain from opossum hunts and other snares of the evil one; to look out that wicked men, of whom this place was choke-full, did not steal the cattle; to rest his pony, Jackdaw, whenever he could safely; and always to bring his cattle home at sundown. If he did all these things, and was generally a good boy, I would give him a cow, from the profit of whose progeny he would very likely become a rich man, when we got back to Squattlesea Mere. He promised to abandon all his sins on the spot. As the cattle stood patiently expectant by the rails, I sent a bullet into the 'curl' of the forehead of a big rough bullock. The rest of the drove moved out with small excitement, and the first act was over.

We flayed and quartered our bullock 'upon the hide,' a 'gallows' being a luxury to which, like uncivilised nations, we had not attained.

I chose a location for a shop in a central position among the tented streets, being chiefly attracted thereto by a large stump, which was a—ahem—butcher's block ready made, divided our animal into more available portions, and with modest confidence awaited 'a share of the public patronage.'

At first trade was slack—the sun became powerful—the flies arrived in myriads—a slight reactionary despondency set in—when lo! a customer, a bronzed and bearded digger. I think I see his jolly face now. 'Hullo, mate! got some beef? Blowed if I didn't think all the cattle was dead! We're that tired of mutton—well, I ain't got much time to stand yarnin'. Give us a bit now, though. Thirty pound—that'll do. Here's a sov'ring. Good-bye.'

Myself.—'Tell the other fellows, will you?'

'All right. Won't want much tellin',' shouted my friend, far on his way.

My soul was comforted. It was the turn of the tide. Another and another came who lusted for the muscle-forming food. Towards evening the news was general that there was 'beef in Ballarat.' The tide flowed and rose until the last ounce of the brindled bullock had vanished, and I was left the owner of a bag of coin weighty and imposing as the purse of a Cadi.

'My word, sir, we'll have to kill two to-morrow,' quoth Ben, 'if this goes on; and however shall we manage to cut 'em up and sell too?'

'Well, we'll see,' said I confidently; 'something will turn up.'

As we returned to our depôt by Wendouree, we met by the wayside a middle-aged man sitting on a log in a despondent mood. He was the only man I had yet seen at Ballarat who was not full of hope and energy. I was curious enough to disturb his reverie.

'What's the matter?' said I. 'Have you lost your horse, or your wife, or has the bottom of your claim tumbled out, that you look so down on your luck?'

'Well, master, it ain't quite so bad as all that, but it isn't so easy to get on here without money or work, and I was just a-thinkin' about going back to Geelong.'

'I should have thought every one could have got work here, by the look of things.'

'Well, a many do, but I am not much with pick and shovel. I'm gettin' old now, and I can't a-bear cookin'. Now, I was as comfortable as could be in Geelong, a-workin' steady at my trade. I was just a-thinkin' what a fool I was to come away, surelye!'

'What is your trade?'

'Well, master, I'm a butcher!'

There *must* be good angels. One doubts sometimes. But how otherwise could this man, an unimaginative Englishman, lately arrived, not easy of adaptation to strange surroundings, have been conveyed to this precise spot, *planté là*, that I might stumble against him in my need? I could have clasped him in my arms.

But I said, with assumed indifference, 'Well, I want a man for a week or two to do slaughtering. You can have five shillings a day, and come home with us now, if you like.'

'Thank ye, master, that I'll do, and main thankful I be.'

When we reached the fallen tree, which, like a South Sea cocoa-palm, supplied nearly all our wants (being fuel, fireplace, house, furniture, and one side of our stock-yard), the cattle were in, the camp kettle was boiling, and Charley, standing proudly by the fire, received my congratulations. Our professional comforted himself internally. We regarded the past with satisfaction and the future with hope, and were soon restoring our taxed energies with unbroken slumber.

Next day we slew two kine, ably assisted by our new man, who, however, looked rather blank at the absence of so many trade accessories. Our bough-constructed 'shop' on the flat became a place of fashionable resort, and the conversion of cows into coin became easy and methodical. Having real work to do, I donned suitable garments, and as I stood forth in blue serge and jack-boots, wielding my blood-stained axe or gory knife, few of the busy diggers doubted my having been bred to the craft. One or two jokes sprang from this slight misapprehension.

'Ah! if you was at 'ome now, and 'ad yer big cleaver, yer'd knock it off smarter, wouldn't yer now?' This was a criticism upon my repeated attempts to sever an obstinate bone with a gapped American axe.

On the first day of my butcherhood I had bethought me of the cuisine of my old friend the Commissioner, which I essayed to improve by the gift of a sirloin. Placing the exotic in a gunny-bag, I rode up to the camp, and said to the blue-coated warder, 'Take this joint of beef to Mr. Sturt with my compliments.' I had no sooner completed the sentence than I saw an expression upon the face of the man-at-arms which reminded me of my condition in life. Gazing at me with supercilious surprise, he called languidly to a brother gendarme, 'Jones, take this here to the Commissioner with the *butcher's* compliments!' For one moment I looked 'cells and contempt of court' at the obtuse myrmidon who failed to recognize the disguised magistrate; but the humour of the incident presenting itself, I burst into a fit of laughter which further mystified him, and departed.

I was now settled in business. I diverted a large share of the trade previously monopolised by my rivals, who now bitterly regretted not having disposed of me by purchase. Every night I went up to the Government camp with my bag of coin, which I delivered over for safe keeping. As many friends were located there, with them I generally spent my evenings, which were of a joyous and sociable character. The conditions were favourable. Most of us were young; we were all making money tolerably fast, with the agreeable probability, for some time to come, of making it even faster.

The exodus from Melbourne was exhaustive. There, daily to be seen in red shirt and thick but very neat boots, stood the handsome doctor of 'our street' by the cradle, for which he had abandoned patients and practice. Next to him, with constant care lowering the ever-recurring shaft-bucket, was a rising barrister. Hotel servants, tradespeople, farmers, market-gardeners, civilians, cab-drivers, barbers, even the tragic and the comic muse, had enrolled themselves among the players at this theatre, where the popular drama of 'Golden Hazard' was having a run till further notice. The ranks of the 50th Regiment were thinned by desertions in spite of the utmost vigilance; while the ships in the bay were likely to be reduced to the condition of the world's fleet in Campbell's *Last Man*.

Pitiable the while was the position of the squatters, especially of those who held sheep. On a cattle station the proprietor or manager, with the assistance of a boy or two, can do much. It is not so with sheep. Particularly was it not so in those pre-fencing days. In vain the sheep-owner doubles his men's wages and removes apparent discontent. He tries to think that matters will go on pretty well till shearing. One night comes a traveller, a wretch with a bag of gold. Next morning a shepherd is missing, and so on.

We gave a little *festa* one evening in honour of a friend who had sold his share in the claim and wisely gone back to follow his profession in town. The conversation had a philosophical turn, and it was debated whether or no the country would come well out of the ordeal to which, particularly on account of its uneducated classes, it was being subjected. Some one expressed an opinion adverse to the result upon national morality and progress.

'I hold a directly opposite conviction,' said Jack Freshland. 'So do all the men who, like me, have seen order produced from chaos in California. "Scum of the universe" was a complimentary description of her population. "Hell upon earth" was a weak metaphor explanatory of her social state. Look at her now—self-regenerate, orderly, honestly progressive in every phase of industry. I don't say that you run no chance of being shot; accidents will happen when fellows' belts and coat pockets are full of loaded revolvers, whisky being cheap. But you run far less chance of being robbed than in London or Paris. When I came away you might leave your valuables scattered about your tent for days. No one dared to touch them. I don't know whether we shall come to ear-marking pilferers and hanging horse-stealers, but this is an Anglo-Saxon population, and in some way, I will stake my existence, order will be preserved.'

'Talking of horse-stealers, I found Fred Charbett's "Grey Surrey" the other day,' said Moore O'Donnell, 'in rather queer company.'

'That's the horse he won the Ladies' Bag at the Port Western Races with,' I cried out eagerly, 'a tremendous mile horse, but no stayer. Had he a large D brand?'

'He had then; and a large S—if that stands for sore back—that ye could see a mile off.'

'He is a flat-ribbed horse,' I explained, 'and any one with a bad saddle might give him a back in a day that a week couldn't cure. How glad old Fred will be to see him again! Who is the ruffian that has him now?'

'One Moore O'Donnell. Maybe ye wouldn't mind putting your interrogation in another form, Mr. Boldrewood, if it's agreeable to ye?'

'A thousand pardons, really—but I didn't understand that you had taken possession of him.'

We all laughed at this, and Jack Freshland said, 'Come, Moore, you old humbug, tell us how you stole the poor fellow's horse. It's all very well for Boldrewood to back you up with his alphabetical evidence. I don't believe half of it. You'll be up before the beak if you don't mind.'

'Give me the laste drop of that whisky,' said O'Donnell, stretching his long legs, 'and I'll tell you all how I compounded a felony, for there is the laste flavour of *that* about the transaction. I was mooning about looking for old "Paleface," when, after a great walk, I came upon the villain in company with a strange grey, also in hobbles. You know what a hot brute mine is: the stranger was about the same. Neither would dream of allowing me to catch him. So, after a long chase, I arrived at home, exhausted and demoralised, with just sufficient strength left to put them into the bullock yard. I refreshed myself from the whisky-jar, and after lunch and a smoke, feeling better, I strolled out to look at the grey. I thought we had been introduced. Of course, there he was, the great Surrey, no less. The last time we met, I had seen a sheet pulled off with pride by a neat groom, just before Fred took him down to the races. Here he was, dog-poor, rough-coated, and with a back fit to make one sick; D on the shoulder, 2B under the mane. Identification complete. "Such is life," thought I. "Just as one's in fine hard condition, with all the world before you, and lots of money and friends, you get stolen, or come to grief, grass-feeding, and an incurable sore back!"'

'Rather a mixed metaphor, if I may be allowed a friendly criticism,' said a dark-haired, quiet youngster named Weston, who had been reading for the bar 'before the gold,' as people distinguished the former and the latter days. 'I don't quite follow who lost the money, or did you or the horse suffer from the sore back?'

'Go to blazes with your special pleading,' shouted O'Donnell. 'Can't a man make the smallest moral reflection among ye, a lot of profligate divils, but he must be fixed to logical exactness, as if he was up for his "little go"? Ye've no poetry in ye, Weston, divil a bit. It's a fatal defect at the bar. Take my advice in time, or I wash my hands of your future prospects. And now hear me out, or I'll stop, and the secret will be buried with me.'

'Go on, Moore; you won't be the last of your line, will you?'

'How do you know, sir? None of your Saxon sneers. The O'Donnell! Ha! ye villain, I'm up to you this time. Next day, as big a ruffian as ever ye seen came up to the tent and asked me "what I meant by stealin' a poor man's 'oss." "See here now," says I, "the stealing's all the other way, it strikes me. He belongs to a friend of mine, who would never have sold him. He may have strayed and got into pound, and you may have bought him out, or you may—pardon me—have stolen him yourself."

'"I bought him off Jem Baggs, as got him out of Burnbank Pound," replied he doggedly.

'"That may be true. I think not, myself. This is what I am going to do. The horse is in my possession, and there he will remain. You can either take him, if you are man enough (and I pointed this remark with the butt of my revolver), or you can summon me before the Bench, or take this £5 note for your claim. Which will you do?" He held out his dirty paw for the fiver with a grin, as he said, "All right, you can 'ave 'im for the fiver. He ain't much in a cart, anyhow."'

'Hurrah!' sung out half-a-dozen voices together. 'How glad old Fred will be to see him again. What did you do with him? Hasn't Bill Sikes re-stolen him yet?'

'I sent him back by a stock-rider next day. He is safe at "The Gums" by this time. I'm dry, though. You wouldn't think it, now! Pass the whisky.'

'I say,' said Maxwell, 'there's a feller which is a poet in this company. Wasn't that a ballad, Aubrey, that you pulled out of your pocket just now, among all those tailors' bills, or licences, or whatever they were? Let's have it.'

This was addressed to a fair-haired youngster who was arguing with great interest and eagerness the relative fattening merits of shorthorns and Herefords.

'Well, it's something in the scribbling line. If you want it, you must read it though; I'll be hanged if I will. Writing it has been quite bother enough.'

'Well,' said Maxwell, 'it's not every fellow who can read, or spell either, for the matter of that. I'll read it myself, sir; perhaps you may find the effect heightened. Now listen, you fellows; a little sentiment won't do none of us any harm. What's it called? H—m!

A VISION OF GOLD

'I see a lone stream rolling down
Through valleys green, by ridges brown,
   Of hills that bear no name;
The dawn's full blush in crimson flakes
Is traced on palest blue, as breaks
   The morn in orient flame.

'I see—whence comes that eager gaze?
Why rein the steed in wild amaze?
   The water's hue is gold;
Golden its wavelets foam and glide
Through tenderest green—to ocean-tide
   The fairy streamlet rolled.

'Forward, Hope, forward! truest steed,
Of tireless hoof and desert speed,

    Up the weird water bound,
Till echoing far and sounding deep,
I hear old Ocean's hoarse voice sweep
    O'er this enchanted ground.

'The acal Wild fancy! Many a mile
Of changeful Nature's frown and smile,
    Ere stand we on the shore;
And yet that murmur, hoarse and deep,
None save the ocean surges keep—
    It is the cradles' roar!

'Onward! I pass the grassy hill
Around whose base the waters still
    Shimmer in golden foam,
Oh! wanderer of the voiceless wild,
Of this far southern land the child,
    How changed thy quiet home!

'For, close as bees in countless hive,
Like emmet-hosts that tireless strive,
    Swarmed, toiled, a vast strange crowd;
Haggard each face's features seem,
Bright, fever-bright, each eye's wild gleam;
    Nor cry, nor accent loud.

'But each man delved, or rocked, or bore
As if salvation with the ore
    Of the mine-monarch lay;
Gold strung each arm to giant might,
Gold flashed before the aching sight,
    Gold turned the night to day.

'Where Eblis reigns o'er boundless gloom,
And in his halls of endless doom
    Lost souls for ever roam,
They wander (says the Eastern tale),
Nor ever startles moan or wail

Despair's eternal home.

'Less silent scarce than that pale host,
They toiled as if each moment lost
   Were the red life-drop spilt;
While heavy, rough, and darkly bright,
In every shape rolled to the light
   Man's hope, and pride, and guilt.

'All ranks, all ages, every land
Had sent her conscripts forth to stand
   In the gold-seekers' rank;
The bushman, bronzed, with sinewy limb,
The pale-faced son of trade, e'en him
   Who knew the fetters' clank.

   *   *   *   *   *

"Tis night; her jewelled mantle fills
The busy valley, the dun hills,
   'Tis a battle-host's repose;
A thousand watch-fires redly gleam,
Where ceaseless fusillades would seem
   To warn approaching foes.

'The night is older. On the sward
Stretched, I behold the heavens broad
   When, a Shape rises dim;
Then clearer, fuller, I descry
By the swart brow, the star-bright eye,
   The gnome king's presence grim.

'He stands upon a time-worn block;
His dark form shrouds the snowy rock,
   As cypress marble tomb;
Nor fierce, yet wild and sad his mien,
His cloud-black tresses wave and stream,
   His deep tones break the gloom.

"'Son of a tribe accurst, of those
Whose greed has broken our repose
   Of the long ages dead;
Think not for naught our ancient race
Quit olden haunts, the sacred place
   Of tolls for ever fled.

"'List while I tell of days to come,
When men shall wish the hammers dumb
   That ring so ceaseless now—
That every arm were palsy-tied,
Nor ever wet on grey hillside
   Was the gold-seeker's brow.

"'I see the old world's human tide
Set southward on the Ocean wide,
   I see a wood of masts;
While crime and want, disease and death,
By rolling wave and storm-wind's breath
   Are on these fair shores cast.

"'I see the murderer's barrel gleam,
I hear the victim's hopeless scream
   Ring through these sylvan wastes:
While each base son of elder lands,
Each witless dastard, in vast bands,
   To the gold city hastes.

"'Disease shall claim her ready toll,
Flushed vice and brutal crime the dole
   Of life shall ne'er deny;
Disease and death shall walk your streets,
While staggering idiocy greets
   The horror-stricken eye!

"'All men shall roll in the gold mire,
The height, the depth, of man's desire,
   Till come the famine years;

Then all the land shall curse the day
When first they rifled the dull clay,
   With deep remorseful tears.

"'Fell want shall wake to fearful life
The fettered demons; civil strife
   Rears high a gory hand;
I see a blood-splashed barricade,
While dimly lights the twilight glade
   The soldier's flashing brand.

"'But thou, son of the forest free!
Thou art not, wert not foe to me,
   Frank tamer of the wild!
Thou hast not sought the sunless home
Where darkly delves the toiling gnome,
   The mid-earth's swarthy child.

"'Then be thou ever, as of yore,
A dweller in the woods and o'er
   Fresh plains thy herds shall roam;
Join not the vain and reckless crowd,
Who swell the city's pageant proud,
   But prize thy forest home."

'He said; and with an eldritch scream
The gnome king vanished, and my dream—
   Day's waking hour returned.
Yet still the wild tones echoed clear,
Half chimed with truth in reason's ear,
   And my heart inly burned!'

'Well done, Maxwell, old fellow; didn't think you could read so well! I haven't been asleep above two or three times. I enjoyed it awfully. Particular down on us. Your underground friend, though, prophesies war, famine, and mixed immigration! Cheerful cuss!'

'Mr. Aubrey, will ye oblige me by coming before the curtain. It's proud I am to know ye. I have seen worse, sir, let me tell ye, in the pages of the *Dublin University Magazine*, where the name of Moore O'Donnell is not entirely unknown. I would like to repate to ye a short ode of my own on— —'

'Rush oh! at Cockfighter's Flat,' burst in a new man—Markham—impetuously. 'That's all the talk now, my boys! They say the gold's thicker than the wash, shallow sinking, and lots of water. Jackson just told me; he's off there to-morrow to buy gold and go to Melbourne with it. I'm away, then. Any of you chaps join me?'

'I don't mind taking a look,' said Maxwell. 'I've half a mind to turn gold-buyer myself. It's a paying game.'

'It's an awfully risky one,' said Freshland. 'A man takes his life in his hand once he's known to carry gold. I know a fellow who started from here for Melbourne a fortnight since, and has never turned up.'

'Perhaps he's bolted,' suggested a cynic.

'Perhaps so,' answered Freshland carelessly; 'but if so, his wife, from her looks, they tell me, is not in the secret. I'm afraid it's the old story,' continued he, gazing mournfully into space. 'I know well how it's done. I can see it all as I sit here. A fellow goes stepping along the road through the Black Forest, whistling cheerfully and thinking of the ounces he has in his belt, or of what has gone down by the escort, of a piano for his wife, of the children who will have grown so, of the pleasant Christmas they will spend together, when, just where the creek crosses the road, One-eyed Dick and Derwent Bill step suddenly out.'

"'Morning, mates," says he, "fine weather after the rain."

"'Thundering fine," growls the one-eyed ruffian. "This yere's a fine day for *us*, anyhow. Done well at the Point, young chap?" As they talk they attempt grim jocularity, but their eyes, cold, sinister, watchful, betray their intent as they close upon him.

"'For the love of God, for my wife and children's sake, spare my life!" gasps the poor fellow; "you shall have every shilling I have in the world."

"'We ain't a-going to hurt ye. Just come off the road a bit, will yer?" says the crafty brute. Pah! I can't bear to think of it. Next summer some bullock-driver finds a skeleton lashed to a tree, in the thickest part of the scrub.'

'I say, Freshland,' I pleaded, 'don't. I've got a couple of miles to walk in the dark to-night. I think I'd rather hear that kind of story by daylight. But I must be off now. We tradesmen, you know! Good-bye.'

I walked back through scattered tents and darksome trees, moaning in the midnight, as the breeze swept through them. I was unable to banish Freshland's horrible tale from my mind, and was decidedly relieved when the yard of our encampment loomed into view. The cattle were lying down, Ben was smoking his pipe on guard, all was safe. Murderers and burglars were exercising their talents elsewhere. I was soon in a land where the mystery of permitted evil troubled me not.

My career at Ballarat was, however, drawing to a close. While we were transacting our *al fresco* breakfast, a 'real butcher' made his appearance with proposals for the purchase of my remaining cattle, and the collateral advantages of stock-in-trade, plant, and goodwill. 'Why had I not come to him in the first instance?' he asked with good-humoured surprise. Some accident had prevented me hearing of him. Mr. Garth laughed, and said he was in a small way compared to the others, with whom I had disagreed. I may say here, that it would be hard to pass through the populous, wealthy, energetic city of Ballarat now, without hearing much about Mr. Garth, owner of farms, mills, hotels, mining companies, what not.

I was pleased with his frank, liberal way of dealing, and augured favourably of his future career. He was the ideal purchaser, at any rate. He adopted, without a word of dissent, my prices, terms, and conditions.

With the conclusion of breakfast the whole affair was arranged. The cattle-edifices, tools of trade, and journeyman butcher were delivered as per agreement; Charley was sent for the horses, Ben was ordered to pack, the route was given, and in an hour we had turned our backs upon Ballarat.

I sent Ben and Charley back to the station, presenting the former with a coveted brown filly, and the latter with a white cow, as good-conduct badges. They reached home safely, after a journey of a couple of hundred miles, a 'big drink' indulged in by Master Ben on the road notwithstanding.

For myself, I went to Melbourne, having business in that deserted village. I had much difficulty in getting my hair cut, by the only surviving barber. The site of my shanty and block now trembles under the traffic of a busy street. The 'lost camp' at Wendouree Lake is valuable suburban property. Steamers run there. Why did I not buy it? If I had taken that, and one or two other trifling long shots, I might have been living in London like Maxwell, or in Paris like Freshland, if a stray Prussian bullet has not interfered with his matchless digestion. However, why regret these or any seeming errors of the past? They are but a few more added to the roll of opportunities, gone with our heedless youth, and with the hours of that 'distant Paradise,' lost for evermore.

MOONLIGHTING ON THE MACQUARIE

There are different kinds of work connected with the management of cattle-stations in the far bush of New South Wales. Some of them strike the stranger as being curious. At any rate, most people have not heard of them before, or if they have, don't know much. Something depends upon *finding* the cattle which you are required to manage. Didn't Mrs. Glass say, before yarning about hare soup, 'First catch your hare'? Right she was! If you'll come with me to the Wilgah brakes, 'Hell's Cages,' and 'Devil's Snuff-boxes' of the Lower Macquarie, you will see the pull of the 'first catch' arrangement. Don't suppose for a moment that ours is a neglected herd. If you were to see the stud animals—chiefly Devons and Herefords, for we found that the 'active reds' could pace out many a mile from the frontage in a dry season, and be back at their watering-place while a soft shorthorn would be thinking about it, and, of course, losing flesh. As I was saying, if you saw our 'Whitefaces' and 'Devon Dumplings,' you wouldn't think that. But those M'Warrigals, that we bought the place from long ago, were careless beggars; thought more of their neighbours' calves—some people say—than minding their own business and doing their proper station work. Now the back of the run is scrubby in parts, and the cattle there are 'outlaws' that increase and multiply. They get joined by other refugees and breakaways—brutes with no principle whatever. We seldom see them, as they have got a nasty habit of feeding at night, like tigers and lions and other wild animals. When we do see them—by day—they break away, scatter, and charge. All the horses and dogs in the country wouldn't get them.

What are we to do? There are some famous bullocks among them—rather coarse, perhaps, but rolling fat—ugly with fat, as the stock-riders say. And as cattle are a first-class price just now, and the feed grand all the way to market, there's no use talking; we must have a shy at them. It won't do for me, a native-born Australian, and manager of my father's best cattle-station, to be beaten by anything that ever wore a hide. Have 'em we must. The new paddock is just finished. We are going to muster the other side of the run—the quiet side—the day after to-morrow, and if we can make a good haul out of these 'scrub danglers' we shall have together as fine a lot of fat cattle as ever left the Macquarie.

And how are we going to do it? There are half-a-dozen as good hands on this Milgai Run, including the black boys Johnny Smoker and Gundai, as ever rode stock-horse or followed a beast. And yet, if we rode after this lot for a month we shouldn't get more than a couple of dozen, tear our clothes to rags, stake our horses, and get knocked off in the Wilgah scrubs—after all get next to no cattle—that's what I look at. Still, there is a way—and only one way—that we may fetch 'em by, and perhaps in one night. I'm going to tell you about it. We must *moonlight* 'em.

It is a strange thing—and I've no doubt it was found out by some rascally 'duffer,' some cattle-stealing brute that went poking about after his neighbours' calves (but the amount of cleverness *they* show when it's 'on the cross,' no man would believe, unless he knew it from experience)—it's a strange thing that wild cattle are twice, ten times, as easy to drive by night as they are by day. Whether they are afraid—like children—whether they can't see so well, or what it is, I don't know. But every old stock-rider will tell you that all cattle, particularly wild ones, are much easier to handle by night than by day. Another reason is, they go out a long way into the open plains to feed at night. Whereas by day they lie in their scrubs like rabbits near a hole, and directly they hear a whip, or a voice, or a stick crack almost, they're off like a lot of deer. Not that I ever saw any; but one thinks about the red deer listening and then popping into fern-brakes and heather-glens. Perhaps I shall see *them* some day, who knows, if cattle keep up?

Well, we had to wait for a day or two, till the moon rose, about ten o'clock. When the moon rises soon after dusk, they keep about the edge of the timber, and are ready to dash back directly they see or hear any one. But when it's dark for some hours before the moon rises, they'll go out far into the plains and feed as steadily as milkers.

Well, we sent word to our neighbours and mustered up about twenty men. We went into the timber at sundown, near a point where we thought they wouldn't come out, and hobbled our horses. We had brought something to eat with us, and made a billy of tea; and after we lit our pipes, it was jolly enough. My stock-rider, Joe

Barker, was one of the smartest riders and best hands with cattle on the river, but, as is sometimes the case with good men and good horses, he had a queer temper. I wanted him to bring his old favourite, Yass Paddy, as good and sure a stock-horse as ever heard a whip. But no, he must bring a new mount that he'd run out of the wild mob!—a good one to go and to look at, but the biggest tiger I ever saw saddled. Joe was put out about something, and I didn't like to cross him. A stock-rider is a bad servant to quarrel with, unless all your run is fenced, or very open. Besides, with his riding, a donkey would have been 'there or thereabouts.'

So we sat and talked, and smoked, and looked about for an hour or two. At last the time came. We pouched our pipes, saddled up, and headed for the plains, making a point for a few trees a good way out, near where the lot we were after often fed. We didn't talk much, but rode far from one another, so as to have a better chance of seeing them. At last Gundai rode up alongside me, and pointed ahead. I looked and saw something dark, which seemed to change line. There were no Indians, no wolves, no buffaloes, in our part of the world. It might have been horses, of course, but we were soon near enough to see tails—not horses'—and a big mob too. Cattle, by Jove! and the heaviest lot we have seen together since the general muster, many years since, just after we bought the station. 'All right, boys! we're in for a good thing.' They were, of course, scattered, feeding about, looking as quiet as store cattle. The regular thing to do was, of course, known to most of us. A couple of the smartest riders must start to 'wheel' them, one on each side. Charley Dickson and the black boy, Gundai, were told off. You couldn't lick Charley, and Gundai was the most reckless young devil to ride that ever broke down a stock-horse. But just at this pinch we want 'em to be pretty quick. Never mind about horses' legs, we look to them afterwards. Off they go like mad Arabs. You can see the dust and dry grass sent up by Gundai's horse's hoofs, like a small steam-engine. We hear the rolling gallop of the heavy bullocks, as the big mob of cattle all raise their heads and make off in a long trailing string—like a lot of buffaloes—directly they hear the first horse. We ride steadily up in line, so as to intercept them in the rush they will be sure to make back towards the scrub. In the meanwhile Charley and Gundai have raced to the two ends of the string, and are ringing and wheeling, and doubling them up together, till the mob is regularly bothered.

Then we go at them, still in well-kept line, and at whichever point a beast tries to 'break' he finds a horseman ready to 'block' him. There is no shouting, whip-cracking, or flash work generally. The great thing is to ride like ten men and be always ready to head or stop a breaking beast, which can be done at night by only showing yourself. No row or nonsense; it only makes the cattle worse. Always be in your own place, and do your work without crossing any one else's line; that's the only way with cattle. Of course we don't mind their running a little wide as long as they are heading out into the plains, and not back towards their scrub forts and hiding-places. So we let them trot a bit, keeping one man ahead to stop them if they get too fast, as they might get winded, and then charge and have to be left on the plains. We keep steadily behind them, while they are streaming out well towards the middle of the plain, and in a direction that by a little judicious 'edging' will land them at the Milgai stock-yard.

Of course there are well-known incorrigibles that have escaped many a muster, and will be sure to try it on now. 'There goes the grey-faced bullock. Look out! Look out!' shouts a stock-rider, as an enormous red bullock, with a speckled Hereford face, turns deliberately round, and, breaking through the line of horsemen, makes straight for 'Hell's Cage.'

I am riding Wallaroo, the best stock-horse on the river—at least that is my belief and opinion. I race at him, and we go neck and neck together for a hundred yards, at a pace that would win the Hack Stakes at a country meeting. Wallaroo's shoulder is jammed against the bullock, his head just behind the brute's great horns. At the batt Greyface is going, of course, he is occasionally on the balance. As I rush the game little horse against him, again and again, I can feel his huge bulk tremble and shake. I am too near for him to horn me, unless he had time to stop and turn, which, of course, I take care that he has not. After a while he edges round a bit, then a little more, then he sees the cattle and makes straight for them as they are moving past in the original direction in front of him. I slacken pace for an instant, and as I do so, drop the twelve foot stockwhip on to him with a right and left, which sends him right up among the tail cattle. He breaks no more for a while, and we are getting on pretty well. We know our direction now. Some of the cattle have got rather blown, and their tongues are out. We round them up, and let them stand for a bit to recover breath.

Off we go again. Can't stay here all night. They can run for miles in the scrub, and why not now? Much more steady this time. Begin to give it up. 'Hullo, what's that?' 'The brindled leader has doubled on us this time.' This was another regular outlaw. He was called 'Leader' because he was never far from the two or three foremost cattle wherever he was. Many a camp had he been on. Many a man had had a turn at him. But the inside of a yard he hadn't seen for years. He generally waited till the mob had gone some distance; when he did turn there was no stopping him. Joe Barker to-day must have a try at him. Away he went. His horse had not been behaving quite the fair thing, and Master Joe was in a great rage accordingly. Away he went, as I said, driving his spurs into the horse, and nearly jumping on to the brindled bullock's back, when he caught him up. He flogged for a bit without trying to turn him, and no man in these parts could use a whip with Joe Barker; he always had it in great order, oiled and lissom, with first-rate hide fall, and the exact thing in crackers. As the whip rose and fell, every cut marking itself in blood on the brindle's quarters, we all knew that he hadn't had such a scarifying for years, if he ever had. This was only to let him taste what the whip, in Joe's hands, was like. He knew, bless you, that it was no good to try and turn 'Leader' at first. After he'd smarted him enough, he went broadside on, and let him have it about the near side of his face. He could sit on his horse at a hard gallop and flay a beast alive. After a bit the brindle began to feel it hot. He turned and made a dangerous rush at Joe. It wasn't so easy to get away as you'd think, because the horse was partly sulky, and had it taken out of him a good deal. We had stopped the cattle, and were looking at the fun. He did get away, however, and flogged that bullock over the face and eyes until he was more than half blinded. Then he turned again and made for the scrub. At him, broadside on, went Joe, still flogging to the inch—forward, backward, every way, all on the near side, till the brindle could stand it no longer. He sidled and sidled away; lastly, he turned right round, and, as soon as he saw the cattle again, made for them like a milker's calf, Joe following up and warming him all the way in.

The fight wasn't over though, for Joe had been punishing his horse for being awkward, and the horse's sides and the bullock's back must have been all of one colour if we could have seen. I mentioned that Joe Barker had the devil's own temper; it carried him too far this time. The horse was a sour, peculiar animal, partly nervous, partly determined, as all the worst buck-jumpers, and what people call vicious horses, are. There are very few really vicious horses. Half of it is ignorance or stupidity on the part of the horse or his rider — generally the last, sometimes both. In this case I think there *was* vice. At the last few strides, as Mr. Leader, regularly blown and bullied, was dashing into the tail cattle, with the intention of working up to the front as usual, Joe gave his horse two or three tremendous drives with the spurs, standing up and letting him have them right. He then brought the double of the whip down over his head, swearing at him for the sulkiest brute he had ever crossed. It wasn't proper treatment for any horse, but he was beside himself with rage; and I made up my mind to speak to him in the morning about it after we had the cattle all safe. The horse took the law into his own hands, or feet, or fingers, or whatever they are. The geological fellows tell you once upon a time horses had three toes, and all but the middle one became unfashionable, and finally hooked it. I know country where a three-toed horse would come in very handy. But Joe's horse showed now he hadn't mistaken his character. He gave a snort as if he had just seen a man for the first time, propped dead, and in a couple of seconds was bucking away, as you may swear he did the very first time he was crossed. I thought it served Joe right, and nobody was uneasy, as he could sit anything with a horse's skin on. But this one kept bucking sideways, front ways, every way, rearing and kicking, and what I never saw any horse but a wild one do, biting and snapping like a dog at Joe's foot every time he turned his head round. Joe, of course, kicked him in the mouth when he got a chance, and the horse was just done when he caught his jaw accidentally in the stirrup-iron — his under jaw. Here he was fixed. He swung round and round with his head all on one side till he got giddy, and fell with a crash before any one could get to him. It was a hard bare place, as luck would have it. Joe was underneath him. We lifted him with his thigh smashed, and a couple of ribs broken. Here was a pretty thing—ten miles from home, and our best man with his leg in two. However, there was no help for it. We let go his horse, put the saddle under his head for a pillow (and, except that this one was rather hot, it isn't such a bad one), left a black boy with him till we could send a cart from the station, and started on.

After this none of the cattle gave any trouble till we were quite within sight of the yards. There was a large receiving paddock outside of these again, into which I intended to put the mob for the night, as I fancied we could get them into the drafting yards better by daylight. But anything of the nature of post and rails is very terrifying to the uneducated 'Mickies' and 'clear-skins.' They are always likely to bolt directly they see a fence. The bullocks might follow them, and if much confusion arose and there was a little timber there, we might lose the lot. So our troubles were not over yet.

But for the wild young bulls and the unbranded heifers born and bred in the thick covert of the 'Cage' and the 'Snuff-box,' both belonging to the infernal regions, I had a different kind of help. As the mob now moved slowly on, the old cows roaring, the calves chiming in, the bullocks occasionally giving a deep low bellow, making, like all cattle off their bounds, noise enough for four times the number, I knew that assistance was not far off. So it turned out, for about two miles from home we were met by two black dogs, walking slowly to meet us. A brace of very powerful and determined, not to say ferocious-looking animals they were. Half bulldog, half greyhound, they took about equally after both sides of the house. They were moderately fast and immoderately fierce, most difficult to keep back from bloodshed. They had required an immense amount of training, which in their case meant unmerciful licking, before they could be brought to obey orders. In their own line they couldn't be beat. They were too slow to follow horses all day, but, as they were fond of cattle work, they always came out a mile or two to meet us, when they heard the whips and the well-known sounds. Danger and Death, as I had christened the brothers, were known all up and down the Macquarie.

Now I felt quite safe for the first time since we had started, and as we closed up a little round the cattle, I looked anxiously for a 'break.' It was not long in coming. A three-year-old bull and a splendid red heifer charged back, and broke in regular fancy scrub style. Danger luckily took the heifer; she was clearing out like a flying doe. Danger was a good deal the quickest on his feet. Death was as sure as his namesake. He had his customer by the muzzle before he had gone any distance, and a loud roar, half of rage, half of pain, told us he was brought to bay. It was not a bad fight. The bull raised him from the ground more than once, and dashed him down with such force as would have satisfied any ordinary dog. But his mother's blood was strong in him, and, after an unavailing resistance, the dog having shifted his hold, and taken to the ear in preference, Micky was half dragged, half driven into the mob, among which, for security, he immediately rushed. Meanwhile the red heifer, rather 'on the leg' and not too fat, forced the pace, so that I really thought she was going to run away from old Danger. But he lay alongside of her shoulder doing his best, and every now and then making a spring at her head. At last he nailed her, and as he stopped and threw all his weight against her, with his terrible grip on her nostrils, her head went right under, and she fell over on her back with such force that she lay stunned. I thought she had broken her neck. When she got up she staggered, stared piteously all round, and finally trotted after the cattle like an old milker. We had only one more break, just as they were going through the paddock rails. Then we had a wing—fine thing a wing, saves men and horses, too—and the whole lot were in and the rails up before they knew where they were going.

Next day we put them in the strong yard, without much trouble, and after drafting the cows, calves, strangers, and rubbish, we had over a hundred of as good fat cattle as ever left our district. We picked out a few of the out-and-outers, including the grey-faced bullock and Leader, and 'blinded' them, after which they travelled splendidly, fed well, and gave us no trouble on the road down. Isn't it cruel? Not particularly. We don't put their eyes out. We run them into the 'bot.' The bot is a 'trevis' or pen, high, strong, and so near the size of a beast that they can't turn round after they've been inveigled into it. Then we can do what we like with them. They may roar and knock their horns about, or kick if they're horses—they can't hurt you. For 'blinding' we cut a broad flap of greenhide, and hang it over the face of any bullock that has bad manners. It is secured above and below. It works wonders. He can't see in front of him, only out of the corners of his eyes. Sometimes he runs against trees and things. This makes him take greater care of himself. He mostly follows the other cattle then, and in a week feeds like an old milker. We were nearly selling Greyface and Leader for a pair of working bullocks before we got down.

Poor Joe was a long time before he got round. He was never the same man again. We dropped in for a first-rate market in town, and so were handsomely paid for a night's 'moonlighting on the Macquarie.'

AN AUSTRALIAN ROUGHRIDING CONTEST

In June 1891, at Wodonga, on the Murray River, in the colony of Victoria—on the opposite bank to Albury, a town of New South Wales—was arranged an exhibition for testing the horsemanship of all comers, which I venture to assert had but few parallels.

Prizes were to be allotted, by the award of three judges of acknowledged experience, amounting in all to about £20. Much interested in matters equine, 'nihil equitatum alienum me puto,' I traversed the three miles which separate the border towns in a cab of the period, and arrived in time for the excitement.

The manner of the entertainment was after this wise. An area of several acres of level greensward was enclosed within a fence, perhaps eight or ten feet high, formed of sawn battens, on which was stretched the coarse sacking known to drapers as 'osnaberg.' This answered the double purpose of keeping the non-paying public out and the performing horses in.

I had heard of the way in which the selected horses were saddled and mounted; I was therefore partly prepared. But, tolerably versed in the lore of the wilderness, I had never before seen such primitive equitation.

About thirty unbroken horses were moving uneasily within a high, well-constructed stock-yard—the regulation 'four rails' and a 'cap'— amounting to a solid unyielding fence, over seven feet in height.

That the steeds were really unbroken, 'by spur and snaffle undefiled,' might be gathered from their long manes, tails sweeping the ground, and general air of terror or defiance. As each animal was wanted, it was driven or cajoled by means of a quiet horse into a close yard ending in a 'crush' or lane so narrow that turning round was impossible. A strong, high gate in front was well fastened. Before the captive could decide upon a retrograde movement, long, strong saplings were thrust between his quarters and the posts of the crush. He was therefore trapped, unable to advance or retire. If he threatened to lie down, a sapling underneath prevented that refuge of sullenness.

Mostly the imprisoned animal preserved an expression of stupid amazement or harmless terror, occasionally of fierce wrath or reckless despair. Then he kicked, plunged, reared—in every way known to the wild steed of the desert expressed his untameable defiance of man, occasionally even neighing loudly and fiercely. 'Twas all in vain. The prison was too high, too strong, too narrow, too everything; nothing but submission remained—'not even suicide,' as Mr. Stevenson declares concerning matrimony, 'nothing but to be good.'

This, of course, with variations, as happens perchance in the married state irreverently referred to.

Before the colt has done thinking what unprincipled wretches these bush bipeds are, a 'blind' (ingeniously improvised from a gentleman's waistcoat) is placed over his eyes, a snaffle bridle is put on, a bit is forced into his mouth; at the same time two active young men are thrusting a crupper under his reluctant tail, have put a saddle on his back, and are buckling leather girths and surcingle (this latter run through slits in the lower portion of the saddle flaps) as if they meant to cut him in two.

This preparatory process being completed in marvellous short time, the manager calls out 'First horse, Mr. St. Aure,' and a well-proportioned young man from the Upper Murray ascends the fence, standing with either leg on the rails, immediately over the angry, terrified animal.

What would you or I take, O grey-besprinkled reader, to undertake the mount Mr. St. Aure surveys with calmest confidence? (We are not so young as we were, let us say in confidence.)

Deftly he drops into the saddle, his legs just grazing the sides of the crush. 'Open the gate!' roars the manager. 'Look out, you boys!' and, with a mad rush, out flies the colt through the open gate like a shell from a howitzer.

For ten yards he races at full speed, then 'propping' as if galvanised, shoots upwards with the true deer's leap, all four feet in the air at once (from which the vice takes its name), to come down with his head between his forelegs and his nose (this I narrowly watched) touching the girths.

The horseman has swayed back with instinctive ease, and is quite prepared for a succession of lightning bounds, sideways, upwards, downwards, backwards, as he appears to turn in the air occasionally and to come down with his head in the place where his tail was when he rose.

For an instant he stops: perhaps the long-necked spurs are sent in, to accentuate the next performance. The crowd meanwhile of 600 or 700 people, mostly young or in the prime of life, follow, cheering and clapping with every fresh attempt on the part of the frenzied steed to dispose of his matchless rider. Five minutes of this exercise commences to exhaust and steady the wildest colt. It is a variation of 'monkeying,' a device of the bush-breaker, who ties a bag on to the saddle of a timid colt, and he, frightened out of his life, as *by a monkey* perched there, tires himself out, permitting the breaker to mount and ride away with but little resistance.

Sometimes indeed the colt turns in his tracks, and being unmanageable as to guiding in his paroxysms, charges the crowd, whom he scatters with great screaming and laughing as they fall over each other or climb the stock-yard fence. But shortly, with lowered head and trembling frame, he allows himself to be ridden to the gate of egress. There he is halted, and the rider, taking hold of his left ear with his bridle-hand, swings lightly to the ground, closely alongside of the shoulder. Did he not so alight, the agile mustang was capable of a lightning wheel and a dangerous kick. Indeed, one rider, dismounting carelessly, discovered this to his cost after riding a most unconscionable performer.

A middle-aged, wiry, old-time-looking stock-rider from Gippsland next came flying out on a frantic steed *without a bridle*, from choice. For some time it seemed a drawn battle between horse and man, but towards the end of the fight the horse managed to 'get from under.'

One horse slipped on the short greensward and came over backwards, his rider permitting himself to slide off. The next animal was described as an 'outlaw,' a bush term for a horse which has been backed but never successfully ridden. She, a powerful half-bred, fully sustained it by a persevering exhibition of every kind of contortion calculated to dissolve partnership. At one time it looked as if the betting was in favour of the man, but the mare had evidently resolved on a last appeal. Setting to with redoubled fury, she smashed the crupper, tore out one of the girth straps, and then performed the rare, well-nigh incredible feat of sending the saddle over her head *without breaking the surcingle*. This is the second time, during a longish acquaintance with every kind of horse accomplishment, that I have witnessed this performance. It is not always believed, but can be vouched for by the writer and about five or six hundred people on the ground. I *felt* the girth, and saw that the buckle was still unslacked.

The rider, Mortimer, came over the mare's head, sitting square with the saddle between his legs, and received an ovation in consequence.

The last colt had been driven into the crush 'fiercely snorting, but in vain, and struggling with erected mane,' and enlarged 'in the full foam of wrath and dread,' when another form of excitement was announced. A dangerous-looking four-year-old bullock was now yarded in the outer enclosure, light of flesh but exceeding fierce, which he proceeded to demonstrate by clearing the place of all spectators in the shortest time on record.

Climbing hurriedly to the 'cap' of the stock-yard fence, they looked on in secure elevation, while the *toreadors* cunningly edged him into the crush, and there confined him like the colts. Here he began to paw the ground and bellow in ungovernable rage. At this stage the manager thus delivered himself: 'It's Mr. Smith's turn, by the list, to ride this bullock, but he says he don't care. Is there any gentleman here as'll ride him?'

With Mr. Smith's natural disinclination for the mount the crowd apparently sympathised. The bullock meanwhile was pawing the earth and roaring in a hollow and blood-curdling manner, as who should say, 'Let me at him; only let me have one turn with hoof and horn.' To the unprejudiced observer the mount seemed one that no gentleman would court or even accept.

However, the Gippslander, removing his pipe from his mouth, calmly remarked, 'I'll ride him,' whereupon the crowd burst out with a cheer, evidently looking upon the offer as one of exceptional merit.

There was no bridle or saddle in this case. A rope was fastened around the animal's body, and with this slender accoutrement only, the stock-rider deposited himself upon the ridge of the red bullock's back. Then the gate was opened, and out he came in all his glory.

No one that has merely observed the clumsy gambols of the meadow-fed ox can have an idea of the speed and agility of the bush-bred steer, reared amid mountain ranges and accustomed to spurts up hill and down, with a smart stock-horse rattling by the side of the drove, always making excellent time, and not infrequently distancing their pursuers amid the forests and morasses of their native runs.

This one had a shoulder like a blood horse, great propelling power, and stood well off the ground, with muscular arms and hocks to match.

He reared, bucked, and plunged almost with the virulence and variety of the colts, and when, after a prolonged and persevering contest, he gradually managed to shift his rider on to his *croupe*, and thence by a complicated and original twist of his quarters dislodged him, it was felt by the spectators that he had worthily sustained the honour of the stock-riding fraternity. Cheers resounded from all sides, as the crowd returning to a centre surrounded the fallen but not disgraced combatant. I think the boys were privately disappointed that the bullock did not turn to gore his antagonist, but he was too much excited for such an attack. He made a bee-line for the fence, which, all-ignorant of its flimsy nature, he did not attempt to jump or overthrow, contenting himself with running by the side of it until he came to the corner, where a gate was cunningly left open for his departure. After a respectable 'cap' had been collected for the veteran, who was more than twice the age of the other competitors, the prizes were distributed, and the entertainment concluded.

As an Australian I may be slightly prejudiced, but I must confess to holding the opinion that our bush-riders in certain departments are unrivalled. The South American 'gaucho' and the 'cow-boy' of the Western States are, doubtless, wonderful horsemen, but they ride under conditions more favourable than those of our bushmen. The saddle of the Americans is the old-fashioned Spanish one—heavy, cumbrous, and, besides the high pommel and cantle, provided with a horn-like fixture in front, to which the lasso is attached generally, but which serves as a belaying-pin and a secure holdfast for the rider in case of need. The tremendous severity of the heavy curb-bit must also tend to moderate the gambades of all but the most vicious or untamed animals. Besides all this, the horses ridden by them are mere ponies compared to the big, powerful Australian colts, and as such easier to control.

But let the stranger, when minded to try his horsemanship, find himself upon a 'touchy' three-year-old, and how insecure does his position appear! He is a good way off the ground, which said ground is mostly extremely hard. The colt is nearly sixteen hands high, and feels strong enough in the loins, if fully agitated, to throw him into a gum-tree. The single-reined snaffle, to which he trusts his life, is of the plainest, cheapest description of leather and iron. The saddle is the ordinary English saddle, fuller in the flap and pads, but otherwise giving the impression of being hard, slippery, and affording but little hope of recovery when once the seat is shaken.

When, with nothing but this simple accoutrement, or perhaps a rolled bag, strapped in front of the pommel, our bushmen ride, as I have described, it must be conceded that no horsemen could be less indebted to adventitious aid.

In the peculiar, strictly Australian department, known as 'scrub riding,' no one not 'to the manner born' can be said to hold a candle to them.

The home of the half-wild herds of cattle and horses is frequently mountainous, thickly-wooded, and rocky. Amid these declivitous fastnesses in which they are reared, the outliers of the herd acquire speed, wind, and activity, which must be known to be believed. Through these interlaced and thick-growing woodlands, down the rocky ridge, across the treacherous morass, away go the cattle or the wild horses at a pace apt to take them out of sight and hearing in remarkably short time. The ordinary horseman, able to hold his own fairly well on road or turf, even in the hunting field, here finds himself hopelessly at fault. Not wanting in pluck, he does his best for a mile or more. But he knocks his knee against one tree, his shoulder against another, and narrowly escapes dashing his brains out by reason of a low-lying branch, which knocks off his hat, and might easily—he reflects—have performed the same office for the head which it covered. He realises the disability under which he labours by reason of not being able to calculate his distance from the unyielding timber in front, beside, around; at the same time to distinguish the route of the fast-vanishing 'mob' (*Anglice*, drove), while all his skill and strength are required to control a stock-horse, if such a mount has been provided for him, which clambers along hillsides and tears down the same with the sure-footedness of a mule, while he leaves the full responsibility of directing his headlong career to his rider. When at the end of several miles the visitor pulls up, he is entirely out of the hunt. Neither men, horses, dogs, nor cattle are within sight and hearing. He is not accustomed to tracking, nor perhaps is the ground favourable to such practice. Nothing is left for him but to follow on as nearly as may be in the direction of the riders, fortunate if, some hours after, he is hunted up by a man sent in search of him, or, more fortunate still, has left all path-finding to his horse, and joyfully recognises the homestead, which comes into sight much sooner than he expected.

In contrast to this exploit, behold the sons of the waste under the same circumstances. Riding along with apparent carelessness, several pairs of sharp eyes are piercing the forest glades in every part of the foreground. One man has descried the outline of a group of slowly-moving forms, or it may be but a single beast, high up a hillside in the gorge of a mountain-range, the depths of a narrow brook, traversed ravine—it matters not. It is the herd they are seeking, or a section of it. The quick-eyed scout gives a low whistle, perhaps holds up his hand; the signal is understood. Bridle-reins are gathered up. No word is spoken, but each man has his horse in hand as they move slowly towards the grazing or stationary outliers. A few minutes bring them nearer, within perhaps good wheeling distance, when a sentinel gets view or winds them, and the whole troop is off like a shot. Each horse, but a minute since stumbling along at a 'stockman's jog' or a go-as-you-please walk, starts into top speed as if for a mile heat. The men, taking a 'bee-line,' ride straight for the fast-vanishing cattle, as if there was not a tree or a rock within miles. How they do it is a never-ending marvel to the uninitiated. But they will not only keep with the outlaws, but out-pace and out-general them; wheeling them at critical places, racing ahead and rounding them up; eventually, with mingled force and diplomacy, hustling them across a country without track, road, or apparently natural features, till dead-beat and defeated they are landed in the high, secure stock-yard, from which some of their number at least will never emerge alive.

THE MAILMAN'S YARN
AN OWER TRUE TALE

'Rum things happen in the bush, you take my word for it,' suddenly broke out Dan M'Elroy as we were sitting smoking round a camp fire, far back in the 'Never Never' one night. The whole tract of country west of the Barcoo was under water that summer. We were all stuck hard and fast, about fifty miles from Sandringham, waiting for the creeks and cowalls to go down. They weren't small ones either—twenty feet deep in some places and half a mile wide. There were a dozen teamsters with wool-waggons, Jim and me and two black boys with four hundred head of fat cattle from Marndoo. A police trooper bringing down a horse-stealer for trial, committed by the Bench there, made up the party. The prisoner was made comfortable—only chained to a log for safety. Here we were, waiting, waiting, and had to make the best of it. We walked about in the daylight, and did a bit of shooting. We'd put up a bough yard for the cattle, more for the exercise than anything else; and to make the time pass we'd taken to telling yarns. Some of them were that curious I wish I hadn't forgotten 'em. But this one that Dan told that night I shall remember to my dying day. He was the mail contractor between St. George and Bolivar Run, a weather-beaten Bathurst native, as hard as iron-bark, who'd have contracted to run the mail from the Red Sea to Jordan in spite of all the Arabs if they'd made it worth his while. He was afraid of nothing and nobody. In his time he had been speared by blacks, shot at by bushrangers, fished for dead out of flooded creeks, besides being 'given up' in fever, ague, and sunstroke in exploring of mail routes through the 'Never Never' country. Hairbreadth escapes were daily bread to him. He seemed to thrive on 'em, but this one must have been out of the common way.

He looked round over the great plain, where we could see the glimmer of water on every side by the light of the low moon, just showing, red and goblin-like. A murmuring wind began to whisper and sob among the stunted myall, swaying the long streamers as if they were mourning for the dead. It felt colder, though we'd piled up the logs on the fire lately, when he filled his pipe and said: 'We'll turn in after this, but you may as well take it to sleep on. It was nigh twenty year ago it happened, yet it comes back to me now as fresh as I saw it that cursed night. You chaps remember,' he said, taking a good steady draw at his pipe, by way of starting it and the yarn at the same time,—'you remember, as I told you, I was running a horse mail between Marlborough Point and Waranah, somewhere about '68. A different season from this, I tell you. No rain for about eighteen months, and when the autumn came in dry, with the nights long and cold, the sheep began to die faster than you could count 'em. I had a fairish contract, and though the mail was a heavy one, I was able to manage it by riding one horse and leading a packer. A terrible long day's ride it was—three times a week—eighty-five mile. Of course I had a change of horses, but I didn't get in till eleven or twelve at night to Waranah. The frosty nights had set in, and sometimes, between being half-frozen and dead-tired, I could hardly sit on my horse. It was getting on in June, and still no rain, only the frosts getting sharper and sharper, when I came along to a sandhill by the side of a billabong of the Murrumbidgee, about ten miles from Waranah. There was a big water-hole there; it was a favourite camping place between the township and Baranco station. I was later than usual, and it was about midnight when I got to this point. Through a weak horse as had knocked up I'd had to walk five miles. I was nigh perished with the cold; hungry too, for I'd had no time to stop and get a feed; and as I'd been in the saddle since long before daylight, you may guess I was pretty well tuckered out. A particular spot, too, when you come to think of it. The sand-ridge ran back from the water-hole a good way (there was a big kurrajong-tree beside it, I remember), and spread out near upon a mile till you got into a fair-sized plain. The ridge—that's the way of 'em in dry country—was covered as thick as they could stand with pine-scrub. An old cattle-track ran right through to the plain, where they used to come to water in the old days when Baranco was a cattle-run. I was dozing on my horse, dog-tired and stiff with the cold, when I came to the water-hole at the foot of this sandhill. I always used to pull up there and have a smoke; so I stopped and looked round about, in a half-sleepy, dazed kind of way. I felt for my box of matches, and I'm dashed if they weren't gone—shot out, I expect—for I'd been working my passage and been jumbled about more than enough. That put the cap on. I felt as if I'd drop off the horse there and then. I never was one for drinking, and I didn't carry a flask. How I'd get on the next couple of hours I couldn't think.

'All of a sudden a streak of light came through the darkness of the pine-scrub to the left of me. It got broader and broader. It wasn't the moon, I knew, for that wouldn't show till nigh-hand daylight. It must be a fire. Somebody camping, of course; but why they didn't stop by the water, the regular place, with good feed and open ground all round them, I couldn't make out. I was off like a shot, and hung up my horses to the kurrajong tree, which stood handy. It was too thick to ride through the pine saplings, and I thought the walk would freshen me up. I started off quite jolly with the notion of the grand warm I should have at the fire, and the pipeful of baccy I'd be able to borrow. It was a big fire I saw as I stumbled along, getting nearer and nearer the head of an old-man pine, the branches as dry as timber, and would burn like matchwood. I could see three men standing round it. As I got nearer I was just going to halloo out, partly for fun and partly for devilment, when the wind blew the flame round, and made one of the men, who was poking a pole into the fire, shift and turn his face towards me. Mind! I was in the dark shadow of the pines. The glare of the fire lit up his face and those of the two other men as clear as day.

'The man's face, as it turned towards where I was standing, had such a hellish expression, that I stopped dead and drew behind an overhanging "balah" that grew among the pines. He seemed to be listening. Another man with an axe in his hand said something to him, when he walked a few steps down the track towards me and stopped. My God, what a face it was! No devil out of hell could have looked more fiendish than he did. It was like no human face I'd ever seen. I began to think I was asleep, and dreaming of a story in a book.

'They were not more than twenty yards from where I stood. My heart beat that loud I was afraid they'd hear it. My hair stood on end, if any one's ever did, while as the tall, dark man began to poke the fire again, and pushed something further into it that was *not a log of wood*, I deuced near fainted, and beads of perspiration rolled down my forehead and face. What did I see that caused every drop of blood in my veins to turn to ice? What the strange man stirred in the fire, making the sparks to fly all round among the red glowing embers, was a *corpse*! There was no mistaking the dreadful shape. One arm stuck out. The legs were there, the skull blackened and featureless, and, Heavenly Father! beyond and in the middle of the heap of glowing embers lay another shape huddled together, and showing no angle of limb or bone. The other man, with a broom of boughs tied together, was busy sweeping in all the pieces of charcoal, so as to prevent the flame from spreading through the tall, dry grass. At a short distance I could make out a tilted cart, such as hawkers use in the bush. "By— —!" said the man with the pole, "I'll swear I heard a stick crack. Any traveller as come to the water-hole and followed the track up, 'll have to be rubbed out, and no two ways about it. It will be our lives against his!"

"'Haven't we had blood enough for one day?" says the other man. "By George! when I think of these two poor chaps' faces, just afore you dropped 'em with the axe, I'd give all we've made ten times over to have 'em alive again."

"'You always was a snivelling beggar," says the tall man. "If you'd had your back scratched at Port Arthur half as often as me, you'd think no more of a man's life than a wild dog's. I believe it must 'a been one or a wallaby as made the stir."

'I've faced a trifle of danger, and seen some "close calls" in my time, but nothing came near that half-hour I spent there till I could make myself steady enough to stir. I couldn't sit; I was too done to stand; so there I had to crouch down and wait till I got the chance to go back on my tracks.

'All the time they kept pushing the bodies into the centre of the fire, without stopping, as they got smaller and smaller. Two of the men were at this dreadful work, while the third was sweeping round every edge of the fire. At last the two men I first saw, sat down on a log close handy and began to smoke. Now was my chance. I crawled from my tree and crept along the cattle-track till I come to where my horses were standing. I mounted one, somehow, and took the other's bridle. I rode steady enough for a while, and then, hustling the poor brutes into a hand-gallop, kept along the road to Waranah till I reached the gate at the boundary of the run. Even then I felt as if I was hardly safe. I looked round and could almost see witches and devils following me through the air, and waving ghosts' arms in every bough of the stunted trees through which the road wound.

'When I saw the lights of the little township, I was that glad that I shouted and sang all the way up to the hotel where the mail was delivered. I had a strange sort of feeling in my head as I rode up to the door. Then I reeled in my saddle; everything was dark. I remembered no more till at the end of a week I found myself in bed recovering from fever.

'I suppose I'd been sickening for it before. What with hot days, cold nights, and drinking water out of swamps and dry holes that were half mud and half—pah! something you don't like to think of—the wonder is we bushmen don't get it oftener. Anyhow I was down that time, and next morning it seems they had the doctor to me. He was a clever man and a gentleman, too, my word! He fetched me round after a month, but I was off my head the first week, and kept raving (so they told me afterwards) about men being knocked on the head and burned, hawkers' carts, and Derwenters, and the big water-hole by Budgell Creek.

'They thought it was all madness and nonsense at first, and took no notice, till one afternoon Mr. Belton, the overseer of Baranco, comes riding into town, all of a flurry, wanting to see the police and the magistrate, Mr. Waterton. This was what he had to say:—

'There had been some heavy lots of travelling sheep passing through the station, and he was keeping along with them for fear they might miss the road and not find it again till they'd ate off a mile or two of his best grass. All of a sudden a mob of the Baranco weaners ran across a plain and nearly boxed with 'em. Mr. Belton gallops for his life—I expect he swore a bit, too—and was just in time to head 'em off into the pine-scrub by the sandhill. They took the old cattle-track over towards the water-hole, he following them up, till all of a sudden he comes plump on a hawker's cart!

'This pulled him up short. He let the sheep run on to the frontage and got off his horse. He knew the Colemans' cart. They always stayed a night at Baranco. When they passed, *a week since*, they were to make Waranah that night. What the deuce were they doing here? Hang the fellows! were they spelling their horses? Feed was scarce.

No! they were not the men to do that. Honest, straight-going chaps they'd always been.

'He walked over to the cart. Something wrong surely! The big slop-chest was open. The cash-box, with lock smashed, was empty. Boots, clothes, tobacco, which they always had of the best, lying scattered about. Where were the poor fellows themselves? If they had been robbed, why hadn't they gone to the police at Waranah and complained? Whoever had done this must have camped here in the middle of the scrub. Then there'd been a fire over by the big pine-stump—an "old man" fire too. Wonder they hadn't set a light to the dry grass? No rain for the half-year to speak of. No; they had been too jolly careful. Swept in the twigs and ashes all round. Curious fire for bushmen to make too—big enough to roast an ox. He stares at the ashes; then gropes among them with his hand. My God! What are these small pieces of bone? Why, the place is full of them. And this? and this? A metal button, a metal buckle—one, two, three—twelve in all.

'It comes back to him now that three travellers left the Baranco men's hut the same morning as the Colemans—one a tall, dark, grey-haired old hand, with a scar across his face. He gets his horse with a long sort of half-whistle and half-groan and rides slow, in a study like, toward the township. The next day the magistrate, Mr. Waterton (he's a squatter, but sits most times when the Police Magistrate isn't on hand), goes out with the Sergeant of Police and the best part of the townspeople of Waranah. He holds an Inquiry. The doctor attended and gave evidence that he had no doubt whatever that the bones formed part of human skeletons. The surface of the fire was raked over, and a lot of metal buttons and buckles—as many as would be used for two pairs of trousers—with other remains of clothing, were found. A verdict of "wilful murder against some person or persons unknown" was returned.

'On the second day after the murder three men crossed the Murray River pretty high up, near a public-house. Their ways were suspicious. One of them fired off a revolver. They had on new suits of clothes, new boots with elastic sides, and no end of tobacco of a queer brand—not known in those parts. Large swags too! The boss of the crowd was a tall, dark man, with a scar and grey hair. He was the man who fired the revolver and used wild language. The police from Crowlands picked up the trail so far. If they had followed hard on, like the Avenger of Blood (as the feller says in the play), they might have run down the murderin' dogs. But the publican had a bad memory. *He couldn't remember* seeing any out-of-the-way travellers cross the river that week. So the police turned back, and lost the scent for good and all.

'A queer enough thing about the matter was, that directly after the Inquiry was published, a telegram was sent from the poor fellows' friends to the sergeant at Waranah. He was to look under the lid of the big slop-chest and he'd find a false top that slid back—very neat made, so that people mostly wouldn't notice it. Behind this was a drawer, and in it notes and cheques. They never kept more than a fiver or so in the cash-box, and told the secret to their relatives before leaving town. Sure enough the sergeant finds the secret-drawer, and in it, after being in the open bush nearly a fortnight, £90 odd in notes and good cheques, which of course he sent to their friends. The villains only got £4 and a fit-out of clothes and tobacco. The police never could get wind of these wretches for years after. However, they dropped on the man with the scar, whose name was Campbell. He was sworn to as the man who left Baranco with the other two on the day of the murder, as the man as had new clothes and tobacco (such as nobody but the Colemans sold in the district) two days after. It was proved that they were all hard up and ragged when they left Baranco. The evidence was in dribs and drabs. But they pieced it together, bit by bit. It was good enough to hang him, and hang him they did. I swore to him as the man I saw at the fire that terrible night. And now, mates, I'll turn in. There's no fear of being burned to bits here, is there? Good-night all!'

DEAR DERMOT

Somehow the days of my youth seem to have been inextricably mixed up with horses. How I loved them, to be sure!—thought of them by day, dreamed of them by night. Books and girls might temporarily enter into competition as objects of engrossing interest; but the noble animal must have had possession of my thoughts for a large proportion of the waking hours.

From boyhood the proprietor of studs more or less extensive, I was quick to discern excellence in other people's favourites. My mind was stored, my imagination fired, besides, with tales of equestrian feats, performed chiefly by Arab chiefs and other heroes of old-world romance. In a chronic state of expectancy, I was always ready to do honour to the legendary steed, so rarely encountered, alas! save in the bounteous realm of fiction.

When, therefore, I *did* fall across 'the courser of the poets,' or his simulacrum, I was prepared to secure him at a fancy price; holding that if I could recoup the outlay by selling a pair of average horses of my own breeding, the luxury of possessing a paragon would be cheaply purchased.

And would it not be? Albeit there are multitudes of people to whom one horse, save the mark, is much like another. For them, the highest joy, the transcendent sensation of being carried by 'the sweetest hack in the world,' exists not. But to him who recognises and appreciates the speed, the spirit, the smoothness, and the safety of the 'wonderful' hackney, there are few outdoor pleasures possessing similar flavour.

It is more than half a century, sad to relate, since I first took bridle in hand. During that time I have ridden races on 'the flat,' over 'the sticks,' and have backed for the first time a score or more of wholly-untried colts. I have tested hundreds of saddle-horses, over every variety of road, at all sorts of distances, in all ranges of climate, and after this extended experience I unhesitatingly pronounce Dermot, son of Cornborough, to be in nearly all respects the finest example of the blood hackney which I ever mounted. The 'sweetest,' etc., he certainly was. Almost too good for this wicked world.

The birth of this unrivalled steed was mainly due to one of the magnates of the earlier Victorian era, himself an example of the strangeness of that destiny which shapes our ends in life. A member of a family of financial aristocrats, domiciled in London and Paris, with which capitals our friend was equally familiar, Mr. Adolphus Goldsmith scarcely dreamed in youth of 'colonial experience.'

But something went wrong with the finance arrangements of his near relatives. A crisis culminated, and the necessity arose for Goldsmith (*fils*) applying himself to the stern realities of life. He had previously performed the strictly ornamental duties of a young man about town. But with a cool perception of the situation, characteristic of the man, and a steadfast determination to conquer adverse fate, the whilom *élégant* of the Bois de Boulogne and the Row looked over the map of the world, picked his colony, giving the *pas* to Victoria, the then fashionable El Dorado for younger sons and *vauriens*, converted the remnant of his fortune into letters of credit, and sailed for Port Phillip.

As an Englishman by birth and rearing as well as adoption, Mr. Goldsmith had sported park hacks and ridden to hounds in his day. He possessed the Englishman's love for horses. Visions, therefore, arose of improving the breed in the new country which he was about to patronise, and incidentally devoting himself to agricultural pursuits.

Distrusting, however, his suitability for the necessary purchases and arrangements, he sensibly cast about for a coadjutor, fully instructed in bucolic lore, to whom he might confide details.

He was successful beyond expectation, inasmuch as he induced Mr. Hatsell Garrard, a gentleman farmer from the midland counties (whose love of all genuine sport had, combined with a run of bad seasons, probably rendered rent-paying temporarily arduous), to accompany him as General Manager to Australia. And whoso recalls his fresh-coloured countenance, his pleasant smile, his shrewd blue eye, his neat rig and bridle-hand, reproduces out of memory's storehouse the ideal yeoman from 'Merrie England.'

Mr. Garrard promptly demonstrated a knowledge of his business by purchasing Cornborough, son of Tramp, a grandson of the immortal

Whalebone. For this sole achievement he deserves a statue, and in that Pantheon which future Victorians may rear for the founders of their prosperity and glory, the square-built, genuinely English figure of Mr. Garrard should find a place. What a responsibility was cast upon him when you come to think of it! How easily might he have chosen an equally blue-blooded, but leggy, rickety, pernicious weed, such as has so often been foisted upon unwary breeders.

Instead of which, he enriched us with the noble, whole-coloured, brown horse, choke-full of the best blood in England, of medium height, but perfect in symmetry, soundness, faultless in wind and limb, temper and courage, fated to be the long-remembered sire of racers, hacks, and harness horses of the highest class—to be honoured in life, regretted, ay, sincerely mourned, in death. For on his unexpected demise, his disconsolate owner was discovered in such a state of prostration and grief that every one thought his wife must be dead, or, at any rate, some relative near and dear.

Truly, the squatter of the 'forties' was from one reason or another a man *sui generis*, with whom the present pastoral era furnishes few parallels. Mr. Goldsmith, in addition to other accomplishments (did he not challenge Charles Macknight to a bout at single-stick, duly fought out within the precincts of the Melbourne Club?) was a musical connoisseur and no mean performer. When the comfortable cottage at Trawalla was completed, albeit stone-paved and bark-roofed, the drawing-room contained a handsome piano, to which, after dinner, the proprietor mostly betook himself. There, in operatic reminiscences and compositions of impromptu merit, he was wont to wander from the realms of reality to a dreamworld of sweet sounds and brighter souvenirs. How one envied him the delicious distraction!

So the Trawalla estate had birth and beginning. It was a first-class 'run' in those simpler times; well watered, with picturesque alternations of hill and dale, plain and forest. The 'shepherded' sheep had unfailing pasture and ample range. There were no fences in those days, excepting around the horse-paddock.

Temptations to over-stocking were fewer, and chiefly—in default of boundary—took the form of an invasion of some neighbour's territory, a trespass which his shepherds were prompt to resent.

Thus, the natural grasses were but moderately fed down, and, with the autumn rains unfailing in *that* district, assumed a richly verdurous garb, scarcely so frequent in the wire-fenced decades. I do not recall the name of the deserving but less fortunate pioneer, the first or second occupant of this desirable holding, from whom Mr. Goldsmith purchased the 'right of run,' with probably a more handful of stock. With cash in hand, he was doubtless enabled to make an advantageous purchase, and thus enter upon his predecessor's labours; once more, as it turned out, to place his foot on fortune's ladder.

Far from London and Paris, Ascot and Goodwood, as he found himself, the erstwhile man about town was not wholly debarred from congenial society. William Gottreaux, another musical enthusiast, was at Lilaree; Hastings Cunningham at Mount Emu; Donald and Hamilton, Philip Russell, and other gentleman pioneers within an easy ride. He became a member of the Melbourne Club, then in Collins Street, upon the site of the Bank of Victoria. The late Sir Redmond Barry was his early and intimate friend. (I took charge of a small package of tobacco, on my homeward voyage, from the Judge, as it seems that particular brand was not procurable in Paris.) When things were settled at Trawalla and the stock manifestly improving, with Cornborough in a snug loose-box, and the sheep increasing fast, the owner of Trawalla found a reasonable amount of recreation, as comprised in frequent sojourns at the Melbourne Club, and the enjoyment of the metropolitan society of the day, quite compatible with the effective supervision of the station.

Thus, on the advancing tide of Victorian prosperity, then steadily sweeping onward, unknown to us all, Trawalla and its owner were floated on to fortune—a gently gliding, agreeable, and satisfactory process. The sheep multiplied, the fleece acquired name and repute—one *couldn't* grow bad wool in that country, however hard you might try. Cornborough became a peer of the Godolphin Arabian in all men's eyes, and the A.G. brand, on beeve-or horse-hide, an accredited symbol of excellence. A purchase of waste land at St. Kilda, made solely, as he informed me, in order to qualify as a legislator, turned out a most profitable investment.

Swiftly the golden period arrived when, after the first years of doubt and uncertainty, it became apparent to holders of station property that nothing prevented them from clearing out at a highly satisfactory price, and leaving the conflicting elements of dear labour, high prices, and a heterogeneous population, to settle themselves as best they might. Mr. Goldsmith, now free to return to Europe, seriously considered the claims of the Rue de Bellechasse, Faubourg St. Germain, as contrasted with Collins Street and the Melbourne Club.

It may be that the owner of Trawalla would have decided upon continuous occupation, with a view to founding an estate, if his sons, who visited Victoria in 1851, had exhibited any aptitude for the life of Australian country gentlemen. But Messrs. Edward and Alfred Goldsmith, who had been educated chiefly in Paris, when they visited their father in 1851, did not take kindly to his adopted country. Cultured, polished young men, yet decidedly more French than English, Parisians to their finger-nails in all their tastes and habitudes, they grieved and irritated their Australianised parent.

Chiefly they lacked the adventurous spirit which would have enabled them to behold, mentally, the grand possibilities of a colonial possession. All their sympathies were with their lost Eden, the Paris which they had quitted. In Victoria they beheld nothing but the distasteful privations of a new country, hardly redeemed from primeval *sauvagerie*. The roads were rough, the beds hard, the cookery—'Ah, mon Dieu!—lamentable, indescribable.'

It was a good time to sell, and though the Trawalla estate of to-day represents a considerably larger sum than Mr. Simson gave for the run and stock, perhaps our old friend was not so far out when he decided to let well alone and retire upon a fair competency.

To that end the stud was sentenced to sale and dispersion; many a descendant of the lamented Cornborough went to enrich the paddocks of friends and well-wishers. I think Mr. Hastings Cunningham bought the greater number of the brood mares and young stock, at an average rate per head.

Now, Dermot was the old gentleman's hack. (Was he old, or, perhaps, only about forty-five? We were decided then as to the time of life when decay of all the faculties was presumed to set in.) I many a time and oft admired the swell, dark bay, striding along the South Yarra tracks with aristocratic elegance, or, more becomingly arrayed, carrying a lady in the front of a joyous riding-party. His owner was *un galant uomo*, and the gentle yet spirited steed was always at the service of his lady friends.

So when, one day at the club, he suggested to me to buy Dermot—more than one lady's horse being required in our family at that time, and only fifty pounds named as the price—I promptly closed.

Dead and buried is he years agone; but I still recall, with memory's aid, the dark bay horse, blood-like, symmetrical, beauteous in form as aristocratic in bearing. 'Hasn't he the terrifyin' head on him?' queried an Irish sympathiser, somewhat incongruously, as he gazed with rapt air and admiring eyes at the tapering muzzle, large, soft eyes, and Arab frontal.

Delicate, deer-like, strictly Eastern was the head referred to, beautifully set on a perfectly-arched neck, which again joined oblique, truly perfect shoulders. Their mechanism must have been such, inasmuch as never did I know any living horse with such liberty of forehand action.

Walking or cantering down an incline, shut but your eyes, and you were unable to tell by bodily sensation whether you were on level ground or otherwise. He 'pulled up' in a way different from any other horse. Apparently, he put out his legs, and, lo! you were again at a walk. No prop, shake, or jar was perceptible. It was a magical transformation. An invalid recovering from a fever could have ridden him a day's journey. No one could fall off him in fact.

He who had no peer was born

amid the green forest parks of Trawalla, at no great distance from Buninyong, or the historic goldfield of Ballarat.

His sire, Cornborough, than whom no better horse ever left England, was a brown horse, like The Premier and Rory O'More; like them, middle-sized, symmetrical rather than powerful. Among the early cracks that owed their speed and courage to him were Cornet, Bessie Bedlam, Beeswing, Ballarat, The Margravine (dam of Lord Clyde), with many others, now half forgotten. Cornet was, I think, the first of his progeny trained. He ran away with most of the two-year-old stakes of the day, to be ever after known as a fast horse and a good stayer. I remember his beating Macknight's St. George at Port Fairy, in a match for £100, and winning various other stakes and prizes. His half-sister, Mr. Austin's Bessie Bedlam, was one of the most beautiful race-horses ever saddled. I well remember her running in old days, and can see her now, stepping along daintily with her head up, like an antelope. She won many a race, and was successful as a stud matron after turf triumphs were over. Beeswing was also good, but not equal to her. Ballarat was a great raking, handsome chestnut mare, bred by Dick Scott, a stock-rider of Mr. Goldsmith's. She must have had a good turn of speed, inasmuch as she won the All-aged Stakes in Melbourne, as a three-year old. The Cornboroughs, like the Premiers, were remarkable for their temperate dispositions. They had abundance of courage, but no tendency to vice of any kind.

On his dam's side Dermot boasted Peter Fin (Imp) as grandsire, and other good running blood. His pedigree was incomplete, thus leaving him open to a suspicion of being not quite thoroughbred. But the stain—the 'blot on the scutcheon,' if such there was—showed neither by outward sign nor inward quality.

Then, as to paces. He walked magnificently, holding up his head in a lofty and dignified manner; his mouth of the lightest—velvet to any touch of bit—but withal firm. He had always been ridden with a double bridle, and showed no provincial distaste to bit and bridoon. If required to quicken his pace from a fast but true walk, he could adopt a rapid amble, so causing any ordinary stepper to trot briskly. And then his canter—how shall I describe it? Springy, long-striding, yet floating, improving his speed at will to a hand-gallop if you merely shook the reins, and as readily, smoothly subsiding at the lightest sustained pull.

With such a horse under you it seemed as if one could go on for ever. Mile after mile fled away, and still there was no abatement in the wonderful living mechanism of which the spring and elasticity seemed exhaustless. The sensation was so exquisite that you dreaded to terminate it. When at length you drew rein, it was, so to speak, with the tears in your eyes.

Then the safety of this miraculous performance. You were on a horse that never was known to shy or bolt, and that *could not* fall down. Nature had otherwise provided. With such a balance of forehand, he may have at rare intervals struck his hoof against root or stone, clod or other obstacle, but trip, blunder, fall—these were words and deeds wholly outside of his being. With legs of iron, and hoofs that matched them well, never once did I know Dermot to be lame during all the years of our acquaintance.

Fortunately for me, and for society generally, he was not quite fast enough for promotion to a racing stable. He was thus enabled to elude the turf dangers and so pass his life in a sphere where he was loved and respected as he deserved.

With regard to his stamina. I rode him a distance of seventy miles one day, being anxious to get home, during the last ten miles of which he waltzed along with precisely the same air and manner as in the morning—with thirteen stone up, too. In addition to other qualities, he was an uncommonly good feeder: would clear his rack conscientiously, and eat all the oats you would give him. I never knew him to be tired, or met any one that had heard of his being seen in that condition.

His graceful, high-bred air, his large, mild eye and intelligent expression, warranted one in crediting him with the perfect temper which indeed he possessed. So temperate was he, that the lady whose palfrey he habitually was (as such, beyond all earthly competition) was in the habit of sending him along occasionally at top speed in company, confident in her ability to stop him whenever she had the inclination.

He was utterly free from vice, either in the stable or out of it. But, if uniformly gentle, he was always gay and free—that most difficult combination to secure in a lady's horse. An angel enclosed in horse hide, such was 'Dear Dermot.' The doctrine of metempsychosis alone can account for such a consensus of virtues—an equine prodigy, a wonder and a miracle. Generations may roll by before such another hackney treads Australian turf. We are not of the school which decries the horses, the men also, of the present day. There are, there must be now, as good horses, as gallant youths, as ever new or old lands produced. But Dermot—may he rest in peace!—was a *very* exceptional composition. And I must be pardoned for doubting whether, as a high-caste saddle-horse, I shall ever again see his equal.

THE STORY OF AN OLD LOG-BOOK

Notwithstanding our share in New Guinea and the debateable land of the New Hebrides, besides the proposed cession of Santa Cruz, the Sydney of 'the thirties' wore the look of being more in touch with the South Sea Islands and the Oceanic realm generally, than at present. The wharves were redolent of the wild life of The Islands and the mysterious land of the Maori. Weather-beaten sailing-vessels showed a sprinkling of swarthy recruits, whose dark faces, half strange, half fierce, were mingled with those of their British crews. Hull and rigging bore silent testimony to the wrath of wind and wave. There were whale-ships returning in twelve months with a full cargo of sperm oil, or half empty after a three years' cruise, as the adventure turned out.

Schoolboys were fond of loitering about among them, wondering at the harpoons, lances, and keen-edged 'whale spades,' at the masses of whalebone and spermaceti, or the carved and ornamental whales' teeth, of which Jack always had a store.

In the forecastle of one ship might be seen the tattooed lineaments and grim visage of a Maori; from another would peer forth the mild, wondering gaze of a Fijian. Bows and arrows (the latter presumably poisoned), spears, clubs, and wondrous carved idols were the principal curios, nearly always procurable.

The whale fishery was at that time a leading industry. Sperm oil figured noticeably among the first items of our export trade. Merchants made advances for the outfit and all necessaries of the adventure, trusting in many instances for repayment to the skill, courage, and good faith of the commander. No doubt losses were incurred, but the lottery was tempting. The profits must have been considerable. Sperm oil, before the discovery of gas or petroleum, was worth eighty or ninety pounds per ton. A large 'right whale' was good for eighty barrels, eight barrels going to the tun. He was a fish worth landing. To get back to the ship, even after hours of hard pulling and the chance of a stove boat, towing a monster worth nearly £1000, was exciting enough.

The crew, like shearers of the present day, were proverbially hard to manage. They did not receive wages, but a share in the net profits—a 'lay,' as it was called. The ship was, in fact, a floating co-operative society. This did not prevent them—for human nature is weak—from committing acts distinctly opposed to the spirit as well as the letter of the agreement. They got drunk when they had the chance. They occasionally mutinied. They resisted the mate and defied the captain. They proposed to take savage maidens for their dusky brides, and to live lives devoid of care in The Islands. It strikes landsmen as a curiously dangerous and anxious position for a captain, who had to confront a score or two of reckless seamen with the aid only of the officers of the ship. Yet it was done. The peril dared, the ship saved, and order restored time after time, by the resolute exercise of one strong will and the half-instinctive yielding of the seamen to the mysterious power of legal authority.

Before me as I write are the well-kept and regularly-entered pages of a whale-ship's log-book, the record of a voyage from Sydney harbour over the Southern main, which bears date as far back as April 1833. In that year again sailed the stout barque, which had done so well her part in bringing us safely to this far new land. Her course lay through the coral reefs and Eden-seeming islands of the Great South Sea; along the storm-swept coast of New Zealand; among the cannibals of New Ireland and New Britain; among the as yet half-unknown region of the Solomon Islands and Bougainville Group. As to the dangers of such a voyage, one incident of the strange races that people these isles of Eden is sufficiently dramatic. A boat's crew had pulled over to an inviting looking beach within the coral ring for the purpose of watering. As the boat touched the beach, stem on, one of the crew sprang ashore with the painter in his hand. A cry escaped him and the crew simultaneously, as he sank to his neck in a concealed pit, a veritable *trou-de-loup*. He hung on to the rope fortunately, and so pulled himself up and into the boat again.

Not a native was in sight. But the treacherous pitfalls being probed and laid bare, the intention was manifest. A line of holes was discovered in the sands, nine or ten feet in depth, cone-shaped and sloping to a narrow point, where were placed sharp-pointed, hard-wood stakes, the ends having been charred and scraped. Sharp as lance-heads, they would have disabled any seaman luckless enough to fall in, especially in latitudes where Jack prefers to go barefooted. Forewarned, walking warily, and 'prospecting' any dangerous-looking spot, they succeeded in unmasking all or nearly all of these man-traps, into which the ambushed natives expected them to fall. They were ingeniously constructed, the top covered with a light frame of twigs and grass, sand being sprinkled over all. Any ordinary crew would have been deceived.

When they reached the village they found the property of a boat's crew, who had been surprised or betrayed. One piece of evidence after another came to light. Last of all, the oars, on the blades of which were marks of blood-stained fingers closed in the last grasp which the ill-fated mariner was to give.

Righteous indignation succeeded this gruesome discovery. A wholesale burning of the town and canoes was ordered. A shower of arrows was sent after the departing boat, as the murder isle was quitted with a distinct sense of relief. It is not improbable that similar experiences have been repeated during the last few years. In those days the 'labour trade' did not exist, and to 'black-birding' was no scale of profit attached.

There is a pathetic simplicity about this unvarnished record of perilous adventure, after the close of half a century. One looks reverently upon the yellow pages which photograph so minutely the daily life of the floating microcosm. The course, the winds, the storms, the calms, the days of failure and good fortune! The huge sea-beast harpooned and half slain, yet cunning to 'sound' deeply enough to pay out all the line, or, the iron 'drawing,' finally to elude capture altogether. Then again what a day of triumph when the hieroglyph show six whales killed and 'got safely alongside.' Midnight saw the boilers still bubbling and hissing; the tired crew with four-and-twenty hours' severe work before them, after, perhaps, half a day's hard pulling in the exciting chase.

Then out of the endless waste of waters rises the lovely shape of the fairy isle. 'Mountain, and valley, and woodland'—a paradisal climate; a friendly, graceful, simple race, reverencing the stranger whites, with their big canoe and loud reverberating fire-weapons; or, on the other hand, sullen and ferocious cannibals, sending flights of poisoned arrows from their thickets, or surrounding the ship with a swarm of canoes, full of hostile savages, eager to climb her deck to slay and plunder unchecked.

It is characteristic, perhaps, of the greater simplicity of manners, and steadfast inculcation of the religious observances of that era, that on board the ship referred to, Divine service was regularly performed on each recurring Sunday. If whales were sighted, however, the boats were lowered; and on one Sunday afternoon two whales were killed. It was obviously a part of the unwritten code of salt-water law that whales were not to be allowed to escape under *any* circumstances, upon whatever days they were sighted by the look-out man. As it was tolerably certain that the ship would be more than once in jeopardy from hostile attacks, a few guns and carronades were mounted; boarding-nettings were not, I presume, overlooked. The old Ironsides' maxim, 'Trust in Providence and keep your powder dry,' was in effect a strictly observed precaution.

How strange it seems to think of the altered conditions made by the passing away of a generation or two! Cold is now the hand which traced the lines I view; stilled the hot blood and eager soul of him who commanded the ship—a born leader of men if such there ever was.

Of the crew that toiled early and late at sea, through sun and storm,—that drank and caroused and fought and gambled on shore when occasion served,—how small the chance that any one now survives!

With reference to the Solomon Group, which has been visited by many a vessel since the barque safely steered her course through shoal and reef, insidious currents and treacherous calm, matters seem to have been much about the same as at present. At some islands the natives were simple and friendly; at others, sullen and treacherous, ready at all times for an attack if feasible; merciless and unsparing when the hour came.

To refer to the Log-book.

'*Monday, July 22, 1833.*—At Bougainville; several canoes came off, trading for cocoa-nuts and tortoise-shell.

'*Monday, July 29.*—Beating along the coast of New Georgia. Canoes came off; traded for cocoa-nuts and tortoise-shell. Shipped Henry Spratt, who left the *Cadmus* last season. [A bad bargain, as future events showed.]

'*August 8.*—Sent the boats ashore at Sir Charles Hardy's island. At 7 P.M. boats returned, having purchased from the natives, who were very friendly, a quantity of cocoa-nuts and a pig. Discovered an extensive harbour on the west side.

'*September 4.*—Sent boats ashore at New Ireland; natives particularly friendly.

'*Saturday, October 5.*—Bore away for the harbour of Santa Cruz. At 2 P.M. cast anchor in thirty fathoms, one mile from shore. There an adventure befell which altered existing relations.

'*Sunday, October 6.*—Sent casks on shore and got them filled with water. Next day got two rafts of water off, and some wood. Purchased a quantity of yams from the natives.

'*Tuesday, October 8.*—Hands employed in wooding, watering, and stowing away the holds. The natives made an attack on the men while watering, and wounded one man with an arrow. Brought off natives' canoes, and made an attack on their town, which was vigorously contested. Another of the ship's company severely wounded. All hands employed getting ready for sea.

'*Wednesday, October 9.*—At 4 A.M. began to get under weigh. Discharged the guns at hostile village. Men in canoes shot their arrows at the ship. Volley returned.

'*October 19*, 1 P.M.—Henry Stephens, seaman, died of tetanus, in consequence of a wound inflicted by a native of Santa Cruz with an arrow. The burial-service read over him before the ship's company. Strong winds and high seas at midnight.

> His midnight requiem, mariner's fitting dirge,
> Sung by wild winds and wilder ocean surge.

The author of *The Western Pacific and New Guinea* (Mr. H. H. Romilly) states in that most interesting work, that in September 1883 a Commission was appointed by M. Pallu de la Barrière, then

Governor of New Caledonia, to inquire into the nature of the arrows, commonly reported to be poisoned, so much in use among the natives of the surrounding islands.

The conclusions arrived at (Mr. Romilly states) by the Commission are only what were to be expected. 'It has long been known to me, and to many other men in the Pacific who have studied the question, that the so-called poison was, if not exactly a harmless composition, certainly not a deadly one. Of course, ninety per cent of the white men trading in the Pacific believe, and will continue to believe, in the fatal effects of poisoned arrows. The Santa Cruz arrow, usually considered the most deadly, is very small, commonly about two feet in length, while the New Hebrides arrows are much heavier, capable of inflicting a mortal wound on the spot. Carteret, more than a hundred years ago, was attacked by the natives of Santa Cruz. Of the ten men hit, three died from the severe nature of their wounds. No mention is made of tetanus. If any of his men had died from so remarkable and terrible a disease, Carteret could hardly have failed to mention the fact.'

With all due respect and deference to Mr. Romilly, we must take the liberty of siding in opinion with the 'ninety per cent of white men trading in the Pacific,' and believe that the arrows *are* poisoned—are deadly and fatal, even when only a scratch is produced. The deaths of the unknown sailor, Henry Stephens, sixty-seven years ago, and of the late lamented Commodore Goodenough recently, *both from tetanus,* surely constitute a marvellous coincidence. It is hard to believe that nervous predisposition was the proximate cause of tetanus in two persons so widely dissimilar in mind, station, and education. Carteret's three seamen possibly died from the same seizure; though, having many other things to attend to, the ancient mariner failed to record the fact.

In addition to the excitement of killing and losing their whales, being wrecked on a coral reef or hit with poisoned arrows, our mariners were fated not to run short of dramatic action in the shape of mutiny.

This was how it arose and how it was quelled:—

'*Thursday, September 1883, off New Ireland.*—At 4 P.M. calm, the ship being close under the land and driving rapidly, with a strong current, farther inshore. The captain ordered the starboard bow boat to be lowered for the purpose of towing the vessel's head round in such a position that the current might take her on the starboard bow, and cause her to drift off shore. The boat was consequently lowered, and the mate ordered Henry Spratt to take the place of one of the boat's crew, who was at that moment on the foretop gallant masthead looking out for whales. Spratt refused to do so, saying that he didn't belong to any boat, and that it was his watch below. He continued to disobey the repeated orders of the mate till the matter was noticed by the captain, who called out, "Make that man go in the boat," when he at length did so, but in an unwilling manner and muttering something which was not distinctly heard.

'On the boat being hoisted up, the captain addressed Spratt in the most temperate manner on the subject of his insubordination, and warned him as to his future conduct.

'Spratt became insulting in his manner and remarks, and ended by defying his superior officers and forcibly resisting the mate's attempt to bring him from the poop to the main deck for the purpose of being put in irons. While the irons were preparing, he bolted forward, and evading every attempt to secure him, stowed himself below in the forecastle. The crew evincing a strong disposition to support this outrageous conduct, the captain armed himself and his officers, and ordered the chief mate to bring Spratt from below. He refused peremptorily, and struck the mate several blows, attempting to overpower him and gain possession of his sword. After receiving two or three blows with the flat of the sword, he was, with the assistance of the third mate, conveyed on deck and made fast to the main-rigging.

'While the prisoner was being made fast, the greater part of the crew came aft in the most mutinous and tumultuous manner, exclaiming against his being flogged, and questioning the captain's right to do so.

'They were ordered forward, and some of them (Murray in particular) showing a disposition to disobey and force themselves aft, the captain found it necessary to strike them with the flat of his sword, and to draw a rope across the deck parallel with the mainmast, warning the crew to pass it at their peril.

'The captain then, calling his officers around him, instituted a trial, and the whole of Spratt's conduct being calmly considered, he was unanimously sentenced to three dozen lashes.

'One dozen was immediately inflicted, and the prisoner was then asked if he repented of his misconduct, and would faithfully promise obedience for the remainder of the period that he should be permitted to remain on board. This promise being given, and the greatest contrition being expressed, he was unbound, and the remainder of his sentence commuted. As, however, he was considered a dangerous character, orders were issued that he should be treated as a prisoner (having the liberty of the deck abaft the mainmast) till he could be landed at New Georgia (the island from which he shipped), or elsewhere, if he thought fit.'

This *émeute*, which might have ended easily enough in a second Mutiny of the *Bounty*,—or as *did* happen when the crew of a whale-ship threw the captain overboard on the coast of New Zealand,—having been quelled by the use of strong measures promptly applied, the ordinary course of events went on uninterruptedly. On September 8 (Sunday, as it happened) two whales were killed. The canoes came off and hailed as usual. A violent gale seems to have come on directly the boiling was finished. They were alternately running under close-reefed topsails, wearing ship every four hours, being at 5 P.M. close under the high land under Cape St. Mary. Pumps going every watch, sea very high, ship labouring heavily—then close to Ford's Group. The gale lasted from Monday to the following Friday at midnight. One fancies that from the 'captain bold' downwards, they must have had 'quite a picnic of it.'

Spratt was what is known to South Sea mariners as a 'beachcomber'—one of a proverbially troublesome class of seamen. He had, probably, left the *Cadmus* for no good reason. However, the treatment seems to have cured him, as on September 1 we find the entry:—'Returned Spratt to his duty at his own request, he having promised the utmost civility, attention, and obedience. Fresh breeze and head sea till midnight,' etc.

On Saturday, April 27, 1833, the good teak-built barque cleared the Sydney Heads, outward bound, and on Saturday, May 10, 1834, at

4 P.M., saw the heads of Port Jackson, and at midnight entered, with light winds from north-east.

'*Sunday, May 11, 1834.* — Calm; the boats towing the ship up harbour. Pilot came on board. [They had come in without one — such a trifling bit of navigation, after scraping coral reefs by the score and being close inshore, with strong current setting in, not being worth considering.] At 5 P.M. came to anchor abreast of batteries. Most of the hands went ashore.'

And here, as 'Our Jack's come home again,' let us conclude this story of an old Log-book.

A KANGAROO SHOOT

Another month has passed. The calendar shows that the midwinter is over, and still the much-dreaded New England cold season has not asserted itself. Such weather as we have had in this last week of June has been mild and reassuring. Certes, there have been days when the western blast bit shrewdly keen, and ordinary garments afforded scant protection. In the coming spring there may be wrathful gales, sleet and hail—snow, even. We must not 'hollo till we are out of the wood.'

In the meantime it is not displeasing to see a trifle of mud again—marshes filling with their complement of water; to hear the bittern boom and the wild drake quack in the reed-bordered pool,—sights and sounds to which I have been a stranger for years and years.

The showers have refreshed the long-dry fallows, and a goodly breadth of wheat is now looking green and well-coloured. But to-day I marked three ploughs in one field, availing of the favourable state of tilth. The ordinary processes of a country neighbourhood are in full swing. Loads of hay, top-heavy and fragrant, meet you from time to time upon the metalled highway. A pony-carriage passes, much as it might do in the narrow lanes of Hertfordshire or Essex. The straggling briar and hawthorn hedges have been trimmed lately. All things savour strongly of the old land, from which the district takes its name. As in England, the guns are now in use and request; and amid my peregrinations it chances that I fall upon a custom of the country, which is partly of the nature of work and partly of play.

Yes, it is a kangaroo drive or battue—a measure rendered necessary by the persistent multiplication of these primeval forms, and their tendency to eat and destroy grass, out of all proportion to the value of their skins.

To this gathering I am bidden, and gratefully promise to keep tryst, divining that certain of the neighbours and notables will attend, with wives and daughters in sufficient abundance to warrant a dance after the sterner duties of the day.

And while on the subject of sport and recreation, how little is there worthy of the name in the country districts of Australia. Fishing is there none, or bait fishing at the best; hunting is a tradition of our forefathers; shooting, an infrequent pleasure. Since the introduction of the railway many of the ordinary travelling roads have been practically deserted. The well tried friend or the agreeable stranger no longer halts before the hospitable homestead; months may pass before any social recreation takes place in the sequestered country homes which were wont to be so joyous. But just at the exact period when such resources were strained, the too prolific marsupial has come to the rescue. He it is who now poses as the rescuer of distressed damsels, and *ennuyées châtelaines*, wearying of solitary sweetness as of old; and yet he is classed by reckless utilitarians and prosaic legislators as a noxious animal! Behold us, then, a score of horsemen gaily sallying forth from a station of the olden time,—one of those happy, hospitable dwellings, where, whatever might be the concourse of guests, there was always room for one more,—well mounted, and mostly well armed with the deadly chokebore of the period. The day is cloudy and overcast; but no particular inconvenience is apprehended. The majority of the party are of an age lightly to regard wind or weather. The conversation is free and sportive. Compliments, more or less equivocal, are exchanged as to shooting or horsemanship, and a good deal of schoolboy frolic obtains. Dark hints are thrown out as to enthusiastic sportsmen who blaze away regardless of their 'duty to their neighbour,' and harrowing details given of the last victim at a former 'shoot.'

As we listen to these 'tales for the marines,' uncomfortable thoughts will suggest themselves. We recall the grisly incident in *The Interpreter*; when at a 'wild-schutz' the Prince de Vochsal's bullet glides off a tree-stem and finds a home in Victor De Rohan's gallant breast. Might such a *contretemps* occur to-day? Such things are always on the cards. May not even the rightful possessor of this susceptible heart be widowed ere this very eve, and the callow Boldrewoods be rendered nestless? No matter! One can but die once. It won't be quite so hot as Tel-el-kebir. Even there survivors returned. So we shake up our well-tried steed, shoulder the double-barrel, and ruffle it with the rest, serene in confidence as to the doctrine of chances.

And now after three or four miles' brisk riding o'er hill and dale—the country in these parts may certainly be described as undulating—we come upon a line of recently 'blazed' trees. These are half-way between a ravine or gully, and the crest of a range, to which it runs parallel. As the first man reaches a marked tree, he takes his station, the next in line halting as he comes to the succeeding one. The distances between are perhaps seventy or eighty yards, and each man stands sheltered on one side of his tree-trunk. The number of guns may be some ten or fifteen. The beaters, horsemen also, have gone forward some time since, and our present attitude is one of expectation.

In about ten minutes a sound as of galloping hoofs is heard upon the western side, of ringing stockwhips, shouts and yells, then nearer still the measured 'thud, thud' which tells of the full-grown marsupial. Bang goes a gun at the end of the line; the battle has begun. A curious excitement commences to stir the blood. It is not so much unlike the real thing. And a line of skirmishers in close quarters with an enemy's vedette would be posted like us, and perhaps similarly affected by the first crackling fire of musketry. Two more shots right and left nearer to our position; then half-a-dozen. A volley in our immediate neighbourhood raises expectation and excitement to the highest pitch. 'May Allah protect us! There is but one Prophet,' we have but time to ejaculate, and lo! the marsupial tyrant of our flocks and herds is upon us in force. Here they come, straight for our tree, seven or eight of all sizes, from the innocent 'joey' to the grim ancient, 'the old man,' in the irreverent vernacular of the colonists.

Now is our time. We step bravely from behind our tree and bang into the patriarch's head and shoulders, as for one moment he arrests his mad career in wild astonishment at our sudden apparition.

He staggers, but does not fall. *Habet*, doubtless; but the half-instinctive muscular system enables him to carry off the balance of a cartridge of double B.

As the affrighted flock dashes by, we wheel and accommodate the next largest with a broadside. It is more effective; a smashed hind-leg brings down the fur-bearing 'noxious animal,' which lies helpless and wistful, with large, deer-like eyes. A smart fusilade to the left reveals that the fugitives have fallen among foes in that direction.

The small arms being silent, we quit our trees, each man scalps his victims, giving the *coup-de-grâce* to such of the wounded as need a quietus. No quarter is given—neither age nor sex is spared. Even the infants, those tender weaklings the 'joeys,' are not saved. It is the horrible necessity of war—a war for existence. As thus: If the kangaroo are allowed to live and multiply, our sheep will starve. We can't live if they don't. Ergo, it is our life and welfare against Marsupial Bill's, and he, being of the inferior race, must go under.

One wonders whether this doctrine will be applied in the future to inferior races of men. As the good country of the world gets taken up, I fear me pressure will be brought to bear by the all-absorbing Anglo-Saxons, Teutons, and Slavs upon the weaker races. Wars of extermination have been waged ere now in the history of the world. They may be yet revived, for all we can predicate from existing facts.

As we go down the line the scalps are collected in a bag. We are thus enabled to compare notes as to success. One gentleman has five kangaroos lying around him; he is not certain either whether an active neighbour has not done him out of a scalp. The collecting business having been completed, a move is made for the horses, hung up out of danger, and another paddock is 'driven' with approximate results.

A good morning's work has been done, and a sufficiency of bodily exercise taken by one o'clock, at which time a move is made towards a creek flat, where on the site of a deserted sheep-station, with yards proper, of the olden time, a substantial picnic lunch is spread. Appetites of a superior description seem to be universal, and a season of hearty enjoyment succeeds to that of action.

The spot itself might well have stood for the locality sketched in Lindsay Gordon's unpublished poem. Strange that the poetic gift should enable the possessor to invest with ideal grace a subject so apparently prosaic and homely as a deserted shepherd's hut.

> Can this be where the hovel stood?
> Of old I knew the spot right well;
> One post is left of all the wood,

Three stones lie where the chimney fell.

Rank growth of ferns has well-nigh shut
From sight the ruin of the hut;
There stands the tree where once I cut
　The M that interlaced the L.
　What more is left to tell?

As we were converging towards this spot before lunch, the smart shot of the gathering was made. A forester kangaroo, demoralised by the abnormal events of the day, came dashing up towards the party. He wheeled and fled as we met, and a snap shot but staggered him. Then one of the party dropped the reins on his horse's neck, and with a long shot rolled him over, dead as a rabbit.

A succession of 'drives' make a partial clearance of each paddock, all being taken in turn. The short winter day, accented by heavy showers in the afternoon, begins to darken as we ride homewards, damp but hilarious. The day had been successful on the whole. Plenty of fun, reasonable sport, manly exercise, and a fair bag. Nearly a hundred legal 'raisings' of 'h'ar' prove that the average has been over ten head per gun. Dry clothes, blazing fires, a warm welcome and sympathetic greetings, await us on arrival. The advantage of bearing trifling discomfort, to be compensated by unwonted luxury, presents itself to every logical mind. The dinner was a high festival, where mirth reigned supreme; while the ball in the evening—for had not all dames and demoiselles within twenty miles been impressed for the occasion?—fitly concluded the day's work with a revel of exceptional joyousness.

If there be a moral connected with this 'study in Black and White' it must be that while most people (excepting the advocates for the abolition of capital punishment) admit that it is a good and lawful deed to clear the 'noxious' marsupial off the face of the earth, we trust that the process will not be so swift as to bring speedily to an end such enjoyable gatherings,—these sociable murder parties, wherein business and pleasure are happily conjoined, as in the battue at which I had the happiness to be present.

FIVE MEN'S LIVES FOR ONE HORSE

'Yes; it does seem a goodish price to pay for a half-bred mare—worth ten pound at the outside,' said old Bill, the cook for the rouseabouts at Jergoolah Station, one wet evening, as the men gathered round the fire after supper, with their pipes in their mouths. It had been wet for three days, so there was no shearing. Very little work for the other men either—half a hundred strong—as the wet-fleeced sheep were best left alone. The shearers were sulky of course. They were eating (and paying for) their own rations. But the ordinary 'pound-a-week men,' whose board, with lodging, was provided for them gratis, were philosophically indifferent to the state of the weather.

'I don't care if it rains till Christmas,' remarked a dissipated-looking youth, who had successfully finished a game of euchre with a dirty pack of cards and an equally unclean companion. 'It's no odds to us, so long's the creeks don't rise and block us goin' to the big smoke to blue our cheques. I don't hold with too much fine weather at shearin' time.'

'Why not?' asked his late antagonist, staring gloomily at the cards, as if he held them responsible for his losses.

'Why not?' repeated the first speaker; "cause there's no fun in watchin' of bloomin' shearers makin' their pound and thirty bob a day while we can't raise a mag over three-and-six—at it all hours like so many workin' bullocks, and turned out the minute shearin's over, like a lot of unclaimed strangers after a cattle muster.'

'Why did ye come here at all?' asked a tall, broad-shouldered 'cornstalk' from the neighbourhood of Penrith; 'nobody asked yer. There was plenty for the work afore you struck in. It's you town larrikins that spoil the sheds blackguardin' and gamblin' and growlin' from daylight till dark. If I was the boss I'd set bait for ye, same's the dingoes.'

'You shut up and go home to yer pumpkin patch,' retorted the card-player, with sudden animation. 'You Sydney-siders think no one can work stock but yourselves. You've no right this side of the

Murrumbidgee, if it comes to that; and I'd make one of a crowd to start you back where you come from, and all your blackleg lot.'

'Put up your hands, you spieler!' said the New South Wales man, making one long stride towards the light-weight, who, standing easily on guard, appeared in no way anxious to decline the combat.

'Come, none of that, you Nepean chap,' said a good-humoured, authoritative voice; 'no scrappin' till shearin's over, or I'll stop your pay. Besides, it's a daylight start to-morrow morning. I've a paddock to clear, and the glass is rising. The weather's going to take up.' This was the second overseer, whose word was law until the 'cobbler' was shorn, and the last man with the last sheep left the shed amid derisive cheers. After a little subdued 'growling,' the combatants, there being no grog to inflame their angry passions, subsided.

'What's that old Bill was sayin' about horses and men's lives? I heard it from outside,' demanded the centurion. 'Any duffing going on?'

'Why, Joe Downey passed the remark,' made answer a wiry-looking 'old hand,' then engaged in mending one of his boots so neatly that he might have passed for a journeyman shoemaker, had it not been an open secret that he had learned the trade within the walls of a gaol, 'that if a man was to "shake" a horse here and ride him into Queensland, he'd never be copped.'

'Oh, he wouldn't, eh? And why did Bill get his hair off?'

'Well, Bill he says, "You're a d—d young fool," says he. "I've seen smarter men than you lose their lives over a ten-pound 'oss—yes, and bring better men to the same end."'

'But he said something about five men,' persisted the overseer. 'What did he mean by that?'

'What did I mean by that?' said the old man, who had now drawn nearer, in stern and strident tones. 'Why, what I say. It's God's truth, as I stand here, and the whole five of 'em's now in their graves as fine a lot of men, too, as ever you see—all along of one blasted mare, worth about two fivers, and be hanged to her!'

The old man's speech had a sort of rude eloquence born of earnestness, which chained the attention of the variously composed crowd; and when Mr. Macdonald, the overseer, said, 'Come, Bill, let's have it. It's a lost day, and we may as well hear your yarn as anything else before turn-in time,' the old man, thus adjured, took his pipe out of his mouth, and seating himself upon a three-legged stool, prepared to deliver himself of a singular and tragic experience.

William James, chiefly referred to as 'old Bill,' was a true type of the veritable 'old hand' of pre-auriferous Australia. Concerning an early voyage to Tasmania he was reticent. He referred to the period ambiguously as 'them old times,' when he related tales of mystery and fear, such as could have only found place under the *régime* of forced colonisation. No hirsute ornament adorned his countenance. Deeply wrinkled, but ever clean-shaved, it was a face furrowed and graven, as with a life-record of the darker passions and such various suffering as the human animal alone can endure and live. Out of this furnace of tribulation old Bill had emerged, in a manner purified and reformed. He gave one the impression of a retired pirate—convinced of the defects of the profession, but regretful of its pleasing episodes. Considered as a bush labourer, a more useful individual to a colony did not live. Bill could do everything well, and do twice as much of it as the less indurated industrialist of a later day. Hardy, resourceful, tireless, true to his salt, old Bill had often been considered by the sanguine or inexperienced employer an invaluable servant. And so in truth he was, until the fatal day arrived when the 'cheque fever' assailed him. Then, alas! 'he was neither to hand nor to bind.' No reason, interest, promise or principle had power to restrain him from the mad debauch, when for days—perhaps for weeks—all semblance of manhood was lost.

However, he was now in the healthful stage of constant work—well fed, paid and sheltered. Cooking was one of his many accomplishments: in it he excelled. While, despite his age, his courage and determination sufficed to keep the turbulent 'rouseabouts' in order. In his leisure hours he was prone to improve the occasion by demonstrating the folly of colliding with the law—its certain victory, its terrible penalties. And of the gloomy sequel to a solitary act was the present story.

'I mind,' he began—pushing back the grey hair which he wore long and carefully brushed—'when I was workin' on a run near the

Queensland border. It's many a long year ago—but that says nothin'; some of you chaps is as young and foolish as this Jack Danvers as I'm a-goin' to tell ye about. Well, some of us was startin' a bit of a spree like, after shearin'; we'd all got tidy cheques; some was goin' one way and some another. Jack and his mate to Queensland, where they expected a big job of work. Just as we was a-saddlin' up—some of us had one neddy, some two—a mob of horses comes by. I knew who they belonged to—a squatter not far off. Among 'em was a fine lump of a brown filly, three year old, half bred, but with good action.

"'That's a good filly," says Jack—he'd had a few glasses—"she could be roped handy in the old cattle-yard near the crick. Lead easy too, 'long with the other mokes."

"'Don't be a darned fool, Jack," says I; "there'll be a bloomin' row over her, you take it from me. She's safe to be missed, and you'll be tracked up. D—n it all, man," says I, "what's a ten-pound filly for a man to lose his liberty over? If it was a big touch it might be different."

"'You're a fine cove to preach," says he, quite savage. The grog had got into his head, I could see. "Mind your own — — business." I heard his mate (he was a rank bad 'un) say something to him, and they rode away steady; but the same road that the "mob" had gone. I went off with some other chaps as wer' inside having a last drink, and thought no more about Jack Danvers and the brown filly till nigh a year after. Then it come out. The filly'd been spotted, working in a team, by the man that bred her. The carrier bought her square and honest; had a receipt from a storekeeper. They found the storekeeper in Queensland; he'd bought her from another man. "What sort of a man?"—"Why, a tall, good-looking chap, like a flash shearer." Word went to the police at Warwillah. It was Jack Danvers of course; they'd suspected him and his mate all the time.

'Well, Jack was nabbed, tho' he was out on a Queensland diggin' far enough away. But they sent up his description from the shed we'd left together, and he was brought down in irons, as he'd made a fight of it. The storekeeper swore to him positive as the man that had sold him the brown J.D. filly—old Jerry Dawson's she was. The jury found him guilty and he got three years.

'Now I'm on to the part of the play when the "ante-up" comes in. You mind me, you young fellers, it *always does* sooner or later. He'd no call to shake that filly. I said so then, and I say so now. And what come'd of it? Listen and I'll tell you—*Death* in five chapters—and so simple, all along of an unbroke filly!

'Now Jack wa'n't the man to stop inside of prison walls if he could help it. He and another chap make a rush one day, knock over the warder and collar his revolver. Another warder comes out to help; Jack shoots him dead, and they clear. *Man's life number one.* Big reward offered. They stick up a roadside inn next. Somebody gave 'em away. Police waitin' on 'em as they walk in—dead of night. Soon's they see the police, Jack shoots the innkeeper, poor devil! thought he'd sold 'em. *Man's life number two.* Jack and his mate and the police bang away at each other at close quarters—trooper wounded—Jack shot dead—mate wounded, dies next day. *Men's lives number four.*

'Who gave the office to the police and collared the blood-money? Friend of Jack's, a pal. Five hundred quid was too much for him. What became of *him*? Job leaked out somehow—friends and family dropped him. The money did him no good. Took to drinking straight ahead, and died in the horrors within the year. *Men's lives number five.*

'Yes; he was the fifth man to go down. Two pound apiece their lives fetched! They're in their graves because Jack Danvers was a d—d fool, and when he was young, strong, good-looking and well-liked, must go and duff a man's mare out of sheer foolishness. He didn't see what was to come of it, or he'd 'a cut off his right hand first. But that's the way of it. We don't see them things till it's *too late*. But mark my words, you young chaps as has got all the world before you— take a fool's advice. *It don't pay to "go on the cross"*—never did; and there's no one has cause to know it better than old Bill James.'

'By George!' said the overseer, 'that's the best yarn I have heard for a year. And if the parson preaches a better sermon when he holds service in the woolshed next Sunday, I'll be surprised.'

REEDY LAKE STATION

The Post-office clock in Bourke Street, Melbourne, is about to strike six, in the month of June 1858. At this 'everlastingly early hour A.M. in the morning' (as remarked by Mr. Chuckster), I am the box-passenger of Cobb's coach, *en route* for Bendigo. The team of greys stand motionless, save for a faint attempt to paw on the part of the near-side leader. The first stroke vibrates on high. Mr. Jackson, with an exclamation, tightens his 'lines.' The six greys plunge at their collars, and we are off.

There was no Spencer Street terminus in those days. We were truly thankful to King Cobb. I, for one, was glad to get over a hundred miles of indifferent road in a day—winter weather, too. We did not grumble so comprehensively as latter-day travellers.

Remembered yet, how, when we came to the long hill at Keilorbridge, the driver let his horses out when half-way down. The pace that we went 'was a caution to see.' The wheel-spokes flew round, invisible to the naked eye. The coach rocked in a manner to appal the nervous. The horses lay down to it as if they were starting for a Scurry Stakes. But it was a good piece of macadam, and we were half-way up to the next hill before any one had time to think seriously of the danger.

Nobody, of course, would have dared to have addressed the driver upon the subject. In those flush days, when both day and night coaches loaded well, when fares were high and profits phenomenal, he was an autocrat not to be lightly approached. It almost took two people to manage a communication—one to bear the message from the other. Silent or laconic, master of his work in a marvellous degree, he usually resented light converse, advice infuriated him, and sympathy was outrage.

The roads were bad, even dangerous in places. Muddy creeks, bush-tracks, sidelings, washed-out crossings, increased the responsibilities and tried the tempers of these pioneer sons of Nimshi. Men of mark they mostly were. Americans to a man in that day, though subsequently native-born Australians, acclimatised Irishmen, and other recruits of merit, began to show up in the ranks.

I remember the astonishment of a newly-arrived traveller at seeing Carter, a gigantic, fair-bearded Canadian, coming along a baddish road one wet day, with seven horses and a huge coach, containing about fifty Chinamen. How he swayed the heavy reins with practised ease, his three leaders at a hand-gallop; how he piloted his immense vehicle through stumps and ruts, by creek and hillside, with accuracy almost miraculous to the uninitiated.

Mr. Carter was not a 'man of much blandishment.' I recall the occasion, when a spring having gone wrong, he was, with the assistance of a stalwart passenger, silently repairing damage. A frivolous insider commenced to condole and offer suggestions in a weakly voluble way. 'Go to h—l,' was the abrupt rejoinder, which so astonished the well-meaning person, that he retreated into the coach like a rabbit into a burrow, and was silent for hours afterwards.

One always had the consciousness, however, that whatever could be done by mortal man, would be accomplished by them. Accidents might happen, but they belonged to the category of the inevitable.

One dark night, near Sawpit Gully, a tire came off. Al. Hamilton (poor fellow! he was killed by an upset in New South Wales afterwards) was off in a minute; found his way to the smith's house; had him back in an inconceivably short time; left word for us to get the fire lighted and blown up—it was cold, and we thought that great fun; and before another man would have finished swearing at the road, the darkness, and things in general, the hammer was clinking on the red-hot tire, the welding was progressing, and in three-quarters of an hour we were bowling along much as before. We had time to make up, and did it too. But suppose the blacksmith would not work? Not work! He was Cobb and Co.'s man—that is, he did all their 'stage' repairs. Well he knew that the night must be to him even as the day when their humblest vehicle on the road needed his aid. As a firm they went strictly by results and took no excuses. If a man upset his coach and did damage once, he was shifted to another part of the line. If he repeated the accident, he was dismissed. There was no appeal, and the managing body did not trouble about evidence after the first time. If he was negligent, it served him right. If he was unlucky, that was worse.

The journey to Bendigo was accomplished at the rate of nine miles an hour, stoppages included. It was midwinter. The roads were deep in places. It was therefore good-going, punctual relays, and carefully economised time, which combined to land us at Hefferman's Hotel before darkness had set in. As usual a crowd had collected to enjoy the great event of the day.

Bendigo was in that year a very lively town, with a population roused to daily excitement by fortunes made or lost. Gold was shovelled up like sugar in bankers' scoops, and good money sent after bad in reckless enterprise, or restored a hundredfold in lucky ventures.

Here I was to undergo a new experience in company with Her Majesty's Mails.

As I rather impatiently lingered outside of Hefferman's after breakfast next morning, an unpretending tax-cart, to which were harnessed a pair of queer, unmatched screws, drove up to the door. 'German Charlie'—his other name I never knew—driver and contractor, informed me that I was the only passenger, lifted my valise, and the talismanic words 'Reedy Creek' being pronounced, vowed to drop me at the door. He had always parcels for Mr. Keene. This gentleman's name he pronounced with bated breath, in a tone of deepest veneration.

Beyond all doubt would I be landed there early on the morrow.

I mounted the Whitechapel, saw my overcoat and valise in safely, and, not without involuntary distrust, committed myself to Charlie's tender mercies. He gave a shout, he raised his whip—the off-side horse made a wild plunge; the near-side one, blind of one eye, refused to budge. Our fate hung on the balance apparently, when a man from the crowd quietly led off the unwilling near-side, and we dashed away gloriously. The pace was exceptional, but it was evidently inexpedient to slacken speed. We flew down the main street, and turned northward, along a narrow track, perilously near to yawning shafts, across unsafe bridges, over race channels; along corduroy roads, or none at all, our headlong course was pursued. The sludge-invaded level of Meyer's Flat is passed. Bullock Creek is reached, all ignorant of reservoirs and weirs, and a relay of horses driven in from the bush is demanded.

A smart boy of fourteen had the fresh team, three in number, ready for us in the yard. He felt it necessary to warn us. They 'were not good starters, that was a fact.' The statement was strictly correct. One horse was badly collar-galled, one a rank jib. The leader certainly had a notion of bolting; his efforts in that direction were, however, neutralised by the masterly inactivity of his companions. After much pushing, persuasion, and profane language, we effected a departure.

That the pace was kept up afterwards may be believed. Sometimes the harness gave way, but as the shaft and outrigger horses were by this time well warmed, they did not object to again urge on their wild career.

We stopped at the 'Durham Ox Inn' that night, then a solitary lodge in the wilderness, a single building of brick, visible afar off on the sea-like plain, which stretched to the verge of the horizon. Woods Brothers and Kirk had at that time, if I mistake not, just concluded to purchase Pental Island from Ebden and Keene, but were debating as to price. The pasture seemed short and sparse, after the deep, rich western sward, but overtaking a 'mob' of Messrs. Booth and Argyle's cattle farther on, I felt satisfied as to its fattening qualities. Each cow, calf, steer, and yearling in the lot was positively heaped and cushioned with fat. They looked like stall-fed oxen. And this in June! I thought I saw then what the country could do. I was correct in my deduction, always supposing the important factor of *rain* not to be absent. Of this, in my inexperience, I took no heed. In my favoured district there was always a plentiful supply; sometimes, indeed, more than was agreeable or necessary.

Kerang was passed; Tragowel skirted; Mount Hope, then in the occupation of Messrs. Griffith and Greene, reared its granite mass a few miles to the south. As Sir Thomas Mitchell stood there, gazing over the illimitable prairie, rich with giant herbage and interspersed but with belts and copses of timber, planted by Nature's hand, the veteran explorer exclaimed with a burst of enthusiasm, 'Australia Felix! This is indeed Australia Felix!'

Steady stocking and an occasional dry season had somewhat modified the standard of the nutritive grasses and salsolaceous plants, at this point advantageously mingled. But that the country was superlative in a pastoral point of view may be gathered from the fact that, upon my first visit to the homestead a few weeks afterwards, I saw five thousand weaners—the whole crop of lambs for the previous year—*shepherded in one flock*. Very fine young sheep they were, and in excellent condition. Of course it was on a plain, but, unless the pasturage had been exceptional, no shepherd could have kept such a number together.

Later in the afternoon my Teutonic conductor, who had been going for the last twenty miles like the dark horseman in Burger's ballad, pulled up at Reedy Lake Head Station. There dwelt the resident partner and autocrat of his district, Mr. Theophilus Keene.

I saw a slight, fair man with an aquiline nose, a steady grey eye, and an abundant beard, who came out of a neat two-roomed slab hut and greeted me with polished courtesy. 'He was extremely glad to see me. He had looked forward to my coming this week in terms of a letter he had received from Messrs. Ryan and Hammond, but, indeed, had hardly expected that I would trust myself to their mail.'

Mr. Keene, whom I saw then for the first time, was probably verging on middle age, though active and youthful in appearance, above the middle height, yet not tall—of a figure inclined indeed to spareness. He impressed me with the idea that he was no commonplace individual.

He carried nothing of the bushman about his appearance, at home or in town, being careful and *soigné* as to his apparel, formal and somewhat courtly in his address. He scarcely gave one the idea of a dweller in the waste; yet the roughest experiences of overlanding squatter-life, of a leader of the rude station and road hands, had been his. He looked more like a dandy Civil Servant of the upper grades. Yet he was more than a pioneer and manager—an astute diplomatist, a clever correspondent, an accurate accountant. The books of the Reedy Lake Station were kept as neatly as those of a counting-house. The overseer's sheep-books, ration accounts, and road expenses were audited as correctly as if in an office. The great station-machine revolved easily, and, though unaided by inventions which have smoothed the path of latter-day pastoralists, was a striking illustration of successful administration.

This large and important sheep property, as it was held to be in those primeval times, had considerably over 150,000 sheep on its books. Reedy Lake stood for the whole, but Quambatook, Murrabit, Lake Boga, Liegar, Pental Island and other runs were also comprised within its boundaries. These were separate communities, and were, upon the subdivision of the property, sold as such. These were worked under the supervision of overseers and sub-managers, each of whom had to render account to Mr. Keene—a strict one, too—of every sheep counted out to the shepherds of the division in his charge.

Mr. Ebden, erstwhile Treasurer of Victoria and for some years a member of Parliament, was the senior partner. He had sagaciously secured Mr. Keene, then wasting his powers on the Lower Murray, by offering him a third share of the property, with the position of resident partner and General Manager. Mr. Ebden, residing in Melbourne, arranged the financial portion of the affairs, while Mr. Keene was the executive chief, with almost irresponsible powers, which he used unreservedly—no doubt about that.

This was the day, let it be premised, of 'shepherding,' pure and simple. There were, in that district at least, no wire fences, no great enclosures, no gates, no tanks. Improvements, both great and small, were looked upon as superfluous forms of expensiveness. To keep the shepherds in order, to provide them with rations and other necessaries, to see that they neither lost the sheep nor denied them reasonable range,—these were the chief duties of those in authority. And tolerably anxious and engrossing occupation they afforded.

Thus the great Reedy Lake Head Station, always mentioned with awe, north of the Loddon, was not calculated to strike the stranger with amazement on account of its buildings and constructions, formed on the edge of the fresh-water lake from which it took its name. The station comprised Mr. Keene's two-roomed hut aforesaid; also a larger one, where the overseers, young gentlemen, and strangers abode—known as The Barracks; the kitchen, a detached building; the men's huts, on the shore of the lake, at some considerable distance; an inexpensive, old-fashioned woolshed might be discerned among the 'old-man salt-bush' nearly a mile away; a hundred acre horse-paddock, surrounded by a two-railed sapling fence; a stock-yard—*voilà tout*; there was, of course, a store. These were all the buildings thought necessary for the management of £150,000 worth of sheep in that day. How different would be the appearance of such a property now!

The special errand upon which I had journeyed thus far was to inspect and, upon approval, to accept an offer in writing, which I carried with me, of the Murrabit Station, one of the subdivisions of the Reedy Lake property, having upon it sixteen thousand sheep and *no improvements whatever*, except the shepherds' huts and a hundred hurdles. The price was £24,000—one-third equal to cash, the remainder by bills extending over three years.

The tide of investment had set in strongly in the direction of sheep properties, near or across the Murray. I had followed the fashion for the purpose, presumably, of making the usual fortune more rapidly than through the old-fashioned medium of cattle. To this end it was arranged that Mr. Keene and I, with one of the overseers whom I had known previously, should on the morrow ride over and inspect the Murrabit country and stock, lying some twenty miles distant from Reedy Lake.

It is held to be bad form in Bushland to mount an intending purchaser badly. It is unnecessary to say that it was not done in this case. No detail was omitted to produce a state of cheerful self-complacency, suited to the distinguished rôle of guest and buyer. When Mr. Keene's famous pony Billy, an animal whose fame was heralded in two colonies, and from the Loddon to the Murrumbidgee, was led forth, I felt I was indeed the favoured guest. He certainly was 'the horse you don't see now,' or, if so, very very rarely. Neat as to forehand, with a round rib and powerful quarter, fast, easy, and up to weight, he was difficult to match. The area from Kerang northwards was known as 'salt-bush' country. But little grass showed except on the edges of watercourses. Bare patches of red sandy loam between the salsolaceous plants did not lead the early explorers to consider it first-rate pasturage. Varieties, however, were plentiful, from the 'old-man salt-bush,' seven to ten feet high, to the dwarf-growing but fattening plants on the plain. The cotton-bush, too, known to indicate first-class fattening country, was plentiful. Perhaps the best testimony to the quality of the herbage, however, and which I was sufficiently experienced to appreciate, was the uniform high health and condition of every flock of sheep that we saw. Nothing could be finer than their general appearance, as indeed is always the case in reasonably stocked salt bush country; no foot rot, no fluke, and, *absit omen*, no sheep-scab. This dire disease was then, unhappily, common in Western Victoria. It had been a fair season. Everything was fit to bear inspection. The wether flock looked like donkeys for size, the breeding ewes were fit for market, the weaners precociously fat and well-grown. Nothing could look better than the whole array.

Besides the salt-bush country, plains chiefly, and a large dry lake, there was an important section of the run known as 'The Reed-beds,' which I was anxious to visit. This tract lay between Lake Boga, a large fresh-water lake on one side, the Murrabit, an anabranch, and the south bank of the Murray. In order to ride over this it was arranged that we should camp at the hut of a shepherd, known as 'Towney,' on Pental Island, thence explore the reed-beds and see the remaining sheep on the morrow.

Pental Island, formed by the Murrabit, a deep wide stream, which leaves the main river channel and re-enters lower down, we found to be a long, narrow strip of land, having sound salt-bush ridges in the centre, with reed-beds on either side. Crossing by a rude but sufficient bridge, we discovered Mr. 'Towney' living an Alexander Selkirk sort of life, monarch of all he surveyed, and with full charge of some ten or twelve thousand sheep turned loose. The bridge being closed with hurdles, they could not get away. His only duty was to see that no enterprising dingo swam over from Murray Downs on the opposite side and ravaged the flock.

The night was cloudless and starlit, lovely in all aspects, as are chiefly those of the Riverina—an absolutely perfect winter climate. The strange surroundings, the calm river, the untroubled hush of the scene, the chops, damper, and tea, all freshly prepared by Towney, were enjoyable enough. After a talk by the fire, for the night air was cool, and a smoke, we lay down on rugs and blankets and slept till dawn. Our entertainer was dejected because he had not a Murray cod to offer us. 'If we had only come last week.' 'Tis ever thus.

That day's ride showed me the reed-beds in the light of sound, green, quickly-fattening pastures. At one angle of the Murrabit, on *my* run—for my run, indeed, it was destined to be—there were two flocks of sheep, five thousand in all, of which the shepherds and hut-keeper inhabited the same hut. It was managed thus. One flock was camped on the northern side of the bridge, one on the other. The hut-keeper, long disestablished, but then considered an indispensable functionary, cooked for both shepherds. £30 a year with rations was the wage for the shepherds; £25 for the hut-keeper.

Then there was a frontage of, perhaps, a mile and a half to the southern end of Lake Boga. This noble fresh-water lake, having shelving, sandy shores, is filled by the rising of the Murray. On the bluff, to the right of the road to Swan Hill, was a curious non-Australian cottage, built by Moravian missionaries, and situated upon a reserve granted to them by the Government of Victoria. These worthy personages, becoming discouraged at the slow conversion of the heathen, or deeming the *locale* unsuitable, sold their right and interest to Messrs. Ebden and Keene. I decided to place the head station close by, and there, I suppose, it is at the present day.

A picturesque spot enough. Northward the eye ranged over the broad, clear waters of the lake, now calm in the bright sunshine, now lashed into quite respectable waves by a gale. Eastward, over a wide expanse of reed-bed, dead level and brightly green, you traced the winding course of the great river by the huge eucalypti which lined its banks. Around was the unending plain, on which the salt-bushes grew to an unusual size, while across the main road to Melbourne, fenced off by the horse-paddock of the future, was a cape of pine-scrub, affording pleasing contrast to the wide, bare landscape.

We returned to Reedy Lake that evening, and before I slept was the contract signed, accepting price and terms; signed in high hope, and apparently with a fair prospect of doubling the capital invested, as had done many another. Had I but known that this particular indenture, freely translated, *should have run thus:*—

'I hereby bind myself to take the Murrabit Run and stock at the price agreed, and to lose in consequence every farthing I have ever made, within five years from this date.

'(Signed) R. BOLDREWOOD.'

Why can't one perceive such results and consequences now and then? Why are so many of the important contracts and irrevocable promises of life entered into during one's most sanguine, least reflective period? Will these questions ever be answered, and where? Still, were the veil lifted, what dread apparitions might we not behold! 'Tis more mercifully arranged, be sure.

Thus we entered with a light heart into this Sedan business, much undervaluing our Prussians. After visiting Melbourne, it was arranged that delivery of stock and station should be taken within a specified time.

I didn't know much about sheep then; what a grim jest it reads like *now*! I had leisure for reflection on the subject in the aftertime. I judged it well to leave the apportioning of the flocks to my host and entertainer. He did far better for me than I could have done myself. I had every reason to be satisfied with the quality of the sixteen thousand instruments of my ruin. There was a noble flock of fat wethers, three thousand strong; for the rest, 'dry' ewes, breeders, weaners, two-tooths, were all good of their sort. After engaging one of the overseers, a shrewd, practical personage, I considered the establishment of my reputation as a successful wool-grower to be merely a question of time.

The Fiend is believed to back gamblers at an early stage of their career. It looked as if His Eminence gave my dice a good shake *pour commencer*. The first sale was brilliant: the whole cast of fat sheep to one buyer (at the rate of £1 each for wethers, and 15s. for ewes) — over six thousand in all. They were drafted, paid for, and on their way to Melbourne in the afternoon of the day on which the buyer arrived. The lambing was good; the wool sold at a paying price, considering the primitive style of washing. Next year, of course, all this would be altered. Meanwhile I surveyed the imprint 'R.B.' over Murrabit on the wool-bales with great satisfaction.

'But surely,' says the practical reader, 'things were going well; season, prices, increase satisfactory. How did the fellow manage to make a mull of it?' There *were* reasons. The cost of a run bought 'bare' is unavoidably great. Huts, yards, woolshed, homestead, paddock, brushyards, lambers, washers, shearers, all cost money—are necessary, but expensive. The cheque stream was always flowing with a steady current, it seemed to me. Fat stock, too, the great source of profit in that district, gradually declined in price. Interest and commission, which amounted to 12½ per cent or more, in one way and another, gradually told up. In 1861 an unprecedented fall took place in cattle, such as had not been felt 'since the gold.' Beeves fell to the price of stores. Buyers could not meet their engagements. The purchaser of my cattle-station in Western Victoria was among these. He was compelled to return it upon my hands after losing his cash deposit. Thus seriously hampered, the finale was that I 'came out' without either station or a shilling in the world. What was worse, having caused others to suffer through my indebtedness.

The Murrabit was then sold, well improved, though not fenced, with twenty thousand good sheep on it, at £1: 5s. per head—£25,000—nearly the same price at which I had purchased; but with four thousand more sheep, and costly improvements added, including a woolshed which had cost £500. The new purchaser paid £10,000 down, and I was sorry to hear afterwards lost everything in about the time it had taken me to perform the same feat. But he had, I believe, the expense of fencing—an economical luxury then so impossible for a squatter to deny himself. In addition to this, that terrible synonym of ruin, sheep-scab, broke out in the district, and in time among the Murrabit sheep. This, of course, necessitated endless expenditure in labour, dressing-yards, dips, and what not. No further explanation is needed by the experienced as to why my equally unlucky successor went under.

Talking of scab—now a tradition in Australia—it was then plentiful in Victoria, with the exception of certain favoured districts, among which the trans-Loddon country was numbered. Now in the days when Theophilus was king, foreseeing the ruin of the district (or chiefly, perhaps, to Ebden and Keene) which would ensue should the disease get a footing, he fought against its introduction, either by carelessness or greed, with all the vigilant energy of his nature.

There are men of contemplation, of science, of culture, of action. My experience has been that these qualities are but rarely united in the same individual. This may be the reason why 'Government by Talk' often breaks down disastrously—the man who can talk best being helpless and distracted when responsible action is imminent. This by the way, however. Mr. Keene did not dissipate his intelligence in the consideration of abstract theories. He never, probably, in his life saw three courses open to him. But in war time he struck hard and promptly. In most cases there was no need to strike twice.

Touching the scab pestilence, this is how he 'saved his country.' Primarily he put pressure upon his neighbours, until they formed themselves into a league, offensive and defensive. They did not trust to the Government official, presumably at times overworked, but they paid a private Inspector £200 a year, furnishing him also with serviceable horses and free quarters.

This gentleman—Mr. Smith, let us call him—an active young Australian, kept the sharpest look-out on all sheep approaching the borders of the 'Keene country.' He summoned the persons in charge if they made the least infraction of the Act, examined the flock most carefully for appearances of disease, and generally made life so unpleasant, not to say dangerous, for the persons in charge, that they took the first chance of altering their route. If there was the faintest room for doubt, down came Keene, breathing threats and slaughter. And only after the most rigid, prolonged inspection were they allowed to pass muster. Why persons selfishly desired to carry disease into a clean district may be thus explained. Store sheep—especially if doubtful as to perfect cleanliness—were low in price in Western Victoria. Near to or across the New South Wales border they were always high. If, therefore, they could be driven to the Murray, the profits were considerable. No doubt such were made, at the risk of those proprietors through whose stations they passed. A *single sheep* left behind from such a flock, after weeks likely to 'break out' with the dire disease, might infect a district. Mr. Keene had fully determined that 'these accursed gains' should not be made at *his* expense.

One day he received notice from Mr. Smith that a lot of five thousand sheep of suspicious antecedents was approaching his kingdom. They were owned by a dealing squatter, who, having country both clean and doubtful, made it a pretext for travelling sheep, picked up in small numbers. 'From information received' just ere they had entered the clean country, Mr. Keene appeared with a strong force, with which he took possession of them under a warrant, obtained on oath that they were presumably scabby, had them examined by the Government official, who found the fatal acarus, obtained the necessary authority, *cut their throats, and burned the five thousand to the last sheep.*

After this holocaust, remembered to this day, it became unfashionable to travel sheep near the Reedy Lake country. He 'who bare rule over all that land' rested temporarily from his labours. They were not light either, as may be inferred from a statement of one of his overseers to me that about that time, from ceaseless work in the saddle, anxiety, and worry, he had reduced himself to an absolute skeleton, and from emaciation could hardly sit on his horse. Nothing, perhaps, but such unrelenting watch and ward could have saved the district from infection. But he won the fight, and for years after, not, indeed, until Theophilus I. was safe in another hemisphere, did marauders of the class he so harried and vexed dare to cross the Loddon northwards. As soon as the normal state of carelessness and 'nobody's business' set in (Mr. Smith having been discontinued), the event foreseen by him took place. The district became infected, and Reedy Lake itself, Murrabit, and other runs, all suffered untold loss and injury. Rabbits came in to complete the desolation. What with Pental Island being advertised to be let by tender in farms, dingoes abounding in the mallee, free selectors swarming from Lake Charm to the Murray, irrigation even being practised near Kerang, if Mr. Keene could return to the country where once he could ride for forty miles on end requiring any man he met to state what he was doing there, he would find himself a stranger in a strange land. Without doubt he would take the first steamer back to England, hastening to lose sight and memory of a land so altered and be-devilled since the reign of the shepherd kings. Of this dynasty I hold 'Theophilus the First' to have been a more puissant potentate during his illustrious reign than many of the occupants of old-world thrones.

A FORGOTTEN TRAGEDY

It is difficult for the inhabitants of settled districts in Australia, where the villages, surrounded by farms or grazing estates, are now as well ordered as in rural England, to realise the nature of outrages which, in earlier colonial days, not infrequently affrighted these sylvan shades. It is well, however, occasionally to recall the sterner conditions under which our pioneers lived. The half-explored wilds saw strange things, when *émeutes* with murder and robbery thrown in compelled decisive action. In the year 1836 immense areas in the interior, described officially as 'Waste Lands of the Crown,' were occupied by graziers under pastoral licenses. Caution was exercised in the granting of these desirable privileges. It was required by the Government of the day that only persons of approved good character should receive them. Being merely permissive, they were liable to be withdrawn from the holders for immoral or dishonest conduct. When it is considered that the men employed in guarding the flocks and herds in these limitless solitudes were, in the great majority of cases, prisoners of the Crown, or 'ticket-of-leave' men, whose partially-expired sentences entitled them to quasi-freedom, it is not surprising that horse-and cattle-stealing, highway robbery, ill-treatment of aboriginals, and even darker crimes were rife.

The labourers of the day were composed of three classes, officially described as free, bond, and 'free by servitude.' This last designation, obscure only to the newly-arrived colonist, meant that the individual thus privileged had served his full term of imprisonment, or such proportion of it as entitled him to freedom under certain restrictions. He was permitted to come and go, to work for any master who chose to employ him (and most valuable servants many of them were), to accept the wages of the period, and generally to comport himself as a 'free man.' But he was restricted to a specified district, compelled at fixed periods to report himself to the police authorities, and he went in fear lest at any time through misconduct or evil report his 'ticket-of-leave' might be withdrawn, in which case he was sent back to penal servitude. The alternative was terrible. The man who the week before had been riding a mettled stock-horse amid the plains and forests of the interior, or peacefully following his flocks, with food, lodging, and social privileges, found himself virtually a slave in a chain-gang, dragging his heavy fetters to and fro in hard, distasteful labour. This deposition from partial comfort and social equality, though possibly caused by his own misconduct, occasionally resulted from the report of a vindictive overseer, or betrayal by a comrade. It may be imagined, therefore, what vows of vengeance were registered by the sullen convict, what bloody expiation was often exacted.

Taking into consideration the ludicrous disproportion of the police furnished by the Government of the day to the area 'protected'—say a couple of troopers for a thinly-populated district about the size of Scotland—it seems truly astonishing that malefactors should have been brought to justice at all. Even more so that armed and desperate felons should have been followed up and arrested within comparatively short distances of the scene of their misdeeds.

It says much for the alertness and discipline of the mounted police force of the day that in by far the greater number of these outrages the criminals were tracked and secured; more, indeed, for the active co-operation and public spirit of the country gentlemen of the land, who were invariably ready to render aid in carrying out the law at the risk of their lives, and, occasionally, to the manifest injury of their property.

Circumstances have placed in my hands the record of a murder which, in careful premeditation, as well as in the satanic malignity with which the details were carried out, seems pre-eminent amid the dark chronicles of guilt.

More than sixty years ago Mr. Thursby, a well-known magistrate and proprietor, residing upon his station, which was distant two hundred and fifty miles from Sydney, was awakened before daylight, when a note to this effect from the constable in charge at the nearest police-station was delivered to him:—

'Last night the lock-up was entered by armed men, and two prisoners removed. One man knocked at the door, stating that he was a constable with a prisoner in charge. I opened it; when two men rushed in, one of whom, presenting a pistol at me, ordered me into a corner, and covered my head with a blanket. I heard the door unlocked. When I freed myself the cell was empty.'

Upon receipt of this information, Mr. Thursby despatched a report to the Officer in charge of Police at Murphy's Plains, distant eighty-five miles. Taking with him the manager of a neighbouring station, and the special constable quartered there (a custom of the day), Mr. Thursby started in pursuit of the outlaws. Their tracks were not hard to follow in the dew of early morn, but near Major Hewitt's station, seven miles distant, they became indistinct. After losing much time the station was reached, and here a black boy was fortunately procured. With his aid the trail was regained, and followed over rough, mountainous country. Mr. Jones, the manager who had accompanied the party, informed Mr. Thursby that five of the convict servants assigned to the owner had run away previously— 'taken to the bush.' They had committed depredations, and had been unsuccessfully followed by the mounted police, whose horses, after coming more than eighty miles, were fagged. However, two of them surrendered themselves next day. One man (Driscoll) was suspected of having spoken incautiously of the leader's doings (a man named Gore), who had vowed vengeance accordingly. Driscoll had been placed in the lock-up, along with Woods, a suspicious character, who said he was a native of Windsor, New South Wales. Gore and the other men were still at large.

After leading the party for some distance through the ranges, the black boy halted, and pointing to a thin thread of smoke, barely perceptible, said, 'There 'moke!' When they came to the fire from which it proceeded, what a spectacle presented itself! On the smouldering embers was a human body, bound and *partially roasted*. It lay on its back, with legs and arms drawn up. The middle portion of the body was burned to a cinder, leaving the upper and lower extremities perfect. Mr. Thursby recognised the features of the man called Woods, who had been imprisoned the day before. The black boy was so horrified that he became useless as a tracker, and as the day was far advanced, Mr. Thursby had the body removed to Engleroi, a station not more than a mile distant.

Here fresh information was furnished. The tragedy deepened. Before daylight on the previous morning, Driscoll had knocked at the door of the shepherd's hut, breathless and half insane with terror, imploring them for the love of God to admit him as 'he was a murdered man.' Nothing more could be elicited from the shepherds, though it since appeared that they could have named one of the murderers. Fear of the 'Vehmgericht' of the day doubtless restrained them — fear of that terrible secret tribunal, administered by the convicts as a body, which in defiance of the law's severest penalties tried, sentenced, and in many cases *executed*, the objects of their resentment. The party decided later on to proceed to Mr. FitzGorman's head station, and on the way arrested and took with them the hut-keeper of the out-station. They did not know at the time (as was since proved) that he was one of the murderers.

On leaving the lock-up, the men had stolen the constable's blue cloth suit, and being informed at Tongah that a man in blue clothes had been met with, a few miles down the Taramba River, Mr. Thursby rode forward with the black boy, leaving the hut-keeper secured, to await his return. Some time was lost, as the tracks were not picked up at once, but on reaching Mr. FitzGorman's station, forty miles distant, at midnight, the man in blue clothes was discovered, housed for the night. He was at once secured. On being questioned, he said his name was Burns, and that he was looking for work. He produced a certificate, which did not impose upon his captor, who knew it to belong to the constable, who, being a ticket-of-leave man, required to hold such a document. In his bundle, when searched, several articles taken from the lock-up were found. Gore the bushranger and murderer stood confessed.

Mr. Thursby was at that time ignorant that the second murderer was already in his hands, but determined to follow up the pursuit, caused Gore to be mounted on one of the station horses, and rode back with as much speed as might be to Tongah. Suspecting the hut-keeper (whose name was Walker) of being in some way an accomplice of Gore, Mr. Thursby had both men lodged in the lock-up. Still unrelaxing in pursuit, and believing that the second murderer might be one of the three runaways from Major Hewitt's station, Mr. Thursby raised the country-side, and took such energetic measures that on the following day they were apprehended.

By this time the shepherds, gaining confidence from the capture of the outlaws, of whose vengeance they went in fear, commenced to make disclosures. The constable identified the hut-keeper (Walker) as the man who, at the point of the pistol, ordered him to stand in the lock-up. Driscoll knew him and Gore as the two men who removed him and Woods from the lock-up. He then went on to state that, after being hurried along for several miles after leaving the lock-up, they halted in a lonely place, where Gore ordered them to make a fire. When it was kindled to a blaze, Gore tied them back to back and blindfolded them. At this time Walker held the pistol. Driscoll heard a shot, when Woods dropped on the fire, dragging him with him. The bandage falling from his eyes, Walker struck him twice on the head with his pistol. In his agony, getting his hands free he ran for his life. He was followed for a considerable distance, but eventually escaped to Engleroi. Half an hour afterwards, Gore came up in search of him. What must have been the feelings of the hunted wretch, so lately a bound victim on his self-made funeral pile, when the armed desperado, who made so little of human life, reappeared? However, he contented himself with compelling Driscoll and the shepherds, among whom he was, to swear under tremendous penalties not to disclose the fact of his presence there.

Gore and Walker were brought before the nearest Bench of Magistrates and committed for trial at the next ensuing Assize Court.

There was not sufficient evidence, though a strong presumption, that the other runaways were implicated in the cold-blooded murder. It appeared to have been chiefly arranged by Gore and Walker—the former in order to be revenged on Driscoll, and the latter to get rid of Woods, who had threatened to give evidence against him for robbery and other misdeeds. No doubt their intention was to murder both men, destroying all evidence by burning their bodies. Driscoll had the good fortune to escape, and was thus enabled to give the necessary evidence at their trial. But though not directly implicated in the graver crime, the remaining three bushrangers—for such they were—lay under the charge of being associated with Gore in committing depredations which had alarmed the neighbourhood for the last six or seven weeks. They had not wandered far from the scene of their freebooting, and after eluding the police on several occasions, remained to be delivered up to justice by a party of civilians—headed, it is true, by an experienced and determined personage, exceptionally well mounted from one of the most famous studs in New South Wales. In that day the bushranger, desperate and ruthless though he may have been, was at a disadvantage compared to his modern imitator. He was mostly on foot. Horses were scarce and valuable. There were few stopping-places, except the stations of the squatters, where an armed, suspicious-looking stranger was either questioned or arrested. 'Shanties' had hardly commenced to plant centres of contagion in the 'lone Chorasmian waste.' The 'Shadow of Death Hotel' was in the future—fortunately for all sorts and conditions of men.

It is a curious coincidence, showing at once the just view taken of the circumstances of the locality and the means proper to lead to the extinction of 'gang robbery' (as the East India Company's servants termed the industry), that Mr. Thursby had just forwarded to the Legislative Council an estimate of the cost of a proposed Court of Petty Sessions at Wassalis. He also 'most respectfully begged to submit for the consideration of His Excellency the Governor a suggestion that a mounted police force would be advantageously stationed there, as well for the protection of the district as for the purpose of connecting the detachments of police at Murphy's Plains and Curban.'

'Many a year is in its grave' since the incidents here recorded affrighted the dwellers in the lonely bush.

It is satisfactory to note that Wassalis was promoted to be a place where a Court of Petty Sessions is holden.

Walker and Gore, being found guilty, were sentenced to death, doubtless by Sir Francis Forbes, the Chief Justice of the day—indeed the first Chief Justice of Australia. They confessed their guilt in gaol, and were duly hanged—let us hope repenting of their crimes. The brother of the magistrate whose courage and energy led to their arrest, frequently visited them in gaol, where they confessed everything. The constable, on recommendation, was promoted. The police station at Wassalis is now organised and equipped with good horses, smart men, revolver at belt and carbine on thigh. Telegraphs in every direction are available for giving or receiving information;

but it is doubtful whether armed and desperate felons, red-handed with the blood of their fellow-men, were ever more closely followed up, more quickly brought to justice, than the murderers of Woods.

THE HORSE YOU DON'T SEE NOW

Many years ago I was summoned to attend the couch of a dear relative believed to be *in extremis*. The messenger arrived at my club with a buggy, drawn by a dark bay horse. The distance to be driven to Toorak was under four miles—the road good. I have a dislike to being driven. Those who have handled the reins much in their time will understand the feeling. Taking them mechanically from the man, I drew the whip across the bay horse. The light touch sent him down Collins Street East, over Prince's Bridge, and through the toll-bar gate at an exceptionally rapid pace. This I did not remark at the time, being absorbed in sorrowful anticipation.

During the anxious week which followed I drove about the turn-out—a hired one—daily; now for this or that doctor, anon for nurse or attendant. Then the beloved sufferer commenced to amend, to recover; so that, without impropriety, my thoughts became imperceptibly disengaged from her, to concentrate themselves upon the dark bay horse. For that he was no ordinary livery-stable hack was evident to a judge. *Imprimis*, very fast. Had I not passed everything on the road, except a professional trotter, that had not, indeed, so much the best of it? Quiet, too. He would stand unwatched, though naturally impatient. He never tripped, never seemed to 'give' on the hard, blue metal; was staunch up-hill and steady down. Needed no whip, yet took it kindly, neither switching his tail angrily nor making as if ready to smash all and sundry, like ill-mannered horses. Utterly faultless did he seem. But experience in matters equine leads to distrust. Hired out per day from a livery-stable keeper, I could hardly believe *that* to be the case.

All the same I felt strongly moved to buy him on the chance of his belonging to the select tribe of exceptional performers, not to be passed over by so dear a lover of horseflesh as myself. Moreover, I possessed, curious to relate, a 'dead match' for him—another bay horse of equally lavish action, high courage, and recent accidental introduction. The temptation was great.

'I will buy him,' said I to myself, 'if he is for sale, and also if——' here I pulled up, got down in the road, and carefully looked him over from head to tail. He stepped quietly. I can see him now, moving his impatient head gently back and forward like a horse 'weaving'—a trick he had under all circumstances. Years afterwards he performed similarly to the astonishment of a bushranger in Riverina, whose revolver was pointed at the writer's head the while, less anxious indeed for his personal safety than that old Steamer—such was his appropriate name—should march on, and, having a nervous running mate, smash the buggy.

To return, however. This was the result of my inspection. Item, one broken knee; item, seven years old—within mark decidedly; legs sound and clean, but just beginning to 'knuckle' above the pasterns.

There was a conflict of opinions. Says Prudence, 'What! buy a screw? Brilliant, of course, but sure to crack soon. Been had that way before. I'm ashamed of you.'

Said Hope, 'I don't know so much about that. Knee probably an accident: dark night—heap of stones—anything. Goes like a bird. Grand shoulder. *Can't* fall. Legs come right with rest. Barely seven—quite a babe. Cheap at anything under fifty. Chance him.'

'I'll buy him—d—dashed if I don't.' I got in again, and drove thoughtfully to the stables of Mr. Washington, a large-sized gentleman of colour, hailing from the States.

'He's de favouritest animile in my stable, boss,' he made answer to me as I guardedly introduced the subject of purchase. 'All de young women's dead sot on him—donow's I cud do athout him, noways.'

Every word of this was true, as it turned out; but how was I to know? The world of currycombs and dandy-brushes is full of insincerities. *Caveat emptor!* I continued airily, 'You won't charge extra for this broken knee? What's the figure?' Here I touched the too yielding ankle-joint with my boot.

That may have decided him—much hung in the balance. Many a year of splendid service—a child's life saved—a grand night-exploit in a flooded river, with distressed damsels nearly overborne by a raging torrent,—all these lay in the future.

'You gimme thirty pound, boss,' he gulped out. 'You'll never be sorry for it.'

'Lend me a saddle,' quoth I. 'I'll write the cheque now. Take him out; I can ride him away.'

I did so. Never did I—never did another man—make a better bargain.

I had partly purchased and wholly christened him to match another bay celebrity named Railway, of whom I had become possessed after this fashion. Wanting a harness horse at short notice a few months before, I betook myself to the coach depôt of Cobb and Co. situated in Lonsdale Street. Mr. Beck was then the manager, and to him I addressed myself. He ordered out several likely animals—from his point of view—for my inspection. But I was not satisfied with any of them. At length, 'Bring out the Railway horse,' said the man in authority. And out came, as I thought, rather a 'peacocky' bay, with head and tail up. A great shoulder certainly, but rather light-waisted—hem—possessed of four capital legs. Very fine in the skin—yes; still I mistrusted him as a 'Sunday horse.' Never was there a greater mistake.

'Like to see him go?' I nodded assent. In a minute and a half we were spinning up Lonsdale Street in an Abbot buggy, across William and down Collins Street, then pretty crowded, at the rate of fourteen miles an hour; Mr. Beck holding a broad red rein in either hand, and threading the ranks of vehicles with graceful ease.

'He can go,' I observed.

'He's a tarnation fine traveller, I tell you,' was the answer—a statement which I found, by after-experience, to be strictly in accordance with fact.

The price required was forty pounds. The which promptly paying (this was in 1860), I drove my new purchase out to Heidelberg that night. One of those horses that required of one nothing but to sit still and hold him; fast, game, wiry and enduring.

When I became possessed of Steamer, I had such a pair as few people were privileged to sit behind. For four years I enjoyed as much happiness as can be absorbed by mortal horse-owner in connection with an unsurpassable pair of harness horses. They were simply perfect as to style, speed, and action. I never was passed, never even challenged, on the road by any other pair. Railway, the slower horse of the two, had done, by measurement, eight miles in half an hour. So at their best, both horses at speed, it may be guessed how they made a buggy spin behind them. Then they were a true match; one a little darker than the other, but so much alike in form, colour, and courage, that strangers never knew them apart. They became attached readily, and would leave other horses and feed about together, when turned into a paddock or the bush.

A check, however, was given to exultation during the first days of my proprietorship. Both horses when bought were low in flesh—in hard condition, certainly, but showing a good deal of bone. A month's stabling and gentle exercise caused them to look very different. The new buggy came home—the new harness. They were put together for the first time. Full of joyful anticipation I mounted the driving seat, and told the groom to let go their heads. Horror of horrors! 'The divil a stir,' as he remarked, could be got out of them. Collar-proud from ease and good living, they declined to tighten the traces. An indiscreet touch or two with the whip caused one horse to plunge, the other to hold back. In half-and-half condition I had seen both draw like working bullocks. Now 'they wouldn't pull the hat off your head,' my Australian Mickey Free affirmed.

By patience and persuasion I prevailed upon them at length to move off. Then it *was* a luxury of a very high order to sit behind them. How they caused the strong but light-running trap to whirl and spin!—an express train with the steam omitted. Mile after mile might one sit when roads were good, careful only to keep the pace at twelve miles an hour; by no means to alter the pull on the reins lest they should translate it into an order for full speed. With heads held high at the same angle, with legs rising from the ground at the same second of time, alike their extravagant action, their eager courage. As mile after mile was cast behind, the exclamation of 'Perfection, absolute perfection!' rose involuntarily to one's lips.

In this 'Wale,' where deceitful dealers and plausible horses abound, how rare to experience so full-flavoured a satisfaction! None of us, however, are perfect all round. Flawless might be their action, but both Steamer and his friend Railway had 'a little temper,' the differing expressions of which took me years to circumvent. Curiously, neither exhibited the least forwardness in *single* harness.

Railway was by temperament dignified, undemonstrative, proud. If touched sharply with the whip he turned his head and gazed at you. He did not offer to kick or stop; such vulgar tricks were beneath him. But he calmly gave you to understand that he would not accelerate his movements, or start when unwilling, if you flogged him to death. No whip did he need, I trow. The most constant horse in the world, he kept going through the longest day with the tireless regularity of an engine.

They never became quite free from certain peculiarities at starting, after a spell or when in high condition. Years passed in experiments before I wrote myself conqueror. I tried the whip more than once—I record it contritely—with signal ill-success. It was truly wonderful why they declined to start on the first day of a journey. Once off they would pull staunchly wherever horses could stand. Never was the day too long, the pace too fast, the road too deep. What, then, was the hidden cause, the *premier pas*, which cost so much trouble to achieve?

Nervous excitability seemed to be the drawback. The fact of being attached to a trap in *double* harness appeared to overexcite their sensitive, highly-strung organisations. Was it not worth while, then, to take thought and care for a pair which could travel fifty or sixty miles a day—in front of a family vehicle filled with children and luggage—for a week together, that didn't cost a shilling a year for whip-cord, and that had *never* been passed by a pair on the road since I had possessed them? Were they not worth a little extra trouble?

Many trials and experiments demonstrated that there was but one solution. Success meant patience, with a dash of forethought. A little saddle-exercise for a day or two before the start. Then to begin early on the morning of the eventful day; to have everything packed—passengers and all—in the buggy—coach fashion—before any hint of putting to. Both horses to be fed and watered at least an hour before. Then at the last moment to bring them out of the stable, heedfully and respectfully, avoiding 'rude speech or jesting rough.' Railway especially resented being 'lugged' awkwardly by the rein. If all things were done decently and in order, this would be the usual programme.

Steamer, more excitable but more amiable, would be entrusted to a groom. Silently and quickly they would be poled up, the reins buckled, and Railway's traces attached. All concerned had been drilled, down to the youngest child, to be discreetly silent. It was forbidden, on pain of death, to offer suggestion, much less to 't-c-h-i-c-k.' The reins were taken in one hand by paterfamilias, who with the other drew back Steamer's traces, oppressed with an awful sense of responsibility, as of one igniting a fuse or connecting a torpedo wire, and as the outer trace was attached, stepped lightly on to the front seat. The groom and helper stole backward like shadows. Steamer made a plunging snatch at his collar; Railway followed up with a steady rush; and we were off—off for good and all—for one hundred, two hundred, five hundred miles. Distance made no difference to *them*. The last stage was even as the first. They only wanted holding. Not that they pulled disagreeably, or unreasonably either. I lost my whip once, and drove without one for six months. It was only on the first day of a journey that the theatrical performance was produced.

But this chronicle would be incomplete without reference to the sad alternative when the start did *not* come off at first intention. On these inauspicious occasions, possibly from an east wind or oats below sample, everything went wrong. Steamer sidled and pulled prematurely before the traces were 'hitched,' while Railway's reserved expression deepened—a sure sign that he wasn't going to pull at all. The other varied his vexatious plungings by backing on to the whippletree, or bending outwards, by way of testing the elasticity of the pole.

Nothing could now be done. Persuasion, intimidation, deception, had all been tried previously in vain. The recipe of paterfamilias, as to horse management, was to sit perfectly still with the reins firmly held but moveless, buttoning his gloves with an elaborate pretence of never minding. All known expedients have come to nought long ago. Pushing the wheels, even down hill, is regarded with contempt; leading (except by a lady) scornfully refused. The whip is out of the question. 'Patience is a virtue'—indeed *the* virtue, the only one which will serve our turn. Meanwhile, when people are fairly on the warpath, this dead refusal to budge an inch is a little, just a little, exasperating. Paterfamilias computes, however, that ten minutes' delay can be made up with such steppers. He smiles benignantly as he pulls out a newspaper and asks his wife if she has brought her book. Two minutes, four, five, or is it half an hour? The time seems long. 'Trois cent milles diables!' the natural man feels inclined to ejaculate. He knows that he is sinking fast in the estimation of newly-arrived station hands and chance spectators. Eight minutes — Railway makes no sign; years might roll on before *he* would start with an unwilling mate. Nine minutes — Steamer, whose impatient soul abhors inaction, begins to paw. The student is absorbed in his leading article. Ten minutes! — Steamer opens his mouth and carries the whole equipage off with one rush. Railway is up and away; half a second later the proprietor folds up his journal and takes them firmly in hand. The children begin to laugh and chatter; the lady to converse; and the journey, long or short, wet or dry, may be considered, as far as horseflesh is concerned, to be *un fait accompli*.

At the end of four years of unclouded happiness (as novelists write of wedded life), this state of literal conjugal bliss was doomed to end. An epidemic of lung disease, such as at intervals sweeps over the land, occurred in Victoria. Railway fell a victim, being found dead in his paddock. Up to this time he had never been 'sick or sorry,' lame, tired, or unfit to go. His iron legs, with feet to match, showed no sign of work. In single harness he was miraculous, going mile after mile with the regularity of a steam-engine, apparently incapable of fatigue. I was lucky enough to have a fast, clever grandson of Cornborough to put in his place. He lasted ten years. A half-brother three years more. The old horse was using up his *fourth* running mate, and entering upon his twentieth year *in my service*, when King Death put on the brake.

Not the least noticeable among Steamer's many good qualities was his kindly, generous temper. His was the Arab's docile gentleness with children. The large mild eye, 'on which you could hang your hat,' as the stable idiom goes, was a true indication of character. I was a bachelor when I first became his master. As time passed on, Mrs. Boldrewood and the elder girls used to drive him to the country town in New South Wales, near which we afterwards dwelt. The boys rode him as soon as they could straddle a horse. They hung by his tail, walked between his legs, and did all kinds of confidential circus performances for the benefit of their young friends. He was never known to bite, kick, or in any way offer harm; and, speedy to the last, with age he never lost pace or courage. 'All spirit and no vice' was a compendium of his character. By flood and field, in summer's heat or winter's cold, he failed us never; was credited, besides, with having saved the lives of two of the children by his docility and intelligence. He was twice loose with the buggy at his heels at night—once without winkers, which he had rubbed off. On the last occasion, after walking down to the gate of the paddock, and finding it shut—nearly a mile—he turned round without locking the wheels, and came galloping up to the door of the house (it was a ball night, and he had got tired of waiting). When I ran out, pale with apprehension, I discovered the headstall hanging below his chest. His extreme docility with children I attribute to his being for many years strictly a family horse, exclusively fed, harnessed, and driven by ourselves. It is needless to say he was petted a good deal: indeed he thought nothing of walking through the kitchen, a brick-floored edifice, when he thought corn should be forthcoming. Horses are generally peaceable with children but not invariably, as I have known of limbs broken and more than one lamentable death occasioned by kicks, when the poor things went too near unwittingly. But the old horse *couldn't* kick. 'I reckon he didn't know how.' And when he died, gloom and grief fell upon the whole family, who mourned as for the death of a dear friend.

HOW I BEGAN TO WRITE

For publication I mean. Having the pen of a ready writer by inheritance, I had dashed off occasional onslaughts in the journals of the day, chiefly in defence of the divine rights of kings (pastoral ones). I had assailed incoherent democrats, who perversely denied that Australia was created chiefly for the sustenance of sheep and cattle and the aggrandisement of those heroic individuals who first explored and then exploited the 'Waste Lands of the Crown.' The school of political belief to which I then belonged derided agriculture, and was subsequently committed to a scheme for the formation of the Riverina into a separate pastoral kingdom or colony. A petition embodying a statement to this effect, wholly unfitted as it was for the sustenance of a population dependent upon agriculture, was forwarded to the Secretary for the Colonies, who very properly disregarded it. The petitioners could not then foresee the stacking of 20,000 bags of wheat, holding four bushels each, awaiting railway transport at one of the farming centres of this barren region in the year 1897. Allied facts caused me to reconsider my very pronounced opinions, and, perhaps, led others to question the accuracy of theirs. My deliverances in the journals of the period occurred in the forties and fifties of the century, and gradually subsided.

I was battling with the season of 1865 on a station on the Murrumbidgee River, at no great distance from the flourishing town of Narandera, then consisting of two hotels, a small store, and a large graveyard, when an uncertain-tempered young horse kicked me just above the ankle with such force and accuracy that I thought the bone was broken. I was to have ridden at daylight to count a flock of sheep, and could scarcely crawl back to the huts from the stock-yard without assistance, so great was the agony. I sat down on the frosted ground and pulled off my boot, knowing that the leg would swell. Cold as it was, the thirst of the wounded soldier immediately attacked me. My room in the slab hut, preceding the brick cottage, then in course of erection, was, to use Mr. Swiveller's description, 'an airy and well-ventilated apartment.' It contained, in addition to joint stools, a solid table, upon which my simple meals of chops, damper, and tea were displayed three times a day by a shepherd's wife, an elderly personage of varied and sensational experiences.

I may mention that the great Riverina region was as yet in its unfenced, more or less Arcadian stage, the flocks being 'shepherded' (expressive Australian verb, since enlarged as to meaning) and duly folded or camped at night. Something of Mrs. Regan's advanced tone of thought may be gathered from the following dialogue, which I overheard: —

Shady township individual—'Your man shot my dorg t'other night. What d'yer do that fer?'

Mrs. Regan—"Cause we caught him among the sheep; and we'd 'a shot *you*, if you'd bin in the same place.'

Township individual—'You seem rather hot coffee, missus! I've 'arf a mind to pull your boss next Court day for the valley of the dorg.'

Mrs. Regan—'You'd better clear out and do it, then. The P.M.'s a-comin' from Wagga on Friday, and he'll give yer three months' "hard," like as not. Ask the pleece for yer character.'

Township individual—'D—n you and the pleece too! A pore man gets no show between the traps and squatters in this bloomin' country. Wish I'd never seen it!'

This was by the way of interlude, serving to relieve the monotony of the situation. I could eat, drink, smoke, and sleep, but the injured leg—worse than broken—I could not put to the ground. Nor had I company of any kind, save that of old Jack and Mrs. Regan, for a whole month. So, casting about for occupation, I bethought myself that I might write something for an English magazine. The subject pitched upon was a kangaroo drive or battue, then common in Western Victoria, which I had lately quitted. The kangaroo had become so numerous that they were eating the squatters out of house and home. Something had to be done; so they were driven into yards in great numbers and killed. This severe mode of dealing with the too prolific marsupial, in whole battalions, I judged correctly, would be among the 'things not generally known' to the British public.

I sat down and wrote a twelve-page article, describing a grand muster for the purpose at a station about twenty miles from Port Fairy, and seven miles from my own place, Squattlesea Mere.

The first time I went to Melbourne I posted it, with the aid of my good friend, the late Mr. Mullen, to the editor of the *Cornhill Magazine*, and thought no more about the matter. A few days after the adventure, my neighbour, Adam M'Neill, of North Yanko, hearing of my invalid state, rode over and carried me off to his hospitable home. I had to be lifted on my horse, but after a month's rest and recreation was well enough to return to pastoral duties. I was lame, however, for quite a year afterwards, and narrowly escaped injuring the other ankle, which began to show signs of overwork. About the time of my full recovery, I received a new *Cornhill Magazine*, and a note from Messrs. Smith and Elder, forwarding a draft, which, added to the honour and glory of seeing my article flourishing in a first-class London magazine, afforded me much joy and satisfaction. The English review notices were also cheering. I thereupon dashed off a second sketch, entitled 'Shearing in Riverina,' which I despatched to the same address. The striking presentment of seventy shearers, all going their hardest, was a novelty also to the British public.

   The constant clash that the shear-blades make
   When the fastest shearers are making play

(as Mr. 'Banjo' Paterson has it, in 'The Two Devines,' more than twenty years later), could not but challenge attention. This also was accepted. I received a cheque in due course, which came at a time when such remittances commenced to have more interest for me than had been the case for some years past.

The station was sold in the adverse pastoral period of '68-'69, through drought, debt, financial 'dismalness of sorts'; but 'that is another story.' Christmas time found me in Sydney, where it straightway began to rain with unreasonable persistency (as I thought), now it could do me no good; never left off (more or less) for five years. The which, in plenteousness of pasture and high prices for wool and stock, were the most fortunate seasons for squatters since the 'fifties,' with their accompanying goldfields prosperity.

The last station having been sold, there was no chance of repairing hard fortune by pastoral investment. 'Finis Poloniæ.' During my temporary sojourn in Sydney I fell across a friend to whom in other days I had rendered a service. He suggested that I might turn to profitable use a facile pen and some gift of observation. My friend, who had filled various parts in the drama of life, some of them not undistinguished, was now a professional journalist. He introduced me to his chief, the late Mr. Samuel Bennett, proprietor of the *Sydney Town and Country Journal*. That gentleman, whom I remember gratefully for his kind and sensible advice, gave me a commission for certain sketches of bush life—a series of which appeared from time to time. For him I wrote my first tale, *The Fencing of Wanderoona*, succeeding which, *The Squatter's Dream*, and others, since published in England, appeared in the weekly paper referred to.

Thus launched upon the 'wide, the fresh, the ever free' ocean of fiction, I continued to make voyages and excursions thereon—mostly profitable, as it turned out. A varied colonial experience, the area of which became enlarged when I was appointed a police magistrate and goldfields commissioner in 1871, supplied types and incidents. This position I held for nearly twenty-five years.

Although I had, particularly in the early days of my goldfields duties, a sufficiency of hard and anxious work, entailing serious responsibility, I never relinquished the habit of daily writing and story-weaving. That I did not on that account neglect my duties I can fearlessly aver. The constant official journeying, riding and driving, over a wide district, agreed with my open-air habitudes. The method of composition which I employed, though regular, was not fatiguing, and suited a somewhat desultory turn of mind. I arranged for a serial tale by sending the first two or three chapters to the editor, and mentioning that it would last a twelvemonth, more or less. If accepted, the matter was settled. I had but to post the weekly packet, and my mind was at ease. I was rarely more than one or two chapters ahead of the printer; yet in twenty years I was only once late with my instalment, which had to go by sea from another colony. Every author has his own way of writing; this was mine. I never but once completed a story before it was published; and on that occasion it was—sad to say—declined by the editor. Not in New

South Wales, however; and as it has since appeared in England, it did not greatly signify.

In this fashion *Robbery Under Arms* was written for the *Sydney Mail* after having been refused by other editors. It has been successful beyond expectation; and, though I say it, there is no country where the English language is spoken in which it has not been read.

I was satisfied with the honorarium which my stories yielded. It made a distinct addition to my income, every shilling of which, as a paterfamilias, was needed. I looked forward, however, to making a hit some day, and with the publication of *Robbery Under Arms*, in England, that day arrived. Other books followed, which have had a gratifying measure of acceptance by the English-speaking public, at home and abroad.

As a prophet I have not been 'without honour in mine own country.' My Australian countrymen have supported me nobly, which I take as an especial compliment, and an expression of confidence, to the effect that, as to colonial matters, I knew what I was writing about.

In my relations with editors, I am free to confess that I have always been treated honourably. I have had few discouragements to complain of, or disappointments, though not without occasional rubs and remonstrances from reviewers for carelessness, to which, to a certain extent, I plead guilty. In extenuation, I may state that I have rarely had the opportunity of correcting proofs. As to the attainment of literary success, as to which I often receive inquiries, as also how to secure a publisher, I have always given one answer: Try the Australian weekly papers, if you have any gift of expression, till one of them takes you up. After that the path is more easy. Perseverance and practice will ordinarily discover the method which leads to success.

A natural turn for writing is necessary, perhaps indispensable. Practice does much, but the novelist, like the poet, is chiefly 'born, not made.' Even in the case of hunters and steeplechasers, the expression 'a natural jumper' is common among trainers. A habit of noting, almost unconsciously, manner, bearing, dialect, tricks of expression, among all sorts and conditions of men, provides 'situations.' Experience, too, of varied scenes and societies is a great aid. Imagination does much to enlarge and embellish the lay figure, to deepen the shades and heighten the colours of the picture; but it will not do everything. There should be some experience of that most ancient conflict between the powers of Good and Evil, before the battle of life can be pictorially described. I am proud to note among my Australian brothers and sisters, of a newer generation, many promising, even brilliant, performances in prose and verse. They have my sincerest sympathy, and I feel no doubt as to their gaining in the future a large measure of acknowledged success.

As to my time method, it was tolerably regular. As early as five or six o'clock in the morning in the summer, and as soon as I could see in winter, I was at my desk, proper or provisional, until the hour arrived for bath and breakfast. If at a friend's house, I wrote in my bedroom and corrected in the afternoon, when my official duties were over. At home or on the road, as I had much travelling to do, I wrote after dinner till bedtime, making up generally five or six hours a day. Many a good evening's work have I done in the clean, quiet, if unpretending roadside inns, common enough in New South Wales. In winter, with a log fire and the inn parlour all to myself, or with a sensible companion, I could write until bedtime with ease and comfort. My day's ride or drive might be long, cold enough in winter or hot in summer, but carrying paper, pens, and ink I rarely missed the night's work. I never felt too tired to set to after a wholesome if simple meal. Fatigue has rarely assailed me, I am thankful to say, and in my twenty-five years of official service I was never a day absent from duty on account of illness, with one notable exception, when I was knocked over by fever, which necessitated sick-leave. It has been my experience that in early morning the brain is clearer, the hand steadier, the general mental tone more satisfactory, than at any other time of day.

A MOUNTAIN FOREST

Excepting perhaps the ocean, nothing in Nature is more deceitful than a mountain forest. Last we crossed through snow, enveloped in mist and drenched with pitiless rain. Now, no one could think evil hap could chance to the wayfarer here—so dry the forest paths, so blue the sky, so bright the scene, so soft the whispering breeze. The shadows of the great trees fall on the emerald sward, tempering the ardent sun-rays. Flickers of light dance in the thickets, and laugh at the stern solemnity of the endless groves. Bird-calls are frequent and joyous. We might be roaming in the Forest of Arden, and meet a 'stag of ten' in the glade, for any hint to the contrary. Forest memories come into our heads as we stride merrily along the winding track. Robin Hood and his merry men, Friar Tuck and Little John! Oh, fountain of chivalry! How indissolubly a forest life in the glad summer days seems bound up with deeds of high emprise; how linked with the season of love and joy, hope and pride, with a sparkle of the cup of that divinest life-essence, youthful pleasure.

'Here shall he fear no enemy,
But winter and rough weather.'

As we thus carol somewhat loudly, we are aware of a man standing motionless, regarding us, not far from a gate, humorously supposed to restrain the stock in these somewhat careless-ordered enclosures. Ha! what if he be a robber? We have been 'stuck up' ere now, and mislike the operation. He has something in his hand too. May it be a 'shooting-iron,' as the American idiom runs?

We continue to sing, however,

'Viator vacuus coram latronem.'

Our treasury consists of half-a-sovereign and an old watch, a new hat and a clean shirt—what matter if he levy on these? He has a dog, however,—that is a good sign. Bushrangers rarely travel with dogs. And the weapon is a stick. Ha! it is well. Only an official connected with the railway line, awaiting the mailman. We interchange courtesies, and are invited to the camp with proffer of hospitality.

We feel compelled to decline. We may not halt by any wayside arbour.

We reach St. Bago Hospice at Laurel Hill before lunch time. Sixteen miles over a road not too smooth. Really, we have performed the stage with ridiculous ease. We are half tempted to go on to Tumut; but twenty-eight miles seems a longish step. Let us not be imprudently enthusiastic. We decide to remain. The hospice has put on a summer garb, and is wholly devoid of snowballs or other wintry emblems. The great laurel, the noble elm, the hawthorn, are in full leaf and flower. The orchard trees are greenly budding. At the spring well in the creek five crimson lories are drinking. They stand on a tray, so to speak, of softest emerald moss, walking delicately; all things tell of summer.

During the afternoon, so fresh did we feel that we took a stroll of five miles, and visited the nearest farmer. As we stepped along the red-soiled path, amid the immense timber, we realised the surroundings of the earlier American settlers. Hawk-eye might have issued from the ti-tree thicket by the creek and chuckled in his noiseless manner, while he rested *la longue carabine* on a fallen log. Uncas and Chingachgook would, of course, have turned up shortly afterwards.

The tiny creek speeds swiftly onward over ancient gold-washings and abandoned sluice channels. Tracks of that queer animal the wombat (*Phascolomys*) near his burrows and galleries are frequent. His habitat is often near the sea, but here is proof that he can accommodate himself to circumstances. Easily-excavated soil like this red loam is necessary for his comfort apparently. Ferns are not objected to. Our host at Bago informed us that one dull winter's evening he observed two animals coming towards him through the bush. He took them to be pigs, until, shooting with both right and left barrels, they turned out to be wombats. He had happened to be near their burrow, to which they always make if disturbed. In confirmation of this statement he presented me with a skin—dark brown in colour—with long coarse hair, something between that of a dog and a kangaroo. The thick hide covers the body in loose folds. The dogs become aware by experience that, on account of its thickness and slippery looseness, it is vain to attempt capture of a wombat. Retreating to his burrow, he scratches earth briskly into his opponent's mouth and eyes until he desists. One peculiarity of this underground animal is, that the eyes are apparently protected by a movable eyebrow, which, in the form of a small flap of skin, shuts over the indispensable organ.

We are politely received at the selector's house. A few cattle are kept; pigs and poultry abound. The father and son 'work in the creek' for gold, when the water is low, and thus supplement the family earnings. Clearing is too expensive as yet to be entered into on a large scale. Want of roads must militate for a while against farming profits in rough and elevated country. A flower-garden and orchard bear testimony to the richness of the soil. But looking forward to the value of the timber, the certainty of annual crops, the gradual covering of the pasture with clover and exotic grasses, the day is not distant in our opinion when the agriculture of this region will stand upon a safe and solvent basis. It is hard to overestimate the value of a moist, temperate climate, and this the inhabitants of the vicinity possess beyond all dispute.

The sun is showing above the tall tree-tops as we sit at breakfast next morning. The air is keen. We need the fire which glows in the cavernous chimney. In ten minutes we are off—ready to do or die—to accomplish the voluntary march or perish by the wayside.

How pleasant is it as we swing along in the fresh morning air. If we had had a mate—one who read the same books, thought the same thoughts, had the same tastes, and in a general way was congenial and sympathetic—our happiness would be complete. But in this desperately busy, workaday land, properly-graduated companionship is difficult to procure.

Still, to those who do not let their minds remain entirely fallow, there is choice companionship in these wooded highlands—that of the nobles and monarchs of literature is always at hand, ceases not the murmuring talk of half-forgotten friends, acquaintances, lovers, what not, of the spirit-world of letters; 'songs without words,' wit and laughter, tears and sighs, pæans of praise, sadly humorous subtleties, recall and repeat themselves. So we are not entirely alone, even were there not the whispering leaves, the frowning tree-trunks, the tremulous ferns and delicate grasses, the smiling flowerets, each with its own legend to keep us company. The sun mounts higher in the heavens; still it is not too hot. The green gloom of the great woodland lies between us, a shade against the fiercest sun-rays. So we fare on joyously. Three hours' fair walking brings us to the end of the forest proper. We take one look, as we stand on a clear hill-top—while on either side great glens are hollowed out like demoniac punch-bowls (the Australian native idiom)—at the mountains, at the oceans of frondage.

We are on the 'down grade.' At our feet lies the Middle Adelong, with deserted gold-workings, sluices, and all the debris of water-mining; a roomy homestead, with orchard pertaining, once an inn doubtless; now no longer, as I can testify.

It is high noon and hot withal. The sun, no longer fended off by o'erarching boughs, becomes aggressive. We have gained the valley and lost the cooling breeze. We request a glass of water, which is handed to us by the good-wife. We drink, and, seating ourselves upon a log on the hillside, commence upon a crust of bread—unwonted foresight this—with considerable relish. As we happen to have Carl Vosmaer's *Amazon* in our hand (every step of the way did we carry her), we tackle an æsthetic chapter with enthusiasm.

In twenty minutes we breast the hill, a trifle stiffer for the rest, and, it may be fancy, our left boot-sole has developed an inequality not previously sensitive. We swing along, however, in all the pride of 'second wind,' and fix our thoughts upon the next stage, eight miles farther on. We have come about sixteen.

We pass another hill, a plateau, and then a long declivitous grade. By and by we enter upon the fertile valley which leads to Tumut. The green valley of river-encircled sward on either side is one mat of clover and rye-grass. We display an increasing preference for the turf as distinguished from the roadway. The sun is becoming hotter. The clouds have retired. There is a hint of storm. The heavy air is charged with electricity. We put on the pace a little. One may as well have this sort of thing over in a condensed form.

Here we stop to look at a man ploughing for maize. Our brow is wet with 'honest——,' whatsy name? We must weigh pounds less than this morning. How far to the Gilmore Inn? 'Four miles!' Thermometer over a hundred in the shade. We set our teeth and march on. We are acquiring the regular slouching swing of the 'sundowner,' it appears to us. There is nothing like similar experience for producing sympathy. We can almost fancy ourselves accosting the overseer with the customary, 'Got any work, sir, for a man to do?' and subsiding to the traveller's hut, with the regulation junk of meat and panmkin of flour. Can partly gauge the feelings of the honest son of toil, weary, athirst, somewhat sore-footed (surely there must be a nail?), when said overseer, being in bad temper, tells him to go to the deuce, that he knows he won't take work if it's offered, and that he has no rations to spare for useless loafers.

It is more than an hour later—we think it more than an hour hotter—as we sight the Gilmore Inn, near rushing stream, hidden by enormous willows. We have abstained from drinking of the trickling rill, hot and dusty as we are. Thoughts of 'that poor creature, small beer,' obtrude, if the local optionists have not abolished him.

In the parlour of this snug roadside inn we put down our 'swag,' and order a large glass of home-brewed and a crust of bread. We certainly agree with Mr. Swiveller, 'Beer can't be tasted in a sip,' especially after a twenty-mile trudge. When we put down the 'long-sleever' there is but a modicum left.

We give ourselves about half an hour here, by which time we are cooled and refreshed, as is apparently the day. Sol is lower and more reasonable. We sling on, by no means done—rather improving pace than otherwise—till overtaken by a friend and his family in a buggy. He kindly proffers to drive us in; but we have made it a point of honour to walk every yard, so we decline. He will leave the valise at our hotel—which kindness we accept. The rest is easy going. We lounge into the 'Commercial' as if we had just dismounted, and order a warm bath and dinner, with the *mens conscia recti* in a high state of preservation.

Copyright © 2023 Esprios Digital Publishing. All Rights Reserved.

www.ingramcontent.com/pod-product-compliance
Ingram Content Group UK Ltd.
Pitfield, Milton Keynes, MK11 3LW, UK
UKHW032212171224
452513UK00010B/609